Hester's Story

Also by Adèle Geras

Facing the Light

Hester's Story

ADÈLE GERAS

ORION

First published in Great Britain in 2004 by Orion,
an imprint of the Orion Publishing Group Ltd

Copyright © Adèle Geras 2004

The moral right of Adèle Geras to be identified as the author
of this work has been asserted in accordance with
the Copyright, Designs and Patents Act of 1988.

A CIP catalogue record for this book
is available from the British Library.

ISBN 0 75285 156 X (hardback)
ISBN 0 75286 504 8 (trade paperback)

Typeset by Deltatype Ltd, Birkenhead, Merseyside
Set in 12.75/14.5 pt Monotype Perpetua
Printed in Great Britain by Clays Ltd, St Ives plc

All the characters in this book are fictitious,
and any resemblance to actual persons living or
dead is purely coincidental.

The Orion Publishing Group Ltd
Orion House
5 Upper Saint Martin's Lane
London, WC2H 9EA

www.orionbooks.co.uk

Many thanks (in alphabetical order) to everyone who helped and encouraged me during the time that I was writing this novel.

Theresa Breslin, Laura Cecil, Broo Doherty, Dian Donnai, Norm Geras, Jenny Geras, Yoram Gorlizki, Jane Gregory, Sophie Hannah, Alex Hippisley-Cox, Erica James, Dan Jones, Ben Jones, Susan Lamb, Judith Mackrell, Linda Newbery, Sally Prue, Marian Robertson, Vera Tolz, Jean Ure and my excellent editor, Jane Wood.

Special thanks this time round to Andy Barnett and Linda Sargent, who provided the last piece of the plot jigsaw.

What do I remember? A window. Me, looking down at the street from a high window. I've been taught the name of this street in case I'm ever lost and have to ask someone to bring me home. Rue Lavaudan. Snow must have fallen in the night because everything is white, except for the shiny, black top of an enormous car. I know how old I am in this scene, because this is the day my mother is going to be put into the ground. I've just had my fifth birthday. I'm not allowed to go to the funeral, but have to stay here with one of the younger maids. Since *Maman* died, my grandmother has been lying in her bed, sick with grief, and I haven't been allowed to play in her room for . . . I have no idea how long it's been, but it feels like a very long time. On this day, the day I remember, she calls me to her at last, and whispers: 'Don't be sad, my darling.'

She is wearing a choker of shiny black beads, and a black hat with a veil. She's been crying. I can see how red her eyes are even through the spotted net that hangs down over her face. 'Your mother will watch over you from heaven.' She squeezes my hand.

What do I remember? I remember thinking, *Maman* might be happy in heaven, but she's left me behind. She can't love me properly. No one else's mother has chosen to leave and go and be with the angels instead. I remember thinking, perhaps I'm not a good enough child to keep her here with me; she'll be happier somewhere else. This thought makes me sad in a completely new way: one I've never felt before, as though my whole body has suddenly been washed in grey and sorrow and cold. Even when this anguish has passed a little, I can still feel bits of the misery in my blood, in my bones and skin and eyes, like tiny pieces of grit, and I know that they won't ever truly go away.

The top of the car. The top of my father's black hat, and *Grand-mère*'s black hat next to it. The hats disappearing into the car and the car driving away. The rest of that morning has gone from my mind entirely, but thinking about it makes me feel cold.

Then I am sitting in *Grand-mère*'s bedroom. I'm perched on a little stool next to her *chaise-longue*. My stool. I love this place. My grandmother has boxes and boxes of jewels which she takes out and spreads all over the satin counterpane and we play princesses and queens and I'm allowed to wear almost everything. I can't keep the big rings on my fingers, but ropes of pearls and amber and pendants of crystal and amethyst, and best of all a sparkling tiara that I use for a crown. I can recall them in detail even now. But this afternoon, *Grand-mère* is serious. Not in a playing mood. She pulls me to her. I can smell her skin like old roses and sunshine.

'Estelle,' she says, 'I have to tell you something. It's important that you understand me, even though I know you're too young really . . .' Her voice fades away and she takes a hankie from somewhere in her sleeve and wipes a tear away. Since my mother went to be with the angels, she cries a lot and so do I – every day when I wake up and realise that *Maman* will not be coming into my room ever again.

'I *will* understand you, *Grand-mère*. I'm a big girl, really,' I say.

'I know. And you are a clever girl, too. Then look at this.' She opens a drawer and takes out a red leather box. She opens it. Inside is what looks like a pile of gold. It glitters in the light as she pulls at it and it turns out to be a chain: links of filigree like the tiniest of leaves, all joined together.

'When I was very young, my father gave me this fine necklace,' she says. 'When my son, your father, married your mother, I had a jeweller cut it into two pieces. Look.' She undoes the chain from around her own neck. It's often hidden by her blouse but now she takes it off and places it next to the one on the dressing-table. The two strands of gold lie side by side on the dark wood. 'I gave your mother the second piece, because she became a daughter and more than a daughter to me. She wore it every day. Now that she is gone, her chain belongs to you.'

She looks at me, and holds my face between her hands. There is something I have never seen before in her eyes, a sort of desperate urgency. She says, 'I'm going to give *you* your mother's half of the

2

chain, my darling, and I want you to promise me something. I want you to promise to wear it forever. Never to take it off. Even when you want to wear other jewels. Will you promise that?'

I nod. I don't mind promising a bit. I think it will be wonderful always to have tiny gold leaves sparkling round my neck, and I say, 'I'll always wear it, I promise.'

'Good girl,' my grandmother says. 'But there's something else I want you to know. When I die, the chain I always wear, this one here, will come to you. I'll arrange for it to be sent to you, wherever you are. And when you get it, you must keep it safe. Really, really safe. I'll send it in a special box and you must keep it there and look after it as though it's the most precious treasure in the world. Will you do that?'

I nod again. The chain isn't like a treasure at all. There's a diamond and ruby brooch my grandmother wears that seems to me much more like something a pirate might hide. This chain is pretty, and I'm happy to have it round my neck – it feels grown-up and important in some way – but secretly I'd rather have something a little more . . . *impressive*. More eye-catching. Perhaps my grandmother sees this in my face, because she says, 'And I want you to promise something else: that you'll give my part of the chain to your daughter, when you have one. Or if you have a son, to his wife, just as I did. This is not just a necklace, my love. Do you understand? It is a way of showing that we're all joined together – you, your mother, and me. And the daughter you will have one day. It's a way of showing we'll always love one another. Do you understand?'

'Yes,' I say, and I do in a way, though loving my mother is getting harder and harder. She's only been dead for a short while and already I've nearly forgotten her smell and how she felt. There are photographs to remind me of what she looked like but, in some of them, she isn't a bit like the person I remember. She's dressed in white with gauzy skirts and she has feathers and flowers and ribbons in her hair and she's pretending to be someone else on a stage. I know these pictures come from a time when she was very young; when she used to dance in the ballet in front of hundreds and hundreds of people. It makes me unhappy to look at them, because although I know that this was not how she was when she was my

3

Maman, I have already lost the image of how she used to be when she was with me. I know better than to say so to my grandmother, but I can't be sure any longer if the feelings that I have for her can properly be called *love*. I say, 'I love you, *Grand-mère*, and when I wear the chain that'll remind me of you.'

'Quite right. And when you're a grown-up lady and have a daughter of your own, you can give her my piece of the chain and . . .' She shakes her head. 'Give her the chain. Pass on the love, *chérie*. Do you promise?'

'I promise,' I say. 'But . . .' A dreadful thought has come to me.

'What, Estelle? What's the matter?'

'Will you die soon?' The words are out of my mouth before I can find a softer way of expressing my terror. *Grand-mère* smiles.

'I have no intention of dying for a very long time. Not until you are quite grown-up.'

I am a little reassured, though I would prefer a definite *no, never, I'm never going to die*, but my grandmother's smile convinces me that I don't have to worry for the moment.

'Don't lose it,' she says. 'And don't tell anyone what I've told you. About my part of the chain. Keep it a secret.'

'Yes, *Grand-mère*. I won't say anything to anyone.'

I mean my father. I won't tell my father. I know that's what she means: *don't tell him*. And I keep my promise and say nothing.

I remember my father sending me away. Telling me that it would be better for me if I left his house and went over the sea in a boat to another country where someone else would look after me. Telling me my grandmother found it too much for her (a lie, a lie. I knew it even then but my mouth was stiff and I couldn't find a word to say) and he had to work and, much as he loved me, he couldn't look after me properly and I'd be far happier with another child of my own age to play with, wouldn't I?

Children have to let things happen to them. I remember a new coat with a velvet collar. I remember a suitcase with my clothes folded in it, and one of my dolls lying on top of them. Antoinette. I haven't forgotten her name. *Grand-mère* coming into my bedroom on

4

my last night at home and sitting at the end of my bed weeping; that hasn't left me. I dream about it to this day. She thought I was asleep and I was too frightened of her tears to tell her I was pretending.

Driving away. That's what's stayed in my mind for nearly fifty years. Turning round in the taxi and looking out of the little window at the back and seeing *Grand-mère* standing on the pavement getting smaller and smaller. The lime trees starting to put out new leaves. Everything blurred because of the tears that keep on falling and falling in spite of my best efforts to be brave. My father sitting beside me, staring straight ahead, his mouth pressed into a line. Stiff. Cold. Not crying a single tear. Everything I'd ever known getting further and further away. Disappearing. Yes. I remember that. I remember leaving home.

19 December 1986

I will not cry, Hester thought. But the phone call had ended only moments ago and she still felt anguished, stiff with pain. She'd been drawn back, too, to thinking about the distant past, which only made things worse. She told herself: I will answer this young woman's questions about the Wychwood Festival, my childhood and my past life as a ballet dancer and I will not on any account cry. She closed her eyes for a moment and breathed in and out slowly, collecting herself in the way she'd learned to do before any performance. Find something – anything – in front of you, she told herself, and fix your gaze on it and you'll keep steady however many times you spin around. The old trick might work for interviews as well as it once did for pirouettes.

'This is the Wychwood Festival's tenth year,' she said. 'Quite an important anniversary, really, and we've got a fascinating ballet premiering here in a few weeks . . . on the sixth of January. It's called *Sarabande* and the music is by my old friend, Edmund Norland. It's being put on by the Carradine Company. There's a competition every year to see who's going to choreograph the ballet and Hugo Carradine is a worthy winner. I'm sure it will be an enormous success.'

'There's a rumour,' said the interviewer, whose name Hester had forgotten (Jenny? Julia? Jean? Something beginning with J. Never mind) 'that Silver McConnell's going to be in it. Is that right? I thought she was going to dance in Paris or Berlin . . .'

Hester suddenly remembered her name as she was flicking through her notebook. *Jemima.* 'I believe she's going to Paris, but it's a Festival tradition to have only ten performances up here at the Arcadia Theatre, so she can fit this in before she leaves. The company arrives on December 27th. It *is* quite an intensive rehearsal period, but everyone seems to enjoy the challenge.'

She forced her lips into a smile. Oh, please, please, she thought, let her stop. Let her close her notebook and leave. Please let there be no more questions.

'I should think that rather cuts into your Christmas celebrations, doesn't it?'

'We don't celebrate Christmas at Wychwood,' said Hester, and realised her mistake even as the words were leaving her mouth. If she didn't move on immediately, Jemima would ask why not, and then . . . Hester couldn't talk about it. Not now and not ever. She found that she was speaking rather more quickly than she normally did, to block any further discussion of Christmas or anything to do with the festivities surrounding it.

'Has George shown you round the Arcadia?' she asked. 'You've met Ruby and George Stott, haven't you? They're such an important part of the Wychwood family. Ruby used to be my dresser, you know, while I was still dancing. I don't know how the Festival would function without them.'

'May I ask you something else, Miss Fielding?' Jemima smiled at Hester, gathering her bag on to her lap as she spoke. Thank God, Hester thought, she's going. She's getting her bag ready. Not long now and then I can be alone again to think. I need to think.

'Yes, of course. Please do.'

'I was wondering . . . I hope you'll forgive me asking, only it's something every one of my readers will be longing to know. Can you say something about why you've never married?'

Hester saw red. It wasn't, she realised with alarm, a figure of speech but something that was literally true. The whole room swam in front of her eyes, as though it had suddenly been flooded with scarlet light.

'Go,' she said, barely able to get the words out at first and then letting them fly from her mouth with an anger she did nothing to disguise. 'Go at once, please. I have never, not through the whole of my career, answered a question like that and I don't propose to start now. This interview is over.'

By the end of this outburst, Hester found she was standing up and pointing at the door. She had a sense of Jemima hurriedly stuffing her notebook into her handbag and backing out of the room, bent nearly double under the blast of Hester's fury.

As soon as she'd gone, Hester sank into the chair and covered her face with her hands. Oh God, here they come. The tears. If I start crying now, she thought, how will I ever be able to stop?

Edmund had phoned her only minutes before her interview with Jemima was supposed to begin.

'Wychwood House,' she had said, picking up the phone as soon as it began to ring. Why was it that people always rang you at a time when you couldn't possibly talk? Hester never gave her name out, just in case the caller turned out to be some sort of a nuisance.

'Hester?'

'Edmund! How lovely to hear from you! What a surprise . . .'

In the second between hearing Edmund's voice and speaking herself, before she had time to adjust what she was saying, Hester knew that bad news was coming. Edmund never phoned. He hated the idea of speaking without being able to see the person at the other end. Telephones were, in his opinion, for emergencies only. She imagined a warning vibration on the line, and the moment between dreading and actually knowing spun itself out, stretched and lengthened for second after second, as though the whole world were slowing to near-stillness. But the words came at last, and as soon as she heard them, Hester wished she'd never answered the phone, never admitted that, yes, she was there and ready to hear whatever was coming.

'Hester, darling, I'm sorry,' said Edmund. 'I'm in Vienna. I've just spoken to Virginia. She phoned me from New York. I knew I had to tell you at once. It's Adam.'

'Something's happened to him?' Part of her wanted to say *what business is that of mine? Adam Lennister has been nothing to me for over thirty years . . . why should I care what's happened to him?* but Edmund, as he always seemed to do, guessed what was in her mind.

'I know you haven't been in touch and so forth, but still. I do feel you must know. You might have seen it in the papers tomorrow anyway, and I couldn't bear the thought of you happening on it, just like that. He's dead, Hester. Adam died yesterday from a heart attack. He didn't suffer any pain, apparently. He was working. In the library of the New York house, because they're always over there for Thanksgiving and Christmas, aren't they? I'm *so* sorry, darling Hester. So sorry . . .'

'Yes,' said Hester. What else could she say? She felt as though all the words she used to know had flown out of her head. Edmund sounded on the verge of tears himself. It reminded Hester of how upset he'd been on the one occasion when they'd really quarrelled. She found that she was clutching the receiver so hard that her wrist and her fingers hurt. Breathing had suddenly become almost impossible, a matter for the utmost concentration. I must say something to Edmund, she thought. He was Adam's best friend.

'Edmund, I don't know what to say. I'm so, I'm so . . .' she managed to stammer, after an effort to move her mouth into the right shape. 'You must be very sad. Would you like to come up here?'

'I'd have adored that, Hester, but I've got to stay here for a couple of days . . . they're doing one of my symphonies and I can't miss it . . . and then of course there's the funeral. I have to go to that. But I'll come straight to Wychwood afterwards. Is that all right? I could get there on the second of January. How does that sound?'

'Oh, Edmund, do come as soon as you possibly can. I can't talk now, because I've got some wretched journalist coming to interview me about this year's Festival.' She laughed, but with no mirth in the sound. 'It's the last thing I feel like doing now.'

'I'll be there soon, Hester. Will you be all right? I'll be thinking of you.'

'I'll be fine. The show must go on, right? I'll see you soon. Goodbye.'

Is this me, uttering such clichés, Hester wondered. *The show must go on*. I don't care, she thought. This cliché is particularly comforting and also true. She believed it. What would become of her if the show *didn't* go on was too dreadful to think about.

The funeral. Virginia would be seeing to it now. Death made a horrifying amount of work. There were so many arrangements, so much to see to – perhaps, she reflected, precisely in order to occupy people who otherwise would want to do nothing but crawl under their blankets and howl and howl like wounded animals.

She tried to recall Adam as he used to be, long ago in the days when he was her lover, but so many images flickered through her mind that a kind of nausea washed over her. Other pictures came and went but the one she kept returning to was that of his dead body. All she could bring to mind was closed eyes and pale skin and white limbs stiff under a cold sheet – not the man whose body she used to know as well as she knew her own.

Hester put the phone down and walked to the window. She pressed her forehead against the glass, and looked out at a garden that was nothing but frost-whitened lawn and shrubs, and leafless trees making strange shapes against the grey sky. Dying isn't the worst thing, she thought, and found that she was trembling. Being buried, that's worse. The idea of burial, the notion that there he would be, real flesh, real bone, gone and underground forever was, as it always had been, an unbearable thought. Hester took a deep breath. It had been years since Adam was anything to do with her. She'd been sure that she'd left him and all the love she used to feel for him far behind, but now that he was dead she wanted to call his name, cry it out aloud, and found that she couldn't.

Her hands were icy cold in the warm room. I must call Ruby. I can't be alone. But I can't . . . I can't tell her. The journalist is coming any minute now. I must pull myself together.

She was brought out of her confusion by Siggy. An enormous ginger and white tom, with gooseberry-coloured eyes, he'd chosen this moment to leave the window sill and jump on to Hester's writing table, treading delicately over her papers. He settled himself against a small pile of copies of the last Wychwood Newsletter, the one that had gone out to Friends of the Festival a few weeks ago. Hester picked up the top copy and glanced at it, happy to be distracted:

As we move into winter, attention always turns to the upcoming Festival and Friends are eager to know who will present the 1987 ballet. This year's competition has been won by Hugo Carradine, the 34-year old founder and choreographer of the Carradine Ballet, who made such a sensation last year with his *Silver Girls*. The projected work for the Festival is called *Sarabande*. Hugo says, 'It's based on an ancient Persian fairytale, but we've built a series of almost abstract variations round the story. It'll be sensual and passionate with lavish decor and costumes in the Bakst tradition. We're very fortunate that Claudia Drake has agreed to dance the principal role of the Princess.'

Wychwood House welcomes the company from 27 December for the customary rehearsal period at the Arcadia, and the first night will take place on 6 January as always and run for ten performances. The Box Office opens on 25 November 1986.

George Stott (Secretary, Friends of the Wychwood Festival and Arcadia Theatre Manager)

'You're getting in the way, Siggy,' Hester said, sweeping her hand gently over his back and putting the Newsletter down. Her table was under the window so that there would always be something interesting to look at if she tired of whatever she was doing: the monkey-puzzle tree and, criss-crossed by its spiky branches, the roof of the Arcadia Theatre, built in a small dip in the landscape a little way away from the house. Every time she looked at it, she felt proud. It had been her idea, her brainchild, and it was now the home of the annual Wychwood Festival which over the ten years it had been in existence, had become a highlight of the ballet calendar. The countryside beyond the garden changed colour with changes in the weather, and today it was how Hester liked it best, with the moors almost purple behind the house and disappearing into clouds in the distance. A flurry of sleet almost obscured her view of the tall, intricately patterned wrought-iron gates.

There was a knock at the door. 'Come in.'

Ruby entered with Jemima close behind her.

'Are you ready, Hester?' Ruby asked. 'This is Jemima Entwhistle . . .' She paused, and Hester knew that she'd noticed that something was not quite right. Ruby always knew when something was troubling her. 'Yes thanks, Ruby. I'm quite ready.'

Then she smiled at the young woman who was hovering near a chair. 'Hello, Jemima, it's nice to meet you. Please sit down.'

Hester's face was still streaked with tears when Ruby came in with coffee and biscuits. She put the tray down and said 'I've brought a drink for you both . . . but what's wrong, Hester? I knew you weren't looking yourself. Where's Miss Entwhistle?'

'I had a call from Edmund,' Hester said. 'Just before you brought her in. He told me that Adam died yesterday. Of a heart attack.'

Ruby knelt down beside Hester and put a hand on her knee. 'Oh, my dear! My poor Hester. How dreadful! How could you think of giving an interview when you'd just been told something like that? You should have cancelled; Miss Entwhistle would have rescheduled it, I'm sure.'

'I didn't want to. I wanted all interviews over with before the company arrives for rehearsals. And I was doing very well. I felt quite proud of myself. She had no idea anything was wrong, but—'

'What happened?' Ruby took the chair opposite her and began pouring the coffee. 'What did she say?'

'She asked me about Christmas, why we don't celebrate it. I changed the subject, of course. Then she asked me why I hadn't married and I just lost my temper and sent her away. Awful of me, really.'

Ruby didn't comment. It would be hard for her, Hester realised, to say anything without mentioning the longest night, 21 December, which was the anniversary that neither of them ever referred to. They managed very well for the most part and the past remained the past, but the dreams were something over which Hester had no control.

For night after night, her sleep would be untroubled, but then, prompted by who knew what, the nightmares would come back; the ones from which she woke with tears still wet on her face. Could you cry in your sleep? Evidently you could. Whatever effort you made to put a terrible experience behind you, however hard you sealed it off in a compartment labelled *do not talk about, ever; do not acknowledge existence of ever*, what you were trying to forget was still there. She had arranged to hold the Festival at this time of year precisely so that she could have all her waking thoughts taken up with that, and now here came the news of Adam's death to throw her plans into confusion. He had been in New York. Hester had no proof of course, but she was quite sure that he spent every year from November till January in the States precisely so as to be somewhere far away when the anniversary occurred, and thus less likely to think of her.

Hester shook her head. 'Let's not dwell on it, Ruby. There's work to be done. It's going to be a good season, I think. We've got a wonderful company coming.'

She stood up and reached for a list which had been half-hidden behind Siggy's curved back and read aloud to Ruby. 'Carradine Ballet Company: Hugo Carradine, Claudia Drake, Silver McConnell, Andy French, Nick Neary, Ilene Evans, and Alison Drake (Ms Drake's daughter).'

When she'd read the names out, Hester smiled at Ruby, doing her best to appear normal, wanting more than anything for things to go back to where they were. She had no desire to mention her feelings. If I talk about the Festival, she thought, then Ruby will humour me. She'll know I don't want to talk about Adam. She took a deep breath.

'It's going to be interesting,' she said, 'to see how Claudia Drake will react to being in the same company as Silver McConnell. Claudia's very temperamental, they say, and she's forever in the newspapers. The photographers adore her. But Silver is by all accounts the new sensation. She's just done Odette/Odile – the best for years, the critics said. They compared her to me. My *Swan Lake* in 1959. Do you remember that?'

'Of course,' said Ruby. 'How could I forget the most famous *Swan Lake* of the last fifty years?'

'You're biased, Ruby! But thank you. In any case, Hugo Carradine was lucky to get Silver McConnell. As I told Jemima Whatsit, it's probably only because we have such a short run that she was able to accept the part. We've got a very starry lot all round this time. Nick Neary's the one who made such a sensation in *La Bayadère* last year, do you remember?'

'The beautiful creature? Yes, I remember him. Too pretty for his own good. He'll be conceited, I shouldn't wonder. They don't have to work so hard if they're handsome.'

'He's a good dancer, though. Very energetic, and technically excellent too.'

'It's going to be a tremendous success, this year, I'm sure. There's quite a lot to get ready in Wardrobe before their costumes arrive. I'd better go and make a start on it, if you're sure you're all right.'

'You go on, Ruby. I'm perfectly all right. I'll stay here for a while.'

Ruby was at her happiest when she was up in Wardrobe. She'd always had what Hester thought of as magic hands. She could take a piece of fabric and turn it, at will it seemed, into almost anything. She could mend a tear completely invisibly. Stains disappeared from garments as though they'd never existed, and her iron nosed its way into ruffles, flounces, and the most difficult of shirts and left nothing but perfection in its wake. Now she organised the wardrobe for every visiting company and looked after the smooth running of the house as well, with Joan and Emmie coming in every day to do the cooking and cleaning.

Hester closed her eyes as Ruby leaned over and kissed her cheek. She wasn't a demonstrative woman and whenever she made an affectionate gesture, Hester was pleasantly surprised and pleased. There aren't very many people I love in the world, she reflected. There's Dinah, who's been such a loyal and lovely friend for so long, and Edmund and Ruby. They love me too, I think. Whenever she brought them to mind, Hester felt as though she'd found a small patch of warmth in a world that seemed to her increasingly chilly. Such a pity that Dinah lived in New Zealand and that their relationship had to be conducted mostly by letter. She chided herself for not including Kaspar Beilin among her nearest and dearest. Darling Kaspar, with his white-blond hair and extravagantly camp style had been her dancing partner for years. Fielding and Beilin were a pair always spoken of together. Since his retirement, a few years after her own, he'd taken up residence in San Francisco and Hester couldn't help dreading what so many of her acquaintances were fearful of these days: AIDS. She shivered and closed her eyes. Make an effort, she told herself. You can't worry about Kaspar now. There is too much to do here with the Festival about to begin. And now there's Adam's death as well. Hester was used to his not being a part of her life, but dead? It was as though a cold hand had gripped her heart.

Ruby smiled at Hester as she was about to leave the room, saying, 'I'll be back in time for dinner. With George, if I can get him to stop what he's doing in the lighting box. Will we see you then? Are you quite sure you won't . . .' Ruby paused to find the right word. 'Brood on things?'

'No, I won't. I'll be fine. I'll just lie down on the *chaise-longue* for a while before dinner. Gather my thoughts.'

Ruby closed the door behind her. Once she was alone, Hester reflected for the thousandth time on how lucky she was to have Ruby here with her, just as she had been for the past thirty-four years. Ruby understood her. She knew better than to jolly Hester along. She knew how important it was for someone to have time to think about things. Ruby was part of the family. What had she said to the journalist? *The Wychwood family.*

The members of the Carradine Company would be here in a few days. Hugo Carradine was an attractive young man, and Hester knew he was overjoyed at the commission. He was talented and successful and well-thought of, with a reputation, even at his age, as a bit of a perfectionist. Dancers, it seemed, were rather in awe of him and he was reputed not to take any nonsense from anyone. Well, there was nothing wrong with that. Hester admitted that she was a perfectionist herself and couldn't really understand anyone who was satisfied with second best. Still, winning in an open competition hinges on such small things. She would never tell anyone that what gave Hugo her casting vote on a panel that was divided between him and another was his choice of music: *Sarabande in F minor* by Edmund Norland. Of course, he may have known that Hester and the composer had been good friends for many years. That wasn't a secret, and if he'd done his research, he'd have found it out. What he couldn't possibly have known, Hester thought, is what that piece means to me, or the circumstances in which it was written.

She remembered the day Edmund had played her the opening melody, how he'd sat at the piano and said *I've written something for you. Listen, Hester. All the sumptuous laziness of the East. Doesn't it make*

you feel better just to hear it? No more Northern gloom for you from now on.
She smiled.

But it wasn't only that, she told herself. Hugo was the best choreographer we saw. And I liked him better than any of the others, even without that private reason. I liked him at once, from the first moment I saw him. His smile was so open, and his warmth and love of the dance so evident in everything he said that I knew he was the sort of person I would enjoy welcoming to Wychwood House. There must be something wrong with me, Hester thought. Even after the shock I've had, I'm still looking forward to all of them arriving. The house is too quiet. It will be good to have it full of dancers again. Full of music and laughter.

Wychwood House had once belonged to a Victorian mill-owner. It was a handsome, square building of grey stone with magnificent wrought-iron gates set into solid stone gateposts; a house with a confident façade and an air of being rooted firmly in the landscape, almost a part of nature. It hadn't always looked like that. When Hester had first seen it, as a very young girl, it was shabby and neglected and the local children used to call it the Witch's House.

It's different now, she thought. Between March and November, three young men from the village came in twice a week to keep the garden looking perfect. Flowerbeds filled with roses bordered the path from the house to the theatre. George loved old-fashioned roses and he was the person who oversaw all the work that went on in the grounds. Hester herself had mixed feelings about flowers of all kinds and roses in particular, though she would never have admitted it. Each individual bloom was pretty of course, but only for a little while before it became overblown and brown around the edges of the petals. Flowers had such a short life and were so quickly less than perfect. Hester preferred shrubs and evergreen trees, and often thought the flowerbeds looked best in winter when the plants had been pruned and nothing but sharp little twigs stuck up out of the black earth.

She loved the garden. She enjoyed walking in it and delighted in the wide sweep of moor and sky that you could see wherever you stood. She had made sure that benches were placed in those spots that gave the best views. Every morning, unless the weather was atrocious, she walked for at least half an hour, through the garden and out to the slopes behind the house. She followed this with an hour at the *barre* she'd had specially installed in her dressing room.

The house had ten bedrooms. Her own was along a corridor and set apart from the accommodation used by the visiting dancers. There was a public drawing room and the kitchen was shared by everyone when the Festival was on. The dining room was only used for the most formal occasions such as the New Year's Eve dinner and the first night party. Ruby and George lived in a small cottage in the grounds. The passageway that led to the Arcadia Theatre went past the door of this room and she could always hear the dancers walking to and from their rehearsals.

Hester had her own sitting room and this room, where she spent most of her time, was known as the Office. The desk stood under the window and she kept the paperwork for both the Festival and her master classes in a mahogany tallboy. A filing cabinet would have looked wrong in a room which resembled in almost every particular dressing rooms she'd known while she was a ballerina. That's why I'm comfortable here, she often thought. It's completely familiar to me. There were no light bulbs around the mirror which hung on the wall near the door, and the smell of greasepaint had been replaced by the fragrance coming from an enormous bowl of pot-pourri, but otherwise it was what she had been used to for years.

She'd always insisted on having a *chaise-longue* in her dressing room and here in the Office she still liked to lie down whenever she needed to read or think. This *chaise* was new, and upholstered in dark red velvet, but the lacquered screen beside it, with its pattern of small boats on perfectly rippled water and conical snow-tipped mountains, was the same one she'd had since 1954. A cream silk shawl, fringed and printed with scarlet poppies, was draped over the other armchair.

The walls, papered in pale apricot, were crowded with framed photographs. There was the picture of her mother she had brought with her from France as a child, a few of Madame Olga, her first teacher, and better than a mother to her; several of her grandmother, darling *Grand-mère*, and many from productions in which she'd appeared. These were mostly of other dancers – her partners, her friends, and members of the *corps de ballet*. There was one exception.

She'd hung the famous Cecil Wilding photograph of herself, the one known as *A Backward Glance* right next to the mirror. Every time she checked to see if her hair was tidy; every time she looked in the mirror to apply her lipstick before going out into the world, she compared how she was now (dark hair cut short in a near shoulder-length bob and highlighted with streaks of red, still excellent skin but, oh God, look at the tiny wrinkles appearing near her eyes!) with the person in the portrait: herself as Aurora in *Sleeping Beauty*. It was taken when she was seventeen. Her head was turned to one side, her hair (very long, in those days) was twisted into a knot at the nape of her neck and threaded with pink and white roses. Her hands were crossed gracefully just below her waist and the ankle-length tulle skirt she was wearing spread out like a pale pink cloud that took up the entire bottom half of the picture. It was, Hester knew, every little girl's dream of what a ballerina *should* look like, which was one of the reasons she loved it. She enjoyed the illusion that it represented.

She'd often thought it would be fun to put up another photo of herself right beside it, showing her sweating after a particularly hard class; hair scraped back and in need of a wash; darned tights; aching calves; torn and bloody feet after hours *en pointe*. But nobody wanted to see that. It was the truth, but who was interested in that when magic was so much prettier? Who wanted to admit that all the effortless grace, the leaping and the flying and the turning were the result of hours and hours of back-breaking work? No one. Everyone liked the illusion. Each time she passed the mirror on leaving the room, she still had the distinct feeling that she was making an entrance, leaving the space that was hers and entering a public stage. Seeing her portrait on the way out to take part in the life outside the Office reminded her of how much she'd loved performing and it gave her courage. She had, she reflected, needed to be brave all through her life, from the very earliest age.

1939

Estelle knew, even when she was a very little girl, that there was something about her which upset her father. Henri was his name – Henri Prévert. He left the house each day dressed in a dark suit. He worked in a bank and *Grand-mère* said his work was very important. He was extremely tall and thin, and when he came into a room he filled it and it was difficult to look at anyone else. And to his little daughter he appeared enormous and she was frightened by his appearance. He reminded her of a scarecrow she'd once seen in a field, who'd worn a hat like Papa and also stood like him motionless, unbending.

He loved *Maman. Grand-mère* told Estelle that he did, and she believed her. Henri was her only child, but she had as much affection for her daughter-in-law as if she'd been her own flesh and blood.

'The love between your parents,' she told Estelle, 'was a mad love. *Un amour fou.*'

Grand-mère looked after everything in the house, so that Henri's beloved wife might have nothing to do but be with him. Estelle's mother was English, and she had no relations except for her second cousin, Rhoda, who lived in Yorkshire. Her mother spoke to Estelle in English from the day she was born, and she found nothing strange about speaking in two languages. One of Estelle's favourite stories was the one about how Papa met *Maman. Grand-mère* used to tell it to her quite often and it was better than any fairytale, because it was true. Helen was a ballerina. She danced in the *corps de ballet*, and when Henri first saw her he fell so in love with her that he couldn't think about anything else. He used to stand outside the stage door every night. After each performance, there he'd be, bearing a bunch of scarlet roses for her. Helen had many fans but this one was different. He looked very serious and he was also much handsomer than any other fan she'd seen. She spoke to him at last, and when she realised how much he adored her, she fell in love with him. They married very soon after they met and she never danced again. *Grand-mère* never said a word about her being sad not to be a ballerina any longer, but Estelle thought that she must have missed wearing all the lovely clothes and dancing on the stage in front of people and hearing them clapping her.

The house in the Rue Lavaudan was tall and narrow. Henri spent much of his time at the bank, but it pleased him to know that his beautiful wife was at home, waiting for him, longing for nothing but his company as he longed for hers.

Helen nearly died giving birth to her daughter, and Estelle's father made sure that the child knew this, even when she was very young. Almost the first thing he said to her was, 'You nearly killed poor *Maman* coming into this world, and you'll tire her out all over again if you worry her now.'

Although Estelle couldn't remember exactly when her father had said this, the words and the feeling behind the words never left her. She understood that he didn't love her, not then and not at any time. Later in her life she understood a little of how this lack of love came about, though she could never forgive it. She, by being born, had changed the body of his beloved wife into something gross and fat and unlovable. She'd torn it into a mess of blood and pain, and then she'd sucked from the breast that was his, that he wanted. How could he look at his daughter and not feel some sort of hatred?

The child loved her mother and she loved her *Grand-mère* and because her father was so busy, busy with his work, he hardly came into her life until after Helen's death. As she grew up, Estelle invented memories of her mother. She made up an idea of her, almost a dream of what she was like, and inserted it into the times she could remember, when *Grand-mère* was her closest companion.

The house was always sunlit. The kitchen had pale yellow walls, and her grandmother liked to bake. Estelle used to kneel up on a chair and help her create patterns with apple slices on the *tartes aux pommes* she made every week. *Grand-mère* sang all the time, small snatches of parlour songs and operettas and the better-known arias from *Carmen* and *La Traviata*. She used to take the little girl for walks in the Jardin du Luxembourg, near the house, where they watched the puppet shows together and then sat on a bench under the trees while she told her granddaughter stories about her own father when he was a small boy. Estelle found it hard to match the person her grandmother was speaking of with the silent papa whose smiles for her touched his lips briefly and never reached his eyes.

On rainy days, *Grand-mère* let Estelle dress up in her clothes and jewels and even wear her high-heeled shoes. Best of all were the hats, carefully put away in striped hatboxes that lived in a special cupboard in the spare bedroom.

'One would need ten lifetimes to wear them all,' *Grand-mère* used to say, picking up a velvet toque, or a neat little red felt circle with spotted netting attached to it, or one of the many straw hats with wide brims she wore in the summer. These were the ones Estelle loved best. They had flowers and bows and bunches of cherries glazed to a dazzling shine attached to the ribbon round the crown, and she felt like a princess when she put one on and paraded in front of the mirror.

They looked at photographs too, and it was on those afternoons, sitting beside her grandmother on the sofa and turning over the stiff grey pages, that Estelle assembled an image of her mother. There were the photographs of her in various productions, dressed in a tutu and wearing a headdress of one kind and another. One of these, the best of all, was the picture Estelle took with her to England. *Grand-mère* put it into a frame and packed it among her clothes in the small suitcase she was taking with her. The photograph showed a pretty lady with her hair piled in an arrangement of waves on top of her head. She was dressed in a practice skirt and was leaning against a wickerwork skip, evidently backstage. A gauzy scarf was wound round her neck and she was smiling. On her feet she wore ballet shoes, and Estelle often wondered who had taken this photograph of her mother, who was obviously on her way to change her clothes after some rehearsal. She was smiling, and Estelle always imagined that the smile was directed at her even though she knew that this was impossible. She hadn't even been born when the photograph was taken.

Helen died of pneumonia at the age of twenty-seven. Estelle was only five but all her life she remembered the sadness she'd felt at the time in the way you remember a distant illness. As she grew older, the pain grew less sharp – not so much a wound anymore but like a hidden bruise, only painful when you prod it.

When Papa announced that she was to be sent to England to stay with her mother's cousin, it didn't occur to Estelle to ask why. Henri did not consult his daughter, but she wouldn't have expected it. You did as you were told, and Estelle wouldn't have dared to object to anything her father had decided. Her grandmother spoke about the decision only once, as they were packing the child's few belongings into a suitcase. Estelle was anxious about Antoinette, her doll.

'I can take her, can't I, *Grand-mère?*'

'Of course, my darling.' She sat on the edge of Estelle's bed, and took the little girl on to her lap. Her eyes were red. Since Helen had died, she had wept so much that this was their normal condition. She said, 'I will write to you every week, Estelle, and you will ask Mrs Wellick to read my letters, won't you? Then soon you'll learn to write yourself, and we can correspond like two real friends, two ladies. That'll be lovely, won't it? Oh, but I'll miss you so much, *chérie*, I will pray for your safety and happiness. And you won't forget your French will you, Estelle? You won't become entirely English?'

Estelle shook her head. 'If I stayed here, I could speak French all the time. Why can't I stay? Why does Papa want to send me to England?'

She had an idea of England in her mind because of what her mother had told her. There was fog there, and rain and white cliffs.

'Because,' said *Grand-mère*, 'he wants you to be with someone nearer your own age. Your mother's cousin has a daughter who's only a little bit older than you. It'll be company for you. I'm getting old, and your father is always busy with his work. And your mother would have been so happy to know you're going to be educated in England. Of course it's best . . .'

Grand-mère's voice faded to nothing and she hugged Estelle to her so closely that the child could hardly breathe for a while. When she let her go, and started talking about Antoinette and how they were going to fit her into the suitcase so as not to crush her dress, Estelle could hear a sort of shaking in her voice and saw her eyes were full of tears. She was blinking a lot, to hold them back.

22

England, when she first saw it, was indeed a place with white cliffs. It seemed to her to be entirely grey – grey skies, grey sea, greyish buildings. They travelled to Yorkshire by train and she stared out of the window as the rain streaked across the glass in horizontal grey lines. When they reached the Wellick house, it was as though Estelle's father disappeared almost before he arrived. One meal, a kiss and a brief hug, and then he was gone in the same taxi that they had taken from the station. Henri had asked the driver to return for him.

The place looked completely empty to Estelle. It was raining when they arrived, and the sky was so low and grey over the purplish hills that she felt she could reach up and touch it. There were a few sheep grazing on the moor and what her father called 'a village' was two streets, a church, a grim-looking grey stone school house, one shop and a tavern of some kind called a 'pub', her father said. Her mother's cousins lived at the far end of the village. On the drive from the station, just before they reached their destination, they passed a big house. Estelle looked at it through the bars of its tall, wrought-iron gates and wondered who lived there. Paula, Estelle's cousin, told her later that it was called the Witch's House and that it had been empty for years, spiders and bats the only company for the ghosts who lived there, and hooty owls nesting in the trees that grew behind it.

Estelle first saw Paula looking down from the upstairs front room window as she and her father got out of the taxi. She had a narrow face, a long nose and thin lips, and her brown fringe fell on to a wide forehead. She looked cross, as though she wasn't a bit pleased that her French cousin was coming to live with the family, and this, Estelle realised quite quickly, was entirely true. Paula thought of her as a nuisance and treated her from the very first with complete disdain and dislike.

Mr and Mrs Wellick – Auntie Rhoda and Uncle Bob – weren't unkind. Estelle only realised much later that they had little aptitude for conversation or laughter and exchanges with them from the very first day were formal and wooden. Whatever came out of their mouths sounded to her like sentences repeated from a reader, or textbook.

This is your room, dear . . . we hope you'll be very happy with us . . . we're sure you'll be a good girl . . . eat your nice tapioca pudding now. And on and on. Those puddings made every meal a torment. Wobbly or gelatinous or gritty white concoctions appeared regularly on her plate and she found them disgusting. As she swallowed each mouthful, she tried hard to think about *Grand-mère's* pastries and lemon mousse, her *pots au chocolat*, meringues and profiterôles – everything delicious she'd ever eaten.

The house was colourless. Curtains of a dark non-colour hung at the windows; the paintwork was a lighter shade of nothing; the carpets were trying to be green but failing miserably. Auntie Rhoda and Uncle Bob dressed to blend into their surroundings in washed-out grey and a thousand variations on beige.

The Wellicks did their best. Bob Wellick went into Keighley every day to work as a clerk in an accountant's office and returned at night. Auntie Rhoda stayed at home and looked after Paula and Estelle.

Estelle felt a desperate longing for France that she didn't have the words to express. On her first night in England she lay in chilly sheets, with Paula asleep in the next bed, and stared at the ceiling. She thought of the taxi, driving away down the road with her father, who never looked back to wave at her, even though she'd stood at the gate for a long time staring after the car. It had truly happened – he'd left her in this place all on her own. Until the moment when she saw the car disappear into the mist that seemed to have fallen while they were drinking tea with the Wellicks, part of Estelle believed that perhaps it wouldn't happen, that Papa would say *Right, my dear. Drink up your milk and come home to Paris with me.*

She felt she was nowhere; not in her home, not in some other home, just in a sort of limbo, a non-place that she would never get used to. Where was *Grand-mère*? Was she thinking of her? Did she miss her? Estelle imagined her grandmother in the high bed at the Rue Lavaudan, with lace-trimmed pillows heaped behind her head, and the thought made tears run down her cheeks. They made puddles under her neck and she was too miserable and scared to call anyone. Also she knew, young as she was, that she didn't want Auntie Rhoda coming to comfort her. She knew that her cousin's presence would make her feel worse, not better, so she swallowed her sorrow and, for many nights after that, she'd wait until Paula's breathing slowed and deepened then cry herself to sleep.

In the end, she became accustomed to her situation and accepted it. She ate, she slept, and eventually she went to school in the village. She became silent because Paula, who was supposed to be her friend and companion, made it quite clear from the moment Estelle moved in that she was quite simply not interested in her. Paula was sly, and Estelle's days were filled with tiny little pinpricks of unkindness that she could not have legitimately complained about without appearing to be what Paula and her friends called a *tell-tale-tit*.

One particularly awful memory stood out from the rest. After Estelle had been in England for about two years, she and Paula were invited to celebrate the birthday of one of Paula's classmates. Estelle was in the class below her cousin at school, so she didn't see much of her there. Nevertheless, Paula's best friend, Marjorie, invited Estelle to the party and she was happier and more excited at the prospect than she'd been about anything for a long time. She understood that Paula wasn't too thrilled at the idea, but she didn't care. She was going to wear her best dress: scarlet velvet, smocked across the bodice, which was a little short. It reminded her of *Grand-mère*, who had done the smocking with her own hands, and Estelle was determined to show it off.

On the afternoon of the party, Paula was even more silent than usual. The girls walked down the village street to Marjorie's house, which was close enough for them to be allowed to walk there by themselves. Paula glanced at Estelle sideways out of her narrow eyes and smiled nastily.

'Marjorie didn't want to invite you really,' she said. 'Her mum made her.'

'How d'you know? You don't know that.'

'Yes, I do. Marjorie told me. She said if it was left to her, she'd never have a baby at her birthday party, but her mother feels sorry for you. So she had to.'

Estelle didn't want anyone to feel sorry for her. She could sense herself blushing with shame and anger. Part of her wanted to run back to the Wellicks and hide in her bed, but the party! Paula had been speaking for days of cakes iced in pink and violet, balloons and lemonade. Red and green jellies. Estelle longed for everything, so she blinked back the tears and walked along beside her cousin. Then, as they were approaching the gate, Paula turned her gaze on Estelle once again and wrinkled her mouth.

'You should've worn something else. An old dress of mine, or something. You look silly in that. It's too small for you and the colour's horrible.'

Estelle answered before she had time to think. The fury that she felt was enormous. It was there, in her chest, like a balloon filling every corner of her body, and when she opened her mouth the balloon exploded and the anger rushed out.

'You know nothing about it,' she shouted at Paula. 'The colour is beautiful and you're jealous because your dress makes you look exactly like a lemon. Yellow and sour. You think I'm going to run home crying because you don't like my dress. Well, I'm not. I'm going to the party, so there.'

Paula didn't answer because they were already at Marjorie's house. She knocked at the door instead, but glanced at Estelle with pure hatred in her eyes. Estelle stood up as straight as she could and put a smile on her face. To herself she said horrible, horrible Paula! I'm not going to let her spoil the party for me. But the fact was she *had* spoiled it, she'd ruined everything. But Estelle wasn't going to let anyone know how miserable she was. All through the games and during the party tea, she smiled and pretended not to notice that Paula and Marjorie and some of the other big girls kept gathering in the corners of the room and whispering. They're whispering about me, Estelle thought. I know they are. I don't care. I don't. I'm just as good as any of them. They're stupid girls who don't know anything. I won't let them make me sad. I won't. She bit her lip and held her head up so that no one would see how she was feeling. She concentrated on what she would say in her next letter to *Grand-mère*; how she would describe the party.

When Estelle first arrived in England, she received a letter from her grandmother every week, and Auntie Rhoda read each one aloud once. If Estelle asked her to read it again later, or on another day, she did, but with a sigh and an air of being tremendously put out. At first, Estelle couldn't write more than a couple of letters of the alphabet, but she used to draw pictures on small pieces of paper and Auntie Rhoda folded them up and sent them in buff envelopes to France.

And then the letters arrived less and less often. War was raging everywhere, and everything became more difficult. Paula enjoyed frightening Estelle with stories of bombs falling on buildings and blowing them up, and sometimes in the evening the whole family gathered round the big radio in the parlour to listen to the news, which Estelle couldn't understand very well and didn't feel able to ask about. Henri wrote to her explaining that, because of the war, it was hard for him to travel to England and that he hoped she was well and not giving the Wellicks any trouble. He also sent letters addressed to Uncle Bob, which Estelle knew contained some money to help pay for her keep. Every time Estelle opened another envelope, she hoped that her father might have written to say *After the War is over, you must come back to France again. You must come home* but he never did.

Each Christmas, the Wellick family went to the pantomime at the Alhambra Theatre in Bradford. It was the annual treat, when even Auntie Rhoda and Uncle Bob took on an air of almost-celebration. When Estelle was nine years old, the pantomime was *Red Riding Hood*, which was one of the fairytales she loved best of all. *Grand-mère* had shown her a picture once, in a big, leather-bound book, of Red Riding Hood in bed with the Wolf. He was dressed in a frilly nightcap, and Estelle could still remember how frightened she was. But she loved the story even though it scared her, and couldn't explain, even to herself, why that should be so. Somewhere near the beginning of the first act a dancer, who was supposed to be some kind of forest fairy, came out on to the stage. Estelle didn't recognise the music but she knew that she'd never heard anything half so beautiful. She was enchanted. She watched this magical person who seemed lighter and more delicate than any human being could possibly be, twirling to the lovely sounds, and swaying like a flower balanced on pointed toes. And the clothes she wore! Estelle drank in the sight of her. She had a garland of leaves in her hair, and the green, gauzy, filmy stuff of her skirts, scattered with thousands of tiny pink flower petals, floated round her legs like mist.

She danced and danced and when it was over, Estelle felt bereft. She thought about nothing but what she had just seen. Those few minutes on a stage made beautiful by apricot and rose footlights remained in her head and, when she was on her own in the bedroom she shared with Paula, for days and days afterwards she tried to mimic the steps she'd seen the dancer take. It looked as though it might be the easiest thing in the world to do and it turned out to be impossible.

The following winter, the big house with the wrought-iron gates at the end of the village had a new owner. Marjorie announced that a lady from Russia had bought it. Her mother had told her that this Russian person, whose name she couldn't remember, used to be quite a famous dancer.

'She won't have anyone to talk to, will she, if she's Russian?' said Paula. 'I expect she can't speak English. Why has she come here?'

'My mum says she's a friend of the Cranleys. You know, they live in that big white house on the way to Leeds. This Russian lady is a friend of Mrs Cranley's son, and he's something to do with the ballet too. I don't exactly know what, though.'

Estelle was fascinated by this mysterious woman. She discovered, from Betty in the shop who knew everything, that her name was Madame Olga Rakovska. She also learned that the house was called Wychwood House. All sorts of stories circulated about Madame Rakovska. She had run away to Paris during the Russian Revolution, fleeing without a penny piece to her name. She had fled with the contents of many bank deposit boxes sewn into her undergarments. She had nothing in the world. She was a rich miser who had rubies the size of birds' eggs hidden under the floorboards. She'd committed a crime and was on the run; and on and on.

Estelle began to see her quite often, walking along between the shop and her enormous house, very upright, in a black coat with a fur collar. The hem of this coat swept the ground as she made her graceful progress along the village street with her head held high and her hands showing white through the pattern of her lace gloves. She had black hair, drawn back into a chignon at the nape of her neck and she sometimes wore a hat that was just like one of Estelle's grandmother's favourites: a small, black velvet creation with a spotted veil hanging down to cover the top half of the face. She longed to talk to her, to ask her whether she still danced sometimes but she didn't dare.

Then, one afternoon when Paula was playing at Marjorie's house, Estelle's curiosity grew so strong that she crept out of the house and ran all the way down the village street till she came to the gates of Wychwood House. The light was beginning to fade and the building loomed very dark and forbidding at the top of the curving, overgrown drive. Estelle took a deep breath and pushed opened the heavy gate. She looked all around, wondering if anyone might stop her, but there was no one.

I should go home, she thought. Maybe all the stories about ghosts are true. Maybe there's something hiding among the shrubs. She made her way up the drive and with every step she grew more terrified. Then she glanced up at the house and her fears vanished in an instant.

Madame Olga had forgotten to draw the curtains in one of the big front rooms. Estelle could see right in and what she saw was a huge space with no carpet on a polished, wooden floor the colour of honeycomb, an upright piano in the far corner and a mirror taking up the whole of one wall. A black rail was fixed to the wall opposite the mirror and, standing with her back to the window, was Madame Olga herself, wearing a long black dress. She was resting the fingers of her left hand on the rail and bending forward at the waist. On her feet she was wearing pink ballet shoes.

From her first glimpse of that room, Estelle knew that her future was there, in that house, with that person. She felt as though she were standing on the edge of a precipice with nothing but blue beneath her, dizzy and longing to jump, but also breathless with dread of something that might be snatched away before she could enjoy it.

She asked Auntie Rhoda about Wychwood House the next day at breakfast, testing out what she felt about Madame Olga. Her aunt was unusually forthcoming.

'I believe that the Russian lady who's bought it is a ballet teacher. I can't think why she's chosen to come and settle here. You'd think a town would suit her better.' There was a spoonful of porridge halfway to her mouth. 'Still, she knows the Cranleys and that must be a help to her. The Cranleys know everyone important round here. That house has been empty for years, and of course it's good to have it lived in again, but still. I don't know whether a ballet teacher is the kind of person we want in this area.' She sighed. 'It's the war, that's what it is. You never got all sorts of foreigners moving in before the war. I don't know how many pupils she'll get, what with the petrol rationing and everything, but some people will still manage to bring their daughters to class, I shouldn't wonder.'

Estelle didn't say a word, but her heart began to beat very fast. She *had* to go there. She had to talk to Madame Olga. She had to meet this ballet teacher, who would teach her how to do all the movements she'd admired on the stage at the pantomime last year. Somehow she knew that asking the Wellicks' permission was pointless. They would refuse, she was sure of it. She vowed to find a way of getting into Wychwood House without telling them. It would be her secret.

Getting to meet Madame Olga was easier than she had dared to hope. There were hours and hours when Auntie Rhoda wasn't really paying any attention to where Estelle was. *Go out and play, dear* was a refrain she heard often.

The following day, terrified at what the strange Russian lady might say to her, she walked again through the black gates, which stood half open. In the bright daylight it was easier to see everything clearly. Overgrown trees loomed up behind the house; all the shrubs needed pruning and the grass was long and ragged. When she reached the porch, she noticed that it was adrift with leaves left over from autumn. She plucked up courage and knocked at the wooden door.

She had to wait quite a long time for Madame Olga to open it. 'Yes?' she said, peering down at the girl standing in front of her. Estelle thought that she didn't look like an ordinary person at all, but like someone who'd just stepped out of a play. Her complexion was perfect, as though she were made of something other than flesh, with her skin pale and smooth and her lips painted perfectly in a shade of red that Estelle later learned she had sent to her from Paris. It was darker than most lipsticks worn by the women she saw every day. Madame Olga had plucked eyebrows, like a film star, and her nose was narrow and slightly curved which, together with her wide-set eyes, gave her the look of a beautiful bird. Her clothes were black, but you couldn't see much of them because she had a shawl or huge scarf or some piece of beautiful fabric in shades of orange and red with a pattern picked out in gold thrown round her shoulders. On her feet she wore ballet slippers of black leather and round her neck there was something Estelle had never seen before – a lorgnette, spectacles on a kind of stick, which she flicked open and then raised to her eyes, looking through them as though she wanted to see right inside you. Through the lenses, her very dark eyes stared at Estelle as if she were reading her thoughts.

'Please, I want to dance. Are you going to be giving lessons? Will you teach me how to dance?' Estelle asked.

'You wish to come for lessons? Classes start in three weeks. Return then, please, and I will enrol you with other girls in beginners' class. There are not so many pupils now. It is the war.'

Estelle was sure, quite sure, that the lessons would start at once and the shock of disappointment was unbearable and made her feel almost nauseous. Madame Olga noticed her dismay and took her hand. 'Come inside, child. Come with me. And please tell me your name.'

'Estelle Prévert.'

Madame Olga nodded and they walked into the house together.

Most of it was dark and gloomy, and it seemed as though there were rooms and rooms hidden away, somewhere where you couldn't see them down long dark corridors and at the top of forbidding flights of stairs that stretched up into the shadows. But Estelle felt, going into the back parlour, as though she were once more at home, in France, in her beloved grandmother's house. She sat in a plump chair upholstered in pinkish velour and took in the ornate furniture, the heavy greenish brocade curtains which looked grand to her, even though she could see they were a little faded and had been mended here and there, and the pale blue walls covered with framed photographs of ballerinas in many different poses. They looked beautiful, every one of them, with their arms and legs making perfect shapes against the painted scenery in the background.

'Why do you wish to learn to dance?'

Estelle hesitated before answering, not knowing how to express her need, her desire. In the end she said, 'I think the steps are there in my feet, but I don't know how to let them out.'

Madame Olga smiled, and said, 'We will go to the studio. Follow me, and please, take your shoes off and go in the socks. We must care for the floor.'

Estelle would have followed her anywhere. They crossed the wide hall and she left her shoes by the door and went into the room she'd seen from the window. She could feel the wood smooth under her feet.

'Good, now stand like this.' Madame Olga threw her magnificent shawl over the back of a chair and took up the first position and Estelle copied her. She nodded, but said nothing and changed to second position and then third and so on and Estelle mirrored every movement. Then she raised her arms, and Estelle followed. Still, Madame Olga said nothing. She moved to the rail.

'This we call the *barre*,' she said. 'Rest your hand lightly, like me.'

Estelle lost track of the time. When they returned to the parlour, the light was fading and suddenly she felt frightened. Surely Auntie Rhoda would be missing her by now? How long had she been here?

'I think I should go home now. It's nearly tea-time.'

'You will please come again. I think you will be a good dancer. Yes.' Madame Olga nodded and Estelle felt as though her whole body might fly up to the ceiling, like a bird, from pure happiness.

Estelle asked Auntie Rhoda's permission that very evening, at supper. Auntie Rhoda stared at her as she spoke. She'd just dished out some mashed potato on to Uncle Bob's plate and paused with her spoon in the air, before plunging it into the potatoes again.

'I don't really think so, dear,' she said, with an air of finality.

'But why not?' Estelle wouldn't normally have dared to ask, but this was too important, and she could feel everything she'd dreamed of sliding away from her. Paula said with satisfaction in her voice, 'Estelle's going to cry.'

'No, I'm not. I just want to know why I can't have dancing lessons.'

'Because even with the money your father sends us we can't afford it and, besides, we know nothing about this person. I don't hold with fripperies like ballet. They make a person think they're better than other people.'

Estelle stared at the mashed potato that Auntie Rhoda had dolloped on to her plate.

'I'm not eating that,' she said, 'and I *am* going to have dancing lessons. I shall write to my father. He'll send more money when he knows how much I want to dance. My mother was a ballerina. I want to be like her and you can't stop me!'

She pushed her chair back from the table and stamped out of the room. Then she left the house in a rage, before anyone could come and fetch her back. Once she was outside she ran all the way to Madame Olga's front door. By the time Madame opened it, after she'd been banging on it frantically for what seemed like ages and ages, Estelle was weeping tears of anger and frustration

'*Moia golubchka,*' Madame Olga said. 'My child!' and she gathered Estelle into her arms and draped her shawl around the child's shoulders. 'Why do you cry? What is the matter?'

'They don't understand. They don't see that I *have* to dance. I must. All Auntie Rhoda cares about is the money. I shouted at her. I have to have lessons.' Madame Olga said, 'Ah, please do not worry about this. You will have the lessons. This I promise you. Go home now and I will speak to this aunt of yours who knows nothing. All will be well. You will see.'

Estelle never discovered what Madame Olga had told the Wellicks. She went to see them while the children were at school and Estelle realised that Madame Olga must have said she wouldn't be asking for any payment. Auntie Rhoda never mentioned the conversation, but took Estelle rather grudgingly into Leeds and bought her a pair of ballet shoes (pink, with lovely satin ribbons to tie) and a dress like a gym-slip with a very short skirt. All the way there on the bus, she'd muttered about what a waste of clothing coupons such purchases were and how impossible it would be to find such items in wartime, but luck had been with them and they'd found everything quite easily.

'This ballet stuff won't butter any parsnips,' she said as they came home. 'Still, I daresay it won't do any harm.'

And so it began. On Wednesday and Saturday afternoons, Estelle inhabited another universe, where music played and her body stretched and lifted and bent and her head was filled with dreams of flying through the air to the sounds that filled every part of her head, even after she'd left the studio. Estelle was one of only four other girls in the class. Petrol rationing was the excuse for the shortage of pupils but Estelle didn't mind. The others were older than she was, and she admired them all and worked hard to copy them in everything they did. All five of Madame Olga's pupils were reflected in the big mirror, moving together, and Estelle would see their reflections and think how pretty they looked, their mirror images moving along with them to the lovely melodies of Chopin or Délibes.

Estelle loved class. She loved the safety of it, the routine; the feeling she had of always knowing precisely where she was. She liked dancing the same steps in the same order and the idea that if she tried really, really hard, she would achieve a perfect sequence of steps and then Madame Olga would praise her.

'Push yourself,' Madame would cry. 'Push yourself to the limit of what your body can do.'

Estelle did, every time she went to Wychwood House. She found that if she concentrated hard enough on what went on in class, she could put everything else into a separate compartment in her head and think about it quite differently – in a much more detached way. As the war dragged on, food was becoming less and less tasty and she dreaded the powdered eggs and the awful day when the sugar ration ran out for the week, as it always seemed to do. But Estelle danced and danced and forgot what was happening in the real world. Auntie Rhoda and Uncle Bob kept the news from the girls as much as possible, and anything Estelle heard about France she somehow didn't connect with her father or grandmother. She learned from a letter about her father's second marriage to a young woman called Yvonne, and found that it was easy not to get upset about such things if she put them in a kind of detached part of her mind. Estelle discovered she had a gift for this, for being able to ignore things that would hurt her if she thought about them too much. She became skilled at keeping a distance between herself and anything too unpleasant to think about.

One day shortly after the end of the war, Auntie Rhoda called Estelle into the parlour for what she called 'a quiet word'. As soon as she saw her aunt sitting rather stiffly at the table with a small package in front of her and a letter in her hand, Estelle understood that something awful had happened.

'Come and sit down, dear,' Auntie Rhoda smiled at her.

'What's the matter, Auntie Rhoda?'

'It's bad news, dear, I'm afraid. Your grandmother . . . I'm so sorry. She was a very old lady, though, wasn't she? We must think of her at peace.' Auntie Rhoda held out the letter and Estelle took it. Her eyes filled with tears as she looked at the tiny black letters of her father's familiar handwriting.

My dear Estelle, I am very sorry to have to tell you that my mother died two weeks ago in hospital. She had been suffering from pneumonia and her end was peaceful and without pain. The funeral was held yesterday. I know how sad this will make you and I am sorry to be the bearer of such news. Your grandmother was most insistent that I should send you this chain. She says that you will know what to do with it, but if you are willing to take my advice (and don't forget that I am still a banker) I would put it away in a safe-deposit box in the local bank. In that way, you will not have to worry about losing it.

'He's written to me too,' Auntie Rhoda said, taking Estelle by the hand and guiding her to a chair at the kitchen table. 'Your grandmother has left you a small legacy, you know.'

Estelle didn't care about her legacy. Her eyes were on the package on the kitchen table. 'Is that the box my father sent?'

'Yes, here it is. We could keep it safe in the bank if you like.'

'No,' Estelle trembled with terror. How could Auntie Rhoda prevent her from keeping *Grand-mère*'s chain? She held out her hand. 'I'll look after it. I won't lose it, I promise. Please let me have it.'

'Well, I can't stop you, I suppose, but I don't think it's very sensible, you know. What if you mislay it?'

'I won't. I wouldn't. I never would. Give it to me.'

Suddenly, the horror of everything struck Estelle and she grabbed the box from Auntie Rhoda's hand and ran out of the room. She fled up the stairs to the bedroom and flung herself on the bed, sobbing and clutching the small box tight in her hand. Rage filled her. How could Papa do such a thing? Write her a letter about *Grand-mère*'s death? If he'd phoned, she could have gone to France, to the funeral. She was old enough to travel by herself. Why hadn't he telephoned? Or sent a telegram? He didn't want me there, she thought. He says *Grand-mère* died of pneumonia but maybe that's not true. Maybe, she thought, Papa didn't want me to meet Yvonne. Maybe Yvonne told him she didn't want me to come. If I'd gone, I could have stood beside the grave in the cemetery and wept and then *Grand-mère* would have known how much I loved her. I'll never see her again.

Estelle sat up and dried her eyes. She pulled Antoinette to her and buried her face in the doll's skirts. Paula was downstairs. She could hear her talking and soon she would be up in the bedroom, asking what the matter was. Estelle fingered the chain she wore always round her neck, the chain her grandmother had given her before she left for Yorkshire. Papa might be a banker, she thought, but he doesn't know me very well. I'll never let *Grand-mère*'s half of the chain out of my sight. I'd never entrust it to a bank. And the idea that I'd ever lose it is ridiculous. Does he think that I'm careless or stupid?

She opened the small round tortoiseshell box. There it was, the chain she had promised to pass on to her own daughter. She knew she had to hide it at once before Paula saw it and started asking questions. If she does, Estelle told herself, I'll just tell her it's none of her business. She got off the bed and hid the box away under her vests, right at the back of her drawer in the shared chest of drawers. It would be quite safe there. Paula wouldn't be interested enough to snoop around for it.

That night she cried bitterly for her grandmother, just as she used to when she first came to the Wellicks, pulling the pillow over her head so that Paula wouldn't hear her. She dreamed all night of *Grand-mère*'s room: the high bed piled with pillows frilled with lace, the hatboxes, the jewels, and her grandmother's voice speaking to her, singing to her, making her feel warm and loved and safe. As soon as she woke up, she remembered the truth and felt chilly and dazed with sorrow. Once she was dressed, she took her father's letter and tore it up into small pieces. She gathered up the bits and went into the back parlour, where she threw them on the coal fire. They acquired glowing, scarlet edges before turning to grey ash. I won't think about it, she told herself. I'll try to forget I ever got that letter. While she danced at Madame Olga's, she pretended *Grand-mère* was still alive, still in her father's house in Paris, and sending good wishes to her granddaughter. Estelle decided that there wasn't much difference between death and distance. What it came down to was not seeing the person you loved. Not ever.

25 December 1986

Alison Drake looked across the table at her mother. Claudia Drake, beautiful international ballet superstar, ta-rah, was pushing two minuscule roast potatoes round her plate. She always did that: arranged her food artistically, nibbled briefly at a couple of things and then rearranged it all over again. Alison debated throwing the remains of the Marks & Spencer turkey roast at her. Her mother, annoyingly, was blissfully unaware of what was going on in her daughter's mind, so Alison decided to say something.

'You haven't exactly made an effort this year, have you? I don't call this a proper Christmas.'

'I can't do a big, elaborate thing,' Claudia said. 'I've explained it to you. I've got to get us ready to go up to Yorkshire on Sunday. Rehearsals start on Monday. I can't leave a whole lot of stuff in the fridge.'

Perhaps it was the ill-prepared and skimpy meal. Perhaps it was the lack of decorations and a tree. Maybe it was her fury at having to drag along with Claudia to the depths of the countryside, but suddenly Alison lost her temper completely and began to shout at her mother.

'It's always fucking rehearsals with you. You never have time for real people and real things because you're so taken up with your stupid ballet and your stupid class that you can never ever miss, oh no, because proper professionals never miss class, do they? And your whole, your whole *ridiculous pretend world* which is more important to you than the real world. I don't care if I never see another fucking ballet ever again in my whole life.'

'How dare you speak to me like that?' Claudia was shouting right back. 'Don't you know that I run myself *ragged* trying to arrange things so that you're not put out? Apologise. Apologise at once, or I shall send you to your room and you can stew there till Sunday for all I care.'

Alison mumbled into her plate:

'I'm sorry I swore at you, but I mean it about the ballet. I *do* think it's boring. I don't see what's wrong with saying that. You're not exactly sympathetic about what I want to do.'

'Well, darling,' Claudia smiled, and Alison knew she thought the worst was over and that she'd won. 'Midwifery, I ask you!' She shuddered. 'All that blood. I don't think I could bear it. Couldn't you find something more – I don't know – more glamorous?'

Alison had been through this before. She decided not to tell her mother all over again that glamour wasn't what she was after. Surely the beautiful Claudia Drake could understand that lesser mortals (i.e. other women and girls) weren't exactly designed for the limelight. She changed the subject.

'What am I supposed to do while you're rehearsing? I don't see why I have to come anyway.'

'You know very well why. Aunt Mavis couldn't have you. She's been invited on a cruise. To Egypt.'

'Your childcare arrangements are crap. Most people have lots of relations. Sisters and brothers and things.'

'It's hardly my fault that I'm an only child. Nor is it my fault that your father is totally inadequate and pathetic. Not to mention the fact that he decided to live in America with his so-called wife, who's a tart with no more brains than your average chicken.'

'Dad *isn't*. He *isn't* pathetic. He rang up last night, didn't he? He spoke to me for ages. You're the pathetic one. And you don't know how clever Jeanette is, or isn't. She's not his so-called wife, either. She's his real wife.'

Claudia pulled a face. 'Oh, per-lease! How clever do you have to be to get a man's attention if you keep the top buttons of your blouse permanently undone and flaunt underwear that's no more than a string and a prayer? Your father is a fool and a bastard and there's nothing more to be said.'

Alison changed the subject. She usually did when it came to talking about her father. The whole matter was too painful to go into, and she tried to avoid it when she could.

'I could stay here on my own. I'm fourteen. That's easily old enough.'

Claudia looked at her pityingly. Alison stared right back, saying, 'What about friends, then? You don't seem to have many of those, do you? Not that *that's* a surprise. And Granny probably died early just so's she wouldn't have to look after me.'

Alison knew that if Claudia were sitting beside her, she'd have hit her. She was breathing deeply: always a sure sign that she was trying not to lose her temper. Her voice, when she did speak, was carefully light and cheerful.

'I have very many friends, as you know, but of course they're performers like me, and so quite unable to help me out by having you to stay.'

How nice of her, Alison reflected sarcastically, not to say anything really nasty. She easily could have done. She could, for instance, have flung the question back: *why haven't* you *got any friends who'll have you to stay for a few days?* She's not asking because she knows the answer. I'm new at that school, and anyway, who's going to ask someone fat and shortsighted (*Speccy Four Eyes*. Couldn't they think of anything more original to call her?) and unpopular to come and spend part of the holiday at their house?

Alison bit her lip, unwilling to show how miserable this knowledge made her. She hated people who moaned about everyone hating them, and in any case, they didn't. Not really. Nobody cared enough about her to hate her, or to bully her. They just don't include me in things, she told herself, and I don't care. She knew this wasn't true, but repeated it anyway in the hope that this would make her feel a bit better. She also knew she wasn't really fat, but just rather taller and more well-built than the daughter of a skeletal mother ought to be. It was the contrast which always made her feel clumsy and heavy.

Alison wondered if her mother regretted keeping her. She could have let Dad take me, she thought. If she had, I'd be living with him and Jeanette in America and she'd be the one I never saw, instead of Dad.

Patrick Drake left them when Alison was five, and from the moment the door slammed behind him forever, Claudia had seen to it that he'd had as little as possible to do with his daughter. I can see what her game is, Alison thought now as she'd thought a thousand times. She's punishing him. She really must have loved him and she's obviously never forgiven him. No civilised divorce for my mum, oh no. She just thinks of him as a bastard who had the cheek to fall in love with someone else. Alison didn't find it in the least surprising that someone had got sick to death of living with Claudia.

Quite apart from her general annoyingness, there was the matter of her schedule. She was on tour for most of the year, and when she wasn't she was at rehearsal or in class or having her photo taken and certainly would hardly ever have been at home looking after her baby or her husband. She'd employed a series of nannies and opted out almost entirely. You couldn't blame Dad for falling in love with someone else. Jeanette was an American student in the class he taught at the Polytechnic, and even though she wasn't as beautiful as Claudia, she was pretty enough, and kind and *there all the time.*

Since Patrick had left, Claudia had dragged Alison all over the world and put her in the charge of so many nannies that often Patrick couldn't see her for months at a time. Alison grew furious whenever she thought about this. How did Mum dare? Until I went to boarding school, she used to take me along to places where home was a hotel room for weeks on end. Before her father moved to America, six years ago, Claudia could easily have asked him to look after Alison on several occasions, but she never did.

Tears came into her eyes and she blinked them away. It was all this thinking about Dad. She saw so little of him now. Because he lived abroad, he couldn't visit often, and he was a rotten letter-writer. He used to send postcards with little poems on them and sometimes presents, but the gaps between letters became longer and longer.

Just before Christmas, Alison had sent him a card she had made herself. She liked the picture on the front, which showed her and Claudia up to their necks in snow, wearing bobble hats, with a Gothic castle in the background. She was less proud of the letter that she'd sent with the card, telling him about the Wychwood Festival in a way that made it quite clear she hated the idea. Maybe I shouldn't have been so negative, she thought. He'll probably think I've become one of those girls who do nothing but moan all the time.

Claudia smiled. 'There's nothing to be done now, Alison, so you will just have to make the best of it, I'm afraid. And it's not for long. I'm not mad about the countryside either, as you know, but it'll be a treat to work with Hugo. Or I think it will. He's such a hard taskmaster and he won't make any exception for me. It's days since I've seen him. He's with his father for Christmas, of course.' She sounded peeved about this, as though she thought that Hugo should have asked her to go with him, Alison thought. Serve her right.

Hugo Carradine had been her mother's lover for two years. She was, Alison knew, more keen on him than she had been about some of her others, because she'd made a point of telling her all about Hugo within days of their getting together. You're a big girl now, Claudia told her. Twelve years old and quite capable of hearing the truth.

'I love him, darling,' she'd said. *Be frank with your children about your feelings*. Alison was convinced her mother had read that in a magazine somewhere. 'I really hope you'll do your best to like him too.'

Alison had told her he was okay and he was, compared with some of the men Claudia'd been involved with in the past. She decided that it was pointless to go on about Wychwood. They would do exactly what suited Claudia. They always did. She helped herself to Christmas pudding. At least I can have as much as I want of this, she thought. Mum won't even allow such stuff anywhere near her plate and, as for brandy butter, well. That was the embodiment of evil.

27 December 1986

Hugo Carradine was sitting in the front stalls of the Arcadia Theatre. A few hours and they'd all be arriving – Claudia and Alison and the other members of the company – but for the moment he was alone here at Wychwood. He'd got up early, left his father's house, and driven to Yorkshire as the light was breaking over the moors. Now he had a short space in which to be alone and able to savour the special atmosphere of an empty theatre. The curtain was open, and the stage glowed a little in the pearly light of the winter afternoon, which filtered down from the small windows set into the roof, high above the flies and the lighting galleries. Here, wooden beams were hung about with the black shapes of the lamps that changed the space beneath them into one magic kingdom after another. When the lighting man slipped a gel, a square of coloured celluloid, into the frame, the colour of everything was transformed.

Colour. Hugo smiled. He looked at the rose-pink velvet curtains and seat covers; the garlands of fat flowers and harps and ribbons all painted gold; the thick carpets in a darker shade of pink and thought it's a bit like a *fin-de-siècle* brothel, but very pretty nonetheless.

Time to go back to the house. He edged out of the stalls and left the theatre, wondering whether to return along the covered walkway which Miss Fielding had told him she'd insisted upon. She had apparently told the architect, 'You can't have ballet dancers freezing their legs off on the way to class or a performance,' and that was that. She was obviously the sort of person who was used to getting her own way, but of course she was quite right. Still, Hugo decided to walk back along the outdoor path, even though it was much longer than the indoor route. The rain had held off, but the wind was strong and it was colder than he'd expected. He pulled his cashmere scarf (a Christmas present from Claudia) close around his neck and set off along the ribbon of road that wound up through the garden.

To his right as he walked, the wide lawn, almost white with frost, stretched to the high hedge that separated Wychwood from the road that ran beside the river. He could see the water, sluggish, brown and slow at this time of year, and the moor rising up from the opposite bank. There was not a sign of human habitation anywhere he looked, though there were plenty of sheep dotted around the slopes in the distance.

'It's deserted!' was Hugo's thought when he'd first arrived at Wychwood. But it was beautiful, and he knew from the full houses that companies always played to during the Festival that no one minded having to travel some distance to get to the Arcadia Theatre. The nearest railway station was five miles away. The taxi firm that served the village consisted of two old Ford Escorts. It really *was* best to come to Wychwood by car. Hester Fielding had thought of everything. She'd managed to persuade the farmer who was her nearest neighbour to sell one of his fields *et voilà* . . . there was a car park tucked away behind the theatre, hidden by a screen of trees and quite out of sight of the house.

There's such a lot of sky everywhere, he thought. It was like a dome over everything and the patterns of cloud and the play of light turned it into something different whenever you looked. All his professional life, he realised, had been spent in boxes of one kind and another. The stage sets in which his dancers moved pretended to be forests, mountainsides, town squares, fairy kingdoms and so forth, but in truth they were nothing but paint on canvas always, and on every side, flat and confining. From the stalls you had an illusion of limitless space. Designers and lighting men were good at creating the lie, but it *was* a lie and that was part of the magic. And the theatre was another box, a larger one with the stage set enclosed within it.

He passed a few flowerbeds on his left. He could see the pruned roses that would doubtless flower in profusion during the summer. Bushes lined the drive, camellias and rhododendrons so well established they were practically trees. Someone had told him that gardeners came in from the village to keep the grounds looking at their best all year round.

Hugo felt an unaccustomed surge of pure happiness pass through him. He was here, at Wychwood, and in a matter of days every critic in the country, everyone who was anyone in the world of ballet, would be sitting in the theatre's pink plush seats, looking at his work; something he'd created, something different from anything they'd ever seen.

He was aware of his reputation. Hugo's wonderful, people said, but his heart's not in anything really avant-garde. He's a romantic when it comes right down to it, yearning for the days of Petipa and Diaghilev. *For Carradine* (Hugo remembered the whole review by heart. You always remember the bad ones) *it's as though the last fifty years had never happened.*

Well, fuck Alasdair Clough, Hugo thought. That bastard's going to change his tune when he sees *Sarabande*. He'd have changed it already if only he'd bothered to come and see *Silver Girls*. Hugo's reinterpretation of *Giselle*, with the Wilis transformed into disco dancers in a Seventies style club had been a huge hit. Somehow the pathos and madness of the original had moved with no problem to the modern setting. The contrast between the music and the decor had been sensational.

Thinking of *Silver Girls* brought Silver into his mind. She was the most exciting talent he'd seen for a long time, though he wondered how far she'd be prepared to push herself. It had struck him during the audition that if she had a fault it was the kind of laziness that goes with great gifts. People who were particularly brilliant often felt they didn't have to make the same effort as everyone else. Well, he thought, she'll soon find out that I expect the best – demand it even – and that I'm not afraid to impose my will on the company. He knew very well that he was known as a perfectionist, but what that meant was a possibility at least of achieving perfection. Hugo wasn't interested in anyone who didn't share his aspirations and Silver would have to adjust to the customs of the company. She was right at the start of her career. He could help build her growing reputation with the part of the Angel in this ballet. Already he was thinking of new steps, new patterns, that he could fit into his vision of the whole to take advantage of her height, her youth and her famous athleticism. He realised he was looking forward to starting work with her, showing her the set and playing her the music for the first time. How would she react to it?

Edmund Norland's piece was perfect, just what he needed. It'd knock everyone's socks off. So far only Claudia had heard it. *Lovely, darling*, she'd said, but she said that about so much that it was hard to know what she really thought of it. She hadn't been in *Silver Girls* because she'd committed to a tour of France with *Nutcracker*, dancing the Sugar Plum Fairy, and although Hugo told her he was devastated not to be able to cast her, secretly he was relieved. Giselle had to be terribly vulnerable and young, sixteen or so, and he'd been lucky to find Ilene to do it. Claudia was thirty-six and, whichever way you sliced it, that was too old for an awful lot of parts these days. *Sarabande* would be okay, he hoped. The Princess in that could be more than a girl. He'd made a point of creating a ballet that would suit Claudia's style; choreographing something that wouldn't be too athletic or taxing where her role was concerned, and he wondered if she was aware that he was, in effect, working round her. Certainly Silver and Nick would have more obviously eye-catching solos and *pas de deux*. All Claudia had to do, for the most part, was react to them. She'd be fine, he was sure of it. The Princess was on stage from beginning to end and that, to Claudia, would mean she was the star. Hugo sometimes wondered about his lover's intelligence, and then immediately chided himself for disloyalty. She was beautiful, she was sexy, and she said she loved him. What more can I ask for, he thought, and then smiled. Just thinking like this meant that in some way he felt justified in asking for more.

He sighed, and resolved to stop worrying about these things until he had to. He had never wanted to do anything else but what he was doing now – making one ballet after another, finding patterns for bodies to move in, urging dancers to leap and turn and be everything they could possibly be. Now he'd been chosen by the great Hester Fielding herself from among dozens of other choreographers and he knew that he had a chance to consolidate his already excellent reputation.

His career had happened almost by accident. As a boy, he'd been keen enough on ballet to start in classes, but by the time he was seventeen he was six foot two and much too tall to become a professional dancer. In any case, he was beginning to read more and more and had started to wonder whether he might not be a writer of some kind, a journalist perhaps. He went up to Queen's College, Oxford, to read English and came back to ballet when a friend of his, who was directing a production of *A Midsummer Night's Dream* needed a short dance for the fairies to perform. He'd asked Hugo to help him. Hugo enjoyed the experience so much; was so delighted to be back in the world of movement and music, and so pleased to find himself in charge of everything that happened, that he made up his mind to pursue choreography as a career.

When he came down from Oxford, he'd managed to find a job as assistant to Julian Flannard in the Flannard Ballet Company, and had done nothing else ever since. Choreography suited him perfectly, and when Julian retired Hugo took over his company and renamed it after himself.

He knew that when he stood in front of a company of dancers he became a different person from the one who walked about in the non-ballet world. He liked his own way and wasn't afraid of putting people's backs up to get it. He'd been known to reduce young dancers to tears in class and at rehearsal, but was so kind and pleasant to them afterwards that no one bore grudges for very long, mainly because Hugo was able to demonstrate how much better this or that dancer was performing now that they were obeying his orders. He was intensely musical, imaginative, and intelligent, and while he never showed off about it, he made a point of being honest with himself. So okay, he had a reputation for strictness, but his dancers always said he was a good listener.

He looked at his watch. Claudia would soon be here and with her what he was beginning to think of as the Claudia Problem. This was complicated, and Hugo hated complications. Frequently, they sorted themselves out if you left them alone, one way or another, but Claudia was a special case. He had begun to wonder lately whether he really loved her. Things she did, ways in which she spoke to poor Alison, had begun to get to him. If ever he dared to chide her, she froze him out or made a scene, spitting at him that Alison was her daughter and none of his business. There had been times over the last few months when he had seriously considered telling her it was all over between them. He had almost convinced himself that this was the best thing to do when the Wychwood competition happened, and then he'd had to cast *Sarabande* and she was perfect as the Princess, and that was how things were.

Claudia never admitted her age in any of the many interviews she gave, and it was quite true that she did look stunning most of the time. But for how much longer would she still be credible as a principal, still be able to dance the roles that required real physical strength and flexibility? It was only a matter of time before she'd have to lower her sights and take on character parts. He didn't want to have to be the one to break that news to her. Hugo sighed. I'll deal with it when I have to, he thought. It's time to go and find something to eat. On his way to the kitchen, he thought about Hester Fielding and how nervous he'd been when he came to the audition. He'd waited for some time in her office before she came in to interview him, fascinated by the photographs that showed her in her youth. In some of the pictures she couldn't have been much more than Alison's age, and when he met her he could still see something of the girl she used to be.

1947

Ballet classes had been cancelled because of the weather. Snow was piled high at the side of the village street and the roads were icy and dangerous. Madame Olga thought it best to declare that the Christmas holidays would last a little longer. Estelle, though, was specially privileged. Because she lived so near Wychwood House, she was allowed to wrap up warm and walk through the village and up the drive to continue practising every day.

Estelle loved these visits, when she had Madame Olga entirely to herself. She would pretend that Wychwood House was her home, and that she didn't live with the Wellicks but here in this place which was still a little mysterious to her. Even though she'd been coming to dancing lessons since she was nine – four years – it was only recently that Madame Olga had started talking to her as though she were more important to her than the other girls who came to Wychwood to learn to dance. During the freezing weather, Estelle had felt herself growing closer and closer to her teacher.

'This is what we do in Russia,' Madame Olga said, sitting down at the kitchen table and smiling at her as she poured the tea. 'I do not have a samovar, but I have my mother's tea glasses.'

'What's a samovar?' Estelle asked.

'It's for the tea. Like, what do you call it, an urn? Yes, an urn. And we will also eat something delicious.'

The chocolates were kept in a drawer of the kitchen dresser. Estelle had no idea where Madame bought them, but she knew that they must have used up lots and lots of sweet rations. They were called *langues du chat*, cats' tongues: long, thin strips of pleasure which they shared while Madame told stories about the good old days when she was still a dancer.

'I wish I could be like you,' Estelle said. She had looked carefully at every photograph on the sitting-room wall, poring over the detail of every costume, every headdress, every pair of shoes. She could recite the names of every ballet and the character Madame Olga had danced in them: *Swan Lake, Sleeping Beauty, Coppélia, Ondine, Firebird*. Especially *Firebird*. Ever since Madame had told the story of the magic golden bird who helped Prince Ivan defeat a wicked enchanter, Estelle knew that the part must have suited Madame Olga better than any other because she looked so bird-like, and because she wore shawls in fire colours – reds and browns and golds.

'You will be a better dancer than me. This I promise you, my child.' Madame Olga took a long sip of her tea and looked sternly at Estelle. 'You do not let them stop you, do you understand? Soon, you will be ready to move on. You must go to London to study and to work. Perhaps very soon.'

'But I don't want to leave you. I want you to be my teacher for always.' Estelle felt a black sorrow weighing on her. Was Madame Olga also going to send her away?

'This would be a pleasure for me, too, but you are a dancer, and you must develop your gift in the best possible way. Next week, you will meet my good friend, Piers Cranley. I have told you about him many times and he is a fine man. His family have been my friends since I came to England. Without them, I would have no friends, I think. They have always helped me. And Piers, he is the best of the family. I have asked him to come and look at you. If he likes you, if he is willing to take you into his company, then you must go. It is the best way.'

'I won't be allowed.'

'You speak of your father? He will prevent you?'

'I don't know. I don't write to him very often. I could ask him, but I think he'd like me to have an ordinary job. To be a teacher, perhaps. Or a nurse.'

'You want to be a nurse? Never!' Madame Olga looked quite shocked.

'No, of course I don't. I want to dance. Just like you.'

'Then we will wait for Piers to come. Everything depends on him. If he thinks as well of you as I do, then you will be in his company. I will arrange everything. You leave such matters to me.'

Estelle spent the next week in a dream. Sometimes she could

imagine herself in London in a proper company with other dancers, working hard in class in the morning, rehearsing in the afternoon, performing in the evening. She knew about the life from Madame Olga. Were there parts for girls of nearly fourteen? Clara in *Nutcracker* was one. And perhaps she could also be one of the cygnets in *Swan Lake*, dancing to that music, the music that went round and round in her head.

While Paula slept, Estelle would lie awake in her bed thinking about the costumes she would wear: jewelled and feathered and silky; organza and tulle. Her ballet slippers would be made of satin and she wouldn't have just one pair, but dozens and dozens. She'd need black and white and pink and blue and red. She'd curtsey in front of the apricot and blue footlights and people in the audience would throw flowers at her feet.

Those were the good dreams. At other times, when she was feeling less cheerful, Estelle had visions of Madame Olga asking permission from her father and being turned away at the door. Or getting a letter from him . . . yes, that was how it would be, because Papa was in France . . . a letter saying, *I will most certainly never give permission for my daughter to become a ballet dancer. She is far too young to leave the Wellick household and live in London at her age. I sent her to England to be properly educated and properly educated she will be. You are wasting your time, Madame.*

By the time the day of Piers Cranley's visit arrived, Estelle had persuaded herself that joining a proper ballet company in London would never happen. She'd be condemned to remain in the life she'd been leading, stuck in the depths of the countryside in the dismal Wellick house until she was twenty-one and could do exactly what she wanted to do. But, of course, by then it would be much too late for her to become a ballerina. She could reduce herself to tears simply by thinking about it.

She didn't tell anyone else what she was feeling. Her friends – Pam and Betty at dancing class and Felicity at school – knew nothing of her ambitions. They'd have thought she was 'showing off'. Wanting to perform on a public stage was the most obvious kind of showing off there could possibly be. They wouldn't have understood it. Estelle knew what they thought of her.

She was shy and rather quiet in class and she never ventured an opinion unless someone called on her specifically. But her answers when she did give them were usually correct and Miss Wilcox noticed this.

'You're a dark horse, Estelle dear. I'm sure you're capable of much more than you're giving, especially in English,' she said.

Estelle just smiled at her. She'd been cultivating an enigmatic, mysterious smile for a long time. Sometimes, as a special treat, Auntie Rhoda took the girls to the cinema in Leeds and Estelle read the film magazines greedily. She used to study the faces – Garbo, Dietrich, Vivien Leigh, Merle Oberon – and notice how they looked when they were smiling. Then she imitated them, and she was good at it. She regarded this as part of her ballet training because Madame Olga had often said how very important *acting* was for a dancer.

'And you, my child, you have the gift,' she said to Estelle, more than once. 'It moves the heart when the audience can feel your emotion. When you are Giselle, I can have your madness and your love in my heart, here!' She would beat on her chest with a fist, and then open her hand and move it through the air, like a perfect white butterfly.

She didn't mean the real *Giselle*. A thirteen-year-old girl in a ballet class couldn't possibly dance the whole ballet on her own. Still, Madame Olga had devised two small solos for her pupil, set to Adolphe Adam's music. She'd told Estelle the story of the ballet in great detail, so that she knew who she was supposed to be and what she was meant to be feeling. In one dance she was filled with joy as she declared her love for Loys, and in the second she had to lose her mind after discovering that her true love was not who he claimed to be. Estelle had no experience of 'madness' or 'love', but she did feel everything deeply. She'd read about these emotions in books, seen them depicted on the screen, and she could imagine and copy the sweetness of first love, then the pain, the confusion, the anguish which she heard in every note of the music. Madame Olga had taught her the technique, the knowledge necessary for each individual step, but Estelle seemed to know by instinct how to use her body to give physical expression to the very strongest of feelings.

Piers Cranley was sitting at the far end of the studio on one of Madame Olga's best chairs. He was wearing a coat over his shoulders because the room was so cold. Estelle was so nervous she could hardly breathe, but as she approached him, she saw that he was rather small and red-faced and was smiling at her in quite a friendly manner. She relaxed a little as Madame Olga took her by the hand and led her right up to where he was sitting.

'This is Estelle Prévert, Piers darling,' she said. Then she turned to her pupil and whispered, 'Curtsey, child. A beautiful révérence, just as I have shown you.'

Estelle was wearing her practice dress and shivering in the cold but she obeyed, bending down low in front of the figure who sat with the light behind him so that it was difficult to see the expression on his face.

'Lovely, lovely,' he said. 'Come closer, child. And don't be frightened. I've come all this way because Olga has written to tell me you're the real thing. Are you?'

Estelle looked at him and wondered whether to be modest. Whether to say something like 'I hope so', or 'I don't know' but thought in the end that it would be better to be honest. She said simply 'Yes,' and looked straight into Piers' eyes. He had a kind expression. She wanted to say 'I *am* the real thing' but didn't quite dare to.

'If you came to dance in my company, you'd have to change your name, you know. We already have a principal dancer called Estelle. Two would be *un embarras de richesses* . . . do you understand French? Well, of course you do. How stupid of me to forget.'

'I don't mind,' Estelle said, and immediately felt a lifting of the heart. How wonderful, she thought, to be able to choose a new name, to begin again, as though you were being reborn. Also, film stars had screen names different from the ones they were born with. It struck her that she was much more likely to be famous with a name other than the one she'd had for years and years.

'*Hester*,' Madame Olga declared, as though she'd made up her mind and the name was a foregone conclusion; as though there could be no other in the world. 'It is very like Estelle. Perhaps it is an English version of the name.'

Estelle tried out the name in her head. *Hester.* She liked it at once. It was as though someone had given her a new dress to try on, and she was happy to find that it fitted to perfection. She nodded.

'We must change the surname too,' Madame Olga continued. 'Both names must be the same. Prévert is "green field" in French, so we have the same in English. *Field . . .*' She frowned and placed the fingers of each hand on her temples, as if deep in thought. 'Fielding,' she said at last. '*Hester Fielding.* Yes. That will be perfect for the lights, for the programmes. For everyone to say. Now, Hester Fielding, please dance as I have shown you for Mr Cranley.'

'Yes,' Estelle said, feeling like *Hester*, trying to *be* like her name. Piers Cranley was leaning forward in his chair as though eager to see what she was going to do. 'I'm going to dance a solo Madame Olga has arranged for me, to music from *Giselle.*'

'I see you're already wearing a gold chain round your neck. You know the story, don't you? How important the chain is in the ballet?'

Estelle – *Hester* – nodded. She wouldn't think of herself by her old name ever again. She was Hester Fielding, now and always.

Madame Olga wound the gramophone and put the record on; the spot where Hester was standing dissolved around her and she was in a village square, dancing, waiting for the harvest feast to begin.

When the music took over, the person she was in her real life became someone else, although she didn't forget who she was or what she was doing. The routines of the dance were complicated and you had to keep the pattern and sequence of the steps in your head and remember what came next and be always aware of what you looked like, what shapes you were creating with your body. You had to be in control, but alongside this, or under it, or wound up with it, was the sensation of being somehow filled with someone else's feelings, hopes, desires, longings. Part of her was transformed into this other person and suffered and loved with her, but she never quite lost a sense of herself; the physical self that was making the movements possible.

When she finished dancing, she looked at Piers Cranley. He was silent for a moment, then he said, 'Olga, my dear, you were right

54

about this as you are about everything. The child is a dancer.' He got up from the chair and came over to Hester, and took her hand. 'Olga must speak to your guardian at once. Will she see her this afternoon, do you think? It's very important that you begin to train seriously as soon as possible.'

Madame Olga asked permission to speak to Auntie Rhoda and Uncle Bob and came to tea the day after Piers Cranley's visit. Even though Madame had lived just outside the village for years, Auntie Rhoda still thought of her as a foreigner and had barely exchanged a single word with her, as far as Hester was aware. Madame Olga hardly ever bought anything in the village shop. Her provisions were delivered in a van that came all the way from Keighley, so she never really met any of the locals.

Auntie Rhoda made shortbread specially, and laid the best traycloth on the tray. Uncle Bob lit a fire in the front room and Hester was instructed to dust every surface. She didn't mind. She pretended she was Cinderella and danced from one piece of furniture to another.

Madame Olga either didn't realise how strange she looked sitting on the sofa in the front room of the Wellicks' house, or else she didn't care. She had on the black dress she sometimes wore for class, but acknowledged the importance of the occasion by wearing her best shoes and wrapping a scarlet chiffon scarf around her neck. She laid her gloves over the arm of the sofa and put her handbag on the floor next to her.

When Auntie Rhoda poured out her tea, Madame Olga took the cup from her and began to speak charmingly, smiling at every word her hostess said even though all she'd managed so far were platitudes like, *I don't know when this cold snap will come to an end. It does make life so difficult* and *I hope you like shortbread.*

Paula wasn't there. She was spending the afternoon at Marjorie's house and Hester was grateful for that. Uncle Bob looked very uncomfortable standing with his back to the fire, holding his cup and saucer in his hand. Madame Olga didn't waste time. As soon as she'd sipped a little tea and eaten her shortbread in a few dainty bites, she began.

'My dear Mr and Mrs Wellick,' she said and she sounded not like herself at all, Hester thought, but like someone dictating the beginning of a letter. 'I come to speak of Hester's future.'

'Who is Hester?' Auntie Rhoda asked and Madame Olga smiled.

'She has not told you? I will explain everything. Hester . . .' Madame Olga pointed dramatically across the room. 'She was Estelle, but she is now Hester.'

Auntie Rhoda looked as though someone were about to attack her from an unexpected quarter: tense, and ready to spring to her own defence if necessary. 'Why is she now *Hester*? I don't understand, I'm afraid.'

'Hester Fielding. This will be excellent stage name.'

'Why would Estelle need a stage name?' Auntie Rhoda asked.

'She did not tell you? She is going to be a ballerina. I hope she will become world famous.'

Auntie Rhoda looked bemused. 'Well, I know she's been having lessons with you, but isn't she a little young to be thinking of—'

Madame Olga waved her hand in the air and interrupted.

'Never, never too young. I am friendly with Piers Cranley, who is manager of the Charleroi Ballet Company. You have heard of it?'

It was clear that Auntie Rhoda had never heard of the Charleroi. Madame Olga went on.

'It is based in London. Mr Cranley, he has money from his family and because of this, his company can put on many ballets and he can afford to hire the very best dancers. Hester is talented. She has a very great gift. Do you not know this? Mr Cranley has seen her dance in my house and he wants her to come to London to join Charleroi's dancers. This will be wonderful training and a chance to dance on stage early, which will be good for her career in the future. All the dancers live in a hostel together. Mr Cranley sees to it that the girls' education is not neglected. There are lessons with a special tutor for a few hours every day. There are about twelve young girls, I think, but Hester will be the youngest.'

Madame Olga drew breath and fixed her dark eyes on Auntie Rhoda, looking hard at her, as though she were trying to hypnotise her. 'This is an opportunity not to be missed,' she went on. 'With ballet, starting to dance on stage as young as fourteen is the very best thing. A great advantage always.'

No one said a word for a long time, but Hester felt as though Madame Olga had taken a hand-grenade and thrown it into the room. She wished for a moment that the matter of her new name could have been introduced a little more gently. She could feel the power of the blast in Auntie Rhoda's indrawn breath, in Uncle Bob's sudden frown and the way he went over to the table to put his cup and saucer down before going to stand next to his wife. A look passed between the two of them.

'This is very kind of you I'm sure,' Auntie Rhoda began, and Hester knew at once that she was going to refuse her permission. It was never going to happen. She bit hard on her lip to prevent herself from crying.

'It doesn't sound to me,' Auntie Rhoda went on, 'like a respectable life for a well-brought up young lady. When all's said and done, you're telling me that Estelle's going to display herself on a stage, wearing very little. She's very young, Madame Olga, and while it's kind of you to take an interest, I'm afraid I couldn't give permission. Perhaps when she's of age.'

'That is too old to train for the ballet, Mrs Wellick. Too old. We must teach the body when it is young. Do you not understand?' A note of anger had crept into Madame Olga's voice.

'I understand perfectly. But I still hold to my opinion. It's not decent, and that's all there is to it.'

'It is most certainly *not* all there is to it. There is more to it, oh, *very* much more. I do not speak of a cheap music hall, Mrs Wellick,' said Madame Olga, properly angry now. 'I speak of Art. High art. Great music. Skill like no other. Beauty. Perfection. How do you *dare* to stop this beauty?'

'I don't know about that,' said Uncle Bob, unexpectedly adding his voice to the argument. 'Beauty or no beauty, her legs'll still be bare for every Tom, Dick and Harry to stare at, won't they?'

Madame Olga stood up.

'Mrs Wellick, I will say this and then I will go. Hester will give me the address for her father. The Charleroi Company goes on tour to

Paris very soon and Piers Cranley will go to see Monsieur Prévert.' She took a small, leather-bound notebook from her handbag and pulled out a pencil. 'This you cannot prevent. Hester, please tell me your father's address in Paris. I will write to him.'

Even though she felt despairing and angry, Hester spoke the words clearly and defiantly into the stifling air of the small room. She glared at Auntie Rhoda and Uncle Bob as Madame Olga carefully wrote down the address. Then she put the notebook away in her handbag and smiled at the Wellicks in triumph.

'Mr Cranley will persuade him, I am sure. And then I hope you will do everything to make it easy for Hester to move to London. I thank you for the hospitality and the delicious shortbread. Goodbye.'

She came over to where Hester was sitting.

'Do not lose heart, child,' she said, putting a finger under Hester's chin and lifting her head. She looked into her eyes and spoke quietly so that the Wellicks, who'd moved to the door, wouldn't overhear what she was saying. 'Do not please think all is over. This is not true. You have seen Mr Cranley. He likes to be obeyed. You will find out when you are dancing for him. He will speak to your father and all will be well. Leave everything to me. Trust me, I will do what is needed.'

Madame Olga picked up her gloves and handbag and swept out of the room. The Wellicks escorted her to the front door and Hester was left alone in the parlour which, in spite of the fire, was dark and cold and just the right place to sit and rage at how things had turned out. In spite of Madame Olga's optimistic words, it was hard not to feel as though there was nothing left to hope for in the world. She'd been foolish to imagine even for a second that she'd be leaving this house. She could taste something horrible in her mouth and she swallowed down the tears that were rising in her throat. She blinked. She wasn't going to give them the satisfaction. They'd have liked nothing better than for her to weep and wail and carry on so that they could say *well, what did we tell you? She's nothing but a child, and not nearly old enough to go to London all by herself.*

'Whatever are you doing in here, all by yourself in the dark?' Paula had come back from Marjorie's house.

'Nothing. Just thinking.'

'Mum said that the Russian lady at Wychwood told her some man wants you to go to London. Is he a white slaver?'

'No, he's the manager of a ballet company. Madame Olga wants me to train to be a ballet dancer in his company.'

Paula burst out laughing. 'Oh, honestly, Estelle, if you believe that you'll believe anything! Company, indeed. You must know what he *really* has up his sleeve, don't you? Whatever Madame Olga says. If you don't, you're more of a baby than I thought.'

'He hasn't got anything up his sleeve. He wants to train me. You wouldn't know about that. Ballet doesn't mean anything to you.'

'You are *so* naïve! Honestly! Once he's got you down there in that London, he'll make you in one of those clubs. You know. Where people take off their clothes. He may even,' Paula's voice dropped and she winked dramatically, 'put you on the streets.'

'I'm not listening to you. You don't know *anything*. He's a friend of Madame Olga's. He's not a white slaver or whatever you called him. He's a respectable gentleman.'

Hester began leaving the room, but then a thought occurred to her. She turned round and shouted at Paula.

'And don't you dare *ever* call me Estelle ever again. I'm Hester now. Hester Fielding. So there.'

Paula called something after her, but Hester had managed to slam the door shut behind her as she left the room. She stood in the hall, uncertain where to go. Auntie Rhoda was washing up in the kitchen. She longed to run upstairs and lie on the bed with her face buried in the pillow, but Paula was almost bound to come in and continue tormenting her. It was too cold to go into the garden or for a walk. She sat on the wooden settle in the hall and stared down at her hands, thinking *I have to go. I have to leave this house and I will.*

The freezing cold weather continued. Icy days and nights, one after the other, went on and on as though spring would never come. Hester's mood reflected the chill outside. She remained in a state of anxiety mixed with gloom for weeks after Madame Olga's visit to the Wellicks, alternating between short daydreams full of glorious possibility and days and days of complete hopelessness.

She lived entirely for her visits to Madame Olga's house. Now that the two of them were planning Hester's future, there were afternoons when they went into the kitchen after class and discussed what would happen for hours. One day, out of the blue, Madame Olga said 'Come with me, Hester dear. I wish to show you something.'

Hester followed Madame Olga upstairs. In all the years she'd been coming for her lessons, all she'd ever seen of Wychwood House was the front hall, the studio and the kitchen. Now Madame led the way up the wide staircase and along a dark corridor and opened a door.

'My bedroom,' she announced. 'No one has been up here to see this.'

Hester looked around. The sage-green velvet curtains were drawn. It was late afternoon and dark outside. Madame Olga hadn't been up here since before the ballet lesson, Hester knew, and this meant that they'd been drawn the whole day, as though she'd decided to do without natural light altogether.

'Sit here,' she said, and pointed to a small stool near the dressing-table. The scent of violets hung in the air.

'I love that smell,' Hester said. 'My grandmother used to smell just like that.'

'I am not yet like a grandmother, I hope,' Madame Olga smiled. 'Only fifty years old.'

Hester couldn't think what to say. She had never considered the matter of Madame Olga's age. 'You look beautiful,' she said.

'You are kind. Never have I been called beautiful before. But always I smell of violets. Now I want to show you this.'

She went to a huge cupboard which reared up like a black cliff against one wall. Panels on each door were carved into a pattern of flowers and leaves, and the handles were made of shiny brass. The doors creaked as Madame Olga opened them and bent to take something from the shadowy darkness within. It was a small leather suitcase, which she put on the bed.

'Come, come here,' she said, indicating that Hester should sit on the bed. She thought of how she used to sit on her grandmother's bed when she was a little girl, and the memory of how they used to play with the contents of the jewellery box brought tears prickling into her eyes. But Hester knew that Madame never wore jewellery. Not even a ring. Nothing. The only time there had ever been a cross word between her and Madame was when Hester, years ago, refused to remove her gold necklace for class. She had threatened to stop coming to ballet lessons altogether if Madame Olga made her take it off.

'What will you do in a real ballet?' Madame Olga cried. 'There is no costume designer, no choreographer in the whole world who will let you wear that around your neck on the stage. Impossible.'

'I'll take it off for performances,' Hester had answered, quite calmly. 'But I will wear it for the rest of the time. I promised my grandmother. And I'll wear it to class.'

Madame Olga had gazed at her pupil and seen how determined Hester was. She never mentioned the matter again. Now she said, 'Open the suitcase.'

Hester opened it, and nearly fell backwards off the bed when she saw what was inside. Her grandmother had jewels, but this was treasure such as only pirates in storybooks possessed. The interior of the case was a twisted mass of intertwined necklaces, glittering, glowing and catching the light – rubies, amethysts, topazes – strings upon strings of them, tangled up with bracelets and brooches and rings set with pearls and jet and onyx, all just lying there in a jumble. Madame Olga plunged a hand into the suitcase and brought it up with lengths of gemstones dangling from every finger.

'Do you see this? All these things? They are rubbish.'

'But they look . . .' Hester couldn't speak. She wanted to say they looked like real jewels; looked as though they were worth more money than she could imagine. Then, a thought struck her.

'Are they pretend? Did you wear them on stage?'

Madame Olga laughed. 'No, no they are real jewels. Men gave them to me. They give when they love you; they give when they stop loving you. They give when they say hello, also when they say goodbye. There have been so many men who have loved me.' She laughed. 'This is my bank. All I have. It's a lot, I think, but I never wear it. Never. It lies here, and when I die, it will be yours. There. One day, you will be a rich woman when I am gone. But now, I will take out some necklace or some brooch for you to buy all the things you will need when you go to London, to the Charleroi Company. What use are these jewels to me? No use.'

'I couldn't . . .' Hester began. 'And my grandmother left me some money of my own when she died. I'll use that.'

'It is good to have more than you need. Do not think of it again. I will give to Piers for you. He will take care of it, I am sure.'

As she spoke, she took out an Easter egg studded with green and red stones, and tiny seed pearls in a pattern which made the initials OR, Madame Olga's own initials. She lifted her lorgnette and peered at them more closely.

'A man,' she said. 'He gave this to me when I danced *Firebird* in Paris. After 1917, the Revolution in Russia. A Frenchman. An aristocrat. Very wealthy.'

Madame Olga held the egg gently in her hand. The rubies and emeralds caught the light. 'This is made by Fabergé, a very famous maker of such things. I have never told anyone what happened. This very rich man falls in love with me. I love him, naturally, or I think I love him, which is the same thing, yes? All is well till I become pregnant. I do not tell him, because I am horrified, and I know if he realises, then he will insist on marrying me. And I am so ambitious. I want so much to be the great, the wonderful prima ballerina. Pregnancy interferes with the dancing. To be a ballerina is not a job, but a way of life. It is for always. I had it taken away.'

'Taken away? What do you mean? Did someone take your baby away?'

'I went to the doctor and he removed the baby. It's called an abortion. Perhaps you are too young to know of such matters?'

Hester didn't answer, but she felt sick as she listened to Madame Olga. 'Do not be shocked. Many, many people, they go to the doctor. I was sad, yes, but it is not so dangerous if the doctor is a good one.'

'But the baby. You're killing your baby, aren't you?'

Madame Olga shook her head. 'It is not a baby when it is so small. So tiny you cannot see or feel it yet as a person. Much better to do what I do, to finish the pregnancy. It is sad not to have a family, but my pupils and my friends, they are the family I have now.'

Hester said nothing, but she wasn't entirely sure that she agreed with Madame Olga. She still missed and mourned her grandmother, and when she was younger, she'd often longed for brothers and sisters, imagining them as versions of herself who would adore her and agree with her and to whom she could say anything. If she could have changed a single thing about her life, it would have been that. She would have wished to belong to an ordinary family, instead of having a mother who had died so long ago that she could scarcely remember her, and a father whom she saw so rarely that she practically never thought of him.

'What happened to the man? The rich man who loved you and was the father of your child?'

'I did not tell him I was pregnant. I left him afterwards, but he begged me to marry him and sent me, oh, you cannot believe what gifts. Including this egg.' She tossed it back into the suitcase and it lay among the other jewels as though it were no more than a stage prop.

Madame Olga stood up and smiled at Hester. 'But when I left him, I said, never again. I devoted myself to the dance. I longed, I cannot tell you how I longed, to be a great dancer. But soon, after a few years, I saw I didn't have the talent for greatness. So I stopped before my age made me stop, and decided that I would spend the rest of my life teaching other dancers who would be great ballerinas for me. I have never put on one of these things after I said goodbye to the man who gave me that egg. Some has gone of what I had. With some, I bought this house. This is the rest.'

'What if burglars come and steal it?'

Madame Olga laughed. 'Who thinks the funny Russian lady who lives in the shabby old house has anything worth stealing? No one. But you are right. This is primitive, to keep it in a suitcase in a cupboard and not even locked. I will take it to the bank, I promise.'

A few days later, Hester heard someone knocking frantically at the Wellicks' front door. She went to open it, but Uncle Bob was on the point of leaving for work and got there before she did. Madame Olga was on the step, waving a small, beige piece of paper. She hadn't even bothered to button her coat and was wearing her indoor shoes, soaked through by the snow which still lay on the ground.

'It's a telegram!' Uncle Bob shouted, and Auntie Rhoda and Paula came running out of the kitchen. Uncle Bob had taken it from Madame Olga who spoke to Hester directly and ignored the others. 'He said yes! Your papa, he said yes. You can go to London and live in Moscow Road . . . oh, I'm so happy. So happy. Now you will be ballerina. Piers is so kind to send telegraph.'

'I would like,' said Auntie Rhoda, 'to read the message, if you don't mind.'

'Certainly! Read it please. I know it by heart and I will tell Hester what my friend says. He says: *Your young pupil's father agreeable stop She should come to London soonest stop Expecting her 24 Moscow Road. Tel. Bayswater 1551. Fond regards Piers.*'

'I can't believe it!' Hester held on to the banister, feeling a little weak. 'He said yes. My father. He's allowing me to go to London . . .'

Hester was so happy that she did a series of *entrechats* in the hall. She could sense that Auntie Rhoda, Uncle Bob and Paula were all staring at her as though she'd taken leave of her senses.

'All will be well now,' Madame Olga said. 'I am going. Please come and see me later, Hester. We have much to talk about. Goodbye, goodbye. Such a happy day.'

She left as swiftly as she'd come. Auntie Rhoda watched her going down the path and then collected herself. 'Well, there's nothing to be done, I suppose, but we have to talk about arrangements. Where, for example, does Mr Cranley think the money's going to come from to pay for all this travelling lark?'

'There's *Grand-mère*'s money,' Hester answered. 'The money she left me. I'll take it out of the bank. It's a lot of money, isn't it? Five hundred pounds. And the money Papa sends – I could have that if I lived in London.'

'Well,' Uncle Bob began, but Auntie Rhoda pushed him out of the door. 'You go off to work, Bob,' she muttered, 'and leave this to me.'

'Leave what?' Hester knew the signs, and felt suddenly faint.

'Come into the kitchen, Estelle,' Auntie Rhoda said, and her mouth had tightened till it was no more than a thin line in her face.

'Hester,' Hester said automatically, though her mind wasn't on her name, but on the *thing*, whatever it was, that Auntie Rhoda was about to tell her. She knew, she was convinced, that whatever it was, it would be bad and worse than bad.

'Sit down there, dear,' said Auntie Rhoda, 'and listen to me. You're not going to like what I've got to tell you, but needs must.'

Hester stared hard at her, saying nothing. Auntie Rhoda looked straight back.

'Some of your grandmother's money has been spent. That's what you need to know. We had to do it. No one could possibly blame us. After all, we spent it on you. You had to have clothes, things for school, shoes, and not to mention all the ballet equipment. Ballet slippers and goodness knows what all else.'

'You spent my legacy? On school uniform? And ballet shoes?' Hester could feel herself growing ice-cold, and for the first time since she'd arrived in England, she was filled with hatred, *real* hatred, for this person who was supposed to have been like a mother to her.

'How much is left?' Breathing in and out was hard. Hester felt as though her chest was filled with rocks.

'About a hundred and fifty pounds. Quite enough to set you up nicely in London, I'd have thought.'

A note of syrupy, false friendliness had crept into her aunt's voice. Hester did the sum. They, she and Uncle Bob, had stolen more than three hundred pounds. How did Auntie Rhoda *dare* to sit there simpering and pretending that all along she'd had nothing but Hester's ballet future in her mind as she spent that money, her money? All at once Hester was quite sure that ballet shoes and school cardigans had nothing to do with it. The money her father sent the Wellicks each month would have paid for those. The money, her grandmother's legacy, had been spent on other things. She stood up.

'It's not true! None of it's true. You've not spent that money on me! It's a lie. You bought a car. It's the car. You used some of my money to help you buy your stupid Austin and you're no better than thieves, both of you, and I'm not spending a minute longer under this roof than I have to. As soon as I get what's left of my money out of the bank, I'm going and I don't care if I never see you ever again. You're horrible and I'll never forgive you as long as I live.'

She burst into tears of rage as soon as she'd finished speaking. Her throat felt raw. Auntie Rhoda sprang to her feet, red in the face and shrieking loudly enough to make the cups rattle on the dresser.

'*We're* horrible? And what about you? How d'you think we feel when you make it so obvious that we're not fit to lick your boots? You think you're better than us, that's your trouble. You always have, too. We take you in when your own father wants rid of you, and what thanks do we get? Not a word, that's what. Not one word in more than eight years. Good riddance to you, I say. Uncle Bob will take you to the bank tomorrow and you can get your money and go and see how far you'll get on your own in London. Not very far, I'll be bound. Now if you don't mind, I've got ironing to do.'

She swept out of the kitchen and left Hester there shaking with fury. She wanted to run after Auntie Rhoda and scream *I never thanked you because I'm not grateful for any of the horrible things you've given me; horrible food, a cold house, no love at all, not even when I was five years old and crying for my lost home every night. Even then you didn't come and cuddle me, never. Not once. I'm glad I never thanked you.*

Paula had followed her mother out of the kitchen, pausing just long enough at the door to smirk before she disappeared. It was clear that she was delighted to see Hester being taken down a peg or two. She'd resented her cousin's interest in ballet from the very first, roaring with unkind laughter if ever she caught Hester practising her foot positions in front of the mirror, or trying to do exercises using the metal bedstead as a *barre*.

I don't care, Hester thought. I'm going to London. I'm going to live in 24 Moscow Road and be a ballet dancer. Madame Olga will help me. Some of her treasure will be used to pay for things I need. She said so. I'm never coming to this place ever again in my life.

For the last two weeks of her stay in the Wellicks' house, scarcely a word passed between them and Hester. She refused to have them help her in any way. When the time came to leave, she got into the taxi with Madame Olga and the Wellicks remained by the front gate.

To have sulked indoors as she left would have made them the subject of gossip among the neighbours, so they pretended they were saying goodbye as though they were a normal family. Hester shook Uncle Bob by the hand, and forced herself to peck Auntie Rhoda and Paula on the cheek. When it was Auntie Rhoda's turn, she said, 'Thank you very much for having me,' as though the last eight years were no more than a birthday party.

As the taxi drove away, Hester sat facing straight ahead and never looked back. She felt lighter and happier with every yard they travelled, as though someone had let go of ropes that had been holding her tight, reining her in.

Saying goodbye to her beloved teacher at Leeds station was quite a different matter. Hester couldn't stop crying as she kissed her, and Madame Olga wiped away the tears with a handkerchief that smelled of violets.

'Do not cry, child,' she murmured. 'It is good, what you are doing. You have a great gift. You must always remember this. I will come to see you dance, do not worry. Piers will invite me and I will come. I will sell more jewels and come many times. I will come to applaud the new ballerina. And you will write to me, won't you? I want to hear every bit of news. Go with God, darling girl.'

'Thank you, Madame. Thank you for showing me—'

'There is no need for thanks, Hester. You have given me nothing but pleasure. I will live through your gift as if it was my own.'

Hester burst out crying all over again. 'But I'll miss you so much. I feel as though you're a kind of mother to me. Better than a mother. How will I thank you?'

'You will thank me with your hard work. That is all I ask. Do not waste your gift. We will meet again soon when you are a ballerina. I will live for that day. Go, go now and find a seat.'

Hester picked up her suitcase. It was the one she'd brought with her to England; the one her grandmother had packed so carefully. Once again it held her clothes, the photographs she'd brought with her from France and her doll, Antoinette. She knew she was too old for a doll, but she couldn't leave her behind at the Wellicks.

She peered through the window at Madame Olga, dressed for the occasion in her coat with the fox-fur collar and the hat with a spotted veil. She was waving and smiling, and Hester waved and smiled back and recognised the sadness that filled her: she felt exactly as she had on the day she had left *Grand-mère*. Loving someone meant leaving them and going far away. That, Hester thought, is how life has arranged it, for me at least.

27 December 1986

Silver McConnell opened her eyes and got out of bed, immediately wide awake. It always surprised her to learn that other people took time to come to life in the morning; that they didn't spring instantly to life. She'd never been what her mum called 'a sleepyhead'. Quite the reverse. Her body managed just fine with a minimum of sleep, and she felt ready for action within seconds of waking up. She was good at catnaps too, and ten minutes with her eyes shut in the dressing room before a performance gave her enough energy to keep her going late into the night.

This morning she was particularly excited, so it was even easier than usual to get out of bed and get started. She was on her way to Yorkshire in a few hours, to join the members of the Carradine Company at Wychwood House. The idea of a big house with a theatre in its grounds appealed to her. The Arcadia was famous in ballet circles. She'd first read about it in a magazine, and had decided there and then that one day she'd dance on that stage, in the place that Hester Fielding, who was one of her all time greatest heroines in ballet, had created after she stopped dancing.

Silver wasn't falsely modest. I'm good, she told herself, whenever she compared her achievements with those of her contemporaries. She felt properly alive only when she was involved in dancing, whether rehearsing, in class, or performing. She was aware of a harmony in every part of her, and it would have been strange if the pleasure she took from the things her body was capable of didn't somehow communicate itself to others. That the critics agreed with her assessment, that her fellow-dancers regarded her with awe and envy, that choreographers were forever asking her to do this or that ballet with them – those were external signs of her success, but her own opinion counted more than anything the world said. From the first day she started in her dancing class as a small girl, everything had come to her with the minimum of effort. She seemed to be able to do whatever was asked of her then, and she still could. But Silver was certain of one thing: she would stop dancing the second she thought that this or that aspect of her work was getting ragged at the edges. Ballet's about perfection, she'd told a television presenter only last month, and she believed that. When she was about fourteen, she'd read a magazine interview with Hester Fielding in which she said that exactly, and Silver had felt more than ever that here was a dancer she could admire unreservedly. They agreed about the important things, and Silver couldn't wait to meet her.

She couldn't understand how someone like Claudia Drake, who'd been so good, could let herself go on dancing when she wasn't really up to it any longer. She was too old. That was the truth, and it was brutal, but far more bruising than giving up forever must surely be trying to regain her youthful glory and failing.

The trouble is, Silver thought, stepping into the shower and turning it on as hard as it would go, she believes her own publicity. That's dangerous. If the papers tell you you're a star and a beauty and can do no wrong loud enough and long enough, it must be easy to believe it. Not me, though, she thought, wrapping herself in a towel and going back into the bedroom. I try to make a point of not believing anything except the evidence of my own eyes, my own body, where the work is concerned.

She'd been uncharacteristically nervous during the audition she did for Hugo Carradine. She didn't normally pin her hopes on things. Roles were frequently offered to her without her seeking them, but this was different, she had thought as she stepped out on to the stage and looked into the darkened stalls. She could just make out the pale oval of Hugo's face.

'I'm going to do the first act solo from *The Bells of Paradise*, which I've just finished dancing at the Sadler's Wells.'

'That'll be fine,' Hugo's disembodied voice answered her. And it was fine, because he'd offered her the part of the Angel, but she'd had the distinct impression that he was a little underwhelmed by her performance. It wasn't anything he said, but Silver couldn't help thinking that he was not one hundred percent bowled over by her dancing, and that irritated her.

The small flat she shared with Gina wasn't the most luxurious place in the world, but Silver was fond of it. It was a vast improvement on the two-up, two-down in the grotty suburb of South London where she'd lived as a child. That was only a couple of steps up from a slum. The streets she'd grown up in were dingy and unattractive, with not a tree to be seen. There was a small park nearby, but the trees and shrubs there had an air of exhaustion about them, as though producing every leaf and flower had been a huge effort. Silver's dad worked as a lorry-driver and was often away. When he did come home he was worse than useless, sitting around in front of the telly for the most part, and hardly taking any notice of her. He loved her well enough, but rather in the way you'd love an exotic pet, a cockatoo or something. He treated her gingerly, as though she might bite, or behave suddenly in ways he didn't understand.

Her two brothers, both older than she was, petted and spoiled her but they didn't understand her either. Her name was her own invention. She'd been called Sylvia at birth, but *Silver* was how she always said it, from when she was tiny, and the word had suited her so well that she'd never felt the need to change it. No one could resist the urge to muck about with it. She tolerated Lone Ranger jokes, and was almost used to 'Silly' – the name that the younger of her brothers always called her.

When she'd insisted on going to a local ballet class, she'd had to put up with a hell of a lot of teasing. Her brothers started it, mimicking her first tentative steps and chortling at their own daring and originality, leaping about in football boots and making what they thought of as ballet movements with their hands. Mum used to shoo them out of the room sometimes, to protect her.

Her mother had been delighted that she had at least one child for whom she could buy ballet shoes and other pretty paraphernalia. Even though the money had been tight, she somehow seemed to find the best bargains from the most unlikely places – market stalls, catalogues, charity shops. Whatever she had to go without (and looking back Silver could see that she probably *had* had to make sacrifices – you never noticed such things when you were a kid) Mum was determined that Silver would be properly kitted out. And, Silver thought, she loved having to knit crossover cardigans in sugary colours like pink or lilac. She even enjoyed sitting in on the class in the draughty church hall where Miss Valerie tried her best. Now her mother was the one who cut out all the bits from newspapers and magazines; who came to watch her dance, who took pride in what she'd achieved. Thank God for Mum, Silver thought. And Miss Valerie too. She hadn't been much of a teacher, but she did realise that I was different, and it's thanks to her that I ended up at the Royal Ballet school.

From White Lodge in Richmond, Silver had gone on to dance small parts and then more important ones, and meanwhile she had grown away from her family. It wasn't that she didn't love them, but she felt that she had less and less in common with them. This made her feel a little guilty whenever she thought about them. She didn't visit them often enough and, although her mother came to see everything, Silver knew she didn't spend time with her when she did, but treated her only as a rather privileged member of the audience. Thoughts that she should make more effort came to her regularly, and she vowed to do better soon, but somehow there was always the next ballet to be rehearsed, and then the next, and the schedules were punishing. But she could phone. Or write. She sat down at the dressing-table and said aloud, 'I will. It'll be my New Year resolution. To be a better daughter. A better sister.'

She sighed, and turned her attention to putting her make-up on. It was a process she relished, because it meant creating a public face, a mask for the world to look at. No one would have believed her if she'd told them, but Silver was unconvinced of her own beauty, and felt she needed to create it. I'm different from what they think I am, she told herself, smoothing on foundation.

She loved the names given to all the shades of make-up. This cream was *Porcelaine* and, as well as blending in perfectly with her skin, it conveyed the right image – delicate, pale and unblemished. From the first time she'd appeared on a stage, she knew that this was how you escaped from yourself. In exactly the same way that she put on a face to dance in, Silver invented a person to be: a smooth, well-groomed, elegant, silvery sort of person to go with her name.

The transformation happened when she was eighteen. At the time, she was living in a pokey room above a launderette, but she had started to buy her own clothes for the first time. Her mother watched, horrified, as she went through everything that was still hanging up in the cupboard in her old room and threw everything on to the bed as though it were so much rubbish.

'What's got into you, madam?' said her mum. 'One minute in that fancy ballet school and living away from home and all this gear's not good enough for you, that it?'

'No,' said Silver mildly. The more her mother spluttered and fumed, the quieter she became. She'd been doing this since she was a little kid, saying nothing or nearly nothing, which always calmed Mum down. It was quite hard to keep up a heated argument if the other person wasn't joining in. 'I've just decided that I don't wear colours any longer.'

'You don't wear colours. Right. Silly me. I thought colours was all there was, but you probably know better.'

'I mean colourful colours, red and blue and stuff. I'm going to wear white, black, grey and beige from now on. And silver of course, for parties.'

'Hmmph!' said Silver's mum, looking cross and bemused. 'What are you going to use for money to buy new clothes? That's what I'd like to know.'

'I won't need to buy much at first. I've got quite a lot of stuff in those colours and I'll just add to it, bit by bit. From markets and charity shops and things. It's amazing what you can find if you know what you're looking for.'

'And what am I supposed to do with this lot?'

'Take it down to the Oxfam shop or something,' said Silver. 'I don't care what you do with it. I just know I don't want it.'

'Maybe Maureen . . .'

Silver looked away to hide her smile. Maureen was her cousin, two years younger than she was, and twice as fat around the waist. Should she point out that Maureen had about as much chance of fitting into her clothes as an Ugly Sister did of getting into Cinderella's shoes? No, I'll shut up, she decided. Let Mum find out when she takes it all over there.

Silver blinked and returned to the present. She frowned into the mirror. The 'strictly no colour' plan had worked well for a number of years, but nowadays she did sometimes add a splash of something here and there for special effect. There was the apricot velvet shawl which she wore with her black silk dress; the moss-green and emerald and turquoise scarves she sometimes tied around her neck or hair, and the satin dress she'd packed to take to Wychwood for the first night party, in a red so dark that it was almost black.

Pale lipstick today, a pinkish shade called *Si la rose*. I'm innocent, she smiled into the mirror. I'm a good girl. I'm going to meet everyone quite soon. I'm hard-working and conscientious. She had three other lipsticks in her bag and one of them, she knew, made her look like something out of a horror movie, a rather attractive ghoul, perhaps. It was almost black and she wore it on occasions when she needed to be strong. Magic wands, that's what lipsticks are, she said to herself and was pleased with that description. Had she seen it in an ad somewhere? Maybe, but it was still quite right even if she hadn't thought of it herself.

A last look in the full-length mirror showed her that she had been transformed into somebody who was ready to meet people and walk about in the world. She took her coat from the hanger in the cupboard and left the room.

As she ate her breakfast, she thought about winter. Most festivals happened during the summer, but Wychwood was different. She wondered whether there would be snow on the moors all around the house. Her first starring role had been as Clara in *The Nutcracker* when she was only just fifteen and that was a wintry ballet, with a set that included specially designed snowflakes which glittered as they drifted down from the flies in the theatre and settled in her hair. 'A magical début' said the papers and more than one couldn't resist 'A star is born.'

Silver smiled and took a sip of coffee. She never minded a cliché when it was also a compliment. She'd gone on to dance almost every major role in the last nine years. Odette/Odile was her favourite; the one she was born to perform. One review had specially pleased her. You couldn't often say that about a critic, but this one knew his onions all right. She had whole paragraphs off by heart. The bit she liked best compared her to Hester Fielding:

Not since Hester Fielding's legendary Odette/Odile of 1959 has there been a performance of the role to match McConnell's. She brings to the double part not only the elegance we expect, but also the almost superhuman power that is the special quality of real swans. She combines grace and poignancy with the hard-edged glamour needed in the dramatic shift of the dual role. It's hard to imagine that she isn't partly a bird. Astonishment is the only possible reaction. Astonishment and wonder.

Since accepting the part of the Angel in *Sarabande*, she'd wondered about the wisdom of taking more than three weeks out of her diary to dance in front of such small audiences for ten consecutive nights. Other choreographers, especially Jacques Bodette, who was waiting for her to finish at Wychwood before beginning rehearsals for *Sellophane in G*, tried to talk her out of it. But she wasn't going to pass up the chance of staying in Hester Fielding's house, of meeting her and dancing in front of her. For years, she'd been watching Miss Fielding's performances on video, over and over again. Her copies of *Swan Lake, Giselle* and *Sleeping Beauty* were almost worn out because she'd played them so often. She had been quite honest with Bodette and he'd understood perfectly.

'*Naturellement*,' he'd said. 'No one would refuse such an invitation. I envy you, *ma petite. La divine* Hester Fielding . . . ' He shrugged his shoulders as if to say, what can you do?

Gina, her flatmate, was now sitting opposite her, tucking in to a plate of cereal.

'You nearly ready?' she said. Gina was a chaotic blonde, who had trouble adapting to the strict discipline of the ballet. 'I hope you've packed a nice thick sweater. Yorkshire's sure to be freezing cold.'

'God, you're a cheery soul this morning! I'm off now. 'Bye!'

Silver leaned over and kissed Gina goodbye. Then she picked up her suitcase and began to carry it down three flights of stairs to the front door.

Claudia changed gear and sighed. She and Alison were driving to Wychwood House and she felt quite disoriented. Anyone would, on a journey into a place where there was nothing to see but moors and more moors (ha! ha!) and only the occasional sheep to break the monotony. It wasn't exactly raining, but misty droplets of water seemed to hang in the air and make everything around slick and moist and chilly. How typical of Alison to pretend to be asleep and leave her with no one to talk to.

'Darling, you're not sleeping, are you?'

'I was trying to. What's the matter?'

'Nothing, only I wanted to ask you something. Something about Hugo. Do you mind?'

Alison sat forward and sighed. 'Go on then.'

'Did you notice anything different about him, the last time you saw him?'

'When was that?'

'Honestly, Alison, don't be obtuse! Just before he went off to his dad's. The other day.'

Alison was silent for a few moments and then said 'Right. He was a bit glittery, I thought.'

'Glittery?'

'I don't know how else to describe it. He was excited. His eyes were all shiny and, well, glittery. Is that all you wanted to say? Okay if I go back to sleep now?'

Claudia nodded absently. Glittery. Yes, that was quite right. He was excited about something, and it was probably that young McConnell girl he'd managed to persuade up to the wilds of Yorkshire. A bit of a feather in his choreographical cap, that was.

She tried to recall the whole conversation they'd had, she and Hugo, as she lay in bed by herself watching him (already up and dressed in his usual black trousers and black polo neck) throw things into his suitcase. At the start, when he'd been incapable of tearing himself away from her for even the shortest time, they'd have stayed in bed together for as long as possible. Going off to his poor old widowed father for a few days wouldn't have got him up so early and so enthusiastically. It was *her*, Claudia was sure of it, though she had no proof. Silver McConnell. Hugo couldn't stop talking about her.

Everyone in the ballet world had been doing nothing but talk about Silver McConnell for the last couple of years. Claudia had followed every review, every interview. It wasn't that she was envious of her success (I'm a star, Claudia told herself repeatedly – I wouldn't change places with anyone), but her youth was something else. Silver had danced Odette/Odile in *Swan Lake* last year at Sadler's Wells and people were still saying how amazing she'd been in the part. Hugo must have seen her then and decided to try and get her for *Sarabande*.

Claudia had made it her business to visit him straight after Silver's audition. Hugo was very excited, that much was clear.

'She's really fantastic,' he told Claudia. 'Just right for the Angel.'

'Where did she get the name *Silver* from? It's surely not what she was born with,' Claudia said.

'No, she was called Sylvia but never could say it properly when she was a kid. Called herself Silver and it sort of stuck. And now it suits her perfectly. She *is* very silvery. You'll see when you meet her.'

'I'm a bit surprised, actually, that our paths haven't crossed before.'

'She's been in Paris with the Opera Ballet there. And yes, she *is* very eye-catching. She was dressed entirely in black and white. Stunning silver earrings, like flashes of lightning, hanging down. White neck, with a very gracefully poised head. Very good skin. What she looks like is a rather stylish portrait of herself in black and white.'

Claudia remembered how he'd smiled. There had been something about his mouth – not exactly a smile just a small, satisfied look that was there and gone before you could fix it properly in your mind – and what it said to Claudia was *he thinks he's found a new star.* Be sensible, she said to herself. You are the principal dancer in the Carradine Company. This was quite true, but there was a tiny voice speaking in her mind, a voice she couldn't quite ignore, saying the unthinkable: *You might be past it as a dancer. Silver McConnell is very young. She's the new prima ballerina everyone's talking about. She'll be at the Festival. What if Hugo brings her into the company permanently? What future will there be for you then?*

No, Claudia told herself, I must try to be positive. I shan't worry about Silver. She's going to do something with Bodette when the Wychwood Festival is over, and once she's with him the Carradine Company will seem very unglamorous in comparison. I'm not going to worry about the dancing. Not yet. She resolved to banish any idea that she might not be able to do her part justice, any fear of being past her best. These things had been troubling her more and more recently, but she wouldn't allow them into her head today. *I'm a prima ballerina. I'm a star. I will think of Hugo, who'll be waiting for me.* And besides, she thought, *I've had all those calls asking me to consider modelling.* At least four magazines in the last six months had tried to persuade her to come on what they called a shoot, with nothing but the best photographers in attendance. *The clothes will look divine on you, Miss Drake. Do say yes* . . . This was a surprise to her, as she thought models had a shorter working life even than dancers, but she'd been assured that her fame as a ballerina would more than make up for her relative maturity.

That was a nice way of putting it: relative maturity. *They probably mean*, she thought, *that I'm on my way to being a wrinkled old crone.* Still, the body was slim enough to be a clothes horse and that, plus her reputation (she was always in the gossip columns of one paper or another), would more than compensate for not being eighteen years old. She'd had to refuse these people, naturally, but it was comforting to know that there was someone out there who wanted her, and would still want her, even when she was no longer dancing.

Alison had gone back to sleep. Hugo was always nice to Alison. He was very likeable and Alison didn't seem to mind him. In fact, things in that area were much better these days. For years, Claudia hadn't had a moment's peace because Alison used to behave quite atrociously to every single man who ventured into the house.

Hugo treated Alison with respect and Claudia admired him for his understanding and kindness, which was more than she could manage. *I am such a bad mother*, she told herself many times, *and the worst thing about me is I* know *I'm a bad mother and can't seem to do anything about it.*

When Patrick left her for Jeanette, she had felt betrayed, belittled and hurt. Only the discipline of having to go to class every day kept her from spending hours grinding her teeth or weeping or plotting hideous revenge. She left the care of her little daughter entirely to the new nanny, Yvana, and pushed herself to the limits of endurance. She worked harder than anyone, tiring her muscles, stretching, bending and forcing her body into ever more demanding postures to distract herself from everything that was wrong in her private life.

The result of her hard work, added to what she knew was a spectacular talent, was stardom. She began to be offered principal roles: Aurora, Firebird, and her most triumphant success, Coppélia. Her image, her face appeared in magazines. Her presence made parties sparkle. Her beauty shone from postcards and billboards. If she had a pound coin for every time the words 'flame-haired lovely' had appeared in the tabloids, she'd be a rich woman. It would be falsely modest to deny it – she was a huge star.

One of the things that went with stardom, Claudia soon discovered, was followers. Men gathered around her whenever she appeared anywhere, flocks of them. Sometimes at parties she had literally to push her way through them. They seemed besotted, as though her perfume was some kind of drug. Most of them were too disgusting for words, but there was occasionally someone who caught her eye and she would single him out and take him home with her.

She was as good at sex as she was at dancing, and it was something, maybe the only thing, that stopped her from thinking. It took her to a place where there was nothing but the sensation in her own blood, her own flesh; somewhere where there were no problems, no disappointments, no quarrels, no spite . . . just skin and mouths and a rush of feelings tingling through her. Claudia loved it and didn't see why she should deny herself the pleasure.

Hugo had been one of the besotted, at least at the beginning. He'd come to watch her in *Coppélia* on the first night and then returned for every single performance. It was a rather hideous production, set in some kind of 1950s suburbia with Dr Coppélius lusting after dolls behind the net curtains. The critics thought it was very daring and it had turned Claudia into a sensation. She still remembered the costume with affection; fishnet tights, and the breasts she often had to bind up when she wore traditional tutus given free rein, so to speak, in a very revealing blouse.

Hugo had pursued her with a dogged persistence that she'd found amusing. He was at every party she went to, and had a habit of standing next to whoever she was talking to and sort of infiltrating himself into the conversation. At the end-of-the-run party for *Coppélia*, she'd finally spoken to him about it.

She'd been talking to someone she really rather fancied when Hugo appeared over his shoulder. He was dressed all in black (black polo neck under his black jacket, black trousers and shoes), his hair fell on to a forehead that was high and pale, and his eyes were the kind that seemed to look not at what was in front of them, but at something beyond. Visionary eyes. She couldn't see what colour they were, but they were gazing at her and it was hard to look away.

The poor young man who'd been murmuring into her ear took one look at Hugo and sloped off in search of someone else.

'Look what you've done,' she said to Hugo. 'He's gone off and I'll probably never see him again.'

'You can do better than him. He's a bore.' Hugo smiled at her but Claudia made a point of not smiling back.

'I didn't find him boring at all. I think I might find you, on the other hand, completely tedious. You've been following me about for weeks.'

'I admire you. I've watched you dance every night. I want to speak to you. I think you're beautiful.'

'I know I am. Everyone tells me that.' Claudia was a little drunk or, she realised, she wouldn't have been quite so frank. 'You'll have to do better than that, you know.'

'I'd like to make a ballet for you,' Hugo said. 'I think you're more talented than anyone has realised and you need me to bring out the best in you. I want you to come and join my company. The Carradine Company.'

'I've never heard of it,' Claudia said. This wasn't quite true. The company had a very good reputation. Hugo smiled as though he knew she was lying.

'You will,' he said. 'Everyone will have heard of us within the year.'

'And you want me to join it? Your interest is entirely professional?' She looked up at him. She knew how she was always drawn to tall men, and a small thrill of attraction flickered somewhere – in her stomach, in her throat – and she considered what it might be like to kiss that really rather lovely mouth.

'No, not entirely. You must be aware of that. It's . . .' he smiled and the melting sensation took hold of Claudia even more strongly. 'It's more personal than that. Can we leave this horrible party? It's smoky and loud and I can't hear what you're saying and I want to be alone with you. Please?'

She hesitated for no more than a second, and then said, 'Why not? Are you going to walk me home?'

'If you like. Let's just get out of here and see.'

Claudia's fingers tightened on the steering-wheel. Oh, that night, she thought, and wriggled in the seat. It was like being sixteen again. Better than being sixteen, because then all she was doing was working, working, working, and on this night, just after her thirty-second birthday, she'd been given her youth back again.

They walked along the Embankment.

'I've never been down here at night,' Claudia said. 'Isn't it beautiful!'

'Like all the clichés you've ever heard: diamond necklaces lying on black velvet and so forth. I've seen everything you've ever been in, you know. I've had to turn into a stage-door Johnny in order to meet you. It's not my habit to go to parties all the time, but you seem to do little else and I was determined to speak to you.'

'Well, here I am. Speak all you like.'

'I meant what I said, you know. I want to make a ballet for you. Would you dance in it, if I did?'

'Yes, of course, Hugo. That would be amazing.'

'It'd have to be something special to do you justice. Something beautiful, like you. Something different, because that's what you are, different.'

Now, driving through the countryside with the darkness pressing at the windows of the car, Claudia remembered how she'd loved listening to Hugo when he was talking about her, how she drank in every word he said. Her mind went back again to that first walk.

'I know what sort of dancer you are,' Hugo said to her. 'And how much more you're capable of being, too. You're thoughtful, and more disciplined than most ballet dancers. Lots of dancers let feeling take the upper hand, but you're so . . . so controlled. Controlled yet passionate. I can see it; so much passion in you, waiting to be exploited. Waiting to be revealed.'

Claudia leaned her weight against his as they walked and smiled up at him. 'I have actually noticed you, you know. At the parties, I mean. Of course, you have an advantage, being so tall. But it's clever of you to know me so well. I mean you to see what kind of a dancer I am.'

'I do,' said Hugo simply.

'But I know nothing about you. Tell me. Tell me everything. You're not married, are you?'

He laughed, as though the mere suggestion was ridiculous.

'Nor am I,' said Claudia. 'Not any more. We're divorced. My husband left me. I do have a daughter, though.'

'Don't sound so apologetic. If she's anything like you, she must be gorgeous.'

I changed the subject then, Claudia recalled. And we talked about everything. His life, my life, my marriage, and his work, his struggle to make dance that was seen, and paid for. Everything. We reached his street after what seemed like hours.

'This is where I live,' Hugo said. 'Come inside. Come and have breakfast. It's nearly morning.'

She stepped into the house without a word and stood in the narrow hall. Hugo reached behind Claudia to close the door and she didn't move and then his arm was on her shoulder, and he drew her to him and kissed her and she collapsed back against the door and they were there for minutes upon minutes, kissing. Claudia felt herself falling, and everything growing dark and hot. Soon, there was nothing in her head but this need, this desire.

Neither of them had spoken. It was, Claudia reflected now, like a ballet. We made our own steps and movements and it was beautiful. I mustn't think about it, she told herself, not while I'm driving. Just the memory of that first night still had the power to turn her weak and faint. This, she remembered thinking, is what my body was meant to do. They made love and then, almost immediately it seemed, they made love again and then they slept and, by the time she woke up and saw his thin face next to hers, she was lost, gone, finished and consumed. In love. This hadn't happened with any of her other men. This was different. She'd never wanted anyone as much as she wanted Hugo when they first met.

That first flush of emotion and lust had gone on for quite a long time. At the beginning, all she'd wanted to do was say his name. To anyone she met. Just the sound of it on her lips thrilled her, and even though she knew how silly it was, she couldn't stop herself doing it. But, as she had known it probably would, the sexual thrill lessened. That was the thing about familiarity – it got to be familiar and then the unfamiliar began to seem desirable.

Claudia blushed as she remembered the recent occasion on which she'd slipped up and been unfaithful to Hugo. A nice young stagehand on the French tour. She used to take off her costume between the matinée and the evening performance and put on a silk robe and meet him in the wings. *Insatiable* was the word that came into her mind. We both were. Remembering it was making her feel randy. That had been one of Dylan's words. Dylan, with his long, blonde hair and hard, muscled thighs and a tongue and fingers that knew exactly what was required.

She couldn't break up with Hugo now. He'd given her this part at exactly the right time, when she'd begun to feel her age a tiny bit more; when every routine was an infinitesimal degree more difficult to achieve than it had been last month. The Princess in *Sarabande*. She would make them all sit up and take notice, she *had* to. If she didn't, it would only be a matter of time before she was doing character parts and then, the next thing you knew, she'd be old and no man would want her any longer. It wasn't a prospect she was prepared to consider.

'This is it, Mum,' said Alison. 'This turning on the right.'

'Sorry, darling, I was miles away.'

'As usual. Lucky I woke up or we'd have been lost. On the moors.'

Claudia didn't answer, but drove through a wrought-iron gate set into tall, squarish gateposts. The drive was long and curved slightly. She was vaguely aware of shrubs on the lawn on either side of the car, their shapes still discernible in the darkness.

'It's huge!' Alison said, as Wychwood Hall came into view. 'And all the windows have got lights in them.'

'Someone's got money to burn,' Claudia muttered. The building stood out black against the night sky. It *did* have a lot of windows, some of which had panels of stained glass set into them. The people living here were clearly unworried about electricity bills. In the portico, another light had been left on to welcome them. The front door was heavy and wooden with an enormous brass knocker. The moors rose behind the house and sleet had just begun to fall. Claudia shivered. She was quite sure that what they'd see when someone answered the door was a retainer of the kind you got in all the best horror movies; white-faced and dressed in funeral clothes.

'Oh my God,' she said. 'What have I let myself in for?'

Alison couldn't sleep. She switched on the bedside lamp, put on her glasses and peered at her watch. Half-past one. Was it possible that she'd been asleep and woken up again? If that's happened, she thought, I won't drop off again now for hours. And I'm hungry. She punched the pillow and lay down again, staring at the ceiling. There were hours and hours to go till breakfast, and how was she going to last out? She looked around. It wasn't a bad room. A bit like a posh youth hostel or a plain sort of hotel. It had its own shower and loo. That was fab. A staircase led up from the front hall to a long corridor and that was where all the bedrooms were. Alison smiled to think of the whole company lined up under their duvets. If there weren't any walls it'd look like one of the junior dormitories at school.

I'm always hungry, she thought and wondered if she was abnormal. One of the most annoying things about being the daughter of a ballet dancer (and there were loads of annoying things, too many to list, Alison reckoned) was not being able to eat properly. Claudia Drake couldn't afford to put on weight, oh no, that simply wouldn't do, so her cupboards and fridge at home never had anything decent in them. She hopes I won't put on any more weight, Alison thought, and that's another reason why there's nothing in the house. That's pathetic! Hasn't she heard of shops? Doesn't she realise I buy a Mars bar every time I go out? She is so *stupid* sometimes.

The whole ballet thing struck Alison as ridiculous. There were all these people: sweaty, hairy *real* people, pretending to be lighter than air and floaty and beautiful and completely unreal. And the joke is they train harder than footballers. They work themselves to death and twist their bodies and feet and everything into positions that are mad. They can't eat properly because that would put weight on, and they can't miss a single day's class because then the whole thing would sort of collapse. Claudia had never missed a class ever. She wouldn't, Alison thought, even miss one if I was taken off to hospital with a burst appendix or something. The ambulances would be screeching to a halt outside the flat, men with stretchers would be tearing up the stairs, in too much of a hurry even to wait for the lift, and Mum would be on the way out, saying *can't possibly stop. Sure you understand . . . class . . . you'll do everything you can, won't you, darlings?* and dazzling them with her smile.

Lying back on the pillows, Alison allowed herself to dream a little. She let herself pretend that she was someone who had a normal mother. And a normal father. A mother who stayed at home so that she could go to day school and come back every afternoon. And a father. That would be the best thing. A father who loved her mother and had a proper job in this country and who loved both his wife and his daughter so much that he'd never, ever go off with someone else and leave them to fend for themselves; a father who was *there*.

I was only little when he left, she thought. I was five, but I remember lots of stuff. We used to go to the zoo and make faces at the animals, copying them. He was funny. He carried me on his shoulders, and swung me round at bedtime before dropping me on to the bed. He used to read books to me. Mum says he didn't and it was always her, but it wasn't. She was always rushing out of the house to be in time for the show. Alison had said that to Claudia once and she'd gone scarlet, which Alison thought proved that she was right. She almost spat at her daughter: *you don't remember anything properly, you were scarcely more than a baby!* Alison smiled to herself. I just shut up about it, but I wasn't a baby and I do remember and it *was* him. He wrote my special book, didn't he? Mum's forgotten all about that. It was a lullaby book, and he typed it out by himself and drew little pictures on each page and stapled all the pages together and I've still got it.

She got out of bed and went to fetch her atlas from the suitcase which was lying open on the floor near the window. If her mother had bothered to ask why she'd packed an atlas, Alison had a story all ready about homework for school, but in fact it was where the Lullaby Book lived, always. The pages stayed nice and flat and who in their right mind would ever think of looking in an atlas when they didn't absolutely have to? She went back to bed, and took the little book out of its safe hiding-place. Then she looked at it, which was quite unnecessary really because she knew the whole thing by heart and had done since she was about three. Still, the tiny illustrations always made her smile. My dad, she thought, was good at drawing pictures and so am I. It's thanks to him I'm good at art and making things. Mum can barely sew the ribbons on her ballet shoes. Now, looking down at the pages, she heard her dad's voice saying the words as she read them:

> Here is a bear who is brown and small
> and wants to speak in a small brown voice
> so you can hear the tales he tells
> of big black bears in caves of stone.
> He whispers gently in your ear:
> Look I am here. You are not alone.

She felt better at once, and put the book away again. If only I wasn't so hungry, she thought, I'd probably be able to fall asleep. A thought occurred to her. She knew where the kitchen was downstairs. She laid the book aside, got out of bed and put on her dressing-gown. Then she stepped out as quietly as she could into the corridor.

There was a dim light shining in the hall. Alison crept down the stairs and into the kitchen. This was the most modern-looking room she'd seen since they arrived. The rest of Wychwood House looked very old-fashioned, but this was big and square with a high ceiling. Every single fixture and fitting was so modern it was practically space-age. Wherever she looked Alison could see white and palest blue and shiny silver. The cooker was an enormous thing – all oven doors and gleaming hotplates, with an extractor hood hanging over it like a canopy of burnished copper.

The fridge was gigantic and white as ice, and it didn't make a loud, humming noise like the fridge in the flat. Alison opened it and nearly let out a yelp of surprise. Someone had taken great care to stock up with every single thing anyone could possibly want. Eggs, bacon, sausages, fruit yoghurts in four different flavours, Greek yoghurt and cream. There were sealed packets of croissants and buns, packets of cold sliced meats, and jars of jam, marmalade, mayonnaise and mustard. There wasn't any fruit or cheese, so they must be somewhere else, maybe in a larder. Granny used to keep things like that in the larder, so maybe Miss Fielding did as well.

She opened the packet of croissants and took out two. People in the company won't be rushing to eat those, she thought as she put them on a special rack on top of the toaster to heat up. Too fattening by half. She took the butter out of the fridge and put it on the table and found a knife in one of the drawers. As soon as the croissants were ready, she sat down and began to eat.

That was when she noticed the cat. He was sleeping in a basket in the corner by the cooker, taking up every single bit of the available space. She got up from the table and approached him quietly, so as not to scare him away. 'You are huge!' she said, crouching down and stroking his back gently. He lifted his ginger head and gazed at her out of pale green eyes. Then he yawned an enormous pink yawn and rested his head on his front paws again. Alison whispered, 'You're a lovely cat. I wonder what your name is?' Then she heard the sound of someone coming towards the kitchen. She froze, crouching on the floor beside the basket.

'Oh, it's you!' said the person Alison had been told to call Miss Fielding. Hester Fielding, whose house this was. The famous dancer; even Claudia admired her. 'You're Alison, aren't you? It was all a bit of a rush earlier on, but I think I caught your name. And you must please call me Hester. I can't bear Miss Fielding. It makes me sound like a Victorian governess. Is anything the matter? Can I help you at all?'

Alison got to her feet in a scramble of confusion, embarrassment and shyness. She was desperate to say everything at once; to reassure Miss Fielding – Hester – that yes, everything was fine, really.

'No, I'm okay. I just. I couldn't sleep, you see, because I was so hungry, and I thought no one would . . . well, I thought everyone else would be asleep. And I would have cleared everything up. Only I couldn't sleep, that's all. And then I saw this cat. He's so big!'

'Siggy's a bit of a monster, isn't he? Don't you worry, though. You finish your croissant. Midnight food always tastes wonderful, doesn't it? I'm just going to make myself a cup of tea.'

Hester Fielding's dressing-gown, Alison thought, looking at her as she set the kettle to boil, was grander than most people's evening dresses. It was made of velvet, or perhaps it was velour, and it was exactly the colour of blackcurrant yoghurt. It swept the floor and was tied round the waist with a kind of sash. Alison noticed (because she always noticed people's figures to see how much thinner than her they were) that Hester wasn't any fatter than Claudia, even though she was older. Claudia had said she was fifty-three, but she didn't look it. *She dyes her hair, of course*, she remembered hearing her mother remark to Hugo. *And quite right too. I intend to be a redhead till my very last breath.*

'That's a strange name, Siggy,' she said, more for something to say than because she really thought it strange. 'For a cat, I mean.'

Miss Fielding – Hester – turned and smiled at her, and Alison immediately felt happier. You couldn't call her beautiful, she thought. Not in the way Mum's beautiful, but it's hard to stop looking at her, and when she smiles, her eyes shine and . . . Alison couldn't express properly what it was exactly, but Hester had a kind of glow about her.

'Siggy's called after Siegfried. He's the prince in *Swan Lake*, you know. We all thought he might be princely when he was a kitten, but now he's so large and lumbering. Not a bit like a prince, at least not a ballet prince. They leap about much more than Siggy's ever done.'

She poured the boiling water into the teapot and waited for a moment before making her cup of tea.

'I hope you enjoy it here at Wychwood,' she said. 'You won't be bored, will you?'

'Oh, no,' said Alison, although for days now she'd been moaning to Claudia that bored stiff would be her permanent state till school started. 'No, I'm sure I'll find lots to do. And I'm going to bed now. I know I'll sleep well.'

'I'm going to write a few letters I think,' said Hester. 'And then try to sleep. It's going to be a busy day tomorrow.'

'Yes,' said Alison. 'Goodnight.'

The croissants were delicious. She picked up the plate she'd been using and washed it at the sink. Which is more, she thought, than my mum will do when she has her breakfast. One of the more irritating things about Claudia was how messy she was. She hardly ever washed up properly either, which made Alison grind her teeth with fury. She always offered to do the dishes when she was at home. You'd think that might please a mother, but oh no. Claudia was forever telling people how domesticated Alison was, only she made it sound like an insult, as though only truly dull people ever bothered with things like housework. That sort of thing, her voice seemed to say, is not for artistic people like me.

'Night night, Siggy!' she whispered as she left the kitchen. Siggy was snoring in his basket and took no notice whatsoever.

Hester lay in bed and thought about Alison Drake. No one would have guessed, to look at her, that she was her mother's daughter, so Mr Drake, whoever he was, must have been dark and stocky. A beautiful mother can be a problem, she thought, and wondered how much her ideas of her own identity, her desire to become a dancer, were bound up in her memories of Helen Prévert. By the time she came to live with the Wellicks, her memories of her mother had already begun to fade, and after that all she had was the photograph she'd brought with her. Hester had had to live up to a vision of beauty and grace caught forever behind glass in a silver frame. Alison, on the other hand, had Claudia in front of her every day and her looks would make almost anyone feel inadequate.

I think of Alison as a child, Hester thought, but she's fourteen. That was how old I was when I started in the Charleroi company and I considered myself quite grown-up and ready to start work.

1948

London was enormous. The cars, the crowds of people on the pavements, the huge, grey buildings – Hester looked out of the taxi window and recognised some of them from newsreels she'd seen. A thin rain was falling and street lamps made the puddles glitter and shine. Mr Cranley had been at King's Cross station to meet her. She caught sight of him standing at the barrier as soon as she started walking up the platform, and waved to attract his attention. He smiled at her, and the nervousness she'd been feeling as the train steamed south (nervousness mixed with excitement, breathlessness at the idea of all the possibilities that lay ahead of her) evaporated at once. Everything was going to be all right.

They didn't pass any theatres on the taxi ride from the station to Bayswater.

'You'll see them all soon enough,' Mr Cranley said. 'Especially the dear old Royalty, our theatre, in Craven Road. Royalty that's rather fallen on hard times, is what I say, but it's a splendid place all the same.'

Hester wanted to say that anywhere would be wonderful after the Wellicks, but didn't quite dare. Mr Cranley peered at her in the half-light of the taxi's interior.

'I hope you're not going to be homesick, are you?'

Hester laughed. 'No, not a bit,' she said. 'Madame Olga is the one person I'll miss and she says she'll come down and see me dance when I'm ready. And I want to say thank you for . . . for everything. I'll work really, really hard, I promise.'

'I know that. I don't take on girls who are frivolous about their dancing and Olga assured me of your determination. Mine is a small company, but a good one. Sadler's Wells and the Festival Ballet often invite my principals to take on roles there, you know.'

He leaned forward as though what he was about to say was

particularly important. Hester thought he looked exactly like someone who had just taken off a Father Christmas costume. His hair was white and his small beard much too neatly trimmed for the part, but his eyes were blue and bright and he had rosy cheeks.

'I noticed something about you, Hester. Something that you may not even realise. Apart from Madame Olga, of course, you're alone. She tells me that you've been alone for a very long time, ever since your father sent you to England and perhaps even longer, for I understand your mother died when you were very young, and who's to tell what that does to a child, eh? We'll never know.'

Hester frowned. What was Mr Cranley going to say? Was he right? The strangest sensation was creeping over her as he spoke, a sense of recognition. Alone. That was exactly what she had been until Madame Olga took an interest in her. All by herself in the world. Suddenly chilly, she rubbed one gloved hand against the other, and shivered. Mr Cranley went on speaking.

'Your father, although he was polite and thank God not a philistine – he did understand about the ballet at least – didn't strike me as a very *warm* person, I must say, and his wife – well, you'll forgive me, but the milk of human kindness is in very short supply there, I fear.'

'I've never met her. I've never been back to France since I left. My father visited the Wellicks three times while I was there.'

'It makes what I'm going to say a little easier then. I hate to speak ill of a person's relations, Hester, but you do seem to have drawn the most impoverished hand in that particular game, don't you?'

Hester nodded. 'But my grandmother was the best grandmother in the world. I remember her.'

'That's something I suppose, but of course she's dead. I don't mean to sound harsh and of course it's not her fault that she couldn't survive to love you, but I know that Madame Olga feels that you're in need of . . . of someone. Olga's an old friend of mine and she's asked me to look after you, and I shall. I mean it. I want you to understand that you can tell me anything, ask me for any help or advice and I'll do my very best to help.'

Hester hesitated. Was it too much? What was Mr Cranley really saying? Could Paula possibly have been right about his intentions? Or was he a father to all his dancers?

'Thank you,' she said at last, 'but . . .'

Mr Cranley laughed. 'I can read your thoughts as plainly as if they were written on your face. You have a very expressive face, which is a great gift for any performer. You're thinking I'll be wanting something in return, and God knows what ghastly ideas might be flitting through your mind! You can forget them. I require no more from you than hard work. I'm a sort of father-figure to the whole company, as they'll doubtless tell you, but you – well, all the rest have perfectly decent parents and grandparents and aunts and uncles and whole coachloads of brothers and sisters. You, not to put too fine a point on it, have not.'

'Thank you, Mr Cranley. I feel . . . I feel as though—'

'Don't bother to say it, Hester. It's not important. And please call me Piers. They all do in the company. Here we are, then. This is it.'

Hester waited on the pavement with her suitcase beside her as Mr Cranley, Piers, paid the taxi driver. She glanced up at the lighted windows of 24 Moscow Road and realised that she hadn't felt as comfortable as this since she'd been a little girl in France. I've been stiff, she thought, as though I've been braced against a storm of some kind. I could be myself at Madame Olga's but that was the only place. But I feel different here.

'You'll be sharing with Dinah and Nell, I believe,' Piers said. 'Lively girls, both of them. Do you the world of good.'

He picked up the case and used the brass knocker in the shape of a lion to bang loudly on the door.

Number 24 Moscow Road looked very grand from the outside. There were three steps up to the front door and a porch with pillars around it. Inside, the hall was rather dark and very far from splendid. Hester found it a little disappointing. A table with a mirror above it took up half of its width. A lounge and a dining room opened off the hall. Later, she was to learn that the lounge was known as the Green Room, which was the name given to sitting rooms in theatres. There were bedrooms on three floors. The principals of the company were on the first and second floors, and the younger members shared rooms on the third floor and also in the attic. Hester found that she had been allocated a bed right at the top of the house, sharing with Dinah Rowland, and Nell Osborne.

'Welcolme to the Attic de Luxe!' said Dinah, the first time she saw Hester. 'It's not much, but it's home.'

Dinah was a tall, pale-skinned girl with a shock of golden hair; Nell was small and gingery, with freckles. They both looked older than she was, by a couple of years she guessed.

Hester put her suitcase down at the end of her bed and looked around. The floorboards were only partly covered, and the rugs were threadbare.

'I can see you don't think much of our decor and who can blame you?' said Nell. She pointed at the rugs. 'You have to use those as sort of stepping-stones to get from the door to your bed if you don't want to risk splinters in your feet.'

Hester smiled. She unpacked her few belongings, marvelling at how little she possessed. Only her clothes and Antoinette, and the tortoiseshell box with *Grand-mère*'s gold chain in it. She propped the doll on the bed, leaning against the pillow, and hoped that Dinah and Nell wouldn't think she was babyish. Neither of them mentioned it.

Hester never told anyone how much she loved the Attic de Luxe. The others moaned about it but she settled in quickly, and soon it was as though she'd always lived there. For the first time in her life she had a tiny space that was entirely her own. She didn't mind the shabbiness of the furnishings and soon grew used to always having tights hanging up over the bath in the chilly bathroom. It took them hours to dry and sometimes she had to put them on while they were still damp. Dinah advised her to squeeze them in a towel after she washed them.

'Not very absorbent though, are they?' said Hester.

'Absorbent? This one's transparent, more like a veil than a towel.' Dinah waved one in front of herself and moved her hips suggestively, like a belly dancer. 'I could be Salome, couldn't I? The Dance of the Seven Towels.'

'When I'm grown-up,' Hester said 'my towels are going to be so fluffy they'll be practically furry. And I'm going to have deep, deep carpets everywhere.'

'Of course you will, ducky!' said Dinah. 'Now get dressed and let's go to the Corner House.'

Lyons Corner House near Marble Arch was Hester's favourite place in the whole of London. The rest of the city was a little disappointing. Never before had she seen a place which was so grey and gloomy. Everyone seemed to be dressed in brown or grey or black and every building was sooty and forbidding. Bomb damage was still visible in many places, and some houses had so much missing that you could look at them and see a wall with the remains of wallpaper still stuck to it, or a mantelpiece sticking out when all around it had vanished.

Dinah and Nell, Hester realised, were the first proper friends she'd ever had. They'd been kind to her from the beginning and Hester never felt at all homesick. There were times when she longed for Madame Olga; longed to walk through the village and through the gates of Wychwood and talk to her about this strange new life. Instead, she wrote to her twice a week, telling her everything – the way Piers' classes differed from hers, the kindness of most of the others in the company to their youngest dancer, and the plans for future productions. And Madame Olga wrote back on blank postcards, in her complicated, spiky handwriting. She offered advice, sent kisses, and begged for more news, more detail. Every time she wrote, she signed the message in the same way: *I think of you all the time and send you my blessings. Olga R.*

During her early months in London, Hester was nervous about being as good as the other dancers in the company. She kept up well during the daily lessons they all had to attend, but dancing was the real focus of her life and sometimes she worried that the other members of the company might not think she was good. For her part, Hester thought she had an accurate idea of her own talents. Sometimes she wondered whether perhaps she might be mistaken, but most of the time she recognised her own gift and was grateful for it. She didn't say so to anyone, but she knew that she would succeed. She had the stamina for the work and the determination to fight, if she needed to, to be acknowledged. She understood that Piers thought highly of her, though he very rarely praised his dancers. It would have been easy for someone with less confidence in their own ability to feel discouraged.

Dinah and Nell showed her the best places to buy ballet shoes and tights and they introduced her to the delights of Lyons, which was exactly the sort of place Hester used to dream about when she thought of leaving Yorkshire. Lining up with Dinah and Nell and paying for whatever she'd eaten or drunk with her own money sent to her directly by her father made her feel grown-up.

The Royalty Theatre was a small island of colour in the middle of all the drabness. The seats in the stalls were blood-red and the curtain a particularly violent shade of crimson, but if you looked carefully, the plush was worn out in places, and there were holes in the curtain near the floor which had been patched and darned more than once.

'Piers never spends enough money on the building,' said Dinah, when she and Hester and Nell were sitting at their usual table in Lyons. 'He'd rather get better costumes for the dancers, or take us all abroad on tour. He says no one minds about worn-out plush if the ballet's good enough.'

She put out her long spoon and helped herself to a bit of Hester's ice-cream. The girls always had the same thing, a triple scoop of ice-cream in three flavours – chocolate, vanilla and strawberry.

'But they might stop coming to the theatre if the seats are too uncomfortable,' said Nell.

'They're not, though,' said Dinah. 'They're not in the least uncomfortable. Just a little shabby. The place isn't dirty or flea-ridden or anything.'

Hester didn't answer, but went on eating her ice-cream. She'd stood in the stalls on the day Piers first showed her round and dreamed of a time when the curtain would open and there she would be, up on the stage, dancing. Nell and Dinah had moved on to talk about the prima ballerina of the company; the same Estelle whose presence had meant that her own name had been changed. This Estelle's surname was Delamere but no one called her anything but Madame P when she was out of earshot.

'What's the P for?' Hester asked Dinah, wondering why she'd never thought of asking before. They'd all had so many other things to talk about that this question had only just occurred to her.

'You can take your pick really,' Dinah answered. 'Pompous, Poisonous, Posh. Any and all of those will do. She's awful and we all hate her.'

'Piers too?'

'Probably. Only he won't tell her so as long as she's dancing up to standard. She *is* rather good, actually, but I don't like her style. Cold, I think she is. You can admire her but never love her, d'you know what I mean?'

Hester nodded, though she wasn't quite sure if she did.

'I think she's ridiculous,' said Nell. 'She's over thirty, for heaven's sake! She must know that there's going to be a time when she can't perform as anything more than a character dancer. Surely she can see her days as a prima ballerina are numbered?'

'No, she can't,' Dinah said. 'You never do know things like that when it's you. You kid yourself that everything's just the same as it always was. It's only the rest of us who can hear the creaking joints during class.'

They laughed, and then left the golden light and warmth of Lyons and made their way to the Underground with their arms linked.

'Another deliciously comfortable night in the Attic de Luxe awaits us!' said Nell.

'Can't wait,' Dinah added, 'to sink into my feather bed.'

Hester, Dinah and Nell didn't really mind how shabby the Attic de Luxe was because they were hardly ever there. They spent most of their time in the rehearsal room round the corner from the theatre, in a dusty hall attached to a church. The room was draughty, high-ceilinged and chilly even in the warmest weather and freezing cold in winter. But Hester hardly noticed the temperature because she worked so hard there, month after month. Piers was not a bit like Father Christmas when he was taking class or going through routines during a rehearsal period.

'I'd appreciate your full attention, Hester,' he'd almost shouted at her once when she'd been daydreaming. She blushed. It wasn't like her to lose concentration, but Piers missed nothing and was often quite fierce with dancers whom he suspected of not attending properly to his instructions. When he was cross with anyone, his face became bright red and he looked as though he might begin to breathe out fire, just like a dragon. One cold morning, when they'd all overslept, Dinah looked at Nell and shook her head.

'You can't go to rehearsal, you know.' She was dragging a brush through her long, fair hair and twisting it up into a knot, anchored with pins. 'You're sick. You've got an awful cough and all you'll do by coming to rehearsal is spread your ghastly cold through the whole company. Piers'll be hopping mad. *Nutcracker* opens next Thursday, remember? At this rate, all the mice and all the flowers will be hacking away in the wings so that you won't be able to hear the music.'

'Shut up, Dinah,' said Nell. 'I'm going. All I need is for Piers to give my part to Simone. She's been eyeing it from the start. This is my very first solo and I'm certainly not going to let a little cough stop me. I've got some lozenges somewhere.'

Nell reminded Hester of a deer, her head often tilted to one side as she looked at you. She wasn't exactly pretty, but her face was very expressive. She laughed a lot, but today, Hester noticed, she had dark shadows under her eyes, her skin was pale and there was a sheen of sweat on her forehead. Hester felt for her. She looked dreadfully ill.

'Lozenges aren't going to help you,' Dinah continued. 'You just wait. Piers will be on to you at once.'

Hester watched anxiously to see what Piers would say when he saw Nell. The girls were standing in rows and Nell was right at the front. Hester couldn't see her face, but Piers had begun to frown and sigh a little, always a bad sign. When Piers sighed you knew that meant trouble. Nell started coughing and spluttering and Piers waved a hand to stop the session.

'Nell Osborne, come here,' he said. Nell stepped forward and hung her head. Hester thought with relief for a moment that he was going to be kind to her. He was going to ask her if she was all right, and maybe tell her to go and get a drink and sit down till she felt better. When he started to speak, his words at first seemed quite quiet. It was only as he went on that the terrifying crescendo crept into his voice:

'You're not well, Nell, are you? No, you're not. I can see it.' He put his hand out and touched her on the forehead. 'You've got a temperature. It's obvious to anyone looking at you that you should have stayed in bed.' His voice grew louder, crosser. 'Not, however, obvious to you, you silly child. Don't you understand that by coming here into this rehearsal room you're endangering all the rest of us – your friends, the production, me, everything we've worked for for weeks. Your stupidity beggars belief. You must go. Now! Go to bed and stay there.'

By the time he'd finished, Nell had tears rolling down her cheeks.

'Stop crying this instant!' said Piers. 'Can't you see I'm worried about you?' He glanced around the room. 'Dinah, Hester, take this shivering wreck and put her to bed at once. Then go to my house . . . do you know where it is? Good. Go and tell my housekeeper to take some food and comfort to this poor invalid and then come straight back here. Ruby'll know what to do. She's used to looking after sick kids. On second thoughts, go to my house on the way to Moscow Road. That's more sensible. Off you go.'

The girls walked through the wintry streets in the freezing wind, and round the corner to Piers' house.

'God, what ghastly weather,' Dinah said. 'We'll all get pneumonia, I bet. Thank heavens Piers lives within spitting distance of the theatre.' She and Hester were on either side of the still weeping Nell, helping her along.

'I'm not going to be well for the show,' she wailed. 'And I might have spoiled the whole thing for everyone. Piers'll never forgive me.'

'Of course he will,' Dinah said. 'He huffs and puffs but he's got a good heart under it all. You can see that. He's going to send his own housekeeper to look after you. It's just that when he's being a choreographer, he sort of becomes someone else. Like a Jeykll and Hyde sort of thing.'

'Here it is,' Hester said. She left Nell leaning entirely on Dinah and went up to the front door to ring the bell.

'What if this Ruby person is out?' Dinah asked. 'What do we do then?'

'You can go back to rehearsal and I'll stay and look after Nell.'

The door opened and a tall young woman stood there, dressed in a tweed skirt and a white blouse. She looked to be in her mid-twenties and Hester was struck by something in her eyes that immediately made her feel better – a sense of calm and kindness, as though she were ready to face anything.

'Can I help you?' she began, and then caught sight of Nell. 'Oh, my goodness, bring that poor child in here.'

'Are you Ruby?' Dinah asked.

'That's right,' the young woman said. 'I'm Mr Cranley's housekeeper.'

'Piers asked us to take our friend home. To 24 Moscow Road. But he said would you please bring round some food and stay with her till she's better.'

'Of course, of course. Come in. Put her down on the sofa in the front room and wait with her. I'll get my things.' She turned to Hester. 'Perhaps we could all go together? Then you can help me carry some food, if you would. I'll get a basket ready.'

Dinah and Hester went into the front room and helped Nell lie down on the sofa. It was the first time since Hester had left France and the warmth of her grandmother's sitting room that she'd been in a room that could have been called properly comfortable. Even Madame Olga's rooms in Wychwood House were frequently cold and the furnishings had seen better days. In Piers' sitting room the walls were papered with a trailing pattern of leaves and berries; the curtains were coppery-red brocade. The lamp standing on a table beside the sofa had a shade made out of stained glass. Hester stared at it, entranced – she thought it was one of the most beautiful things she'd ever seen.

'He doesn't exactly go short of anything, does he?' Dinah remarked as she laid Nell on the sofa, making sure that her shoes didn't touch the upholstery. 'Us up in the Attic de Luxe and him here in all this. He must be rolling in money.'

Hester hardly heard what she was saying. She was gazing at the gilded clock on the sideboard, at the gorgeously-coloured rugs on the carpeted floor (rugs on top of carpet, the height of luxury!), at the engraved invitations propped up against the ornaments on the mantelpiece, and thinking how wonderful it must be to sit in here with the lamp lit and bask in the firelight. There was no fire in the hearth at the moment, but she could imagine just what it would be like.

'Here I am,' said Ruby, coming into the room with baskets hanging from each arm. 'If you could take this, please?' She smiled at Hester. 'I'm sorry, I don't know any of your names.'

'I'm Hester Fielding,' Hester said, taking one of the baskets from Ruby. 'And that's Dinah Rowland. Nell Osborne is the one who's ill.'

Ruby smiled and nodded. Hester didn't notice as it actually happened, but remembering it a short time later, she realised that as Ruby looked into her eyes for the first time, she'd known at once that here was someone she could trust.

Ruby came to the Attic de Luxe every day while Nell was ill. She sat with her while Hester and Dinah were at lessons or at rehearsal and then she went back to cook for Piers. She didn't speak a great deal and Hester thought she was pleasant, but rather quiet. She didn't tell them much, but Hester knew she was Scottish from her accent. She had four brothers and sisters and told Hester once that she sent almost all her wages home to her mother, to help her.

'Are you happy to live in London, so far away from them?' Hester asked her.

Ruby smiled at Hester and thought for a moment before she answered. 'Sometimes,' she said, 'I'm happy to be away from all that fuss, but sometimes I do miss them. Yes, sometimes I miss them dreadfully.'

After three days in bed, Nell was almost herself.

'I'll be going back to rehearsal tomorrow, Ruby,' she said. She was lying on her bed looking quite different from the invalid who'd been sent home only days ago. 'I feel much better. It's thanks to you looking after me. And all the lovely food.'

Ruby shook her head. 'You'd have got better whatever I did, I expect. You're young and healthy.'

'But it's much more fun being ill when there's someone to chat to and take care of you,' said Dinah. 'I think it's jolly nice of you, Ruby.'

Ruby said nothing, but went on working at her tapestry. Hester had noticed that she always had something to sew or stitch when she came to Moscow Road. One whole afternoon she'd spent darning the holes in their tights to such perfection that Dinah exclaimed, 'Your darns are beautiful, Ruby! They make the undarned bits of the tights look awful. How d'you do it? I'd never have the patience.'

Once Ruby had left them, Hester, Dinah and Nell gossiped about her.

'Is she pretty?' Nell wondered. 'I can never decide. Sometimes she looks quite plain.'

'She doesn't make enough of herself,' Dinah said. She was a great believer in enhancing what Nature had given you, and was forever trying to rouge Hester's pale cheeks or put curlers into her hair. 'I wonder if she's sleeping with Piers.'

'No!' Nell and Hester exclaimed together. Sex was something that Hester had known a little about for a long time, but the details of what went on between men and women, and also between men and men sometimes, she learned about from Dinah and Nell. It was a topic of endless fascination and they often discussed it as they lay in the Attic de Luxe with the lights out. It was easier to be frank when it was dark. At first, Hester had hardly believed what she was being told, but she was used to it all now and their talk was much less inhibited. Nell went on, 'No, never. I'm sure Piers prefers men. Aren't you? I mean, what about Anton and Miles and Jeremy? Don't you think he'd prefer them?' The girls dissolved into giggles again. Homosexuality was against the law, of course, but everyone in the company knew about these three men. Dancers, in any case, according to Dinah, were always assumed by the general public to be queer, whether they were or not. The truth of the matter was some were and some weren't and Hester was curious about it – and when she thought about it, didn't quite know *what* she thought about it.

'Will you be all right?' Hester whispered to Nell.

They were in the dressing room at the Royalty Theatre, getting ready for *Nutcracker*. Hester was one of the children in the party scene at the beginning and one of the flowers later on, when Clara visits the Land of the Sweets. She was so excited before this very first appearance on stage that she could hardly put her lipstick on without her hand shaking. She'd thought about inviting Madame Olga to see the show and discussed with Dinah and Nell whether it was worth her while to come all the way to London just to see her running across the stage with a crowd of other people, and they decided it wasn't. Still, Hester found it so hard to write that particular letter. In the end she was honest. She wrote, *I'd love you to come and see me dance for the first time, but it's a very long way for such unimportant parts, so perhaps you'd better wait till I'm doing a solo. Piers says it won't be so long now . . .*

Nell had a short solo in the ballet. She was one of the Oriental dancers in the Land of Sweets scene. Madame P was to dance the Sugar Plum Fairy.

It seemed to Hester that Nell was unusually quiet. They'd all come early to get ready. Piers was insistent that no one should be rushed, no one should panic at the last moment and so, by the time the curtain was ready to go up and the overture was coming over the Tannoy, everyone had been ready for hours. Hester had asked Nell whether she was all right but got no reply. Now she asked again. Nell just nodded and then there was no time for any more conversation. They were on stage. The Christmas tree stood in the corner, heavy with gold and red decorations that shone under the stage lights, and they were transported to Clara's house, where they danced about, waiting for Dr Drosselmeyer to appear.

This part, which didn't require anything too much in the way of suppleness from the person who performed it, was traditionally taken by Piers.

He was dressed entirely in black when he appeared on the stage, and Hester was surprised by how frightening he looked. He wore a black suit and had blackened his beard as well and added a tall black hat. You could hear the children in the audience gasp when he made his entrance, and when he exited the applause went on and on.

Children from a local school were playing the mice. They were gathered in the wings and did a lot of squeaking. Dinah said they'd been chosen because they were so good at it. Piers tried his best to stop them giggling and squealing.

'If you brats don't keep absolutely silent out here,' he told them, 'I shall personally mince every last one of you and serve you up on toast in the interval. Ssss!?'

Hester was scarcely aware of anything beyond the brilliantly-lit box in which she found herself. She was transported, transformed. She was at one and the same time herself and not herself, but a child, and then a flower, and although she knew with the conscious part of her mind that she was remembering steps she'd worked on for hours and hours during rehearsals, there was something in her that transcended her body and lifted her out of her ordinary, everyday self as soon as the music began.

During the interval, there was no sign of Nell.

'Have you checked in the toilet?' Dinah said.

Hester was on the point of answering, when Piers stormed into the dressing room.

'Hester! I want you to change into Nell's costume right away. You've watched the solo she does in Act Two, haven't you?'

Hester nodded. Her chest felt constricted, as though her heart had grown too large and was trying to break through her ribcage. 'You look like a confused rabbit, Hester. Hurry up now and get Nell's costume on. You're dancing instead of her in Act Two.'

'But where . . . ?'

'Taken ill, of course. Gone to my house to be looked after by Ruby. Perfect timing.'

Dinah said 'Don't worry, Piers. I'll get her make-up done. She'll be ready.'

Piers nodded and rushed from the room, presumably to warn the rest of the company that there would be a new Oriental dancer appearing tonight.

'Your big chance, Hester,' said Dinah. 'Stay quite still or I'll be drawing black lines down your cheeks instead of round your eyes.'

'But why didn't he ask Simone? Or you? What if I don't know all the steps?' Mixed with her fear was the feeling that Dinah had more right to a solo than she did. She'd been in the company longer. Surely she ought to have been chosen?

'You do,' said Dinah. 'You've watched Nell do it often enough. He didn't ask Simone because you're better, that's all. And you're better than me as well. I don't mind, Hester, really. Open your mouth for the lipstick.'

'But what about Nell?'

'What about her? She's not Madame P. She'll be thrilled for you. Not everyone in this company is a jealous bitch, though I grant you there are some people who might be trying to trip you up!'

'Oh, God, what if I'm a disaster, Dinah? What if I let Piers down?'

Dinah had finished her work with the mascara and the lipstick. She brought her face very close to Hester's and took her by the chin, looking directly into her eyes.

'You don't know, do you?'

'Know what?'

'That you're different, Hester. You're not like the rest of us. We're not bad, but we're ordinary dancers. You've got something even now that no one else in the company has. Not one of us.'

'What do you mean?'

'You've got star quality.'

'I don't know what that is.'

'Neither do I,' Dinah smiled. 'But I think I can recognise it when I see it. Go on, get out there and show them.'

I have never felt, Hester thought, anything to compare with the mixture of terror, exhilaration, panic and bliss that I'm feeling now. The music was like a wave carrying her in. She rode this wave, and wore it and inhabited it so that, after a few notes, it became no more than an expression in sound of what she, her body, her face, were expressing as she moved. The audience disappeared and yet she never forgot them. She lost herself in the steps and yet she had them as clear in her head as though she were following a map. Her body did things that she'd tried and tried to do and failed. Suddenly, the shock of performance brought all her strengths to a place where she was able to use them. Then, when the dance was over, and the applause woke her from a kind of trance, she realised that she was back. Back in the real world, out of the magic kingdom she'd inhabited as long as the dance went on.

When she came offstage at the end of the curtain calls, the whole company gathered round to kiss her and exclaim at her performance. Estelle passed her on the way back to her own dressing room and even she felt bound, by the general excitement, to say something.

'Well,' she said, looking down her parrot nose. 'You've had your path smoothed before you, and no mistake.' A sour smile passed over her features. 'You will go far.'

'Thank you,' Hester answered, understanding that however grudging it was, this was Estelle's best effort at congratulation.

'Wonderful,' said Piers, blowing kisses at the whole dressing room as he came in. 'Get your street clothes on, everyone, and we'll all go out for a slap-up meal at Gino's. Rave reviews in the press tomorrow, I'll be bound.' He came up to Hester and took her aside, speaking quietly.

'You did very well, dear. You really were quite good on the whole, and I'm pleased with you. Now please wait here for a moment, Hester. Don't go anywhere. You have a visitor.'

'Me?' Hester was astonished. 'I don't know anyone. Who can it be?'

'A surprise. You like surprises, don't you?'

Hester nodded. She knew it had to be Madame Olga. Oh, how she hoped she was right, and it *was* really her and that she'd seen the ballet and been proud of her.

She sat in front of the mirror, still in Nell's costume, looking not a bit like herself. I'm a dancer, she thought. A real dancer. This is going to be my life forever. I must remember always how happy I am now, this second. I mustn't forget how it feels. Dinah and the others were ready to leave. 'Will you wait for me?' Hester asked.

'We've been spoken to,' Dinah answered. 'Given our orders and told to leave you alone to meet this visitor of yours.'

There was a knock at the door just as she'd begun to wipe off her greasepaint with a large ball of cotton-wool.

Piers never simply came into a room. He *entered*, as though he were stepping on to a stage in a starring role. On this occasion he had his arm around the shoulders of someone wearing a black silk dress and a fur stole.

'Madame Olga!' she cried. 'How lovely! I knew it was you! When did you come? I'm so happy to see you.'

'I'll leave you alone for a moment,' Piers said. 'I'll be back in five minutes to take you to the restaurant. Olga will be joining us of course, for the party.'

He left the room as dramatically as he'd come into it. When they were alone, Madame Olga came up to Hester and hugged her.

'I'm crying, Madame! I can't help it. I've missed you so much.'

'Do not cry, child. Do not cry. This is such a happy day for me. I have missed you, too. You cannot imagine how I think of you, up there in Yorkshire; how cold and dull it is without you. My house is empty.'

'And I think of you, Madame. All the time. It's nearly two years since I left Yorkshire, can you believe it's been so long? I wait for your letters every day and I'm sorry if I'm not writing as much as you'd like. I know how you love details and gossip but there's so little time. Piers makes us work so hard. Everything's so busy always. Class and the production we're getting ready and the next one being planned.'

'Of course, of course. I understand. This is the work of a ballet company. I am drinking in all the letters from you, believe me. I read many times, many times.'

'How did you know that I was dancing a solo? Did Piers tell you? How could he have done . . . he only told *me* in the interval.'

'That was a treat for me. No, I came by myself. I tell myself, why for are you sitting in the dark in Yorkshire when you can come to London on the train? I wanted to see you so much. Now I have wonderful surprise. Wonderful! I am so proud of you. I am proud of myself for teaching you so well, and for putting you here in this company where you grow and bloom like a rose. Yes, like a rose.'

'Will you stay in a hotel? My digs are a little—'

'Do not worry. I am like a queen here. I stay with Piers in his house like an honoured visitor. But the greatest pleasure is to see you, child. My heart is full when I see you dance. I am so proud. Very, very proud.'

At the Royalty next morning, everyone crowded round to read the reviews in the newspapers. No one noticed Hester except for *The Times*. At the end of a generally mediocre notice came two glorious sentences: *Young Hester Fielding has made a very promising beginning in the world of ballet. We wish her good fortune.*

'There you are,' Dinah said, as she held out the paper for Hester to read it again. 'Your name in *The Times*. You're on your way. Nothing more to worry about.'

'But,' said Hester, 'I may not do another solo part for ages. Don't forget I only stepped in because Nell was ill.'

They went off to class together. Madame Olga had arranged to come in and watch and then the girls went with her to Lyons Corner House for lunch. Hester wanted to show off her favourite haunt. She accompanied Madame Olga to King's Cross in a taxi and wondered, as the train pulled out of the station, when she would see her dear teacher again.

Hester danced Nell's part for three performances only, and then it was back to the *corps de ballet*, one of many, not chosen to dance on her own. She had been at the Charleroi for nearly two years, and Piers made a point of treating her just as he treated the others, but she *did* know. She knew she was different and also that she was being trained to be different, and that Piers was waiting for the right moment and the right part.

Dinah and Nell enjoyed teasing Hester about not having a boyfriend. She was nearly seventeen now and had been with the Charleroi Company for almost two years. All the other girls were forever flirting with one or other of the young men in the *corps de ballet*, whom Piers called 'the boys'. The young women were known as 'the girls'.

'I think you could do worse than Stefan Graves,' said Dinah one day, as they were resting after a particularly gruelling class. Hester's hair was plastered to her head with perspiration and she felt that she would never be able to walk again. She decided to ignore Dinah's remark, at least until she had got her breath back. Stefan Graves was, in Hester's opinion, not particularly good-looking. She wondered sometimes why she was so different from everyone else. Surely at her age she should have experienced something of what all the others talked about constantly? They always appeared to find this or that young man 'thrilling' or 'so handsome', but she'd never felt the remotest attraction to any of them. Perhaps I ought to ask Dinah about it, she thought, but she said only, 'I think his eyes are a little too close together.'

'You're too fussy, Hester. He's tall, isn't he? And quite strong. And what's more, he's nice and quiet, unlike Miles and Jeremy, for instance. The trouble with you is, you never give yourself the chance to find out what someone is like. You have to make an effort.'

'I think there's something wrong with me.'

'What *do* you mean?' Dinah stopped packing away her ballet shoes. 'You're very attractive. Anyone would think so. There's not a single thing wrong with you that I can see.'

'I don't find it easy . . .' Hester hesitated. 'Well, what I mean is, I don't understand about sex.'

'You do know what happens, don't you? I don't have to tell you that surely?'

Hester blushed. 'Of course I do. Only it seems so unlikely. So remote from anything I've ever felt. I look at all the boys here and I just . . . I can't imagine. You know. Doing any of that stuff. Even kissing someone like that, on the mouth. I can't think how it might feel.'

'What about film stars?' Dinah was looking a little concerned now. 'Have you never had fantasies about them?'

'Yes, of course, but that's just what they are. Fantasies. That's not real. I've never had fantasies about anyone I know. I'm sure it's that I'm not like everyone else and I'll die an old maid.'

'Nonsense.' Dinah stood up. 'Let's go and get a cup of coffee or something, I'm parched. You'll meet someone soon, I'm sure. But you have to give yourself a chance. Get to know people. Go out with them if they ask you. Let yourself relax. I promise you, you'll know. You'll know at once when you meet the right person. It's like nothing else in the world, believe me. You go melty all over and want to dissolve and kissing is bliss, utter bliss when it's someone who makes your heart turn over.'

Hester laughed. 'Gosh, you're soppy, Dinah! But you might be right, I suppose. There's one thing I do know though. That person isn't Stefan Graves.'

When they came back to the church hall later in the morning, Hester and Dinah went to sit next to Nell. They whispered together while Piers took the boys through a routine he'd devised to help them with their jumps. Hester said, 'The thing about Stefan is, he's too quiet. I always feel he's looking right through me.'

'He's not looking through you,' Dinah said. 'He's mooning. Boys always do that when they like the look of you but don't have the bravery to speak up about it.'

'Well, I wish he did. He's there whenever I go down the corridor or come out of the cloakroom. I can feel his eyes on my back. I mean, he seems to follow me with his eyes the whole time and whenever I turn a corner, he's there. If I go and fetch something from Wardrobe, or go offstage into the wings, he's waiting for me.'

'Dinah's right. He's probably just shy,' said Nell. 'You shouldn't be too hard on him without knowing what's what. He's mad about you, Hester. I think he doesn't dare speak to you. You ought to be kind and say something to him. Make the first move.'

'I couldn't, Nell. It's not that I don't like him or anything, but I just don't . . . well, I'm not a bit drawn to him. I would hate the idea of going out with him. And the thought of kissing him makes me — well, it doesn't make my heart flutter.'

Dinah and Nell burst out laughing.

'Girls!' Piers turned from his work with the boys and frowned at them. 'This is a ballet company, not a circus. Kindly keep quiet or leave the room.'

'Sorry, Piers,' said Dinah. 'We'll be totally silent I promise.'

'That I doubt,' said Piers, 'but keep it down, please.'

'Piers,' Hester whispered, 'wouldn't like it if I went out with Stefan either. That's another reason for not getting to know him better, as you put it.'

Piers' attitude to what he called 'romantic attachments' was well-known. He wasn't against them in principle, but in his company he was of the opinion that they distracted the dancers from the main business of their lives which was, as far as he was concerned, to dance every night and think about dancing all day long. Hester remembered what he'd said to her years ago, when she first arrived in London:

'I can't forbid you to fall in love,' he'd said. 'But I do try to discourage it. Love takes up the whole of one's head in a way I don't really approve of. And whatever you do, please try not to get entangled with anyone who's – how shall I put it? – problematic. Likely to cause trouble to the rest of us. But I want to emphasise to you, as I emphasise to all my girls, that if you do get into difficulties . . . *of any kind at all* . . . do you understand what I'm saying, child? you can come to me for help. I will always help you.'

Hester decided to deal with Stefan herself. She had asked herself over and over again what was the best thing to do, and in the end, she decided to speak to him directly.

One morning after class, when Piers was taking some of the other dancers through a complicated routine, she and Stefan found themselves at the far end of the rehearsal room together. Hester knew that this was not accidental. She had come down here to rest and he had followed her.

She sat down on one of the hard chairs and looked at him. He was standing in front of her, looking awkward. For a moment, Hester wondered whether Dinah might be right – she was too fussy – but as she looked at him, she knew that Stefan was utterly wrong for her. Not only did he not make her feel 'melty' in the way that Dinah described, she actually felt a kind of revulsion when she thought of him touching her. She couldn't help it. It must be the absolute opposite of sexual attraction. She would be honest and tell Stefan there was no hope. She would try to be as kind as she could, but she had to make him stop following her around. She spoke quietly. Piers hated people chattering in the background.

'Stefan,' she said. 'I'm not sure what you want to say to me, but I would really much rather you didn't, well, didn't stare at me like you do.'

'But I'm not . . .' Stefan began, stuttering a little. 'I only . . .'

He paused and Hester waited for him to continue. He said, 'I like you, Hester. You must have seen that. I dream about you.'

'Please, Stefan. I understand, I do honestly, but you see, I don't dream about you. It wouldn't be fair to you if I said anything else. Do you understand? I'm sure you could find another girl who . . .' She couldn't think what to say next.

'I don't want any other girl. Only you.'

'I'm so sorry, Stefan. There's no kind way to say this, but I'm not interested in you in *that* way. And I'd rather you stopped following me, if you don't mind. Do you?'

Stefan hung his head and sighed. 'I wasn't doing any harm. You can't stop me looking. Thinking.'

'But it's only going to hurt you, isn't it, Stefan? Wouldn't it be better if you turned your attention somewhere else?'

He shuffled his feet and looked at Hester. Then he looked away.

'Right,' he said. 'I'll try not to annoy you again.'

'Thank you,' Hester said. Then she rose from the chair and walked as quickly as she could to the other side of the room.

'Where have you got to, Hester?' Piers called. 'I need you now, please. Come and line up here with the others.'

'Coming, Piers,' said Hester. As she bent and swayed and moved through the routine, Hester felt for the first time in her life as though actions, her words, could be powerful; could be used to achieve what she wanted. But I wish I could meet someone who made my heart beat faster. I won't believe in it till it happens to me.

The first night of *Sleeping Beauty* came after six weeks of rehearsals. Piers had chosen Hester as the Bluebird and she had a short solo at the very end of the ballet. She was also Simone's understudy for the demanding part of Princess Aurora.

'You can't expect it to happen twice,' Nell said. 'Someone dropping out and you taking over. Simone's as tough as old boots.'

'Doesn't matter,' Dinah said. 'She'll know the part backwards when she comes to dance it later. Which she will, no two ways about it.'

'I'm happy enough to get the Bluebird,' Hester said. 'I've enjoyed every minute of rehearsing for this production.'

Madame Olga was already in London and had sat in on the dress rehearsal and watched class on the morning of the première. Once again, she was staying with Piers, and once again she was coming to the cast party after the performance. Hester could hear her own heart racing as she got ready for the first act. She felt a mixture of terror and excitement. She'd had to learn not only her own solo, but also the routines for the *corps de ballet*. Since the Bluebird only came on at the end of the ballet, Hester had to pull her weight (Piers' words) in the first two acts as well. There was a lot to remember.

During the interval, Dinah and Nell helped Hester into her Bluebird costume.

'Gosh, I'm tired,' she told them. Nell made her hold her head to one side while she used hidden hairpins to skewer the blue feathered headdress into the mass of Hester's hair, which had been twisted up on top of her head and gathered into a net.

'Piers,' said Dinah, 'isn't the sort of manager to waste resources. There aren't enough of us, that's the trouble.' She was busy fastening a kind of apron around Hester's waist. It was sewn with blue feathers which matched those on the headdress. She sighed. 'Wouldn't it be wonderful to have enough money to pay for different costumes for every single part? I can't wait for clothes rationing to be over. It'll be such a relief not to have to make do with a basic tutu and add all kinds of other stuff on top of it.' She stepped back to consider the finished effect. 'Well, you look about as much like a Bluebird as you ever will. Flap your arms a bit, go on.'

Hester obliged, giggling a little. She'd been a guest at the Princess Aurora's christening in Act One, in a tutu with some glittery organza over the skirt; then a guest again, with a rose-sprinkled apron this time, at Aurora's sixteenth birthday, and now she was ready for her solo. Piers had a habit of celebrating someone's first proper part in a ballet by giving the dancer a new pair of shoes. Hester's were made of sky-blue satin, and she thought she'd never in her life seen anything quite as beautiful.

The applause at the end of her solo was deafening. Somehow she'd summoned all her remaining energy for the short routine and, at times while the music was lifting her, she almost believed it was possible truly to take flight.

'Thank God,' said Piers, who was waiting in the wings as she came off stage. 'Not a single feather on stage. I do hate my birds shedding. Remind me to tell you of a *Swan Lake* which looked as though everyone was moulting to Tchaikovsky.'

The celebration at Gino's restaurant went on until the early hours of the morning. Madame Olga and Piers left before the others, and after they'd gone, Hester glanced around the table and suddenly felt as though she were outside her own body, looking down at everything. The voices, the laughter, the lights of candles stuck into Chianti bottles on every table were far away and she almost fainted.

'Are you okay, Hester?' said Nell. 'You look most odd. Very pale. Has it all been too much?'

'I don't know. I did feel funny for a bit, as though – I don't know how to describe it – as though there was a huge cliff by my feet and nothing but empty space and I was about to fall. All of you, the tables, everything were all far away and I was, I don't know. Afraid, I suppose. I expect I've had too much wine.'

'You've only had half a glass. And you added water to that,' said Dinah.

'I'm just tired,' Hester said. 'And a bit sad because Madame Olga's going off early in the morning and I'll miss her. Don't worry, I'll be fine tomorrow.'

In the Attic de Luxe, Hester undressed and got into bed in a daze of exhaustion. She felt like weeping, and didn't really know why. All evening people had been saying nice things to her, and each time she'd felt like bursting into tears.

'Good night, both,' said Dinah, already sounding as though she were half asleep.

''Night,' said Nell.

''Night,' Hester said. 'Thanks for helping me this evening.' And then there they were at last, under cover of darkness, all the tears she'd been holding back for the last few hours. They rolled out of her eyes and into her hair. She turned over and hid her face in the pillow, hoping the others wouldn't hear anything, if they were still awake which she doubted. Why, she asked herself. Why are you crying? This should be one of the happiest nights of your life. How can you? What would you say if someone asked you what on earth you had to weep into your pillow about? I'd tell them I was missing *Grand-mère*. She would have been so happy tonight if she could have been there, sitting in the front row next to Olga and Piers. I was a success, *Grand-mère*, and you weren't there with me. That's why I'm crying.

The gold chain, *Grand-mère*'s gold chain, fell forward against Hester's chin and felt cool against her skin. She turned over on to her back and fingered it gently, leaf by leaf.

28 December 1986

Alison was walking across the hall when she met Hugo on his way to the kitchen for breakfast. A woman was on her way out of the house, too. She was tall and slim and the coat she was wearing was white and fluffy. She must be one of the dancers in *Sarabande*, Alison thought. I'd look like a polar bear in a coat like that.

'Hello, Alison,' said Hugo. 'How's everything? Hello, Silver. Have you had breakfast yet? This is Silver, by the way, Alison. Silver McConnell, this is Alison Drake. Claudia's daughter.'

'Hi!' said Silver, and surprised Alison by grinning and putting out her hand to be shaken. She smiled at Hugo and said, 'I'm going for a walk before class. I want to have a look at the garden.'

'Nice to meet you,' Alison muttered and then, realising that she'd muttered, began to smile to make up for it. She wanted to say something about how Silver looked exactly like her name, but Hugo spoke to her before she'd thought of how to put it.

'Off exploring?'

'Yeah,' Alison answered. ''Bye, Silver. 'Bye, Hugo,' and before she could say anything else, Hugo had gone into the kitchen and Silver had closed the front door behind her. Alison was left alone in the hall.

The wooden floor here was polished and shiny, and a staircase led up to the corridors where all the bedrooms were. Hester – Alison still felt strange thinking of her like that, even in her own head – had her own private rooms. The carpet on the wooden floor was gorgeous: maroon and peacock and pink and chocolate brown in complicated patterns of trees and flowers. The rest of the woodwork was almost black. The curtains were burgundy and gold, with tiny little glittery bits woven into them. The whole thing looked like a stage set or something. Alison could easily imagine a sword fight taking place on that staircase.

What was it that Hugo had said about 'exploring'? Alison thought he was being stupid. Now, though, it seemed like something a bit more interesting to do than lie about indoors. She'd noticed the theatre as they drove up last night. That'll do, she thought. I'll go and explore that.

She opened the front door and made her way along the gravel path. Yes, there it was. It looked like some kind of doll's house. Fancy having a theatre in your garden! Fab or what? When she got there, she was a little surprised to find the front door unlocked. She stepped into the foyer, which was quite deserted. It had pinky-red carpets, wall to wall, and a ceiling decorated with gold-tipped twirly bits. A chandelier hung above her – quite a small one, but very pretty, with crystal drops. To her left, a staircase curved upwards, to the circle she supposed. Soon, they'd all be here, ready for the first rehearsal. And the pep-talk from Hugo before that.

Hugo wasn't bad. Not compared with some of Mum's men, who'd been ghastly. A few of them had done a good job of pretending Alison didn't exist, and in some ways, she thought, they were right. I've been at boarding school for three years so it's quite easy for everyone to forget all about me for weeks and weeks. I bet Mum's longing for the twelfth of January when I'll be off her hands. Tears came into Alison's eyes and she blinked them away. Stop it, she told herself. Don't be pathetic. It was pathetic to want someone's love and approval so much. She'd been ultra-brilliant at hiding this and she was pretty sure Claudia thought she didn't have much time for her. So I'm good at *something*, Alison thought. My mum doesn't know how I really feel about her. Great. Fantastic. Also, she doesn't know the first thing about me. Everything that's important in my life she scoffs at. She makes fun of the fact that I want to be a midwife, and keeps going on and on about squalling babies and blood and how could I think of living my life with no one looking at me and applauding. That's not what she says, but it's what she means.

Alison turned and made her way up the stairs. This brought her to the theatre bar, a long room complete with bar stools and a mirror behind the bottles. There were windows all along the opposite wall and, at the far end, two glass display cabinets. She went over to the first one and gazed at a white dress with a long, gauzy skirt and a bodice covered in tiny, white satin roses. It was draped against some dark blue velvet and next to it was a garland, also of white roses, but these were bigger and there were leaves made of dark green velvet sewn in among the flowers. Alison read the words on the card lying next to the garland: *This is one of the costumes worn by Hester Fielding in the famous 1957 production of Giselle.*

It wasn't all that hard to imagine the lady she'd met last night wearing such a wispy, skimpy dress. The waist was ridiculously tiny and wouldn't have fitted a normally shaped child. Alison had seen *Giselle* a couple of times when her mother had been one of the ghosts, the Wilis, who dance to their death the men who betrayed them in life.

The other cabinet was full of ballet shoes, laid out in rows on some more blue velvet. They were all satin, but of different colours – pink, white, black, lilac and red. You could see that they were worn, but the ribbons had been arranged to lie artistically in twists and curls. The card read *Shoes worn by Hester Fielding between 1950-63.*

Ballet dancers were funny, Alison reflected. There were stories about them taking off their shoes at the end of a ballet only to find them bloodstained inside from all the wear and tear on their toes. Thinking of this now made Alison wince. It was revolting! Claudia's old shoes had never had any blood in them, thank goodness.

Between the cabinets she noticed a door. It would have been easy to miss it because it was so well disguised to look like part of the wallpaper, but there it was; a small, gold handle gave away the secret. Alison opened the door and began to go up the narrow, rather steep stairs she found behind it. Perhaps I'm not allowed to be here, she thought, and then realised that if anyone had wanted her to keep out, it would have been locked. The keyhole under the doorknob had a gold key in it, just like in a fairytale.

At the top of the staircase, she found a corridor, with doors to several rooms leading off it. She opened the first one she came to and stepped back, horrified. Someone was in there already, sitting on a chair at the far end of the room.

'Oh, gosh, I'm so sorry,' she said. 'I didn't realise that there was anyone up here. I'll go . . .'

'No, no, dear, don't worry.' The person on the chair stood up, and Alison could see that she'd been crying. She was busily wiping her eyes with a hankie and then she put on the glasses she was holding in her other hand. 'I was just about to go back to the house. I know who you must be. Miss Drake's daughter, Alison. Am I right?'

Alison nodded, wondering how this woman knew this.

'I expect you're wondering how I know who you are. I'm Hester's companion. Ruby Stott, but everyone calls me Ruby. I was Hester's dresser for years and years, and there's no standing on ceremony in the theatre, is there?'

'I'm sorry if I'm not supposed to be here,' Alison said. 'I was just looking round. It's . . . it's lovely.'

Ruby seemed more like a teacher at school than someone connected to a theatre or a ballet company. She had a kind face and grey hair and she was wearing a grey tweedy skirt and a pale blue cardigan over a white blouse.

'This is Wardrobe,' Ruby told her. 'We're very lucky to have all this space. We're over the auditorium now. The rehearsal room is next door. Much bigger than Wardrobe, of course. Both this room and the rehearsal room have very thick soundproof floors, but still, Hester insists that no one must be here during performances.'

'It's great,' Alison said. The costumes – hundreds of them, or that's what it looked like – were hanging in a cupboard with no doors, so that you could get at them more easily. She could see long, filmy skirts, and the stiff short skirts of tutus sticking out; there was lots of velvety stuff in bright colours; tights rolled into small bundles and piled up on a shelf on the other side of the room, and dozens of pairs of pink, blue, beige and black ballet shoes. These were stacked together next to the tights.

It was amazing how many shoes ballet dancers needed, Alison thought. There ought to be a way of making them stronger. Her mother would never wear any of this lot. Claudia Drake took her own shoes with her wherever she went, in a special suitcase. Alison used to play with them when she was a little girl, pretending that they were animals. She gave them names and arranged them in exactly the way they were arranged here with their ribbons nicely wound round and neatly tucked in.

'What's in that box?' she asked, pointing to a small trunk standing next to the shoe cupboard.

'Ribbons,' said Ruby. 'You can never have too many of them, I've found. They've all sorts of unexpected uses.'

'May I look?'

Ruby nodded and Alison lifted the lid. She gasped when she saw what was in the box. There must have been thousands of them, all rolled up and in every colour she could imagine, as well as a few she hadn't ever thought of – like a grey one which had strands of sparkling black woven through it and a white one sprinkled with red stars. 'They're fantastic, Ruby! Where did you find them all?'

'I've been collecting them over years. Whenever I'm in a shop that sells them, I buy whatever catches my eye.'

'They're beautiful,' said Alison. 'Really lovely. Are you going to be using some on the *Sarabande* costumes?'

'No, I think most of those are coming by road, later this week. Though your mother did tell me last night that she's brought hers with her.'

'Has she?' Alison said, doing her best to remember. 'I don't really know.' Then it came back to her: Claudia prancing round the lounge in what looked like peacock-blue chiffon tracksuit bottoms. Could that have been part of a costume? She'd had a kind of bra on top, with sequins all over it . . . yes, it had to be a costume, because even her mother, who wore really silly clothes sometimes, wouldn't have dared to go out in something like that. 'I think she did try on some blue outfit.'

Alison went to stand in front of a full-length mirror that took up most of one wall. She noticed Ruby looking at her and turned round.

'I'm sorry, I'll go in a minute. I don't know why I was looking at myself. I never do normally. I hate mirrors.'

'Why would that be?' Ruby asked.

'Because I'm not good-looking. My mum thinks I'm ugly. She's never said, of course, but she must think that. She's very beautiful, you see. She thinks I don't come up to scratch. I'm a disappoint-ment.'

'I'm sure she doesn't think anything of the kind. And you know full well you're not a bit ugly.

'Yes, I suppose I do really. It's just that my mum is so beautiful. It's intimidating. She says I don't make the best of myself. That's practically as bad as being ugly according to her. I don't want to wear contact lenses. And I'll never be a ballet dancer. I'm the wrong shape, sort of square and short.'

'Well, I think you look fine. Unless, of course, you've ambitions to be a ballerina. Perhaps you're not quite small enough for that. But I don't think you're that interested in dancing. Am I right?'

Alison laughed. 'Can you honestly see me in a tutu? Such a stupid sort of dress, isn't it? No, I hate ballet. Well, not hate it really, only I'm bored by it and I can never see the point of anything that goes on. It's well, like a kind of silly game with its own rules and if you don't understand them and obey them, you're made to feel thick and insensitive.'

Ruby nodded. 'I've never been very interested in the dancing side of it myself,' she said. 'Though I've spent more than half my life in the theatre. I did like working with a lot of people, though. It's hard to be lonely if you're part of a ballet company.'

'My mother says that in companies she's been in, the other dancers aren't really friendly. She says they'd cheerfully trip you up in the wings for a chance to take your part, most of them.'

'I expect there are always folk like that, whatever job you're in. It's not something particular to the ballet.' She took some hangers off the rails and began putting them into a wicker skip in the corner.

'I must get on, Alison. It's been lovely talking to you, and if you ever feel like helping me, I'd be glad of the company. There's always plenty to do. Are you good with a needle? You'd be amazed how many rips the dancers make in their costumes, even over a short run. And I like to wash things before a production,' she explained. 'Everything gets dusty hanging up here, even if it looks clean. That's why this lot is going in the skip. George'll help to take it down to the laundry room in the basement. He's my husband,' she added.

Alison glanced out of one of the small windows. She could see the path up to the house.

'It's really nice here, but I should go back now,' she said. 'My mum'll wonder where I've gone, I expect.'

'Then I'll come with you and lock up.'

They went down the stairs together. Looking at everything in Wardrobe had distracted her for a while, but now she remembered:

Ruby had definitely been crying before. What was that about? It always came as a shock to Alison when adults wept. Claudia didn't count. She burst into tears all the time, and often for no good reason, but people who dressed like Ruby and looked sensible and who seemed so *together* didn't usually cry. She was so easy to talk to. Alison had never spoken to anyone about what her mother thought of her, but Ruby invited it by wanting to listen, by looking really interested in what you were saying. She wasn't the sort of person, though, who'd want to let you know what was troubling her. You could tell.

Alison decided to go to the first rehearsal. For one thing, she didn't have anything else to do. After she came back from Wardrobe, she'd looked for Siggy, but couldn't find him in any of the public rooms. He must have gone to the private bit of the house where she wasn't allowed to follow him. She didn't feel like being the only person in the whole of Wychwood House, when everyone else was at the Arcadia. You couldn't call it spooky or anything, but still. It might be quite lonely and, anyway, it would be interesting to see what Hester wore during the day. If her dressing-gown was anything to go by, it would be something spectacular.

There was a chair pushed up against the wall, in the corner, and Alison sat down on that. It was like being back at school, she thought. Everyone else was already sitting down. They'd arranged themselves in a rough circle in the middle of the room. They were all waiting for Hester to appear – all except for her mother. What had become of her?

She looked at each person in turn. Andy French was like a good-looking elf, with slanting eyes and a rather pointed nose. He had a wicked smile and Alison reckoned he was probably the company joker. She'd met someone like him in every school she'd been to, someone who loved gossiping, talking back to the teacher (or Hugo, Alison thought, in this case). Someone who enjoyed sending people up and generally creating mischief. They were okay, jokers, as long as they liked you.

Ilene Nolan and Silver McConnell sat together, chatting quietly.

Ilene was tiny and very fair and Silver, Alison decided, was like someone out of a movie. Alison was used to ballet dancers, and took their grace for granted, but Silver, in black tights and long-sleeved leotard, made everyone else look clumsy. Alison felt like a sack of potatoes just looking at her. She turned towards the door, expecting Claudia to come throught it at any moment. She couldn't have overslept, because Hugo would have woken her up. Maybe she wasn't feeling well? Perhaps, Alison thought, I ought to go and look for her.

The men were dressed in shabby-looking sweatshirts and ancient tracksuit bottoms, and they had sports bags which now lay under a table in a corner of the room.

'God, everyone, sorry sorry sorry . . .' The door next to where Alison was sitting flew open and a man stood in the doorway. He waited till everyone was looking at him, and only came forward when Hugo waved him to a chair. Alison watched him as he sat down. This must be Nick Neary. He was the only member of the company she hadn't met. He was very good-looking, with light brown hair, highlighted with ash-blonde streaks. His eyes were greenish-blue, like sea water. Hugo got up then and coughed a little, which meant he was going to say something.

He came to the centre of the circle of chairs to speak. Alison tried to concentrate on what he was saying, but her gaze kept straying to where Nick was sitting. She made a big effort and looked at Hugo instead.

He was very tall and thin, like a rather elegant bird. He had dark eyes and hair, rather sharp features, a high forehead and a wide mouth and he always wore the same clothes, dark polo necks and dark trousers. You couldn't call him handsome exactly, Alison thought, but he had a smile which changed his whole face. He looked round at everyone, and then began to talk about the ballet.

'*Sarabande* is a fairytale,' he said. 'As you all know, I've choreographed it around a piece of music by Edmund Norland called *Sarabande*. It's quite a short piece, so the jazz composer, Frank Marron, has devised some wonderful variations on the original. For the performances, we're very lucky to have the Mike Spreckley Trio accompanying us on piano, bass and drums. They're fantastically in demand, as you know, but they'll be here in time for the dress rehearsal. What that means is that you won't have too much opportunity to dance to live music, but I've got a good tape till the guys arrive. All of you will soon get to know every note better than anything you've ever heard, I promise you. It's great stuff. Claudia is the Princess, Ilene is her Nursemaid, Andy is the Fool, naturally,' – here Hugo paused for laughter, which arrived on cue – 'Nick is the Lover and Silver McConnell is the Angel. You'll all know Silver by reputation of course, and we're very lucky that she's got the time in her schedule to dance with us at this Festival.'

Alison watched Silver bend her head to acknowledge the smiles that everyone was beaming at her. She wondered why Hugo didn't seem bothered about her mother's absence. Maybe they'd had a row and she'd told him she wasn't coming. Hugo went back to talking about *Sarabande*.

'There's not that much of a story, really. It's just a fable about a princess who has to decide between the pleasures of the world and love and so forth, and the attractions of death. No contest there, really, but the piece does emphasise something we don't often see on a stage, and that's how attractive the idea of death can sometimes be. The action is divided into ten scenes. None of these lasts more than ten minutes. I'll go over them with the individual dancers later when we map out the rehearsal schedule but, basically the Princess is urged by her Nursemaid to go out and enjoy life; the Fool shows her all sorts of diversions; the Nursemaid tries to persuade her of the joys of domesticity and marriage; the Princess meets the Lover; they fall in love; they dance with the Nursemaid and then with the Fool. Then the Angel of Death makes an appearance and tries to seduce the Princess away from the Lover. The Lover and the Angel dance together, vying for the Princess's favours. She chooses Love in the end, and the Angel has a final farewell solo. Then the others rejoice; the Princess and the Lover have a *pas de deux* which merges into an ensemble dance for the finale. And in a sort of coda, the Angel and the Princess dance together when the Lover is asleep, each of them knowing, of course, that they will meet again when Death returns to claim her at the end of her life.

'Shortish ballets are the tradition at Wychwood, and of course we start at half past seven so that after the performance there's time for people to get back to civilisation before the restaurants shut. And on the first night, of course, there's the Twelfth Night party that Hester traditionally hosts for the company, Friends of the Arcadia and other honoured guests. She does, by the way, like being called Hester rather than Miss Fielding.'

'How come you know so much, Hugo?' Andy asked. 'I thought you moved in the real world with the rest of us plebs, not in these posh circles. I'm a bit of a fish out of water, me. All this grandeur. Not my usual scene, I can tell you.'

Hugo laughed. 'I came to last year's first night, just to get to know the set-up. It's been an ambition of mine to win the Wychwood competition and I can't tell you how thrilled I am to be here, and with such amazingly talented dancers, too. No, I mean it. This is going to be a tremendous production, but I'll just say this. I expect one hundred percent commitment from all of you. All the time. I don't have any patience with slackers, as those of you who've been in the company for some time know very well. In return, of course, I'm at your disposal whenever you want to talk things over, or ask questions and so forth. Okay?'

He paused to see if anyone had anything to say, but everyone was nodding and smiling so he carried on. Had they all noticed that Claudia hadn't arrived yet? That, Alison thought, didn't show one hundred percent commitment, but she was sure that Hugo wouldn't quarrel with her in front of the others. He carried on with his talk. 'The set's been designed by Aubrey Godfeld, and later on you can all have a look at the model. It's in the props room. It's simply beautiful. I felt we had to make up for the simplicity of the story and the brevity of the piece by going all out for lavish decor and costumes.'

'When'll those be arriving, Hugo?' Ilene asked.

'Should be here the day after tomorrow. You'll have a good few days to get used to them, don't worry. Right, are there any questions?' Hugo glanced at his watch. 'Hester will be coming to welcome us all officially in a moment. She'll also take the first class. That's another tradition.'

'I knew about that one!' said Andy. 'I read an article about her in a magazine somewhere. Look, I've worn my untorn T-shirt in her honour!'

He stood up and did a pirouette and everyone laughed. People began pushing the chairs back against the walls and getting the room ready for Hester's arrival. The men had taken off their tracksuit bottoms and stuffed them into their bags. Everyone was now wearing leotards and tights and Alison watched Nick in his beige T-shirt and black tights and wondered what it would be like to have him as a dancing partner.

Ballet dancers took ages getting ready. It was always such a palaver. They had to change their shoes, tie up ribbons on those shoes, get their hair out of the way in elasticated hairbands, and on and on.

'Hester's coming,' Hugo said over his shoulder. He held the door open and she walked in, smiling and glancing from one person to another. She went to stand next to Hugo who stepped forward to introduce her.

'Right, everyone. This is Hester Fielding, and she needs no introduction from me. I know I speak for everyone when I say how thrilled and proud we are to be here, and how determined to make this year's festival the very best ever. Hester's going to say a few words and also very kindly take the first class. Ladies and gentlemen, Hester Fielding.'

Hester, Alison saw, wasn't in anything half as magnificent as the dressing-gown she'd worn last night, but still, she seemed like a person from a magazine. Her trousers were black and silky and with them she wore a high-necked sweater of very soft blueish-mauve wool. She stood up very straight and managed to have her hands in a position that made them look beautiful. I'd never know where to put my hands if I had to get up and make a speech in front of everyone, Alison thought.

Hester began to speak in a soft, rather low voice. Alison sort of listened, but she was also looking at everyone and seeing if she could work out what they thought about everything. Silver was gazing at Hester with something like adoration in her eyes. Ilene and Andy were leaning forward as though they could learn how to be living legends like Hester Fielding just by listening to her.

'Hello, everyone. I'm really delighted to welcome you all to Wychwood House, and the Arcadia Theatre and I won't bore you with a lot of talk, but I just want say this: please treat the house as your home and be very happy while you get the ballet ready. I'll take this first class, but then I'll leave you to your own devices, so that I can have a wonderful surprise at the dress rehearsal. I'm going to find it really hard not to sneak in and watch rehearsals because I'm always so curious to see how everything's coming on, but I *am* rather busy organising the master classes that start here in February. So have a wonderful time, all of you, and thank you for coming to Wychwood. I'm sure *Sarabande* is going to be wonderful.'

Alison applauded with the rest. It's odd, she thought. I haven't been a bit bored, and I'm glad I came and didn't stay behind in the house all by myself. She noticed that the dancers had begun to warm up at the *barre*, bending and stretching. Look at Silver, she thought. How can anyone get their body to do that? She'd put one leg up on the rail and then leaned her whole body forward over it, so that her head was touching her knee. The others were touching the floor with their hands, or practising yoga-type lunges to loosen up.

Then Nick caught sight of her looking at him and came over to where she was sitting.

'Hello!' he said and smiled right at her. 'I don't think I know you, do I? I'm Nick Neary. What's your name?'

'Alison Drake. I'm Claudia's daughter.'

'Oh, right. Hugo did say she was bringing a kid. I thought he meant a little kid. Silly of me. Do you like ballet?'

Alison hesitated. It wouldn't do to be too honest.

'I don't mind it sometimes. I've never thought of doing it myself though.'

(Oh, God, you stupid thing. How could you say something so mad? As if anyone with an ounce of sense would imagine someone as fat and galumphing as you wanting to be a ballet dancer!)

'I often think of doing all sorts of other things, actually. Like being a film star. That would be far less work, I'm sure.'

Alison thought: You'd be brilliant. 'Yes, ballet is hard work. Lots of people don't realise.'

Hugo was looking as though he was about to get everyone into line to start the class. Nick smiled at Alison and then out of the blue, stretched his hand out and touched her arm lightly.

'Smashing to talk to you, Alison. But duty calls, right?' he said, indicating Hugo and Hester with a movement of his head. He liked her. He seemed to like her. Happy, she thought. I'm feeling happy.

'Now,' said Hester, standing in front of the dancers. 'Is everyone ready? I'm going to begin with the steps which are the basis of everything. This is the routine my first teacher, Olga Rakovska, used to take me through every day, when I was about nine years old. It still works, I think—'

At that moment the door of the rehearsal room opened and Claudia came into the room in a great hurry. Alison knew she was flustered because her hair was still down over her shoulders and she was a little red in the face. It did look as though she'd overslept. She was about to rush over and take off her coat and get ready when Hester stopped speaking and stared at her. 'I am not in the habit of saying things twice, so I'm afraid you've missed the beginning of this class. We will all have to wait now, while you change into your shoes. It's a waste of our time.'

'I'm so sorry,' Claudia began. 'I overslept.'

'Please don't oversleep again. Real professionals don't oversleep. I'm not prepared to give my time to a company where the principal thinks she can turn up whenever it suits her.'

'I said I'm sorry,' said Claudia, in what Alison recognised as her 'dangerous' voice, the one which was extra sweet and cloying and which signalled the fact that she might very well lose her temper. 'I don't think I've missed very much, have I?'

Her mother's smile would have blistered paint. Alison wondered whether Hester could sense just how furious Claudia was. No, probably if you didn't know her, you'd never guess.

'You have missed the beginning of my class. I believe you've also missed the talk Hugo's given to the company. Not very much at all.'

Alison looked at Hester with admiration. She was clearly not going to be bullied by Claudia or by the threat of a temper tantrum. She continued to speak, but to the whole company now.

'While we wait for Claudia to get ready, I'd like to say this. I expect the highest standards from any dancers who come here to

Wychwood. I don't tolerate second-best. I am impatient with excuses. I believe that real dancers come to class on time, work hard, think of their colleagues and, above all, think of the ballet that they're going to be putting on. It's a cooperative venture and that means that everyone has to work together. I hope you all agree.'

Everyone was nodding, and by now Claudia had taken her place right in front of Hester, ready to start the class. Hester smiled at her. 'Good. Now we can begin. We'll start with *demi-pliés*, please.'

They went into a routine they must have practised hundreds of times. Alison listened to the instructions – *pliés, entrechats, demi-pliés, jetés* – but now that her mother was busy doing the exercises with everyone else, she could look at Nick again. She watched him going through the movements, marvelling at how graceful he was. She could still feel the touch of his hand on her arm. He had made it seem as though he really liked her.

Bitch, Claudia thought, watching Hester leave the room after the class. How dare she pull me up in front of the whole company, as though I was some kind of naughty schoolkid? The cheek of it! Doesn't she know who I am? For God's sake, what did I miss? Precisely nothing. Hugo's pep talk (big deal!) and a few clichés from Madam, probably. Bloody living legend! I'm the star now. I'm the one with my face on the cover of *Vogue*, not her. Her days are over and what is she now, when all's said and done, but a festival director. And that's it. The ballet could go on perfectly well without her, but it would collapse without me. I should have said something. I should have told her what's what.

As she thought this, Claudia knew that would have been quite impossible. The whole future of *Sarabande* would have been placed in jeopardy. I might be selfish, but I wouldn't want to spoil Hugo's big chance. She congratulated herself on her maturity. She had to admit that part of her reason was her own desire to dance the role of the Princess. She knew that if Hester put pressure on Hugo, he'd have no hesitation in giving the part to someone else. He was always saying it: *Nobody's indispensable*. The mere idea of being pushed out of the cast made Claudia want to cry. This was her chance to stop all those who, she knew, were starting to talk about how much longer she would be able to dance, speculating about how old she was, just out of her hearing. No, she would behave herself and all would be well. That cow they all thought was so marvellous would have to admit how good she was. She imagined the scene – Hester presenting her with flowers, Hester saying, *that was wonderful. I couldn't have done it better myself.*

The rehearsal proper had begun now. She was waiting for Hugo to call her, and was only half-attending to the routines he was going over with Ilene and Andy. Nick was right on the other side of the room and looked deep in thought. Probably an act, Claudia reckoned, like most things he did. But he was undoubtedly gorgeous. She looked at his long legs and wondered about him. She'd heard that he was gay, but he seemed always to have an eye for any pretty girl who happened to cross his path. She began to feel, as she looked at him, the first stirrings of an all too familiar sensation: new desire. She sat up straighter, wondering whether there was anything else in the whole world as thrilling as the possibility it presented. It was like having tiny little thrills uncurling green roots all through her veins. She could feel them. Pull yourself together, she told herself. Concentrate on the rehearsal.

The music droned on. It was a bit too modern for Claudia's taste. Tchaikovsky was her very favourite and almost everything after Rimsky-Korsakov and the divine *Schéhérezade* too tuneless in her opinion. She never said so to Hugo because he loved anything where the melody was completely unhummable. Where, in fact, there was no melody. You couldn't say that about the *Sarabande* music but it wasn't exactly *Swan Lake* and it took some concentration fitting the steps to the notes.

'Let's do your entrance now, Claudia,' Hugo said, turning to her. She went to stand in front of him and he turned the music on for her first entrance.

'No, Claudia. No, no and again no. We've been through this, haven't we? Three steps and then a pause. Listen to the music. It's all there. Do it again, please.'

Claudia went through the entrance again, but her mind wasn't on it. She would have to have a word with Hugo. For a moment there, he'd nearly lost his patience with her and if she'd said it once she'd said it a thousand times to more choreographers than you could count on the fingers of both hands: *I don't do conflict situations in the rehearsal rooms. I don't respond to bullying, so you can forget it or I walk.* Most of them got the picture immediately and fell over themselves to be nice to her. Hugo was sometimes just plain bossy and there was no need for it. You got better results from being kind, she thought, and she'd have to tell Hugo about it before it became a problem.

He wasn't one to lose his temper. He was cleverer than that. He was rather obviously exasperated with some of the things she was doing. And okay, perhaps she hadn't been working as hard as she could have, but it was early days on this ballet. Tons of time yet to get it right, and who'd arrived at dead of night yesterday and had overslept and not managed to get breakfast before bloody class started? Now she came to think about it, it was Hugo's fault she was late. He could have woken her, couldn't he? She did have a memory of someone shaking her shoulder, but that had been too early altogether and she'd gone back to sleep. She'd be more focused tomorrow.

After Hugo had finished with her, she went to sit down again. For a wonder, Alison was here. She was gazing at Nick like a mesmerised sheep, but at least she was in the rehearsal room and behaving herself quite well. That's thanks to me, Claudia told herself. It sorted her out forever, true enough, but I was pretty savage that day. How old was she? Maybe nine or ten. She'd been getting on my nerves all afternoon. *What is there to do, Mummy? I don't want to play with my dolls. I don't want to go and see what Joanie upstairs is doing. I don't want to watch TV* and on and on till Claudia thought she was going mad. She'd lost it completely: yelled at the poor kid with the full force of her lungs and her face red and twisted up with anger. She could remember how it had felt even now, her mouth tight and her hands clenched to stop herself from actually hitting Alison as she shrieked at her.

There's nothing to do, and I don't care if you do think you're hard done by. Bloody well find a book or something and shut up. Just shut up. Above all, I don't want to hear that voice of yours droning on and on as if it's my fault you can't find ways of keeping yourself occupied. God, your father doesn't know how lucky he is sometimes to have left all this behind him. Maybe I should pack you off to them, him and the Jeanette person, and see how you like it there, eh?

Alison, to give her credit, had given nearly as good as she got and screamed right back. *Okay, okay I'm going and I'll never ask you what to do ever again. I'll please myself and I shan't care whether you like it or not and if you're horrible to me just once more I'll go to the papers and tell them their precious ballerina is a witch who's cruel to her only daughter and then see how many of them will want to take your picture. I hate you!*

Claudia smiled. That had been intelligent of Alison. A trump card. She'd hugged her and kissed her immediately, of course, even summoning up some tears, and gone into an over-the-top routine of love and devotion and pretended stress over something or other, apologising, promising never to say anything like that ever again, and it had worked. Sort of. Alison never did have to go to the press, but Claudia knew she wasn't taken in for a moment. Still, she never bothers me with demands for entertainment, Claudia thought, so it worked out rather well.

She often wondered whether she really loved her daughter. Or whether she loved her properly, in the way that other people seemed to adore their offspring. When she was pregnant, she longed for the birth of the baby. She spent hours imagining how wonderful she'd look in photographs, with a pretty little child at her side. No one had told her how much sheer hard work babies were and, of course, it was just her luck to have given birth to the most difficult baby in the world. Claudia recalled so many battles to get the baby to eat, so many nights broken by her crying, that it was a wonder, quite frankly, that she'd come out of it feeling anything remotely resembling affection for her daughter.

She sighed, and consoled herself with the thought that of course she must love Alison. Of course she did. It was just that the love was so often overlaid with irritation that it was hard to know sometimes exactly what she felt. At least here at Wychwood there was no need to worry about her. She had a huge garden to wander about in, an enormous house to explore (even if there were bits of it which were private rooms and therefore out of bounds) and a cat to keep her amused. And now, it seemed, she might even be developing a crush on Nick. She'd be okay.

Having decided that, Claudia put Alison out of her mind entirely and considered Nick again. I could look at him for hours, she thought, and bent down to take off her ballet shoes to hide the blush that was suffusing her face at the thought of that body pressed close to hers. Being a redhead had its disadvantages.

The man who had just come into the kitchen to join the company for lunch looked like someone's idea of a nice granddad. Or an elderly uncle, Alison thought. He was too old to be any kind of dancer, though he was certainly thin enough. Hugo stood up and pushed his chair back and went over to shake hands with the new arrival. They came to Hugo's end of the table and sat down there. Where did the extra chair appear from? It seemed to have materialised out of thin air. No, Andy had simply moved down a place and left a space between him and Nick.

'Okay, everyone,' said Hugo, 'here's someone I want you to meet. This is George Stott, who's the lighting manager, the front of house manager and also secretary of the Friends of the Wychwood Festival. A very important person as you can see. He's Ruby's husband, for those of you who've already met Ruby.'

George smiled and said 'Good afternoon, everyone. It's good to have you here and I hope you all enjoy the time you spend at Wychwood. Hugo's been very kind about me, but what I'm really good at is making things run smoothly, so if you've any problems, don't hesitate for a second. I'll be happy to help in any way I can.'

He sat down and poured himself a drink from the jug of orange juice in the middle of the kitchen table. Then he began to help himself to cold meats and salads, and turned to Alison.

'I don't think I've met this young lady. Is no one going to introduce us?'

'Alison is my daughter,' said Claudia, in a way which made it sound, Alison thought, as though she was anything but pleased about this.

'Delighted, I'm sure,' said George and smiled at her. Alison smiled weakly back. The conversation went on around her. Ilene and Andy were discussing Hester.

'Incredibly chic,' said Ilene. 'How old she is she? Fifty?'

'Fifty-three,' said Andy. 'I looked it up. She used to go about with Edmund Norland, who wrote the music for *Sarabande*. Bet you didn't know that.'

'By "go about" do you mean "sleep with?"' Ilene asked.

'Don't think so. Don't really know. She never married, I know that much. And her partner, Kaspar Beilin, who's in San Francisco now with his own company, never made a secret about being gay. Don't forget, the press were a whole lot more discreet in those days. You could do all sorts of stuff in private that would end up on the front page of the tabloids if you did it today.'

'What have you done that might have ended up on the front page, then, Andy?' said Claudia, overhearing the end of his remark.

'Front page? Moi? Never in a million years. No one would give a damn about my love life. It's stars they're after. Stars like you, Claudia.' He beamed at her, and Alison saw how her mother relaxed and smiled happily for almost the first time that day, just because Andy made a flattering remark. Putrid and pathetic. She put out her hand to pick up another bread roll – they really were delicious, freshly baked and with a proper golden crust, and there was even butter to go on them – when Claudia said, in a voice that seemed to Alison to ring out in the enormous kitchen and rise up to the ceiling and sort of hang there before floating down into the ears of every single person in the room:

'Oh God, darling, not *another* roll, surely? You've had more than enough. Here, have a tangerine or something.'

Alison felt burning hot all over. She put the roll back, and said nothing. I wish I could push her face into her plate and get squashed lettuce leaves and tomato pips all over it. I wish I could take this knife and tear up her stupid pink tracksuit with it. She noticed that everyone else had suddenly begun to chat more loudly and energetically than ever to cover up their embarrassment. No one said anything to her but she saw Hugo looking at Claudia with something like horror on his face and Silver looking at Hugo and then leaning forward to say something to George.

Alison took a tangerine from the fruit bowl in the middle of the table, peeled it and ate it without tasting a single mouthful. Then Nick got up from the table. As he left the room, he turned and looked straight at her and winked. He didn't say a single word and yet Alison understood. The wink was his way of saying, *Mothers, honestly!*

Hester was waiting for Hugo in the Office. They'd agreed at the interview, shortly after he'd been given the commission for this year's Festival, that he'd come and keep her up to date with everything that was going on in rehearsals. She would never have sat in on them, but liked to know that all was well and in particular that the choreographer was happy with the arrangements at the Arcadia.

The company was still at lunch. You would never know, Hester thought, from the silence all around, that the house is full of people. That's the thing about putting on a ballet, it occupies your time. Today was a little exceptional, but on other days, rehearsals would be taking place during the afternoon.

Edmund had sent her another postcard. She had a whole collection of them, lined up on the mantelpiece, so that she could imagine him in Vienna. Today's postcard was of a Baroque building, with curlicues and gargoyles and bits and pieces of ornamentation everywhere, but she'd had formal flowerbeds from a palace, street scenes, a portrait of Johann Strauss, and quite a few works of art from museums and art galleries. He'd written almost every day. Today's message, in perfect, tiny writing, said:

> Do you remember the 1963 tour? Sitting in a café just down the road from this church and eating a cake that was more cream than sponge? No ballet dancer worth her salt would dare to do such a thing now. Hope you are bearing up, Hester. Only a few more days till Jan 2nd. I'm off to New York tomorrow. That won't be easy. Much love E.

Someone was knocking. Hester put the postcard down and called, 'Come in.'

Hugo put his head around the door. 'Is it convenient? Now, I mean, for our chat.'

'Yes, yes of course. Do sit down.'

She admired the way Hugo didn't make a production out of finding a place to sit, but simply went straight to the armchair and put his folder full of notes (he was reassuringly well organised) on the floor beside him. She said, 'Some choreographers I've had up here haven't enjoyed their daily talk with me, you know. They thought, some of them, that I was being bossy. Controlling, one of them called it.'

'Not at all,' said Hugo. 'I don't mind a bit. In fact, it'll be good to talk to you about problems I can't discuss with individual members of the company.'

'I'm glad you see it like that. I enjoy keeping in touch, that's all. And sometimes it's easier to talk to someone who's not so close. But tell me a bit about yourself first. Tell me about your parents.'

'My mother died last year. I'm adopted, which of course makes not a scrap of difference to my grief or to how I miss her. She and my dad told me about the adoption very early on, so it's never been an issue. They were my parents and that's how I've always thought of them. They were both architects, in partnership together, and my father's a bit lonely now. I don't see as much of him as I ought to, because he lives near Newcastle and I'm down in London with the company. Still, we had a good Christmas together.'

'But you had to rush off and leave him almost immediately afterwards. I'm so sorry.'

'He understands that this commission is a great honour. And he was impressed by the mention of your name. You're the one dancer even people who've never been to the ballet have heard of.'

'Very kind of you to say so.'

Hugo waved a hand around the room, at all the photographs on the walls.

'No one's forgotten, though. It's all on film. Silver McConnell told me that you were the real reason she took the part in *Sarabande*. She worships you, you know.'

Hester laughed. 'It's ridiculous, really, but knowing something like that still gives me a thrill, even though I haven't danced professionally for years. It's good to be remembered. I teach a lot of master classes and I do still go through my basic class routines every day, but I'm very far from what I was. Look at this . . .' Hester pushed her shoes off and pointed her stockinged toes towards Hugo. 'Who on earth with any sense would deform their feet like this? Look how horrible and lumpy and contorted they are; that's the punishment for all that dancing. All those classes. Those hours *en pointe*. It's insane.'

'But beautiful. While you're doing it anyway. Very beautiful.'

'Thank you, but there's a price. Lumpy feet. Pains in my joints, too, which'll probably get worse as I get older. Oh, don't listen to me. I'm just in a gloomy mood. Let's talk about Silver McConnell. She's very promising, I believe.'

'Silver's my first problem. She's very talented. In fact, I think maybe *too* talented. She creates a fantastic effect without having to work nearly as hard as some.'

'I expect she will – work harder, I mean – after you've shown her what you want, won't she?'

'I'll have a try. I'm just off to rehearse with her now.'

'If she's a real ballet dancer, and not just superficially gifted, then she'll understand what you're trying to do. Let me know what happens.'

'I will.' Hugo stood up. 'And thank you for listening. I'm going to look forward to these meetings with you. Really.'

'Me too,' said Hester. She watched him leave the room and realised that it was true. She liked him. She, too, was looking forward to the next day's meeting. But what had come over her suddenly? Showing him her feet? She'd never done anything like that before. She picked up the postcard from Edmund and added it to the others on her mantelpiece. She imagined herself telling him all about how she'd stuck out her stockinged feet without a second's hesitation and how he'd laugh the laugh that seemed to come from the very heart of him; the laugh that had enchanted the whole of the Charleroi company from the very beginning.

1950

'Everyone, I'd like you to meet Edmund Norland,' said Piers, coming out on to the stage at the Royalty Theatre. The members of the company were sitting in the stalls. Hester, Dinah and Nell were right at the back, which was the best place to sit when Piers was giving one of his pep talks. They were in the middle of rehearsing for *Giselle*, and Hester still occasionally thought she must be dreaming, hugging herself with pleasure at the realisation that she, Hester Fielding, was going to dance the principal role. She was seventeen years old, and going to dance Giselle! She still could hardly believe her luck and had to pinch herself every day as a reminder. Piers told her it was something of a gamble but that he'd chosen her because she was the only person who was both young enough and good enough. Estelle was dancing Queen of the Wilis, Miles was Loys and Dinah was thrilled to have been cast as Bathilde. Piers had promised Hester that Madame Olga would be there on the first night. Hester turned her attention from daydreaming about *Giselle* to what was happening now. Piers had this young man on stage with him and Dinah was whispering in her ear.

'Who is he? He's rather nice, isn't he?'

Hester looked at the young man standing beside Piers. His fair hair fell over his forehead. He seemed pleasant enough and certainly he was full of smiles for his audience.

'He's all right,' she whispered back.

Piers was in full flow now. 'Mr Norland is a composer. A wonderful composer, naturally, and please don't think what I'm about to tell you is influencing me in any way. He genuinely is the new Tchaikovsky and he's written a ballet for us. It's *Red Riding Hood*, and I intend to put it on for Christmas, straight after we finish the *Giselle* run. It's already September, so you'll understand that we don't have a great deal of time. Mr Norland's come to this rehearsal to give me his opinion on who might be a suitable heroine. I have my own ideas of course, but Mr Norland insists on meeting the company. I told him we were like a big family here, and he is about to be included in it, for better or for worse. So please do your best work today, and bear in mind that we have a special guest in the audience. Right, everyone, off you go to prepare yourselves.'

As they were getting ready for the stage rehearsal, Nell told them more about Mr Edmund Norland.

'Magda Volsky's his girlfriend – you know, the principal dancer in the Westhaven Company. She's very skinny and foreign. Quite funny-looking actually, but not a bad dancer. Not that I've ever seen her, of course, but that's what I've heard.'

'You always know so much, Nell!' Hester said. 'How do you manage it?'

'She gossips to everyone,' said Dinah. 'You must have seen her.'

'Well, yes, in our company,' said Hester, as Nell threw a powder puff at Dinah and laughed. 'But I didn't know she knew about other companies as well.'

'You'd be surprised what I know,' said Nell. 'I'm a mine of information.'

During the rehearsal, whenever she wasn't on stage, Hester stood in the wings and looked at Piers and Mr Norland in the third row of the stalls. Piers was right. The Charleroi Company *was* like a family. Piers was the father; Dinah and Nell and some of the young men were like her brothers and sisters, the older dancers were like cousins, and Estelle P was a rather nasty great-aunt. There were occasional arguments, of course there were, between members of the family but, on the whole, you could depend on them. And you loved them, too, Hester realised. Only Madame Olga was dearer to her than Dinah, Nell and Piers.

The theatre itself was a home and more than a home. The stage was a magic place that could become anywhere. No more than a box, really, enclosed by curtains and scenery and lit by lamps which shone a coloured light on you and changed you into a ghost, or a young peasant girl or . . . the flats were up for the last act of *Giselle*, all mist and gravestones and blue shadows, but Hester was already imagining a forest, thick with green trees which might hide a wolf. She wanted to be Red Riding Hood, and she was determined to make a good impression on this Edmund Norland, who seemed to have some influence on Piers. She stepped out into the light, and transformed herself into Giselle.

Edmund Norland very quickly became Edmund. He was always in the Royalty after that first day. Sometimes he leaned against the wall of the rehearsal room while Piers took a class; sometimes he came to Lyons Corner House with Hester, Dinah and Nell; he often came to Gino's in the evening, and occasionally he was to be seen with the foreign-looking Magda. When she was there, he was very attentive to her, but when he was alone with the members of the Charleroi Company, he didn't seem to miss her very much.

Then, one day in early October, at the end of a rehearsal Piers said, 'Dinah, Nell, Hester and Mona. Could I have a word, please?'

The dancers looked at one another, as if to say, what have we done now? Piers saw this and laughed. 'Not to worry, darlings! This is a treat for you. A party, no less. It's Edmund's idea, but it's a good one, I must say.'

The idea may have been good, but it was also exhausting. The four of them had been chosen to perform some dances at a birthday party for someone called Virginia Lennister. She was the wife of a friend of Edmund's and she loved the ballet. In fact, Piers told them, she had invested in the Charleroi Company. She was a wealthy American and lived in a grand house near St Albans.

'And you're going to have to rehearse my little dances as well as *Giselle*. Do you think you're up to it? I've devised a few simple things for you to do that will nevertheless impress Mrs Lennister. Nothing too demanding and all set to the pretty Chopin music that partygoers will be expecting. My own little *Chopiniana*!' He laughed. 'How does that sound to you?'

It sounded wonderful to all of them. Dinah said, 'I've seen the house. It's ever so grand. And I've heard of Adam Lennister. He's a writer, but I'm not sure what he writes.'

During rehearsals, they found out more from Edmund.

'I've known him for years,' he told them. 'We were at school together and he used to write poems. I set some of them to music once. Now he's a biographer and a very good one, though his books aren't exactly moneyspinners. Still, Virginia's got enough for both of them. The house is quite beautiful. Wait and see. You'll all have a grand time.'

On the day of the party, Piers and his dancers arrived in the enormous car that Mrs Lennister had sent for them. In the boot was a small skip full of tutus, ballet shoes, make-up and assorted headdresses and jewellery. Edmund was already at Orchard House and was going to meet them before the party started to go over the moves, though it wouldn't be a proper rehearsal.

'Blimey,' said Nell as they drew up in front of Orchard House and she took in the ivy-covered façade. 'I didn't think there were houses like this so close to London. And there must be an orchard too, right? Round the back, perhaps?'

'Come along, ladies, enough gossiping,' said Piers, but he couldn't resist adding, 'It is rather fine, isn't it? They've got quite a nice flat in London as well, only she likes the country. Well, so would I if I could live in this sort of style. My experience of outside London is that things are usually unspeakably Spartan.'

A elderly man in evening dress – Hester guessed he must be the butler – showed Piers into the drawing room and then led her and the others upstairs.

'One law for the rich and another for the poor,' Dinah whispered to her, as they were shown into one of the guest bedrooms.

'There are refreshments for you in the kitchen when you're ready,' said the butler. 'Take the back stairs to the basement.'

'Thank you,' Hester said. 'That's very kind.'

Once the butler had left the room, they hurried to take their coats off. Dinah went to sit at the dressing-table.

'I wouldn't mind living here for the rest of my life,' she said, as she applied dark red lipstick. 'If this is one of the guest rooms, imagine what the main bedrooms are like.'

The others sat on the bed, tying up the ribbons on their ballet shoes. The *toile de Jouy* wallpaper; the four-poster bed; the dressing-table which wore a flounce of fabric that matched the pale blue chintz curtains – they'd stared at everything for a long time before daring to put their costumes down on the bed, and their tatty cigar-boxes full of broken stubs of greasepaint on to the spotless surface (wood, covered by a sheet of glass) that lay in front of the mirror.

As soon as they were ready, they went down the fine main staircase, craning their necks to see what they could of the rest of the house on their way to the back stairs. In the kitchen, where food for the party was being prepared, no one took much notice of them, except for one kind young woman who was in charge of pouring their tea and making sure they had some sandwiches and cake to go with it.

'My name's Ella. I'll be looking after you. You're to come in again after the dancing, and then you'll get something a bit more filling.'

Her eyes shone as she watched the dancers eating. 'I'm going to try and watch your performance, if that's all right. From the gallery, where I won't be seen. I love the ballet. I go to Sadler's Wells whenever I can.'

After tea, they followed Piers to the ballroom. A huge expanse of parquet flooring, polished to a high shine of golden-brown, stretched from the door to a raised platform. Chandeliers hung from the ceiling like clusters of gemstones, and the whole of one wall was made up of windows on to the terrace and the garden. Hester could see trees at the far end of a long sweep of lawn. Was that the orchard? Edmund was already at the piano, which was placed to one side of the stage, but got up to meet them as they made their way across the parquet. A woman was standing next to him: fair-haired, with very piercing blue eyes and a small, thin-lipped mouth which seemed to have difficulty in smiling, as though it were a skill she hadn't quite mastered.

Edmund introduced them to their hostess. 'This is Virginia Lennister. Piers you know, of course, and these are Dinah, Nell, Hester and Mona,' and before long, they were up on the stage and the music surrounded them. Hester went through the moves with the others, wondering why Virginia Lennister had been so chilly. This was her birthday party, and she was supposed to be the one who loved ballet. It was in her honour that Piers had put this sequence of dances together, so why had she been so unwelcoming? Maybe,

Hester thought, it has nothing to do with us and she's annoyed about something quite different. Later, she learned that a kind of guarded hostility was Virginia's natural manner, that she found it hard to relax, and even harder to show any of the normal signs of happiness.

After the performance was over, Hester took longer than the others to change out of her tutu. Nell, Dinah and Mona went down to the kitchen leaving her still taking off her make-up. Edmund had delayed her. He'd gone on and on about how wonderful she'd been until she interrupted him.

'You're very kind, Edmund, but I must go and get changed. We're expected in the kitchen for supper, I think.'

'I know, I know. But here's what I wanted to tell you. You're going to be dancing Red Riding Hood in my ballet. Piers and I agreed really, but I insisted. I told him I'd go on strike if you didn't get the part, not let him do it. No, seriously, I didn't but I would. And it's going to be such fun, isn't it?'

'Is that true? Am I really going to be . . . after *Giselle*? Red Riding Hood? I can't believe it.'

'It's perfectly true. He's telling the company tomorrow about all the casting. Of course, no one can start rehearsing till *Giselle* is up and running but the sooner the better really.'

'Thanks, Edmund. I'm so grateful to you, really. I can't tell you.' She flung her arms around Edmund's neck and hugged him.

'Go on, then,' he said, smiling. 'Better get into your clothes and go for some supper.'

By the time she reached the guest bedroom, the others were nearly dressed. She mumbled something, but Dinah was too sharp to be fobbed off.

'You've been with Edmund, haven't you? Can't fool me. What's he been telling you?'

'I don't think I'm supposed to let on, but I'm so excited. Please keep it to yourselves, though.'

'Go on, then,' said Mona. 'The suspense is killing me.'

'It's his ballet. *Red Riding Hood*. I'm going to be doing the name part.'

The others kissed her and congratulated her and Mona said, rather sharply, Hester thought, 'Well, that was obvious to me from the very first time Edmund came to the Royalty. I could see he was impressed with you. Did he tell you the rest of the casting, by any chance?'

'No,' said Hester. 'We're going to be told tomorrow.'

Hester changed the subject, and then the others left her to get ready and went downstairs without her. While she dressed, Hester wondered whether she had imagined an edge of envy in Mona's voice. Dinah and Nell were amazingly generous and never seemed to resent her success, but Mona? It was hard to tell, but here she was, about to take on another leading role, straight after Giselle. Perhaps there were some other members of the company who were good enough to dance the part, but she was just as good as they were. She knew that now. She felt herself suddenly filled with a sort of power. I'm going to do it, she thought, peering at her face in the mirror. I *will* be a good dancer. Maybe even a great one. Yes. I can do it. She went on getting ready with a thrill of happiness running through her veins. Let them be resentful, she thought. I don't care. I only care about the part, the ballet; trying to be as good as I can possibly be.

On her way downstairs she took a wrong turning and found herself in a long corridor. One door was open and a light was on inside. Whoever was in the room must have heard her because a man's voice called out, 'Hello?'

She hesitated for a moment and then took a deep breath and stepped into the room. The person who'd been sitting at a desk in the corner stood up and faced her. He was very tall and pale. That was Hester's first impression. His eyes were dark and he smiled at her.

'I know who you are, you're Miss Fielding, one of the dancers. I'm Adam Lennister.'

'Oh,' she said. This was Virginia Lennister's husband. The writer. Hester found that the proper responses had died in her mouth and instead, there was a pulse beating somewhere in her head. This man was beautiful. His face was like the face of a statue come to life: a perfectly straight nose and lips that seemed carved into exactly the right shape. His dark eyes were fringed with ridiculously long lashes – the longest Hester had ever seen.

'I'm sorry, I'm lost, I think. Silly of me. I thought I'd worked it all out before.'

'It's a confusing house. I know it too well to lose myself in it, though I try sometimes. Like now, for instance.'

'And I've disturbed you. I'm so sorry.'

'Not at all. I've been hiding in here since the dancing finished. Parties aren't really my sort of thing, but my wife likes them and so . . . Do sit down for a moment.'

He went back to his chair at the desk, indicating to Hester a sofa where she should sit. She didn't lean back, but positioned herself on the edge.

'You look as though you're about to take flight. Don't worry. I won't keep you long. I wanted to say how much I enjoyed your performance. Virginia's very fond of ballet, and Edmund, your accompanist, he's also a great fan.'

'You're not, then?'

'Well, I didn't think I was. To be honest, I haven't seen all that much. But tonight . . . well, I *would* like to see something else. Edmund says you're going to be doing *Giselle* at the Royalty. Is that so? He and my wife describe it as tragic and romantic. Would I like it, d'you think? I love the Romantic poets.'

'*Giselle*'s my favourite of all the ballets,' Hester said. 'Not that I've seen that many, of course. And I suppose I'm biased because it's the first time I've danced a principal role.'

'If you're the star of the show, then I'm sure I'll like it.'

Hester was at a loss for how to answer this. She was breathless, as though her heart were being squeezed, as though her ribcage were tightening around it, and she thought that if she tried to speak, her voice would come out squeaky and unnatural. Was this what Dinah and all the others were trying to tell her about? They hadn't conveyed the force of the feeling, but Hester thought that maybe it was. Maybe this was the attraction she was supposed to have felt for other men, but never had. He'd spoken to her. She had to answer, before he realised how she was feeling.

'I don't know how to say what it is I like about the ballet. It just makes me feel as though I'm in a world that's perfect. Beautiful. Not like the real world.'

'Yes,' he said and fell silent, his shoulders slumped. I must leave, Hester thought. She stood up.

'I ought to go.' Her voice came out as a whisper. 'You must be tired.'

'No, I'm not tired,' he said and stood up. 'Will you do me a favour?'

'Yes?'

'Please call me Adam. Next time we meet?'

'Of course. Adam. I'm Hester.'

'Hester,' he said, on an outgoing breath, like a sigh. She wanted him to say it again, and miraculously, he did.

'Hester. I'll come and watch you dancing in *Giselle*. I promise.'

'Thank you.' She turned and almost ran from the room. Her face was burning. He wants to see you performing, she told herself. He's only interested in you as a dancer; nothing more than that. He's discovered that ballet is enjoyable and that's the beginning and end of it.

She had forgotten, after all that, to ask him the way to the kitchen, but she found it in the end, blundering through corridors and down staircases without paying any attention to where she was going. When she got there, Dinah, Nell and Mona were tucking into smoked salmon and potato salad, and there was peach melba waiting for them all on the dresser.

'Where've you been?' Mona said.

'We were just about to send out a search party,' Dinah added. 'You look hot and flustered.'

'No, I'm fine,' Hester said, surprising herself with how normal she sounded.

Hester thought that dancing Giselle, the part she had always loved more than any other, would distract her from her own emotions, but the ballet seemed to mirror so many of her feelings that by the time the day of the first night arrived, she was in a state of such anxiety and elation and excitement that she could hardly go through the ordinary motions of breakfast and class and talk with her friends. There was a fitting in Wardrobe just before lunch and Hester stood for a long time with her arms above her head while the wardrobe mistress took the bodice in with pins.

'You've lost a little weight since the last time you wore this,' she said, not altogether approvingly.

'I haven't been meaning to,' Hester said. 'I eat all the time.'

But I think I may be in love, she said to herself. This must be what it feels like. I'll speak to Dinah. I must tell her. Everything.

She found her friend in the dressing room.

'Dinah, can I tell you something?'

'What's the matter, Hester? You look as though you've seen a ghost.'

'No, it's worse than that. I think I'm in love. I think I'm feeling all those things you said I'd feel.'

'Wonderful! How wonderful! Who is it? Anyone I know?'

Hester hung her head. 'That's the problem. It's Adam Lennister. What am I going to do?'

Tears began to slide out of her eyes and she wiped them away with the back of her hand.

'Has he . . . ? Since we danced at his house, have you seen him?'

Hester shook her head. 'He's written to me. He's coming to the first night. He wants to take me to dinner. I want to go, but it would be wrong, wouldn't it? He's married, Dinah!' She was almost wailing. 'I'm sorry. I'm being stupid. I can't go to dinner with him.'

'But you want to, don't you?' Dinah was looking very serious. 'And you will, I think. You have that look about you.'

'What look?'

'The look that means you'll do what you want to do whatever I say to you. Whatever I warn you about. Whatever anyone advises. I'm right, aren't I?'

Hester bit her lip. Dinah was right. She'd known, from the first letter (he'd written to her three times since they'd first met, and she knew each message by heart) that she would do whatever he asked her to do. She said, back-tracking, 'I don't suppose, really, that there's anything wrong with going out to dinner with someone.'

'So you won't be coming to Gino's with the rest of us? That'll be a shame.'

'No, I'll be there. He didn't mean tonight. His wife will be with him for *Giselle*. And I wouldn't miss a first night party at Gino's. What would I say to Madame Olga? Adam . . .' She blushed. Just saying his name made her feel most peculiar, as though parts of her were shifting in her body. She went on, 'He's asked me to dinner the day after tomorrow.'

'Be careful, Hester.' Dinah looked grave. 'I mean it. You could be hurt so badly.'

'I will be, I promise,' Hester said. 'And I'll try not to be hurt.'

Hester was doing her best to sound normal when she didn't feel normal at all. This, what she was experiencing now, was more like suffering from a fever. She should have felt happy but she was miserable. At least Dinah knew what was going on now. The shame, the secrecy that would have to surround any relationship with Adam would be hard to bear. She could never tell Madame Olga about him, that was certain. She was in London for the first night of *Giselle* but Hester knew her opinions about love in general and for dancers in particular. It was, she often said, a disease dancers should never allow themselves to catch. She'd been warning Hester against it for years. And now Dinah had warned her all over again. Adam was married. I ought to tell him I won't see him but I can't. I want to see him. I don't care if it is only over a dinner table. Adam Lennister. She repeated his name in her head, over and over again.

Hester stood in the wings and closed her eyes. She blushed with pleasure as she remembered the bouquet of cream roses that had been delivered to the dressing room just half an hour ago. Nell had searched out one of the big vases that were kept in the props department and joked about a secret admirer because there had been no card with the flowers. I know who they're from, Hester thought. No one but Adam would have sent them, and only he wouldn't have put his name on a card, for all the obvious reasons. I won't think about that side of it, Hester thought. Not now. All that matters is, he's here. He's going to be looking at me soon. She would dance every step, every single one, just for him. She shook her head. The ballet had started. The *corps* in their peasant costumes were celebrating the harvest. It was time for her to forget about everything but what she had to do on stage.

The familiar music swelled into the auditorium and filled the darkness around her. Her heart was beating very fast. The skirt of her costume was striped in pale green and white, her blouse was white, with a modest round neck, and around her waist she wore a wide, tightly laced black belt that emphasised her slimness. *Grand-mère*'s chain had been judged by Piers too delicate to use as the chain Loys gives to Giselle. She'd left it in an empty cleansing-cream tin in the cigar box she used for all her make-up. This was where she always hid it when she was performing. Hester took a deep breath and stepped out into the light.

Madame Olga said she cried all through the ballet. She was still dabbing at her eyes when she came backstage to congratulate Hester.

'Superb! Superb!' she said. 'I can die a happy woman now that I have seen you dancing Giselle. You were so touching! Such pain, in the mad scene. And the flower! Ah, that was something very special.'

'Thank you,' Hester said, catching Madame Olga's eye in the mirror. She was taking off her make-up. The performance had exhausted her. Not the dancing so much as the emotion. That's because I'm feeling so much of what Giselle feels, she told herself, and shivered as she remembered the petals falling off the flower and on to the stage: *he loves me, he loves me not, he loves me.*

Piers, who was also in the dressing room, praised the whole company. 'I think the reviews will be wonderful, my dears. They will doubtless say you're a star, Hester, and you must remember that half the time they don't know what they're talking about. You mustn't believe the good things and you also mustn't believe the bad things the critics say. I'm the only one you should pay attention to, because I'm the one who knows when you're dancing up to your best standard.'

'And was my Giselle up to scratch?'

'It'll do, my dear. It'll do!' He smiled at her as he left the room, and according to Dinah what he'd said was high praise.

After much talk and laughter, all the others went off to celebrate at

Gino's. Dinah was the last to leave. She looked closely at Hester and asked, 'Are you all right? You're in a dream half the time these days. We're off now. Are you coming? Shall I wait for you?'

'No, I'm fine. I'll be there in a moment. It's just that it takes it out of you, all that *feeling* on stage. I need time to recover.'

The room felt echoey after Dinah had gone. The costumes hanging on a rail under the window were like ghosts – different colours, different textures, but each one bringing to mind the person who'd just discarded it; something that only a short while ago had been part of a living and moving body and was now still and silent. All the ballet shoes had been put away on the shoe shelf. They were lined up together – black and white satin, brown leather, and mauve silk for the Wilis – and looked like pretty flowers, with their ribbons tied neatly around them. The fragrance of talcum powder and several perfumes hung in the air. She was alone. She didn't have to pretend any more.

She rubbed cream into her face and gazed at the roses which seemed to her to be almost luminous. Adam. Not tomorrow but the next day, after the performance, she was going to have dinner with him. And that's all, she told herself. Nothing else. No one can possibly object to me eating with him. I'll behave well. I'll be careful. Dinah will be proud of me. She wiped the grease off her face and put on her street clothes.

On the third night of the run, when they were in the wings together just before the first act curtain, Dinah said, 'Oh, my word! Just guess who's sitting out front.'

'Who?' Hester put her eye to the tiny gap in the stage-left edge of the curtain through which the cast always examined the audience before a performance.

'There, in the fourth row. It's him, isn't it?'

'He's been to every performance.'

'It's tonight, isn't it? You're going to dinner with him.'

Hester nodded. 'His wife's in the country.'

'And if she was in London, I'm sure she'd be joining you, wouldn't she?'

'Stop it, Dinah! You know she wouldn't.'

'I'm not going to say another word, Hester. But do take care.'

'I'm sick to death of being warned, Dinah. I know what you think. But I can't help it. I want to see him again.'

They went to a small Italian restaurant a long way away from the theatre. Adam had sent her a letter telling her exactly where his black car would be parked.

'I'm so sorry about the cloak and dagger stuff,' he said, turning his head to smile at her as they drove off.

'I understand,' Hester said, and then couldn't think of anything else to say. For a wild moment she thought, this isn't going to work. We have nothing in common. He's too old. What will we talk about?

Adam broke into her thoughts. 'It's awkward, isn't it? Knowing how to begin a conversation with someone who you feel you know so well and yet really don't know at all. Do I sound as though I've taken leave of my senses?'

'No,' said Hester. 'I feel just the same. As though I know you very well, but I don't, do I?'

'I've been out front every night, you know.'

'Yes, I've seen you. We've got a hole in the curtain we look through. We get quite a good view of who's in the audience.'

'Did you look for me?'

Hester nodded, unable to speak.

'Right,' said Adam. 'This is it. I hope you like Italian food.'

'Yes, lovely,' said Hester, reflecting that she didn't care what the food was. They were going to sit at a table together and talk and she'd be able to gaze at him as much as she wanted. She was determined to enjoy every second of their time together.

'Tell me all about it,' Dinah whispered as Hester crept into bed. 'I've not been able to get to sleep. You're awfully late.'

'Can't tell you now. We'll wake Nell up.'

'Rubbish! You know you could play a trombone in her ear and not wake her. Come on, I want to know every single detail.'

'There's nothing to tell. We talked, that's all.'

'What about?'

'His schooldays. He and Edmund were at school together. We talked about his work and how difficult it is to sit down every day and just write and how he wished that writers were like ballet dancers and could have the discipline of class. That made us laugh – the idea of a writers' class. Pens out, in first position. Paper in fifth position. Eyes down.' She giggled.

'Hilarious!' said Dinah. 'Clearly you had to be there to get the full effect.'

'You're the one who asked. I'm happy to stop right there.'

'No, I'm sorry, truly. Go on. What else?'

'He wanted to know about me. No one else has ever asked me so many questions. I told him all about my grandmother. I've never spoken to anyone about that, about how I felt when I left her. I nearly started to cry.'

'And he consoled you? Put his arm around you?'

'No, he was on the other side of the table. And I controlled myself before it got too bad.'

'Did he kiss you goodnight when you parted?'

'Yes, but just a kiss on the cheek. Very proper.'

She was lying. She was still reliving that scene in her mind, over and over again. How he'd walked her from the car to the porch. It was so late that no one would see them, she knew.

'Goodnight, Hester,' he'd said and leaned down to kiss her on the lips. It was the lightest of kisses, and yet she felt it like a brand, burning into her flesh. 'Till next time.' She'd had to restrain herself. She'd wanted to ask, when is the next time? When will I see you again? He said, 'Tomorrow. Can you come out with me tomorrow? I feel like camping outside the theatre and waiting all through the night. But I won't. I won't embarrass you. I'll wait patiently.'

Dinah said: 'Are you seeing him again?'

'Tomorrow.'

'And the next day, I daresay.'

'If he asks me.'

Dinah sighed. 'You're a lost cause. The damage is done.'

'What do you mean? What damage?'

'You're too far gone to come back again. That's what I think.'

Hester didn't answer because what Dinah said was true. She *was* too far gone. She said, 'I must try and sleep now, or I'll be a wreck tomorrow and so will you and Piers will kill us.'

'You're right. I'm off to sleep and I advise you to do the same. If you can. Sweet dreams.'

''Night!' Hester stared into the darkness and thought about Adam. She ran a finger over her mouth and shivered. Dinah's right, she thought. I won't be able to turn away from him. I should, I know I should, but if he wants me, I won't be able to stop myself. She tried to imagine how it would be when she saw him again. She was sure he would kiss her. Yes, he would kiss her. Her mouth fell open and her eyes closed and she abandoned herself to fantasies that made her tremble and feel hot all over.

'Where are we going?' Hester peered through the windscreen. They were travelling in Adam's car along the Embankment but a yellowish mist hid every familiar landmark, veiling the glitter of the lights along the river.

'I'm taking you to the flat. I'm going to cook for you tonight. I'm sick of restaurants, aren't you?'

'We've only been four times.'

'But four nights in a row. I don't think people were designed to eat out so often. Sometimes it's a treat to stay home.'

'I don't mind where we go.'

'You'll like the flat. It's got a wonderful view of Chelsea. At least when it's not foggy.'

Hester said nothing. Part of her felt as though whatever was going to happen had been arranged. Choreographed – and a voice in her head said, don't go. Ask him to take you home. She knew that once she went into his flat, once she allowed herself to be taken there, she was agreeing to something. She wasn't objecting. She wouldn't be able to say, he tricked me. He seduced me. He lured me to his flat. The truth is, she told herself, I want to go. I want to be alone with him. I want him to kiss me properly. I want him. I can't help it. It's wrong but I'm not going to stop myself. I won't pretend I don't know what's going to happen.

Adam took her arm as they stepped into the lift. It was one of the creakiest, oldest lifts Hester had ever seen, and seemed reluctant to crawl up to the third floor. It was also tiny.

'Hester . . .' Adam said, and his arms were around her before she could answer. She turned her face up to his and then his mouth was on her mouth and she forgot entirely the small, fluttery movement of his lips on hers when he'd kissed her every night as they said goodbye. This, this hungry breathing-in of one another, *this* was a kiss. Along her arms and legs and through her body, she felt as if the blood was rushing too quickly along her veins.

Adam stepped away from her as the lift opened, and they walked silently to his door. Once they were inside, he led her to a sofa in the lounge and drew the curtains closed. She wished someone would tell one of them, either her or Adam, what the next move was. She knew the right way to behave. Here she was, alone with a married man in his flat and his wife was far away. She ought to go. She ought never to have come. She could stand up and walk to the door and ask him to drive her back to Moscow Road.

Adam didn't say a word. He came to sit down beside her on the sofa and drew her into his arms. *He* has to do it, she thought. He has to show me what he wants. I can't tell him. I don't know what to do unless he starts. Unless he shows me. But please, please let him say something now. I want him. Can I tell him how much I want him?

'Hester,' he said at last. 'Hester, are you sure? I don't want to make you do something you'd regret.'

'I won't. I won't regret it. Please.'

Adam stood up and pulled her gently to her feet. They were standing beside the sofa and before she knew what was happening, her coat and skirt were on the floor. He was too slow, *too* gentle. She stepped away from him and pulled off her jumper, impatiently, swiftly. She was naked under the thin wool and she came to him and wrapped her arms around him and then he was kissing her and she almost fainted with pleasure. He kissed her mouth and then her neck and then her breasts, and she made a sound in her throat halfway between a groan and a sigh, and they moved together as though they were only one body down on to the sofa again. It was there – there, ready for them to lie on – and her heartbeat was so loud that she could hardly hear what he was saying, hear her own name repeated over and over again, and then he went on kissing her everywhere, all over her skin till it shone and burned and part of her thought, no, I can't be doing this it's wrong and I want to do it and I can't stop. And then there were no more words anywhere and nothing but her own nerve-endings and a singing in her head and her body swept by a tide of desire which obliterated every conscious thought, every doubt, everything but this feeling which hurt her and filled her and which she wished would never stop. Never never never.

A few days later, Edmund and Hester were sitting together in Lyons Corner House.

'You're not eating, Hester,' he said. 'You told me this was your favourite place in the whole of London and that was your favourite ice-cream but you haven't touched it.'

'I'm sorry, Edmund. I know. I'm rotten company, only I'm so . . .' She reached for a hankie in her coat pocket and couldn't find one.

'Here, have mine.' She took it, and wiped away a tear that had threatened to fall on to her cheek.

'Thanks. I thought you might not notice . . .'

'Not notice how miserable you are? You must be joking. Your face is very revealing. Your emotions are there for anyone to look at. It's what makes you such a great performer.'

'I'm not miserable. I've never been happier in my life. In some ways . . .' Her voice trailed off. Edmund, across the table from her, took her hand and held it. He'd invited Hester to tea yesterday, after the *Red Riding Hood* rehearsal. Now that they were face to face, the normally voluble Edmund seemed not to know what to say.

'Edmund . . .'

'Hester . . .'

They spoke in unison and laughed.

'May I speak first, Edmund? Only if I don't speak now, I won't dare later on. I'm making a huge effort not to get up and run away. Don't look so worried. I'm not going to.'

She picked up the long, silver spoon, scooped up a little ice-cream and ate it. Edmund waited for her to speak, not touching the scone on the plate in front of him. 'It's Adam Lennister. I'm in love with him. We're in love. I don't know what to do.'

As soon as the words were out of her mouth, the tears came. They welled up in her eyes and she made no effort to stop them. They ran down her cheeks as she picked up Edmund's handkerchief.

Edmund moved his chair nearer to hers so that he could put an arm around her shoulders. 'You can cry all you like. No one's looking. We're in luck because there's hardly anyone here.'

'What am I going to do? He's married. But he loves me. He says he does. He says . . . doesn't matter. But I can't stop myself. I can't . . .'

'Have you . . .' Edmund stopped, unable to say the words.

'Yes. A week ago. I can't concentrate on anything, Edmund. It's unbearable. I think of him in class, at rehearsal. All the time. It's only when I'm being Giselle that I manage to put him to the back of my mind, but then when I come offstage I'm longing to see him so much that I can't get my breath. Have you ever felt like that? Sort of exhausted just with *wanting* someone?

'Well, not quite in the way you describe it, no. But I've had my moments.'

'I feel so stupid. God, isn't it frightful how life imitates the silliest kind of romance? I'd think this was laughable if it wasn't happening to me. I honestly didn't think I was that interested in men. Dancing was everything.'

She put her head down on the table and put her hands over her hair, trying to disappear. Edmund leaned in to whisper, 'Don't, Hester. Please stop crying. It's all right. It *will* be all right. I promise. I'll look after you. Do stop crying. They'll chuck us out,' he went on, trying for a lighter tone, trying to make her laugh.

Hester sat up and used Edmund's hankie again to dry her eyes.

'I'm so grateful to you Edmund. You've become such a good friend to me so quickly. It's such a comfort to talk to you. But how can you say it'll be all right? It won't be. How could it? I'm hurting Virginia Lennister and I don't even know her.'

'You can't help it sometimes. You can't help falling in love. But you just have to, well, do the best you can. What does Adam say about this?'

Hester shook her head. 'We don't talk about it. We hardly talk . . .' She blushed, remembering the three occasions when she and Adam had been together, since the first time. How they'd barely managed to close the front door of his flat behind them and greet one another before it began, the heat and the love and all the things they did to one another, the wash of feeling and emotion that didn't allow any room for discussion. Hester thought of how hard it was to leave him, how he clung to her, how her whole body felt like a melting candle for hours afterwards. How guilty she felt when she remembered what she'd just done, when she thought of what Madame Olga would have said if she could have seen her. Hester shook her head. Edmund, understanding some of what she meant, was also a little red in the face.

'He and Virginia haven't got the best marriage in the world,' he told her. 'They're not terribly well suited, but they've been together for some years. And, of course, Adam doesn't make all that much money, so he's somewhat financially dependent on her. If it wasn't for Virginia, they couldn't possibly live the way they do. I think he'd be quite happy spending a lot more time in London, but Virginia loves Orchard House. I don't think she's slept more than a couple of nights in their flat, whereas he often uses it when he's up here burrowing about in libraries. And it sounds a strange thing to say in the circumstances but Adam's a very honourable person. Very loyal. Does that sound mad? Also, of course, he's much older than you are.'

'You're as old as he is, aren't you? You don't seem all that much older than me.'

'He's actually two years older than I am. He's twenty-nine. I'm not saying age matters necessarily but you know how people talk.'

'You mustn't say a word!' She grabbed Edmund's sleeve. 'Not to a soul. Not to Piers, not to anyone in the company. Dinah's the only person I've told. Above all, don't tell Adam. I promised him I wouldn't tell. I couldn't help it, though. I needed to say something to someone. Please say you won't breathe a word. Promise me.'

'I promise,' Edmund said. 'But it'll come out, you'll see. Someone will cotton on in the end. In fact, I'm surprised they haven't already. Adam is sure to confide in me eventually. Come along, now. It's time for rehearsal. Are you feeling up to it?'

'It's the only thing I can do, the one thing that distracts me from everything else.'

'Then come along, Red Riding Hood. I will make sure you get to the Royalty and don't get waylaid by Big Bad Wolves.'

Edmund tucked Hester's arm under his as they made their way along the Bayswater Road. How lucky I am to have him as a friend, she thought. How kind he is. And maybe he was right. Maybe things would work out for the best. How could love such as she was feeling be anything but good?

28 December 1986

'And a step and bend and lean over a little . . . that's it. And back and up . . . Silver, concentrate. You look as though you're miles away.'

'I'm not miles away, Hugo. I'm right in front of you.'

'You know very well what I mean. Not concentrating. Now try that sequence again.'

Silver's mouth tightened, and she looked at him with evident incomprehension. She's not used to being told she needs to try harder, Hugo thought. She's been spoiled. Well, she's met her match now. I'm not going to let her get away with being slack. He scrutinised her carefully as she moved. 'Better. Could be more than just better, though. Could be spectacular. And will be, if I have anything to do with it. Okay, let's move on. Nick, you come in now, please, just move towards Silver from upstage right . . . that's it.'

Nick Neary was excellent, which was a great relief. Silver needed to depend on him, and although the Lover wasn't exactly the Angel's partner in the conventional sense, the best *pas-de-deux* in the ballet were the two they had together, as they fought over the Princess.

'Okay, Silver, you have to be magnetic and menacing at the same time. You're going to win in the end, because Death always does, but Nick has to be serious competition. Nick, I want you to show the precariousness of love and all that.'

'No problem, Hugo. Precariousness of Love is my middle name.'

Hugo and Silver both laughed and Hugo said, 'Okay. Just once more and then we'll break for today.'

He pressed the switch on the tape recorder and music filled the rehearsal room. Silver closed her eyes as she went into the short routine that she'd been learning this afternoon. Hugo could see that she still wasn't giving it the one hundred percent effort that he expected of his dancers. Where had she been trained? She'd told him at the audition that she admired Hester Fielding more than anything; how could she say that and yet not be prepared to work her socks off? He knew that her relaxed attitude was that of the truly talented. She was so naturally good, so able to succeed with the minimum of effort, that she hadn't ever had to put in the sweat that went with absolute perfection. Well, he thought, she won't be able to get away with that for long. Not with me in charge. He watched her as she kept count of the steps, following the blocking out of the moves they'd just done, but she was holding something in reserve and she needed to give herself completely to the music. This tune, this theme, was Silver's — the Angel's variation on the dance that was at the centre of the whole ballet, the Sarabande itself: stately, dignified, passionate all at once. It was written for wailing saxophones and brass, and as Silver raised her arms above her head, Hugo knew he wouldn't be satisfied till he could almost see feathers growing out of her skin and imagine that she had wings that might stretch out and carry her up and up as she took flight. She stood on point and lifted her right leg so high that it almost touched her ear. Nick was holding her. She was definitely one of the most gifted dancers Hugo had ever encountered and he would get her to fulfil her potential if it was the last thing he did. The audience had to believe she was capable of flight.

'Bloody hell, Silver,' said Nick, when they were finished and pulling on jumpers and leg warmers for the walk back to Wychwood House. 'I've heard of high kicks but that's amazing.'

'I can only do that if I know you're there, so thanks. I couldn't do it without you.'

'Thanks, both of you,' said Hugo. 'It's going to be great.'

'Got to run,' said Nick, who had hurried to the door.

'Right,' said Hugo. 'Silver, may I have a word?'

'Yes, okay,' said Silver. She had pushed her ballet shoes into her bag and was buttoning up her cardigan. She smiled up at Hugo. 'I'm getting the hang of it, I think.'

'Yes, you are, but I have to say, Silver, I don't think your mind is entirely on the work. Am I right? Is there something worrying you?'

Anger flared in her eyes.

'You're joking, aren't you? Not entirely on my work? What are you saying? That I'm not up to scratch? No one else has ever complained about my dancing. I very nearly didn't take this job, you know. Jacques Bodette is waiting for me. I hope I'm not going to start wishing I hadn't agreed to dance with your company?'

Hugo deliberately made his voice gentle: 'Don't be angry, Silver. I'm not attacking you. I just think that you've been getting away with less than your best.'

'I don't believe it! What on earth are you saying? Are you saying you're sorry you offered me the part? I'm not staying here if I'm not wanted.'

'Of course you're wanted, Silver. Please don't misunderstand me. What I think is that you're much better than anyone realises. Even you. I think you have it in you to be someone really . . . ' Hugo paused to find the right word. 'Really legendary. But it's going to take phenomenal work.'

'What the hell do you think I've been doing all morning?' Silver looked as though she would happily throw her huge handbag at his head. She was keeping her temper, but only just.

'It's a waste of your energy to be angry, Silver. We're on the same side. All I'm trying to do is make you see that up to now you haven't even begun to reach the heights you're capable of.'

'And you're the one who's going to get me there, are you?'

'That's right. I am. I just need you to help me a little.'

'You're wrong, you know. Does anyone ever tell the great Hugo Carradine that he's wrong? I bet they don't. But you are. And I'll prove it to you. Of course I'm ready for the work.'

'Then I'll see you at rehearsal tomorrow, Silver. You're going to be wonderful.'

He left the room, feeling her eyes on him, almost feeling the grimace that she was undoubtedly making behind his back. Let her pull faces, he thought, she'll thank me in the end. She is going to be something that hasn't been seen for a generation.

Who the bloody hell did Hugo Carradine think he was? Silver was so furious at what had just happened that, for at least thirty seconds, she was already packing in her mind – throwing her suitcase into the back of her car and getting away from this hellhole. Then she calmed down a little, and took a deep breath. No way. She was not going to give up this chance. Not for Hugo bloody Carradine and not for anything else either. She wasn't going to let Hester Fielding get the story from her pet choreographer, not if she had anything to do with it. He'd put it about all over the place that Silver O'Connell couldn't cut the mustard when it mattered, and before long those clacking tongues that made sure every single rumour or story found its way everywhere would have done the damage and her reputation would be ruined. She pulled her scarf round her neck and squared her shoulders. There was nothing for it but to put up with his nonsense as best she could. She couldn't get over how different he was once he was in charge. Like a lot of men, really. Just give them some power and watch how they become tyrants. He'd been such a sweetie at the audition. So flattering too. *You're quite the most promising young dancer I've seen in years* were his exact words. What had happened since then?

As she walked back along the outdoor path, Silver tried hard to admire the garden, which was more like a park than the garden of a private house. It must take an awful lot of work to keep a place like this looking good. The wind was bitter and she put her head down to avoid the worst of it. She tried to think of the last time anyone had criticised her and couldn't. Ever since she'd started dancing, there had been nothing but praise from every single person she came across. Silver looked up and saw the clouds dark over the moors and, for a split second, she allowed herself to consider whether what Hugo said could have any truth in it. Impossible. Didn't she always try with one hundred percent of her energy and intelligence? A tiny voice, somewhere so deep in her mind that she hardly heard it, was saying, *you've always been able to do it with no effort. No one's noticed till now, that's all* but Silver paid it no attention and turned her mind, deliberately, to other things.

Sod Hugo. He'll soon see what he's got in me, she told herself. Everyone said she was the best. How come all of them were wrong and he was right? The opposite was probably true. And in any case, it was too late for him to find a substitute, so he'd never actually get rid of her. He was as stuck with her as she was with him. It wasn't any wonder he was saddled with a prima ballerina who was past it. And not only past it, but really cruel too. That remark at lunchtime to her kid about the bread roll when Alison was far from skinny was just plain unkind. It showed that Hugo had very poor judgement if he was in love with a creature like her. Other dancers probably steered well clear of him. Even as she was thinking this, Silver knew it was nonsense, but she allowed herself to be comforted by the thought that he wasn't nearly as famous as Jacques Bodette, who thought she was incomparable. He's forever saying it, and I believe him, Silver thought. Why shouldn't I?

I'm safe, Alison thought. Mum's there in the theatre, going over something with Hugo, and she'll be there till suppertime and I can go wherever I want. She was walking along the path without looking where she was going, and she'd been out for ages and ages. She wondered at first whether to be worried or upset by the fact that not a single person in the whole world, right now this minute, knew where she was. No one, she thought, gives a shit about me, and that's the truth. I could go and drown myself in that river and I bet Mum wouldn't even miss class the next day. I bet she'd even be pleased. Well, I'm not going to give her the satisfaction of having her photograph taken weeping and wailing over my grave. She's not worth getting all steamed up about.

This was a sentiment that Alison had persuaded herself of over many years. She couldn't remember exactly when it was, but about two or three years ago she'd come to certain conclusions. The main one was that she had to look after herself because no one else would if she didn't. She'd made all sorts of plans and her head was usually buzzing with dreams, like her favourite at the moment – of herself getting on a plane and taking off to go and find her father in America. She had his address. She wrote to him from time to time. The last letter had been just before Christmas, and now as she remembered it Alison blushed a little. It had been nothing but moaning from beginning to end: moaning about Claudia, moaning about having to go to Wychwood for over ten days, moaning about school, and on and on. Thinking about it, she could imagine her father sighing and tearing it up and putting it into the wastepaper basket. They called it the trash in America which made it sound even more rubbishy.

I haven't forgiven her for that remark at lunchtime. She thinks I forget all about the things she says a second or two after she says them, but just because she's a butterfly brain it doesn't mean that I am. I remember every single nasty remark she's ever made, and I wish I could tell her so. There ought to be a button I could press and then they'd all spool out, as though they were on a tape, recorded forever in my memory. I could say them to her one after another. That'd make her sit up. Maybe I will one day, too.

There was a light shining out of the downstairs window of a small house just ahead of her. She hadn't seen it before. She must have walked right past the theatre without knowing it and be at the back of it. Yes, that was right. Alison turned and saw the outline of the Arcadia, darker even than the nearly black sky.

The house or cottage or whatever it was looked a bit like Hansel and Gretel's house made of gingerbread and sugar and sweets, she thought. The house in the middle of the forest. She shivered a little and then said, half aloud, 'This isn't a forest, and Hansel and Gretel is a fairytale. Grow up, will you?'

She was just about to turn round and walk back the way she'd come, when the door of the fairytale cottage opened and she could see someone silhouetted against the light.

'Alison? Is that you?'

'Oh, Ruby! Yes, it's me. I didn't recognise you at first. I thought . . . never mind. I don't know how I got down here. I was just walking about.'

'Well, now that you're here, you can come in for a cup of tea with me, and then we'll go up to the house together.'

'Thank you. Is this where you live?'

'That's right. Me and George. You met him at lunchtime. He's still in the theatre, but he'll be by for his tea. Come along in. You must be cold out there.'

Alison found that a verse from her father's book was repeating itself in her head:

> Here is a doll
> dreaming of walking
> down the path to another house.

She dreams of a party
and drinking tea
and all the friends
she has gone to see.

She followed Ruby into the house and closed the front door behind her.

'I'll go and fetch the tea things. You sit down here, Alison, and make yourself comfortable.'

She left the sitting room then, and Alison could hear cup and saucer noises from the kitchen, which was down a small corridor. As she looked around the room, she noticed that in this cottage too, there was no sign of Christmas anywhere. It had struck her as strange when they arrived last night there wasn't a single card or decoration anywhere in Wychwood House, and no sign of a tree either. Hester must have got rid of everything on Boxing Day, which was most peculiar. And here in Ruby's cottage it was the same. She wondered whether she could ask about it and decided she probably couldn't. She went over to the mantelpiece to look at the photos that were lined up there. One or two of them were of Hester. You could see that it was her, even though she was young, because she was dressed in ballet clothes and hadn't changed all that much, really. The picture Alison liked best showed five children sitting on a bench in a park, or perhaps it was a big garden. The eldest girl had a kind of beret on, and she looked about fourteen. She wasn't smiling, but all the others in the photo were. Two of the littler children were boys and two were girls. The baby girl was sweet as anything, like a doll, and she had a bit of hair caught up in a ribbon. When she heard Ruby coming in with the tray, Alison turned round.

'I love this picture. Is it of your children?'

'No,' Ruby answered, putting the tea things down on a table between the sofa and the armchairs on the other side of the fire. 'That's me and my brothers and sisters. I'm the eldest.'

'You're lucky.' Alison took the cup of tea Ruby handed her and bit into buttered scone. 'I wish I wasn't an only child.'

'I used to wish I was,' Ruby smiled. 'Then I was ashamed of myself at once of course, but still, I couldn't help it. I always felt I was the one who had to look after them, be responsible for them. Too much for a young girl I suppose it was, looking back. I didn't think so at the time. I thought it was my duty, that's all.'

She set her cup down on the table and took out a piece of canvas from a basket lying beside the fire. 'You don't mind if I do my tapestry?'

'No, it's lovely. I like the colours. Is it a picture of anything?'

'Well, I don't have a printed pattern, if that's what you mean. I just seem to know what I want to do next.'

Alison noticed, as Ruby spoke, that there were cushions with tapestry covers on every chair; there was a firescreen pushed up against the wall which Ruby must have made as well.

'You do it jolly quickly,' she said.

Ruby smiled. 'Years of practice in dressing rooms here and there. I used to do it to keep myself busy while I was waiting to do a change of costume, or when a dress rehearsal went on into the night. They do that quite often.'

Alison helped herself to another scone and remembered briefly how furious she was with her mother. If she could see me now, she'd have a fit, Alison thought. I don't care though. It's delicious and I'm hungry. She watched Ruby's silver needle pricking in and out of the canvas, and wondered if she dared to ask why she'd been crying earlier, in Wardrobe. Would Ruby get upset and throw her out? How should she put it? Perhaps it would be tactful to pretend she'd never seen it. Ruby looked up from her tapestry.

'There's something troubling you, Alison. Am I right?'

'Well, not troubling me exactly, only – well – I wanted to ask you something and I don't know if you'd like me to. That's all.'

'Ask away.'

She couldn't. She couldn't ask about the crying. Instead, she said the first thing that came into her head. 'Why don't you have decorations or a tree up still? It's only just been Christmas.'

The silence that followed seemed to go on for a very long time. Ruby appeared to be completely absorbed in her tapestry and it was such ages before she lifted her head that Alison was on the point of saying something else, something quite different, to change the subject and make everything all right again. But Ruby spoke before she was able to think of the right words.

'We have never celebrated Christmas here. Not at any time since I started working for Hester. She . . . well, she's never really had a chance to, what with being someone who always worked on Boxing Day, all through her life as a dancer. It just didn't seem worth it, somehow, to put everything up and then not be able to appreciate it properly. And for the last ten years, of course, there's been the Festival. What with a company on the point of arriving and then the rehearsals and so forth, it never seemed . . .' She paused. 'Appropriate. There's always a party after the first night, and that's sort of taken the place of Christmas here at Wychwood.'

Alison nodded, only partly satisfied. 'I expect you have the turkey and things, don't you, even though there's no tree?'

Ruby shook her head and looked straight at Alison. 'Salmon, usually. Hester doesn't like Christmas pudding. And besides . . .' She shook her head. 'It's such a sad time of the year, isn't it? The longest night and all the trees looking so bare and nothing much in the garden. We're busy arranging the Festival. We try not to notice the dark days.'

'You were crying before,' Alison said, and the words were out of her mouth almost before she was aware of what she was saying. 'In the theatre. I wanted to know why you were, but I didn't dare to ask. It's none of my business, but—'

'Och, that was nothing to get upset about. I should have explained at once, I suppose, but I hadn't met you then. I was thinking of an old friend of ours, mine and Hester's, who died recently, that's all. Adam Lennister, his name was. He died far too young. I think it must have been passing the *Giselle* costume in the bar that put me in mind of him, because that was his favourite ballet. That's all.'

'I expect a Christmas tree and decorations wouldn't be right if you're in mourning, would it?'

'No, I suppose this year, Adam's death has made a celebration less possible than it usually is.'

Ruby resumed her stitching. Alison wondered again whether what she'd just heard was the whole story. There was nothing sinister or strange about being sad when someone you knew died. That was quite normal, but there was something in the way Ruby never once looked at her while she was speaking, and her eyes sort of moved from side to side in a way that Alison thought looked like someone who wanted to run away. She'd had a lot of practice with Claudia, who was always varnishing the truth, and she was almost sure that Ruby had been crying about something quite different; something she didn't want to talk about. Or maybe she was crying about more than one thing and had only told Alison about the most obvious one.

'Hello, ladies,' said someone, and Alison jumped up from her chair.

'You've met Alison, haven't you, George?'

'What a nice surprise. Come to have tea with us, have you?' said George. 'I hope you've kept a scone or two for me.'

He sat in the other armchair and Ruby took the tray out to the kitchen to make fresh tea for him. He picked up a scone and ate it in three swift bites.

'I had no idea when I married her that Ruby was such a good cook, but if I had, that would have been a very good reason to propose, I reckon. Have you had one?'

'Yes, they're lovely.' Alison racked her brain for something to say but found herself suddenly tongue-tied. She didn't have to worry, though, because George was someone who chatted away whether you joined in or not. He was just finishing a story about when he was in the army and had got in trouble with a sergeant for nicking someone else's cigarettes or something, when Ruby came back with the tea.

'I was just talking to that Nick chap, Ruby,' he told her. 'He's got a lot of good stories to tell about some of the London companies.'

Alison, who'd almost fallen into a doze, what with the warmth of the fire and the lovely food and the softness of the cushions in the armchair, sprang to attention mentally when she heard Nick's name mentioned. Alison knew that it was completely stupid and ridiculous to think that Nick might ever be interested in her, even if he wasn't gay, which she thought he might be. She was almost sure she'd heard Ilene mentioning something about this to Andy. Nick was just being friendly when he smiled at her and touched her arm. He's nice to everyone, she thought, and then something truly hideous occurred to her. What if he fancied Claudia? Lots and lots of men did, Alison knew that. Being nice to her daughter was a thing some of them did to make her like them. They weren't to know that this wasn't going to impress her.

Alison stifled a sigh. She could practically *see* a mood of misery and chilliness creeping over her. It looked like a grey, shapeless ghost and Alison knew that it was about to engulf her and then the pleasant feelings she'd been having, sitting here drinking tea with Ruby and her husband, would all disappear in a moment.

'Are you coming, darling?' Claudia was in a seductive mood. Nick had shaken her up rather. He was without a doubt the most gorgeous young man she'd seen for ages and he was having a predictable effect on her. She couldn't wait to rehearse their *pas de deux* tomorrow. Those long fingers holding her waist, his breath on her neck. She shivered. Hugo could have distracted her, but he was sitting at the small table in the corner of their bedroom, rather too preoccupied with the papers in front of him. That was his problem. He was dedicated. It didn't seem to matter a scrap to him that she'd arranged herself on one of the twin beds in a way that would have driven any normal man crazy. No, he was taken up with thinking about tomorrow's rehearsals and probably that Silver person. He clearly thought she was the cat's pyjamas, and saw her as the new, the young – yes, the *young* – up and coming star. Well, Claudia thought, there's time enough for him to worry about that tomorrow. He ought to be paying some attention to me now. She lay back on top of the duvet, with her breasts almost entirely exposed, and sighed. Hugo was running a hand through his hair and pretending he hadn't seen her.

'You're more interested in your scribblings about tomorrow's rehearsal than you are in me.'

'Not at all, darling.' But he sounded so far away that Claudia knew she was right. 'I'll be there in a second. I've just got to finish the notations for tomorrow's scenes.'

She closed her eyes and waited. Like this, it was easy to imagine that someone else – Nick – was going to come and stretch out beside her. She knew that lovemaking was probably the last thing on Hugo's mind, but she was beginning to feel more and more as though she needed, *had* to. And here he was, Hugo, lying next to her on the counterpane. He stroked her neck and whispered in her ear, sending tremors of pleasure through her body. She would keep her eyes tightly closed . . .

'Show me that you love me,' Claudia whispered, sliding her body under his.

'You're making it difficult for me to say no, Claudia. We'd better try to keep it quiet though. We're all so on top of one another in this house.'

'I'll be completely silent. I promise. Oh, Hugo, I want you so much. Please . . . please.'

She felt his arms around her. He was pulling her closer to him.

'Claudia,' he said, and then he was stifling her moans with his kisses. 'Sssh,' he said. 'Sssh, darling.'

'Oh,' said Claudia and moved her body in rhythm with his. 'Oh, Hugo darling, I won't . . . I can't . . .'

Much later, when they'd retired to their separate beds, Hugo fell asleep at once, but Claudia lay awake for a long time. During their lovemaking, she had found it very easy indeed to forget about Hugo altogether and use her imagination to conjure up Nick instead. That was bad news, wasn't it? That was the beginning of the end when you started imagining another lover. What if nothing came of it? She loved Hugo. She did. She'd been happy with him for a long time. Why did that have to change? Maybe it didn't. Maybe she could have her cake and eat it. But what if Nick wasn't interested? That wasn't a thought that would allow her to get to sleep, so Claudia deliberately turned her mind to other things, Nick's arms, for example, pulling her back against him. The smell of his body as they danced together. She went over the steps of the *pas de deux* in her head. Tomorrow they'd be dancing together. Please, she thought, as sleep overcame her, let me dream about him.

29 December 1986

'It's a bloody disaster!' Hugo sat down heavily on a chair in the rehearsal room and Silver could see he was having to make a huge effort to stop himself from kicking something. At his feet, three large boxes lay open, their contents spilling out on the floor. Silver saw some ragged feathers stuck to a mass of damp chiffon. That was my outfit, she thought. And that Harlequin-type colourful thing must be the Fool's costume. The props had been badly damaged. Scarlet roses made from some kind of plastic had been snapped off a couple of bushes. Goblets had huge dents in them. Baskets of fruit had been crushed. It was all a hideous mess.

Everyone was standing around, not quite sure what to say. It was clear that Hugo was in such a state that any remark might make him worse instead of better. Claudia stood behind him and Silver could see that she was dying to put a calming hand on his shoulder. At least this would give him something else to worry about and maybe get him off her back a bit. She wasn't looking forward to being told off for not pulling her weight in front of other members of the company. It was bad enough when they were on their own. She wondered whether to say something comforting about the costumes and decided it was probably safer to shut up. Ilene and Andy had huddled together in a corner and were whispering to one another. Nick was the first to dare to speak.

'Surely there's something we can do? We can get compensation, can't we? Insurance and so forth?'

'Fat lot of good insurance'll be when our costumes and props are ruined. I doubt very much if we can get replacements in time. New Year's Eve the day after tomorrow and then New Year's Day and then there's only a couple of days to the dress rehearsal. These aren't ordinary costumes out of stock. They've been specially made and Molly, the person who made them, is out of the country. I suppose we *could* send someone down to London to get some stuff off the rail at one of the theatre costumiers but it won't be the same. It won't be the *Sarabande* I intended.' He frowned and ran a hand through his hair. 'I don't want to depress anyone, but honestly, I don't know where this leaves our production.'

'How did it happen?' Everyone was wondering about this, but only Claudia was brave enough (or foolhardy enough, Silver thought) to ask.

'I should have thought that was obvious,' said Hugo, fixing Claudia with a look that would strip paint. 'Some stupid bugger left these boxes out in the rain at the station or something and everything's soaked through. Colour's run on the costumes and they've been torn. Look — and many of the props are broken. Not just wet, but stuff snapped in pieces. Disaster. I don't know what to do.'

Andy said, 'We ought to unpack everything, oughtn't we? To see the extent of the damage.'

Hugo sighed. 'I suppose so.' He glanced round the room in despair and his gaze fell on Alison who was sitting on a chair in the corner. I know why she's here, Silver thought. She tries to hide it, poor kid, but it's clear as clear. She's got a crush on Nick and she'll come to every single rehearsal, just in case she gets a smile out of him or something. Maybe I should put her straight.

Alison put up her hand, as if she were in a classroom.

'What is it, Alison?' Hugo sounded irritable.

'Sorry, Hugo, only I thought that if you asked Ruby, she'd know what to do. About the costumes, I mean.'

He sighed, and then said, more as a way of humouring Alison than because he thought it was a good idea, you could tell, 'Okay, okay, maybe she can. D'you know where she is?'

'She's in the laundry room in the basement, up at the house. Shall I go and fetch her?'

'Go on then. Meanwhile, the rest of you, let's get this lot packed away till Ruby gets here and do some actual dancing. At least that can be up to scratch even if nothing else can.'

Alison ran out of the room in search of Ruby, and Andy and Ilene made their way to the space marked out on the floor to represent the

Princess's room. Nick sat down and waved to Silver from the other side of the room and made a rueful face at her.

'Right,' said Hugo. 'When you're quite ready, Nick – thank you – I'll concentrate on this. Sorry, Andy and Ilene, this has eaten into your time a bit, but let's make a start.' From the tape recorder came the up-tempo, jig-like music that accompanied the Fool's dances.

'Right, Andy, sprightly, sprightly. God, you look like a pensioner on sleeping pills. Lively, for Heaven's sake!'

Silver wondered what would happen if Claudia came and sat next to her. She'd want to chat but Hugo couldn't bear a background of chattering during rehearsal and, in any case, what would they say to one another? Claudia had hardly spoken to her since they'd arrived at Wychwood. It would be hard to shut her up without annoying her. How was she supposed to do that? Claudia was, however, too clever to make Hugo crosser than he was already. She signalled Silver with a tilt of her head that clearly said 'come outside and have a natter', and left the room. Silver followed her out and found her already settled down in one of the chairs outside the rehearsal room.

'Come and have a chat,' she said to Silver. 'I can't bear sitting there in silence and watching other people go through their stuff, can you? Plus I reckon Andy and Ilene'll appreciate being left to themselves, right? It *can* be a bit intimidating to be watched sometimes, don't you think?'

'Yes, I suppose so,' Silver smiled. What Claudia meant was *it would put these lesser dancers off to have a prima ballerina like me seeing Hugo directing and correcting them.*

'Poor Hugo!' Claudia went on. 'Those costumes and props mean such a lot to him. He's *so* taken up with every detail, d'you know what I mean? Actually, I made a point of bringing my own costume with me, so I'll be wearing what I was supposed to wear all the time. It's better, I've found, to be safe than sorry.'

'Hmm,' said Silver. What could she possibly say? She struggled to find something. 'Ruby used to be Hester Fielding's dresser, didn't she? And there are lots of costumes upstairs in Wardrobe. Someone who was here at last year's Festival told me about it. I expect she'll find some things we can all wear.'

Claudia smiled at Silver and waved a hand, indicating that all talk of costumes bored her to tears. She leaned forward. 'Actually, I wanted to ask you about something else. Or someone else, really.'

'Who's that?' What was she after?

'Nick Neary. Do you know him? I can't think why our paths have never crossed. He's very good, isn't he?'

'Yes, excellent. What can I tell you about him? He's okay. I've done a couple of things with him.'

'Is he gay?'

There. That was it.

'Bi, I think. He's had boyfriends in the past, that I know for a fact, but then last year he had a thing with Lucy Bradshaw.'

'Really? You surprise me. Such a skinny, wretched-looking creature.'

Silver laughed. 'It's not as though the rest of us are plump, though, is it?'

'No, but you know what I mean . . .' Claudia indicated her generous bosom. 'In certain areas a bit extra is always very welcome.'

She laughed a deliberately sexy sort of laugh.

Pathetic, Silver thought to herself. Can it possibly be that Claudia had her eye on Nick? What about Hugo? She couldn't surely be planning anything while they were all living so much on top of one another? She said, not bothering to hide the fact that she was changing the subject 'Your Alison's a nice kid.'

'Oh, she's fine with other people,' Claudia said. 'It's only when you're her mother that you get the rough side of her tongue. And her father's buggered off to the other side of the Atlantic with his fancy woman, so of course I bear the brunt of everything. D'you mind if I ask you something?'

'Not at all,' Silver said, and wondered *what now?*

'I read somewhere that you're going to Paris to dance with French Opera Ballet again next year. Is that right? Amazing for you if it is.'

'Yes, I'm doing *Swan Lake* with them. In April. Just as a guest, though. I'm not joining the company. But I've got to do *Sellophane in G* for Jacques Bodette first, when this is over.'

'Oh, I see.' Claudia rummaged in her huge handbag and Silver could have sworn that she sounded disappointed. Why on earth, she thought, would Claudia care what I do when *Sarabande* is over? Could she be jealous? That's what it looks like. She knows she's getting older and she hates it. Does she think that Hugo might replace her with me? Maybe I ought to reassure her and tell her how useless he thinks I am, but why should I? Let her worry. She was so horrid to Alison and a bit of fretting won't kill her.

'Don't let it worry you, Hugo,' said Hester. 'I know exactly how you feel at this moment, as though the whole ballet is going up in smoke. It's easy to lose perspective, but do remember it's the dancing that everyone's coming to see when it comes right down to it.'

She was sitting on the *chaise-longue* with her shoes kicked off and her legs tucked under her. Siggy was curled up at the other end.

'I know, I know.' Hugo took a sip of the sherry that Hester had poured for him. He sighed and ran a hand through his hair. What a theatrical gesture, Hester thought, and wondered briefly whether Hugo wouldn't have made a wonderful dancer. She pulled her attention back to what he was saying.

'You're right, of course. I could redesign the whole thing to be minimal and have the whole cast dressed in black leotards and so forth, but the whole point of *Sarabande* is the glorious Bakst-like set and costumes that I had specially designed. The words I used when briefing her were things like "ornate" and "opulent" and "rich". We need a physical look that matches the music, which is like – well, you know what it's like. Luxurious and sweet and, like I said, opulent. We simply won't get the same effect in black T-shirts.'

Hester laughed. 'I'm sure you don't need to be so concerned. Isn't Ruby going to help sort it out?'

He nodded. 'Then you've nothing to worry about. She'll repair the damage, I promise you. She's much, much more than a wardrobe mistress. More like a magician. It'll be fine. Relax, Hugo, and tell me how the rest of the production is shaping up. How's Silver doing, for instance?'

'She's making a lot more effort, but now I sense a kind of resentment, underneath. Almost as though she's saying okay, I'll do it, because he says I must, but I'm sure as hell not doing anything willingly. She looks at me as though she's a rebellious teenager and I'm trying to dock her pocket money or something. But I'm getting there. I need her to look as though she's flying. She'll be wearing wings, of course, which will make a difference.'

'Those'll probably slow her down somewhat. Some *entrechats*, and *fouettés en tournant* might be effective.'

'Yes, that's a good idea. I have got her doing a great deal of running . . . *bourrés* galore.'

'Exhausting!' said Hester.

'She'll manage, I think. The rest of the cast are fine and Nick is outstanding.'

'I'm so glad.' Siggy had jumped off the *chaise* and gone to sit on Hugo's lap. 'Push him off if he worries you.'

'Not at all.' He stroked the cat that was stretched across his legs. 'I'm greatly honoured that he's chosen to sit on me.'

Hester closed her eyes for a moment. Hugo said 'Are you okay, Hester? I'm not tiring you, am I?'

'No, no, not at all. I'm just, well, a bit sad, I suppose. Tomorrow, someone I once knew very well is being buried. That's all.'

'I'm so sorry. Are you going to the funeral? And here I am going on and on about myself and my trivial problems.'

'No, it's quite all right, really. I hadn't – haven't – seen him for years and years. And the funeral's in America so it's out of the question. But Edmund, Edmund Norland, that is, will be there. He can tell me about it when he gets here after New Year.'

'I can't wait to meet him. I really hope he's happy with what I'm doing to his music. I'll leave you now.' He stood up. Siggy slid his body into the seat Hugo had just left and curled up with a low purr of satisfaction.

Ruby came in almost as soon as Hugo left and stood leaning against the desk.

'I'm glad you're not the sort of person who'd turn a cat out of his chair,' Hester said. 'Hugo thought he was being honoured when Siggy jumped on his lap. I didn't have the heart to tell him that was his way of asking to sit in the armchair. He's been telling me about the costumes. Are you going to be able to manage?'

'I'm sure I will. Some of the costumes are fine and I'm sure I can fix the damaged ones. There's not much we haven't got, but I'll go into Leeds and buy a few things I still need. I might take Alison with me. I came to see how you are, Hester.'

'Oh, Ruby, how kind you are! I'm fine. Truly. I go hours and hours without thinking about it at all. But with the funeral tomorrow, of course my mind does go back . . .'

'You shouldn't let it,' Ruby said gently. 'You should look forward to seeing Edmund very soon.'

'Yes, I know. I am. I do think of that, but all sorts of other thoughts spring up. Then I have to make a real effort to concentrate on the future. There's lots to occupy me here at the moment, but still . . . What about you, Ruby? Are you managing?'

'Me? Why, of course!' Ruby spoke as though her mental state, her inner composure, were not in the least relevant.

'You look a bit pale, that's all. Are you sure you're not getting one of your headaches?'

'No.' Ruby looked towards the door. She's going to leave soon, Hester thought. The conversation is edging towards territory she doesn't like. Sure enough, when Ruby spoke again, it was to say goodbye.

'I must go, Hester. If that's all right with you. I only popped in for a moment. George'll be wanting his tea.'

'Yes, do go, of course. I'll see you later. Don't worry about me.'

Ruby glanced back as she left the room and Hester saw something in her eyes, a kind of sorrow or fear, or perhaps a mixture of the two. She'd picked up on this many times in the years they'd been together, but hadn't been able to bring herself to ask Ruby about it. What would she have said? She knew that confession wasn't something Ruby approved of. She believed in people keeping their emotions under control.

Hester sighed. Maybe it's nothing, she thought. Maybe she's just sad, like me, to think of Adam with earth piled up and covering him. She shivered. She wouldn't cry. She absolutely refused to cry for Adam.

30 December 1986

Thick snow had fallen overnight, and Alison wondered whether she and Ruby would still be able to get into Leeds today. She'd been looking forward to the trip, but the snow was exciting too. Alison noticed the first flakes drifting down yesterday as she was drawing the curtains before she went to bed. She made the same wish she always made when she saw it coming down: please let it lie. Please let the world be transformed when I wake up. Now, everywhere she looked, there was nothing but white and more white outlining the branches on every tree; covering the grass and the paths, and blanketing the curve of the moor. It's lovely, she thought. If I started making a snowman, would anyone else join in? They'd probably be too busy with rehearsals to do anything that was just for fun.

The snow had changed everything. The lawns, the paths, the trees, and the moors in the distance didn't really look white, but had shadows on them that were blue and mauve and grey and there was a silence surrounding her that was more than just quiet. It felt as though a muffling blanket had been thrown over everything. Siggy had obviously been out, at least for a while. There were his paw prints leading to one of the flowerbeds and then back again to the house but, as far as she could see, she was the first human to step out after breakfast.

Waking up and finding the whole garden draped in snow was brilliant. She looked at the footprints she was making in the white expanse, and then she looked at the moors behind the house, melting into a mass of greyish-purple clouds. It won't turn to slush here under thousands of feet and wheels and artificial lights, she thought. I must remember all the colours and try and put them down on paper later so that I don't forget. Would it be better in watercolour? Probably, but crayons were what she had available and she would have to make do.

'Hello!' Alison turned round at once to see who was calling her. Hester was striding towards her, as though she wanted to say something to her. She was dressed in a dark blue coat and a woollen hat knitted in shades of red and pink. When she spoke, streamers of white vapour came from her mouth.

'I saw you as I was coming back from my walk. Isn't the snow wonderful? I love Wychwood when it looks like this. Mind if I join you?'

'No, of course not,' Alison answered and immediately wondered what they were going to talk about. Hester fell into step beside her and they walked down the drive in the direction of the theatre. The sun had just risen and pale rays were lighting up the moorside. The sky wasn't really blue, more a sort of very pale grey, but the snow glittered where the sunlight caught it and some of the trees had branches that were tipped with gold. The crunching of their boots on the path was the only sound in the landscape.

'I've always liked the snow,' Hester said. 'Maybe you could make a snowman near the house. Has anyone suggested it?'

'They're going to be busy rehearsing, I expect. They're always rehearsing. If they're not at class.'

'It must be most peculiar to anyone who isn't involved, I know. The thing is, they haven't got long and Hugo seems to be a perfectionist.'

'My mum is too. She's never happy with what she does. She's always moaning about not having enough time to do things. It's okay. I'm used to her rehearsing all the time.'

'Are you bored, Alison?'

'Oh, no, not at all. It's lovely here. I thought I might be bored, but I'm not.'

They walked together through the gate and down the village street.

'I used to live there when I was a little girl.' Hester pointed at a very ordinary house, set back from the road. 'With my mother's cousins. The Wellicks, they were called. I wonder where they are now.'

'Don't you know?' Alison burst out, and then wondered whether she sounded a little rude.

'We've lost touch, I'm afraid. I wasn't very nice to them when I was a girl, I think. They did their best to look after me. I see that now, but at the time, well, I didn't want to leave my grandmother and everything I knew and Yorkshire was very different from what I'd been used to in France. I couldn't have been the easiest child in the world to look after.' She smiled. 'I went to London when I was fourteen to study ballet and only came back here long after they'd left.'

Alison thought about this. She'd never really considered the possibility of simply leaving someone you didn't like. What would it be like to leave Claudia? She shivered. I wouldn't know where to go, or what to do on my own. Dad would most likely look after me so I'd be okay, and maybe I should do it, she told herself. Mum and I are always fighting. Would I miss her if I lived somewhere else?

'I don't think I'd be brave enough to leave home,' she said finally.

'It's different for you,' Hester said. 'You have your mother. Mine died when I was five and the Wellicks couldn't really take her place, however hard they tried.'

'That's awful,' Alison said, and stopped in the middle of the road to look at Hester. She seemed so glamorous, so self-possessed. It was hard to imagine her as a small child, with no mother to take care of her. Just thinking about it made her want to cry.

Hester nodded and went on walking, looking down at her feet. 'I was lucky, though. My first ballet teacher became a sort of mother to me. She was Russian. Olga Rakovska was her name and Wychwood was her house. She left it to me when she died.'

'Did you have a father?' As soon as she spoke, Alison realised both what a stupid question it was (*of course she had a father, you idiot*) and also that it was probably cheeky to ask someone she hardly knew about such things. Hester didn't seem to mind, though.

'I didn't get on very well with my father. I hardly saw him after I was five. I suppose he must have loved me in his way, but I can't remember him ever showing me that he did.'

'How horrible for you! My dad loves me, but he's in America so I don't see him very often. I wrote to him and told him we were here. He usually writes back.'

'Don't worry. The post's always delayed around Christmas. I expect he's written back and the letter's been held up.'

Alison nodded. 'Maybe.' She changed the subject because she didn't want to say anything nasty about her mother to Hester, who was probably like everyone else and filled with admiration for Claudia. 'I'm going to help Ruby with the costumes and things. We were supposed to be going into Leeds this afternoon, but maybe we won't be able to with this snow. I like working with my hands, which is lucky, because I couldn't ever be a ballet dancer.'

Hester stopped walking and looked at Alison. 'There's nothing wrong with *not* being a ballet dancer, you know. It's very easy for those of us who do it to forget that there's a whole world of normal people out there . . .' She waved a gloved hand in the air '. . . who eat normally, are all sorts of different shapes and sizes and don't spend their nights flying through the air dressed in chiffon and satin.'

'I suppose so. But I always feel fat and clumsy next to Mum.'

'You're not fat and clumsy. You must know that. Just a normal person. And if you don't have ambitions to dance, I don't see that it matters what size you are. D'you know what you want to be when you leave school?'

'I'm going to be a midwife.'

'Really? That would be . . . interesting.'

Alison thought she could hear a change in Hester's voice, but perhaps she'd imagined it.

They'd reached the end of the village street and Hester turned in the direction of Wychwood House.

'I think we should go back now,' she said, and Alison nodded. They talked a little on the way back, about *Sarabande* and how she'd known the person who composed the music since she was a young girl, but Alison had the impression, she wasn't quite sure why, that something had changed. Did I say anything to upset her, she wondered, but couldn't think of what it might have been.

1951

Hester lived for Sundays. That was the only day of the week when there were no rehearsals, no classes, no dancing of any kind to take her mind away from Adam and how much she loved him. For the rest of the week, she had to survive without him for the most part, though he sometimes came to the evening performance and waited till everyone had left the theatre before taking her to dinner somewhere far from the Royalty. They tried to be discreet, but Hester had begun to think that Piers had his suspicions. Once, during class, he remarked on Adam's new-found love of ballet. He spoke casually, but she felt that he was looking at her searchingly, trying to find out what was going on.

'You girls who danced at Virginia Lennister's party made a convert, didn't you? Adam's here almost every night. But then I suppose he might be coming to keep Edmund company.'

Sundays were theirs; hers and Adam's. That was the day that Dinah and Nell spent with their parents, and both of them left the Attic de Luxe early in the morning. Hester waited till they'd gone and then she bathed and dressed as though she were getting ready for a performance and at ten o'clock she walked to the end of Moscow Road, where Adam always waited for her in his black car.

They hardly spoke as they drove to the flat in Chelsea. But as soon as the door had closed behind them they relaxed, and Hester pretended, as she did every time she was with him, that they were a married couple. That this was their home, and that they were spending Sunday together as man and wife. She never mentioned this dream to Adam, but apart from that, there was nothing they didn't speak about.

'I wasn't very good at being a kid,' he said, tracing the veins on the back of her hand with his fingers. 'My parents sent me away to boarding school when I was about ten and somehow, every time I went home for the holidays, they seemed more and more distant, as though they had nothing to do with me. They were killed in a car accident when I was thirteen. I was terribly shocked, then sad, but in a disembodied way. I liked school, or heaven knows what would have become of me. Edmund helped. He's younger than me, so he didn't have that much to do with me at school, but his parents were friendly with mine so after they died I spent holidays with his family. We're more like brothers than friends, in some ways. I tell him everything, normally. I suppose one day I'll have to . . .'

'He knows about us already. I told him,' Hester said, turning in the bed and leaning on her elbow and looking down at Adam. 'Are you angry? I wanted to talk to someone who knows you.'

'How could I ever be angry with you? Kiss me. Edmund won't say a word. He's fond of you, you know.'

She concentrated on the kiss. Should I tell him about what Edmund said about everyone finding out in the end, she wondered. She was finding it hard to think, with Adam's mouth on hers, with his body pressed against hers.

As they lay in the wide double bed, peaceful after lovemaking, she said, 'I sometimes think I've never really talked to anyone before. I used to tell my grandmother everything, but that was when I was such a tiny child. Just babbling, really, I suppose. And then Madame Olga, of course. I spoke to her, but that was mostly about the ballet. *She* was the one who used to tell *me* things. Well, she'd had so many adventures. Lovers, and so forth. I had nothing to tell her in exchange.'

Adam laughed. 'You could speak to her about us. D'you think she'd be shocked?'

'Of course she would! Not because of what you think, though. I'm sure the fact that you're married wouldn't be the thing she objects to nearly as much as that you might steer me away from the ballet. I have to do my best to fulfil my potential; she's always said that, and I want to, as well, only . . .'

'Only what?' Adam picked up her hand where it lay outside the blankets and began to kiss it, moving his lips up and up her arms.

'I get distracted easily. You're distracting me now. I was thinking about my dancing and suddenly I can only think of you, and what you're doing.'

'You like it, don't you?'

'Oh yes.' Hester said. 'Oh yes, I do. I love it. Please don't stop.'

Much later, she sat at the kitchen table, fully dressed. She'd begun to feel the creeping sadness that always came over her as the day began to slip away towards the time when she'd have to leave Adam and resume what she thought of now as her other life; her normal, everyday life, where she had to hide emotions that might betray what many would think of as disgraceful behaviour. Was it, though? Was what they were doing so wrong when it made them so happy? If they could keep it a secret, and if no one ever knew about it, how could they be hurt? Hester was thinking of Virginia. If Adam's wife found out . . . this was something she dreaded and yet, at the same time, there was a tiny voice in her head, which usually spoke to her as the time of her parting from Adam approached. This time, she couldn't help herself. The words were out of her mouth before she could stop them.

'Adam, what would happen if Virginia found out about us?'

He gazed at her and didn't answer for a few moments and Hester's heart thudded with dread. Finally, he spoke. 'She'd be very hurt. In spite of the distance between us, she's possessive. It doesn't matter to her that she doesn't have a good relationship with me, but she would hate someone else to be having one, I'm quite sure. Still . . .' He paused. 'It's going to have to happen, isn't it? If we're going to be together. I'll have to tell her one day. Ask for a divorce. And when I do—'

Hester stared at him, hardly daring to breathe. Was he proposing to her? Was this *marriage* he was speaking of? Adam laughed.

'You should see yourself! You look as though I've said something really shocking. I want to marry you and be with you for the rest of my days. In fact, I can't imagine a life without you. There. Should I go down on one knee?'

'No. No of course not. But yes, I'd love to marry you. Oh, Adam, I've been so afraid.'

'What of, my darling?'

'Well, there's so much. You not loving me any longer. Virginia finding out. You deciding you're too old for me. There's so much to worry about that I don't know where to begin.'

'I shan't stop loving you, Hester. No matter what happens. Not ever. I promise.'

'Really?'

'Truly.'

'I'll have to go soon.'

'Don't go yet. Come here. Kiss me.'

'Dinah and Nell will . . . will be . . .' she meant to say, 'back from their parents' or 'back in the Attic de Luxe' but the words were stifled by his mouth and she gave herself over to sensations that would have to last her for a whole week. *I shan't stop loving you, Hester. Not ever. No matter what happens. I promise.* The words echoed in her mind. What *would* happen? What did he mean? She shivered. Why did everything have to be so complicated?

'Hester, is that you snoring?'

'No, Dinah,' Hester whispered. 'It's Nell.'

'Why aren't you asleep, then?'

'I don't know. Why aren't you?'

'I'm worried about you, that's why.'

'Me?'

'We can't talk like this.' Just enough light filtered under the door for Hester to see that she'd sat up in bed. 'Let's go downstairs. Everyone else is asleep. We can make a drink and take it into the Green Room.'

'We'll be exhausted in the morning. What'll Piers say?'

'I won't tell him if you won't. Come on, we're not getting any sleep here anyway.'

Hester pulled on her dressing-gown and tiptoed behind Dinah downstairs to the kitchen.

'I'll make the tea. You bring that tray over here.'

Moscow Road was organised like a bed and breakfast establishment. Some of the dancers had their own bedrooms and others shared, but the large front room, always called the Green Room, acted as a lounge for everyone. The furniture had seen better days, and so had the carpets and curtains, but the room was comfortable in a faded sort of way. A large oval table stood in the bay of the window, and Dinah put the tray down there and poured the tea. She handed a cup to Hester, who was perched on the edge of one of the armchairs. Dinah looked searchingly at her and said, 'You look as though you might suddenly jump up and run away. Okay, I'm not taking no for an answer. Tell me what's going on with you and Adam.'

'You know what's going on. I told you. You and Edmund are the only people I have told. I couldn't bear to hide anything from you.'

'But it's serious, isn't it? It's not just the sex.' She ticked the points she was making off on her fingers. 'You're in a dream all day long. You don't hear what people are saying to you half the time. I know you see one another every Sunday. Then there's the matter of how you look.'

'How I look?' Hester was longing to discuss Adam with Dinah. How wonderful to be able simply to speak his name whenever she felt like it; tell another person how much she loved him, how she dreamed of a whole life with him, how golden the time was when they were together and how grey and dim the world looked when they were apart. Edmund wouldn't like talking about anything like that. It didn't seem to be the sort of thing you told a man, but Hester wondered whether Adam would confide in his friend, now that he knew she'd already told him everything.

'You look,' said Dinah, 'like a rosebud that's just opened up. Or as though there's a light somewhere inside you that's shining out of your eyes. Oh God, that sounds ridiculous. But you know what I mean. You had the same look during Act One of *Giselle* when you were supposed to be in love. Passionately in love.'

Hester nodded. 'I am. I'm in love.' Dinah leaned forward to hear more.

'Is it wonderful? Is it as glorious as you expected it to be?'

'Better. I can't describe how being with Adam makes me feel. Please don't tell anyone else, though, will you? Not even Nell. Do you promise?'

'Of course I won't tell.' Dinah took a strand of her hair, and twisted it round her finger. 'Oh, Hester, you poor darling! What are you going to do?'

'Do?'

'Well,' Dinah closed her eyes. 'What's going to happen? What if Piers finds out? He'll murder you both. He won't care about the morals of it, but he'll be furious if your dancing suffers.'

'My dancing won't suffer. I won't let it. It's the one thing . . .' Hester paused and Dinah said, 'What? The one thing what?'

'That won't suffer. Nothing's going to stop me from dancing. I'd die if I couldn't dance. Don't worry about that, Dinah. Really. That's not what's on my mind.'

'Nor me. Not really. I'm thinking of something else. Something that hasn't occurred to you, obviously.'

'If you mean his wife, I think about her all the time. I feel so guilty and bad and, well, just horrible in every way. I do, really.'

'But not bad enough to stop you making love to her husband.'

Hester could feel her eyes brimming with tears. 'Don't say that. I can't help it. I'm – I can't help myself. If I could, I would, I promise you. If I could love Edmund, for instance, I'd be so happy, but I can't. I'm just paralysed with love. When I'm with him, Dinah, oh, it's impossible to describe, but I feel as though every skin cell and nerve end is tingling and vibrating and just almost exploding. I don't know how to stop them, those feelings. When I'm away from him I feel as though I've been imprisoned. Except when I'm dancing. I just live for the times when we're together. It's awful. It's wonderful. I don't know what to do.'

Dinah said nothing for a few moments. Then she sighed. 'It's like an illness, isn't it? I know. I do understand, but I've got to warn you of a couple of things. I don't mean to be a spoilsport or anything, but I'm a bit older than you—'

'Only eighteen months or so.'

'Don't interrupt. You do realise, don't you, that there's no future for the two of you. Has he spoken to you about the future? Has he mentioned it?'

Hester smiled. 'Yes. Today he told me he was going to divorce his wife. He's asked me to *marry* him, Dinah. Really. I couldn't believe it at first, but he meant it. He's going to tell Virginia everything. That's what he said.'

'You do know, don't you, that they say anything sometimes? Men, I mean. They say what they think you'd like to hear. That's what I wanted to tell you. Listen to me, Hester, and don't get cross, okay?'

'I won't. Promise.'

'He's not going to leave his wife. He maybe thinks he is, at this very moment, but he won't when it comes to it. Have you forgotten Orchard House? Think of what he'd lose if he left his wife for you. And you should ask him if he's still sleeping with her.'

'He couldn't be. It's impossible. You don't know, Dinah. You don't know how we . . . he would never . . .'

'I'm sorry, Hester. I know what it must seem like to you, but they do, you know. Sleep with their wives, I mean. If only to keep them from becoming suspicious, from finding out what's going on. You must see that.'

Hester sat in the chair and felt as though her body was turning to stone. That hadn't crossed her mind. Adam and Virginia, in a bed like that one they'd all sat on in the guest bedroom at Orchard House; Adam and Virginia together, doing things that Adam and she . . . oh God, it made her feel ill to think about it. How would she live with these new pictures in her head?

'He doesn't see all that much of her,' she whispered at last. 'They live almost apart.'

'Almost,' said Dinah, 'but not entirely. Ask him, if you don't believe me.'

'Never. I'd never ask him. I'd be frightened to hear the answer. Oh, Dinah, I can't go on like this. What's going to happen to me?'

'You're going to drink that tea and come to bed. Everything will look brighter in the morning. It always does.'

'Class and rehearsals and then a performance,' Hester said. 'At least I don't have time to think too much.'

'Tell me about Mr Lennister,' Dinah said. 'He's so handsome. D'you enjoy yourself when you're with him?'

'Well, of course I do. I told you.'

'No, I don't mean that,' Dinah said. 'I mean fun. D'you have fun?'

Hester said nothing for a few moments. Dinah's question made her think about the way she and Adam spent their time together. They only ever met in his flat. They made love. They cooked meals and ate them. They'd been for walks, long walks. Nothing else. They'd never been to the cinema, or an art gallery. Apart from Edmund, she'd never met any of his friends. *It's not his fault*, she told herself. *It's not my fault. We have so little time together that we don't want to waste it doing normal, mundane things.* She knew what she wanted, more than fun, more than entertainment, more than conversation: she wanted to lie next to Adam and cling to him and smell his skin and his hair and drink him in at every pore. She wanted to be part of his flesh, as he was part of hers.

'No,' she answered Dinah finally. 'I don't suppose you would call it fun. But we're together so seldom. It's all a bit . . .'

'Passionate?'

'Yes, I suppose that's it. Intense. It takes up my whole head, every minute when I'm not dancing.'

'Let's try and sleep, okay? Otherwise you won't be dancing up to standard tomorrow and then Piers'll be after you.'

Dinah led the way upstairs and Hester followed. I can lie in my bed till morning, she thought, and pretend. I can imagine his body beside mine. I can think what it would be like to wake up and find him sleeping beside me. She slipped into bed, and listened as Dinah's breathing grew heavier and slower, and then she closed her eyes. If she concentrated, she found she could still feel the touch of his hands on her skin. The memory of him inside her and his mouth on her mouth made her whole body ache. She was weak with the delicious pain of longing for him.

'Hester? Are you crying?'

'No,' she whispered, trying to swallow the tears that had started to slide down her cheeks in the dark. She knew that if she moved to find a tissue, or if she sniffed, Adam would realise and then—

'You are,' he said, tracing a finger over her face. 'My darling girl, you're crying. Don't, Hester, please. Please don't cry.' He turned towards her and tried to gather her into his arms again, but she shook him off.

'No, really.' Hester was anxious to keep her voice even and normal, even though she felt like howling aloud. 'I'm all right. I'll be all right.'

'But what is it? What is it, my darling? I can't stand to see you unhappy. Tell me.'

Hester shook her head, unable to speak. How could he possibly make her happy when everything was so completely ghastly? But she had to say something, anything, or he'd go on and on and then she'd have to get up and go, and she didn't want to waste a minute of her time with him because they weren't going to be able to be together until well into the new year. She sniffed and took a deep breath.

'Dinah's leaving. She's had a good offer from a company in Cardiff and she'll have the chance to dance principal roles. Of course she's got to go, because it's wonderful for her, and I'm happy for her sake. But I'll miss her so much and it won't be the same, not living in the Attic de Luxe any longer. Nell's moving downstairs to another room and so am I. It's hard to believe that we're not the most junior dancers in the company any longer.'

'That's a shame,' Adam said. 'I know how close you are. Poor Hester. But you'll keep in touch, won't you? By letter and so forth. And I'm still here and I love you. You know that, don't you?'

She nodded in the dark. She didn't point out to him – she didn't dare – that it was some weeks since he'd promised to ask his wife for a divorce and now, well now, he'd done something for which she would find it hard to forgive him. For a moment, thinking about the hideousness of it, Hester wondered whether it would be sensible to keep quiet and not say anything, but she was filled suddenly with rage and she sat up in the bed and the words came pouring out of her before she could stop them.

'If you want to know the truth, Adam, mostly I'm crying because I'm so angry. I'm angry with *you*.'

'Me?' Adam sounded genuinely shocked. 'What do you mean?'

'You've arranged for us to go out to dinner after the first night of *Red Riding Hood*. Me and you and Edmund, and your wife. How *could* you? Don't you know that every second sitting at that table will be torture for me? How can I look her in the face? Didn't you think for one moment how it would feel to me, to be sitting there with her?

189

You obviously didn't or you couldn't have fixed up such a nightmare. And after the first night, too. How am I supposed to dance when I know that's waiting for me afterwards?'

She flung herself back against the pillows and covered her face with one arm. Adam put out his hand and turned her towards him, so that they were lying with their faces almost touching. She could feel his breath on her skin.

'Hester, my darling, I had to do it. I couldn't get out of it. Virginia asked particularly to meet you when she heard you were dancing the name part in *Red Riding Hood* and it was she who insisted it would make a wonderful Christmas treat for us on Boxing Day, and wouldn't it be fun to eat together afterwards and ask Edmund too. Now how could I possibly say no? Wouldn't that have given the whole game away? "No, sorry, darling, we can't go out afterwards because the ballerina you're so keen on is my mistress."'

'Yes, I understand,' Hester said coldly, turning away from Adam in one swift movement and flinging herself out of bed. 'I should have thought of that. You'd have been quite powerless in that situation. I do see, of course.'

'You *are* angry, Hester. Oh God, don't be angry. Forgive me. Please, Hester, my love. How could I possibly—'

'I know. You couldn't. You couldn't let *darling* Virginia suspect anything.' She bit back a remark she was just on the point of making, about how he'd promised to tell his wife about them; promised to ask for a divorce. I won't, she told herself. I won't do that. I'll never mention it again and let's see if he does. And *mistress*. Hester supposed it was true, but how wounded she'd felt when he said it. She had foolishly imagined that she, Hester Fielding, was more than that. Special. Different. Not like all those ordinary people who were sleeping with someone else's husband. How naïve! How stupid! Dinah would say *I told you so* or *what did you expect?*

She sat on the side of the bed, pulling on her stockings, trying not to start crying again, wanting only to be out of Adam's house and in the street, going home to Dinah and Nell and then getting up tomorrow and concentrating on getting herself ready for the first night. On what she was meant to care about: the ballet. Everything she'd been working so hard for over the last few weeks.

'Stop it, Adam,' she said. He'd crossed over to her side of the bed, and put his arms around her waist as she sat there, and then he began to kiss her naked back, and touch her breasts gently, and pull her towards him, murmuring into her skin words she couldn't hear but which sounded like her name, and *please*, and *love* and all the things that made her weak when she heard them. She leaned into his body, loving how his lips were moving over the skin of her back to her neck and then her ear.

'Come to bed again, Hester,' he whispered. 'You don't have to go yet. I'll drive you home later. I can't bear it if you leave now. Please, darling Hester. Come here.'

She let herself be drawn into the bed again, into forgetting everything but their bodies. As he began to kiss her everywhere, everywhere, she thought fleetingly of how often they seemed to use sex in order not to have to think; not to have to confront reality or consider what their situation was, or was going to be, but then her thoughts began to unravel and soon she forgot everything; every last word that had been in her mind to speak melted away and disappeared.

'I've got a present for you,' Adam said later. 'For Christmas.'

'And I shall try and find one for you that won't give anything away if your wife comes across it.' Hester laughed, to show that she was no longer sulking about the first night dinner; that she was going to be a good sport and pretend like mad for the sake of – what? She wasn't quite sure, maybe the *status quo*, that she was no more to Adam than someone who'd just danced the main part in one of Edmund's ballets. 'What's this? May I open it now?'

'Yes, I want you to. I want to look at your face when you see what it is. And I want to think of you when you use it.'

She undid the wrapping carefully. The gold paper was slippery under her hands. Inside was a robe made of black satin with the image of a golden dragon embroidered on the back. The dragon's head was near the shoulder and a shimmering, scaly tail twisted and wound down towards the hem. It was the most beautiful garment Hester had ever seen that wasn't a costume to be worn on stage. The black and gold seemed to slip and glitter and shine in her hands.

'Oh!' she said, as she turned it over and over, stroking the fabric, loving it, loving the opulence of it, the luxury and splendour. 'Oh, how lovely! I shan't want to wear it at all, it's so beautiful. But I will. I won't even wait until Christmas. I'll wear it tonight and it'll remind me of you every time I put it on. It's . . . I can't describe what it makes me feel. Where did you find it?'

'There's a shop near the British Museum. I saw it in the window and knew it was made for you. Do you like it? Really?'

'I love it, Adam. I'll treasure it for ever, I promise you.'

'I love you, Hester. You know that, don't you?'

'Yes,' she answered. 'Of course I do.'

Even as she said it, she wondered whether she believed her own words.

Red Riding Hood opened on Boxing Day. The theatre was full of children and parents and everyone seemed pleased to be there, but Hester was too worried about what would happen after the show to be anxious about the ballet itself. She took off the gold chain, wrapped it in a handkerchief and hid it carefully, as usual, in the cigar-box where she kept all her make-up. Her costume (a peasant outfit *à la Giselle* with a silk hooded cape over the top) was pretty and Edmund's music was a joy to dance to. She thought about her first entrance, with the forest painted on flats on each side of the stage and the backdrop showing a path through the trees with a little house in the background. During rehearsals, she'd occasionally imagined *Grand-mère* as the person she was going to visit, but this was impossible once she'd seen Miles as the wolf. Both in his dress suit in the forest and later in the grandmother's dress, the effect was comical.

'We do not want droves of mothers fleeing the theatre with their screaming tots terrified of the Wolf,' Piers said.

Hester stood up and left the dressing room. What would happen after the ballet was over, she wondered for the hundredth time, but she pushed this to the back of her mind and set out for the wings to make her entrance stage left.

Dinah was helping Hester to dress for the dinner she had been dreading, and was right in the middle of putting up her hair. She had pushed Piers, and all the others who'd been congratulating Hester on her performance, out of the dressing room a few moments before. Adam and Virginia were waiting in the theatre bar. Edmund was coming to fetch Hester.

'Stop twitching and sit still,' Dinah said. 'I'm going to make your hair into a sophisticated upswept whatsit but I can't if you keep turning this way and that.'

Hester was sitting on the stool in front of the mirror, wearing her dragon robe.

'I'm just checking my eyes, and my lips. Are they okay? You don't think I've got too much make-up on?'

'No such thing, I don't think.'

'Of course there is! I don't want to look brassy and artificial.' Hester peered at her image in the mirror and grimaced.

Dinah laughed. 'You don't. You look dewy and virginal.'

'I don't! Do I really?'

'Yep. An accident of your features and colouring, I suppose. Also elegant and cool. All the good things you're supposed to be according to the best magazines.'

Hester's eyes met Dinah's in the mirror. 'I'm terrified, Dinah. What am I going to say to her?'

'You'll be fine. Edmund will talk a mile a minute and you don't have to speak much if you don't feel like it. Just blush winsomely and tuck in to your smoked salmon or steak or whatever you're having.'

'Hester? Are you decent?' Edmund stuck his head around the dressing-room door. 'Oh golly, you look fantastic. We ought to go now. Are you nearly ready?'

She nodded. She had put on a hyacinth-blue silk blouse with long, full sleeves and a black pencil skirt. On her feet, she wore black satin court shoes. She'd borrowed a black velvet cape from Wardrobe. She pulled it around her and joined Edmund at the door.

'Are you okay, Hester?' They were in the corridor leading down to the stage door.

'I think so. I hope so.'

'I'll be there, you know. You can talk to me, whenever you're feeling . . . well, whenever you like.'

Hester flung her arms round Edmund's neck and kissed him on the cheek.

'You're so good to me! I don't know how I'd manage anything without you. I'm dreading this evening so much, you can't begin to imagine.'

Edmund smiled. 'Well, if your dread has this effect, I might wish you'd be scared more often. But nothing bad will happen. It'll be perfectly all right, you'll see. I know how hard it'll be for you, but take my advice and pretend. It's easy when you're used to it. Pretend you're just another ballerina who hardly knows Adam. Pretend you've only just met. Okay?'

They were now outside the stage door and she couldn't say what she was thinking, but it occurred to her that Edmund wasn't going to feel exactly comfortable either. Hester didn't know whether Adam had confided in him, but she had, and he would be aware of the hidden meanings in everything. Hester was grateful for his affection and support and realised suddenly how much she relied on him. All through the rehearsals for *Red Riding Hood*, during raucous meals at Gino's with the rest of the cast, and on the rare occasions when they were alone, he directed a strong, steady warmth of friendship at her which never wavered and never altered. She tried out her happy smile, and kept it fixed on her face as she stepped out of the stage door to meet Adam and his wife, while her heart thumped painfully in her throat. It'll soon be over, she thought. It'll be all right.

Edmund and Hester were on one side of the table and Adam and Virginia on the other. The restaurant was the sort of place which Hester would have enjoyed describing to Dinah and Nell once she got home, but she wasn't paying the surroundings the attention they deserved. She vaguely took in walls covered in something like dark red velvet, pink-shaded lamps everywhere and white china that sparkled and shone on pink linen tablecloths. I'll have to tell Madame Olga something about it, Hester thought. She knew how infuriated her old teacher was to have been prevented from coming to the first night by a bad attack of flu. A good description of this restaurant would cheer her up. The food was probably delicious as well, though it could have been *papier-mâché* as far as she was concerned. Virginia, on the other hand, she could have described to her friends in detail because, while everyone was talking, Hester looked at Adam's wife and saw how pretty she was: fair, with blue eyes that were lighter than she remembered and long, curly blonde hair twisted up on top of her head with tendrils falling elegantly down on to her shoulders. She was wearing a plain white dress in heavy silk and her arms and throat were bare; her fur stole hung over the back of her chair.

Hester found the sight of her a kind of torture. She couldn't help it. When she looked at Virginia, all she could see was her naked body in the throes of making love with Adam. There was the high bed she remembered from Orchard House and Virginia spreadeagled on it, and then her and Adam together hot, panting, sweating, writhing. She began to feel weak and slightly nauseous.

'I'm sorry, I'll be back in a moment,' she said. 'I must just . . .' She picked up her handbag and stumbled towards the Ladies' Room. When she got there, she locked herself into a cubicle and sat on the seat for a long time, trying to bring her breathing under control. In and out, in and out. Gradually, she began to feel more like herself. Someone was knocking on the cubicle door.

'Hester? Are you in there? Are you all right? It's Virginia.'

Oh, God, no, she thought. What shall I say? What shall I do? She called out, 'Fine, thanks. I'll be out in a minute.'

'I'll wait for you,' Virginia spoke with an American accent. I'll have to go out and face her, she thought. Face all of them. She stood up and opened the door and went to wash her hands.

'I expect I'm tired,' she ventured, trying hard to smile.

'Don't look so anxious, Hester, really. It's quite understandable after your performance. Which was great, by the way. I'm so jealous of your talent. It must be wonderful to be able to dance like that. You're like . . . like a flower, or thistledown or something. Light and beautiful. But of course I know what hard work it is. You make it seem so easy.'

'Thank you,' Hester said. 'It does take it out of you a bit, especially on the first night.'

'We'll be going home soon, I'm sure. It's quite a long drive down to Orchard House.'

She nearly asked her why they weren't staying at the flat, and then caught herself in time. She was perfectly sure that she wasn't supposed to know of its existence. Virginia was applying lipstick in the mirror and rattling on in a way that surprised her, because she remembered her as being rather quiet. They'd been drinking wine. Maybe it had gone to Virginia's head.

'We could stay in the flat, of course,' she went on. 'Adam has a place in Chelsea he uses when he's working late and so on, but I only really feel comfortable in the country. And it's important I should feel comfortable because, well, I shouldn't say this to you, I don't suppose, and you'll think I'm brash and vulgar and running off at the mouth, as we say in the States, but the thing is, we've been trying for a baby for the longest time and tonight – well, tonight is a good night for it, let's just say that. So I really want to get Adam home as soon as possible and in the mood, if you know what I mean.' She giggled and led the way out back to the table. Hester went after her, trembling. Virginia Lennister half-drunk and giggling. A good night to *try for a baby*. They'd been trying *for the longest time*. It took all her self-control to sit down again and go through coffee and the paying of the bill with something like an ordinary expression on her face.

As they were leaving the restaurant, Hester whispered to Adam, 'Never phone me again. Never write. I don't ever want to see you. Not ever.'

'But why?' Adam whispered back urgently. Edmund and Virginia were walking a little ahead of them, towards the car.

'Because you're a liar. Nothing but lies from beginning to end. You've no intention of leaving your wife. I no longer believe a word you say.'

'That's nonsense, Hester, you know it is. I love you, dammit. I *will* tell her. As soon as I can. I promise.'

'And when *can* you? When she's told me herself how you've both been *trying for a baby?* You want everything, don't you? Me and your wife and a baby. Everything. Well, you can't have me. I'm a dancer and I can't concentrate on my work if I'm worrying about you all day long. My work is more important than you are. You're going to become *not at all* important to me.'

He couldn't answer, because they'd caught up with Edmund and Virginia. Hester sat in silence in the car all the way to Moscow Road, staring at the backs of their heads: Mr and Mrs Lennister, who were going home together. She felt as though every drop of blood had congealed in her veins. Deliberately, she turned her mind to tomorrow's class. Piers would take the cast through the first night notes; he'd polish everything that needed attention before the next performance. She wouldn't give Adam another thought. She'd forget about him and never think of him again.

'Goodbye,' Virginia said as Hester left the car when they reached Moscow Road. 'Thank you for *Red Riding Hood.* It was such a success, wasn't it? You must be so proud to be a part of that.'

'Goodbye,' Hester said. 'Yes, good night. And thank you.' She ran up to the porch and let herself in quietly, unable to stop hearing in her head that voice, Virginia's voice, sighing into Adam's ear, grunting and moaning; both of them frantic and loud in their lovemaking. She went up to the Attic de Luxe and fell into bed, wondering how to deal with the misery that was crushing her under its weight.

Between Boxing Day and Twelfth Night, Hester moved through the hours like an automaton. She came to life only when she was dancing. Apart from that, she walked about in a numbing fog of unhappiness.

Dinah left for Wales on the second of January and Hester felt, as she waved after the taxi from the front porch of 24 Moscow Road, that this was a recurring image in her life: someone leaving in a big black car, someone getting smaller and smaller as they grew further and further away; someone gone for ever who used to be there. She wiped away a tear that was rolling down her cheek and chided herself. Don't be so melodramatic and selfish, she told herself. You're not saying goodbye to Dinah forever. You'll stay in touch.

She'll write and so will you. It's not like leaving *Grand-mère*. Not at all. But the sensation of being at the same time bruised and icy-cold was there, just the same. That never changed, however long it had been since Hester was that small child, saying a proper goodbye for the very first time.

A few days after Dinah's departure, she and Nell moved downstairs to single rooms. Hester felt very grown-up. Suddenly she was one of the senior dancers in the company, a principal with, according to everyone she spoke to, a dazzling career ahead of her. The reviews for *Red Riding Hood* were ecstatic. Adam wrote to her every day and she tore his letters up and threw them away, though not before she'd read them. He phoned her every night at Moscow Road and she always put the phone down at once. He sent her bunches of cream roses which she gave away to other dancers. He sent messages via Edmund. Then, one night, he was waiting when she came out of the stage door.

Hester hesitated for a moment when she caught sight of him and tried to walk in the opposite direction, trying not to see his face. But he ran after her, and in the end she couldn't stop herself from turning and running towards him; from burying her face in the fabric of his coat, and weeping with anguished longing as he held her. They didn't say anything in the car. Later, he told her he couldn't live without her. He promised again to tell Virginia that he was leaving her. He was going to marry Hester. He was. Did she believe him? Did she think he really would? She no longer knew, but she couldn't bear to go on alone, not seeing him, not being with him. She had to believe there was a future for them.

For the very first time, Hester stayed in the flat all night, wrenching herself out of Adam's embrace with barely minutes to spare before that morning's class. As she got ready at the back of the church hall, Piers looked at her somewhat askance and asked, 'Night on the tiles, Hester, dear?'

Hester smiled weakly. Her whole body felt as though it were made of jelly. She tied the satin ribbons of her ballet shoes round her ankles and stood up to take her place with the others. She asked herself over and over again as her body went through the familiar routines, should I have let him talk me into staying? He didn't have to do much persuading, she recalled. All he has to do is be near me. Every single part of me wants to be his and I don't have the strength to keep my distance. She remembered how they'd torn their clothes off and fallen into bed like famished creatures—

'Concentrate, Hester,' Piers sounded cross. 'You're not paying attention.'

Hester said nothing and blushed. And bend and *entrechat* and bend and *plié*. She wrenched her thoughts away from Adam and tried to fix them on what Piers wanted her to do.

The Charleroi company left London at the end of March 1952. They were going to Birmingham, Cardiff, Newcastle, Manchester, Glasgow and Edinburgh and then back to London. For weeks, Hester's life was a succession of train rides, and digs where she had to share chilly and sometimes rather grubby rooms with Nell and Mona. The inadequate radiators in these places seemed to be forever draped in wet tights which were often still a little damp when she put them on in the evening. She took her doll, Antoinette, with her everywhere, and even though she remained in the suitcase, Hester liked knowing she was there. She would never have dared to cuddle her, but there were times, when she was missing Adam dreadfully, when the temptation to take her out and hold her tightly in bed was almost overwhelming.

Coppélia was one of Hester's favourite ballets, and Swanhilde was a part she loved. The way she transformed herself each night into a moving, dancing doll, with round eyes and stiff limbs was something like magic. The children in the audience always gasped when they saw the trick being played on the sinister and rather pathetic Doctor Coppélius, and even after many rehearsals and performances Hester would sometimes find herself shivering a little at the sight of the Chinaman, and the other automata in the Doctor's workshop, staring at her from the shadows. The costumes and the make-up were so convincing that she could scarcely recognise dancers she'd known for years. This production was one Piers was very proud of, and with good reason.

Throughout the tour, Hester wrote to Adam nearly every day. She had to admit that when it came to talking, to conversation, she had always found it easier to talk to Edmund than to Adam. Her conversations with her lover were too intense, every word too fraught with meaning. She used to spend hours every Sunday night going back over everything they'd said, trying to extract significance from each word. Edmund was funnier than Adam and more easygoing, and he and Hester laughed a lot together. She knew that, whatever happened, he was on her side, and the knowledge was comforting.

All the letters that Adam wrote to her while she was out of London she kept in a beautiful wooden box that Dinah had given her before she left the company. He was a good writer and found a thousand different ways to say that he loved her, but sometimes Hester wondered whether she should believe him. She stared at the thin lines of ink arranged in the neat italics of his beautiful handwriting and didn't know what would happen to the two of them. And there was something else. It had been more than five weeks since her last period. Her cycle was always very irregular, however, so she tried not to worry too much.

Coppélia opened in Cardiff in the third week in April. Until Hester saw Dinah after the show, she'd forgotten just how very much she'd been missing her. She came to see the ballet and took Hester out to dinner afterwards, and they arranged to meet for coffee the following morning before class. As Hester waited for her friend, it occurred to her that she must have eaten too much the previous evening. Suddenly, she felt very sick indeed. She took a deep breath and the nausea passed, but when Dinah arrived, she took one look at Hester and said, 'Are you feeling okay? You look quite green, you know.'

'Fine, really,' Hester answered. 'I ate too much last night, that's all. I'm not used to it. Are you having coffee?'

'Yes. I'll just go and fetch it.'

Once they were sitting down facing one another across the table, Dinah said, 'Hester, please don't be cross but I think . . . well, you're never ill. Not in all the time I've known you. Could you possibly be pregnant?'

Hester laughed. 'No, Dinah, I'm sure I'm not. Just because last night's fish and chips didn't agree with me, you shouldn't leap to conclusions.'

'Hmm. Fine. I won't pry. It's none of my business. But I'm going to give you something. Just in case.'

She opened her own handbag and produced a notebook and a biro. She wrote something on it and tore out the page. 'If you ever *do* find yourself pregnant, this is a name and address which might be useful. Don't say a word to anyone, but keep it by you for emergencies.'

Hester took the piece of paper and folded it up. She held it a little away from her as though it were contaminated. 'I'm lying. I am a little worried. I've missed a period, or at least, it's very late. But this person is an abortionist, is he?'

'That sounds so ghastly. Like "butcher" or "murderer". He's a doctor, that's all. He's helped out a great many people in the company over the years. And he's not too expensive. What if you are pregnant? You can't afford to have a baby now, Hester. Think of your career. You're going to be a star. A world class star and you can't ignore that. You have a duty to your art.' Dinah laughed. 'Listen to me! I sound worse than Piers, but you know what I mean. You really don't want to mess up your life with a baby.'

Hester frowned. 'I hate the thought of abortion. I think it's . . . it's hideous. Just the thought of it . . . a baby.'

'It's not a baby, Hester, not right at the start of things. Not really. You shouldn't think of it like that.'

Hester stirred the remains of the coffee in her cup, making a figure-of-eight pattern in the dregs. 'If I am pregnant,' she said, avoiding Dinah's gaze, 'I wouldn't be the only person involved. The father . . .' she couldn't bring herself to say Adam's name. She took a deep breath. 'The father would have some say in the child's future, don't you think?'

Dinah took her hand. 'You're in love, Hester. You're not seeing clearly. I promise you that if you did get pregnant, the person who'd be keenest for you to visit the address I've given you is Adam.'

Suddenly Hester was furious. 'You've no right to say such things.

You've no idea, Dinah. He loves me. He really, truly does. He'd never . . .' She took a deep breath. 'I know how it looks to outsiders. I know he said ages ago that he'd leave his wife and he hasn't yet, but he will. I'm as sure of that as I am of anything.'

'Then I won't say another word. I refuse to fall out with you over a man. Just keep that bit of paper safe. Now, let's get you to class or Piers will be having kittens.'

After that day in Cardiff, Hester was sick every morning, and she began to acknowledge that her missed period, together with the nausea meant that she was pregnant. Dinah thought she was. But she'd never once had to miss class, so perhaps this wasn't the proper morning sickness that came with pregnancy. No one she knew had ever been pregnant, so there was no one she could ask about this. How was that possible? She'd lived since she was fourteen with ballet dancers, that was how. Since she'd been in the company, only about three people had left to get married; had given up dancing. She wondered if Dinah herself had used the address she'd given to Hester. No, that can't be, she told herself. I'd know about it if she had. She wouldn't have kept it from me.

Hester lay in bed, suddenly terrified. What was going to happen to her body? Perhaps the changes had begun already. There might be something growing and growing, secretly, there in the silent darkness within her, and she wouldn't know about it for ages. She longed for *Grand-mère*, who would have comforted her and looked after her and told her what she needed to know. She would have brought Hester a *tisane* in one of the yellow cups that she remembered from her earliest childhood. She would have made her feel better. Dinah was in Cardiff and Edmund, who would have listened to her and soothed her fears and cheered her up, was in America overseeing the music for a production of *Red Riding Hood* in Chicago and wouldn't be back for months. Hester sometimes felt as though she were quite alone in the world – apart from Adam. But she was terrified of what his reaction might be to the news. What would he say?

Every evening, as she danced Swanhilde in one theatre after another, she was aware of changes in her own feelings. Part of her, most of her, shrank from the idea of a baby. Dinah was right about the dancing. How would she go on performing? What would become of her career if she had a child? She didn't think she was brave enough to face the shame of being an unmarried mother. The very words sounded disgraceful to her ears. Piers would sack her, that much was certain. Was there another ballet company in the world that would employ her once the newspapers had spread the story? But the most important question of all was, could Dinah possibly be right about what Adam would say? It occurred to Hester that on the contrary, perhaps *this*, pregnancy, might be the very thing to give him the courage to confront Virginia with the truth that he was intending to leave her.

She went over it often in her mind. He'd been promising her for months and months that he'd speak to Virginia. He kept on telling Hester that he was going to – really, truly – and yet he hadn't. Why hadn't he? She tried not to ask herself this question, because she didn't like any of the possible answers. He was cowardly. He was lazy. He was undecided. He didn't really want to spend the rest of his life with Hester. That was the worst answer of all.

But a child. Surely that would make a difference? Wouldn't he love her even more if she was expecting his baby? The fact that Virginia had not succeeded in her wish to become pregnant, Hester regarded as both a good omen and also an indication that Adam made love to his wife very rarely. Just thinking about them together still had the power to fill her with a kind of anguished rage.

By the time the company was ready to leave Edinburgh, she'd missed a second period. I'll find a doctor in London, she told herself, and then I'll know for certain. Then, she lost herself in dreams of Adam saying *I'll take care of you now. You must see my doctor. It's my child you're carrying.*

The letters flying between them grew more and more passionate the closer they were to seeing one another again. In the latest, Adam proposed a special celebratory dinner in a quiet restaurant, just the two of them, on the Sunday after she got back to London. This was to be followed by a night, a whole night together, in the flat.

As Hester dressed for dinner with Adam, she made a face in the mirror. She was trying to put up her hair and acknowledging for the thousandth time how much she missed Dinah. Her friend would have helped her. She poked in a couple of pins and sighed.

'I can't seem to do it on my own,' she said aloud.

She giggled. Talking to yourself was a sign of madness, wasn't it? Well then, Hester thought, I'm crazy. She no longer knew what she thought. There were times when she was so happy that she felt as though her whole body was full of champagne and might begin to fizz and explode. At other times, she was lost in a fog of despair and misery. She was quite sure now that she was pregnant and she knew exactly when the baby had been conceived: on the last Sunday before the tour, over eight weeks ago. Since then, Adam's letters were the only thing that gave her the strength to endure not seeing him for so long. She had no idea what she felt about the pregnancy, about having Adam's baby, but she knew she'd have to tell him as soon as they met, and she found herself dreading it. What did that say about her own feelings?

Hester looked in the mirror and told herself that what she saw would have to do. She picked up a scarf and went to the front door of 24 Moscow Road to keep watch for the black car.

The car was there when she opened the door. She could see Adam's face through the window, his nose and his chin and the dark hair falling over his forehead as he turned his head to look for her. She opened the door and slid into the seat beside him and for a few moments they clung to one another, unable to speak.

'Hester, darling darling . . .' Adam nuzzled her neck and she found she was almost crying as she ran her hands through his soft hair, smelling his smell which she'd thought she'd remembered and now realised that she'd forgotten completely.

He pulled away from her and smiled. 'Let's go, Hester. I'll get carried away if we sit here any longer. Food, to calm us down a bit, right?'

Hester nodded. She couldn't find the right words. Adam was here. There was nothing to be afraid of. They'd live happily ever after. It would be all right. Everything would be all right. The baby . . . she nearly blurted out the news right there in the car, but managed to restrain herself.

The restaurant was dark and lit with lamps on every table, even on a May evening. Adam and Hester sat right at the back of the room. A velvet curtain hung down behind her chair and it occurred to her that Adam had specially asked to sit there because she could duck behind it if anyone he knew appeared suddenly. He was ashamed of her. Was that true? She was being over-sensitive, but on a beautiful early summer night, they could have gone to a place with a garden, or sat at one of the tables near the window. Adam didn't want anyone to see them together. That was how it struck her, and she chided herself for being unkind. In all probability, he'd chosen this place as a treat because the food was wonderful and also extremely expensive. She'd known him long enough to realise that he liked to show off his — *Virginia's* — wealth.

'You can't imagine how I've missed you, Hester,' Adam said, holding her hand as they finished their coffee. 'Are you ready to go now? It's been so long.'

'Yes,' she said. The meal had gone by and they'd chatted all through it without Hester really knowing what she was talking about. They didn't say anything important. Nothing private, either, although Adam didn't take his eyes from her face and towards the end of the meal, stretched his hand out under the tablecloth and ran a finger down her thigh till she thought she might faint from the bliss of it.

But being pregnant had changed her. Before she'd left on tour, she'd have been the one wanting so desperately to make love to Adam that she could scarcely swallow her food. Now, perversely, even though she felt the clothes on her body only as irritating things that got in the way of them touching one another, the fact that he was so obviously longing to take her to bed made it seem to Hester as though that was *all* he was interested in: sex. He doesn't want to talk, she thought, conscious that she was feeling sulky for no good reason. It's my hormones, she told herself as they walked together to the car. Once we're alone, once we've made love, it will be easier to speak. I'll tell him then.

The flat was full of flowers. He'd bought dozens of cream roses and placed them in vases everywhere. He carried Hester to the bedroom, over the threshold like a bride. Like *his* bride, Hester thought, as the fragrance of more roses overpowered her.

She closed her eyes as she lay back on the bed and let Adam unbutton her blouse.

She'd expected him to tear at the fabric in his eagerness, but he went slowly, kissing her breasts as he undressed her and Hester cried out with longing for him. She could feel the satin counterpane sliding and smooth against her skin as they made love and afterwards she felt heavy in all her limbs as she curled herself round Adam's body.

'Adam,' she whispered. 'I want to tell you something.'

'Mmm,' he answered, half asleep.

Hester was breathless. The words were simple, but suddenly they seemed like stones stuck in her throat. The silence between them swelled and grew and she thought she could almost see it, hovering over the bed. She closed her eyes and let the sounds come out. 'I'm pregnant, Adam. I'm going to have a baby at Christmas.'

He sat up at once and swung his legs down on to the carpet beside the bed. Then he covered his face with both hands and shook his head. Hester was sitting up on one elbow, and she saw him, saw his reaction, and knew in that second that everything – all their love and passion and dreams and fantasies – was about to collapse around her, and that nothing either of them could say from that moment on would alter anything.

She was sitting upright and staring at the wall when he turned to face her. He took her left hand in both of his.

'Darling, forgive me. A bit of a shock, that's all. I don't know what to say. Are you sure?'

Hester nodded. Adam sighed and looked at the ceiling, then at the floor and then at her.

'I thought you'd be pleased. I thought—'

'I know, I know, but you must see that . . .'

'What?'

'I can't tell you what to do, of course, but I can't—'

'Can't what?'

He was twisting the sheet in his fingers. 'It's hard to say this, Hester. I love you so much. You must know that. But I can't leave Virginia. There. I should have told you months ago, but I always put it off because I couldn't bear the possibility that you might leave me.'

She felt icy cold. 'Why can't you leave *her?*' To herself, she sounded petulant and sulky, like a spoiled child.

'I can't. It's not that I don't love you, Hester, you know I do, but I've been married to Virginia for years and there's a history and a past that I can't just . . . well, I can't abandon her. She had a miscarriage. Two weeks ago. It's the latest in a series that's gone on for years and years and now there's no more hope. She can't have children, and she's, well, she's bereft. How could I leave her now? You must see that I can't. Imagine what her feelings would be if I married you and in six months' time, a baby appeared. It would kill her. She's not . . . well, there's a possibility that she might try to kill herself. I can't do that, Hester. I'm sorry.'

Frozen, Hester thought. I wish I could be frozen and never come to life again.

'Of course I'll help you in any way I possibly can,' Adam went on. 'Financially and so forth. If you decide to keep the baby. Or if you decide not to . . .'

Hester sprang out of bed. 'It's none of your damned business whether I keep the baby or not. I'll make up my mind without telling you. I'm never going to see you again. I can't believe what you're saying. *Financially and so forth* as though I were some business person you'd only just met. You're a bastard, Adam, and there's nothing else to say. You've never, ever had the slightest intention of leaving Virginia. You've lied to me from beginning to end. You never loved me, you just wanted to *fuck* me.' She was shrieking so loudly that her throat hurt. She never said such things. The obscenity tore at her, made her feel dirty and disgusting. 'I'm a doll. That's all I am. I've had practice now at being that. I know all the moves a mechanical doll has to make. Like this, like this.'

She began to dance, to go through the steps she knew by heart from *Coppélia*: the little dance Swanhilde did when she was pretending to be nothing more than an automaton. She moved about jerkily on the bedroom floor, stark naked, and Adam stood up to stop her, to take her in his arms.

'Don't touch me,' Hester screamed at him. 'Don't dare to touch me. That's what you want me for, to be your fantasy doll, to do everything you want in bed. Things I bet Virginia won't do, am I right? I, on the other hand, know how to make all the right moves. You're no better than Doctor Coppélius. You're sick. And you've been sleeping with *her* the whole time we've been together. It's disgusting. *You're* disgusting.'

Adam spoke calmly. 'She'd have guessed I was seeing you if I hadn't made love to her. Can't you understand how difficult this is for me?'

'Difficult for *you*? I can't believe what you're saying. No, I don't understand that. Not at all,' she shouted. She began dressing, pulling her clothes on frantically with no care or thought. 'I don't give a damn about you any longer. I've wasted these months. I've probably ruined my whole life. It might be that I'll never dance again.'

'No, surely—'

'What do you know about it? Nothing! I'll get fat and slow and no one will want to employ me.'

'You don't need to have this child,' Adam said, in a voice so soft that she could barely hear it. 'I know a doctor—'

'Abortion? You'd kill the only child you're ever likely to have? Are you *that* wicked? I didn't think you'd be capable of such cruelty.'

'It's not a baby, Hester. Not yet. Not to me.'

'Well, it bloody well *is* to me.' She sat down on the end of the bed and began to cry. 'Or it was, till I told you. Now it's a part of you and I don't know whether I want to have it anywhere in my body. At this very moment I wish I could tear it out with my own hands and flush it down a drain. I wish I could have a miscarriage. I wish I'd never seen you. I wish I could die.'

'Stop, Hester, stop. You'll be all right. I'll look after you.'

Hester stopped crying at once and stood up. She took a handkerchief out of her handbag and blew her nose. Act, she said to herself. Play a part. Dignity. Act dignified. In control. Don't let him see how much every bit of you is hurting. She gathered herself together in the way she'd grown used to doing just before making an entrance. She was ready.

'No, Adam,' she said, surprising herself with the steadiness of her own voice. 'Thank you very much. I don't want your help. *Financially and so forth* or otherwise. I don't want to see you ever again. I don't want you to write to me. I want you to disappear. That's all. I'm going to try and forget I ever knew you. Go back to Virginia and I hope you rot away with regret. You won't. You find it very easy, don't you, to push things aside that don't fit in with your life, so put me out of your mind. Forget about me. I'll make bloody sure you never lay eyes on your child. If I decide to have it, that is. I might abort it. I might kill it because I hate you so much. You can wonder all your life what your child would have been like because I'll never tell you. And if you dare to come anywhere near me again, I'll go straight to Orchard House and tell Virginia everything. I mean it, too. I'll describe every detail. Everything we've done together. She'll love that. That'll help her get over her miscarriage, won't it? Maybe I'll let her know anyway about *our* baby. How would you like that?'

Adam was white. 'You wouldn't, Hester . . .'

'Probably not.' Hester smiled. Oh, how calmly she was speaking! 'Not because I want to spare you pain, but simply because it would make me as vile and uncaring as you are. But you'll have to worry forever, won't you, in case I change my mind. I'm going now. I'll find a taxi on the main road.'

'I'll drive you home.'

'I'm never stepping into that car again. I'll find a taxi.'

'Then I'll wait with you until you find one.'

While they waited for a taxi to appear, neither of them said a word. Hester felt as though she were holding back a flood. If she moved or spoke, all the tears would come rushing out and drown her. When the taxi drew up beside them, she got into it without a word and without looking behind her. Right up to the last second, she was waiting. Part of her wanted him to say *no, no come back it's all a dreadful mistake of course I'll leave Virginia and we'll live together forever and look after our baby don't go I can't live without you I can't I can't don't go.*

He said nothing of the kind. She heard a kind of groan as she slammed the taxi door shut. She gave the driver her address. I can't cry here, she thought. I must wait till I get home.

She lay on the bed at 24 Moscow Road and tried to weep but the tears had formed a rock in the middle of her chest. She could feel them, solidified into a painful weight that made breathing difficult. I must sleep, she told herself. How will I go to class tomorrow if I don't sleep?

All night long, Hester moved between nightmares. It wasn't clear to her whether she was asleep or awake, but she was sweating and feverish and pictures appeared in her head: Adam and Virginia dancing together round the ballroom at Orchard House; herself and Adam kissing; her baby, turning in a kind of blue mist somewhere inside her where she was hardly aware of it, a monster to remind her of Adam. A beloved child to treasure when she had no one else to love. She imagined something being torn from her womb with huge, silver tongs and she shuddered. She couldn't do it. She longed not to be pregnant; she prayed that maybe if she danced and danced and pushed her body to the limits of which it was capable, she, too, might miscarry. Lose the baby. How wonderful that would be! If she could be rid of every part of Adam forever and ever, but paying money to have it, him, her, the baby, torn out of her – she didn't think she had the courage to do that. She turned over in bed and buried her face in the pillow. Oh, God, she thought, let me sleep. The light was already there, behind the curtains, and her eyes felt raw and painful. How would she face this new day? Every other day? Her whole life? Hester began crying all over again.

30 December 1986

'I can't tell you how grateful I am to you, Ruby,' said Hugo. He'd come to Wardrobe before the day's rehearsal began to check what needed to be done on the costumes. 'I'm going to try and claim compensation of some kind from somewhere, but meanwhile the dancers have to be dressed in something. I don't know what I'd have done without you.'

He was sitting in the chair opposite Ruby, who was making a list in a small notebook.

'I've made a note of what has to be done,' she said. 'It won't be too bad, really. I'll be going in to Leeds later on, with Alison. We were going this morning but it would have been a bit of a problem driving in all that snow. I'm glad a bit of a thaw's set in now. The wings for the Angel will be the most work, I suppose, but I've had an idea. It may not be as eye-catching as the feathers you had before, but most of those are ruined. Any that aren't I'll use here and there. You'll be surprised, I think, and I hope the surprise is a pleasant one.'

'I'm sure it will. I also think, by the way, that it's very noble of you to say Alison can help you with all this. She's not a bad kid.'

Ruby put her pen down and looked at Hugo. 'I'm not being noble. I'm happy to have her help. She seems sensible and she's rather good with her hands, I've noticed. And, well, I shouldn't say anything, I know, but I think that she feels a little unappreciated, if that's the right word. I'm sorry. It's none of my business, really.'

'No, no, you're quite right. I try, but Claudia and I don't discuss it very often. I mean, because Alison isn't my daughter or anything, I feel as though I mustn't interfere too much, though it's true that sometimes she does go a bit far. Like that awful remark she made to Alison at lunch yesterday.'

Ruby nodded. 'I can imagine it must be awkward for you.'

'Exactly!' Hugo beamed. 'That's it exactly. It's awkward. If I say too much, then I'm seen as butting in and taking over her father's role and if I say nothing, I feel guilty. Sometimes, I swear, I see Alison looking at me as if to say, *why don't you do something?* Have you got children of your own, Ruby? You seem to know an awful lot about young people.'

'No, no children. I've got four younger brothers and sisters though. I did my fair share of looking after them when I was a girl.'

'I do think it's surprising, though,' Hugo said, absently twisting a piece of fabric in his fingers, 'that Hester never married.'

Ruby was silent for a moment. Then she said, 'She had her fair share of suitors, and turned them all down. She was totally dedicated to the ballet, and she travelled a great deal. She was very close to Kaspar Beilin of course, but only as a friend and a partner. There was a time when they were one of the most famous couples in the world. She was a star. I don't think many men would have enjoyed playing second fiddle to someone like Hester.'

'I'm astonished she didn't marry when she was very young, before she became really famous. She must have been even more lovely than she is now. She's not exactly beautiful, is she, but just manages to be somehow extraordinarily attractive. Almost luminous. Oh, that sounds silly, but you know what I mean. I suppose I'm a bit starstruck. I just think she's completely wonderful and I'm full of admiration for what she's done here. It meant so much to me to win this competition.'

Ruby smiled and nodded, but said nothing. She picked up her pen again and began to write things on her list. Hugo took the hint.

'I'm sorry, I'm blathering on in my usual fashion and I'm disturbing you. In any case, they'll all be arriving downstairs for the rehearsal any minute. I'll see you at supper, I expect. 'Bye now.'

Claudia was waiting for Hugo when he arrived in the rehearsal room.

'Darling, whereever have you been? I've been looking for you since lunchtime.'

'Hello, Claudia.' He kissed her briefly and then held the door of the rehearsal room open for her and followed her in. 'No one's here yet. Did you see anyone on your way over? We need to get going.'

'You sound harassed, sweetheart,' said Claudia, coming up to him and putting her arms around him. 'No, not harassed, really,' he replied. 'Just sorting out the mess over the costumes. Ruby's going to be invaluable. It'll be okay I daresay, but I can't deny it's thrown me for a bit of a loop.'

'You poor pet!' said Claudia and stroked his hair. *Pet!* When did she start calling him that? Maybe she'd always done it and he'd been so besotted that he'd never noticed. Now, it set his teeth on edge and it was all he could do not to wince. His feelings for Claudia were changing, and he wondered briefly why this was and whether it had anything to do with his worries about her capacities as a dancer. He was finding it hard to concentrate. He was waiting for Silver. Where was she anyway? They were to go over the Angel's first entrance, the first time she danced with Claudia, and he really hoped that today when he had the two of them to contend with, she'd make a bit more effort.

Claudia was still speaking. She hadn't stopped while he'd been thinking of Silver, but he wasn't really listening. Now that he'd tuned in to her words again, he found she had moved on to talking about her costume.

'I knew I was right to pack it with my own clothes. I like having my costume with me. It makes me feel safe. I *will* still be able to wear it, won't I? It won't clash with something Ruby's cooking up for the others or anything? I completely refuse to wear something *makeshift*. Something that wasn't designed for me.'

'Don't worry, Claudia. It'll be fine. You'll look wonderful, I'm quite sure.' He wondered how they could fill the time till Silver arrived. When did that happen? When did finding subjects of conversation become difficult? There was no doubt about it. His relationship with Claudia was coming to a natural end, and he wished that she were the kind of person to whom he could simply say *Claudia, it was great, but it's over now. I used to love you, but I don't any longer.* Unfortunately, she wasn't. She would, in Alison's words, throw a wobbly. At any other time that wouldn't matter, or it wouldn't matter so much, but now he had *Sarabande* to consider. He wasn't about to mess that up.

'D'you know where Alison is?' Claudia was asking him. She'd

gone over to the chairs and was making a big production out of putting up her hair and getting her ballet shoes on.

'Yes, she's going to be helping Ruby with the costumes and props. They're going into Leeds later on to get something from the shops. Ruby says she's very sensible and good with her hands.'

'Thank Heavens for that. I was really worried, you know, about bringing her with me. I didn't want her doing her usual sulky number in front of the whole company.'

'She's only sulky with you, you know. With everyone else, she's really quite amiable.' A thought occurred to him. 'Do you love your daughter, Claudia?' he asked.

'What an extraordinary question! *Of course* I love her. I should have thought that was obvious. Look how I put myself out for her! I'm really quite hurt that you feel you need to ask me a question like that.'

'Well, I'm sorry, Claudia, only you don't show it. I think you could be nicer to her. I've wanted to say something to you about it for ages . . .' His voice faded away as he saw Claudia's face turning pale and her mouth tightening. Oh, God, he thought, what on earth am I doing? I must be mad. Why did I have to speak up now? She's furious. We're going to have a full-scale row and Silver'll walk in at any moment.

'Don't be angry, Claudia. I don't mean that you're unloving or anything, of course I don't. Just that I think you could be a little softer to her when you speak to her. That's all. Honestly. That's the only thing I meant. Teenagers are very sensitive, aren't they?'

Tears now stood in Claudia's eyes. 'I don't know why you're not worried about the way she speaks to *me*! *I'm* just as sensitive as she is. And what's more I have to dance; to put myself through all kinds of stress that she knows nothing about.'

At that moment, Silver arrived and Hugo was profoundly grateful. All he needed now was a real row with Claudia. As it was, she smiled radiantly at Silver and blew a kiss in her direction while at the same time making a big deal of starting on her warm-up exercises at the *barre*. She wanted Silver to see how self-possessed she was, and more than anything else, Hugo knew, she wanted to impress Silver with her professionalism.

'Hello, Silver,' he said. 'We're nearly ready to start.'

'I'm sorry I'm late. I was talking to George. He's awfully nice but it's hard to get away from him.' She smiled at Hugo and he smiled back and walked across to where the ghetto-blaster was waiting to be turned on. He pressed 'play' and the Angel's first theme filled the room.

'I'm ready now,' Silver said, stepping on to the floor and taking up her first position. Hugo nodded and said, 'Okay, we're going to take it from the beginning, but before we do, I just want to show you a sequence I've thought of that we might put in a little later in the scene. It's going to require a bit of work. Let's begin with a *chaine en tournant* . . . good, then *bourrés* over to the top right of the stage . . . that's it.'

He watched her, and knew that while she was clearly trying harder, there was still much more of herself that she wasn't giving. What was he going to have to do to change that? He certainly wasn't going to tick her off in front of Claudia. He'd have to have a word with her afterwards. These were new steps so perhaps he ought to see how they worked out when she'd had time to absorb them and work on them a little.

'I'm so sorry, I didn't realise there was anyone in here,' Hester said, coming into the drawing room. Silver sprang up at once from the armchair by the fire. 'Would you rather be alone?'

'No, no, not at all. In fact, I've been longing to talk to you ever since we came to Wychwood. You're one of my heroines. Really. Now I'm blushing. I'm sorry, only it sounds so silly.'

'I think it's kind of you to say so, and I promise you, it never sounds silly to me.' Just then there was a knock on the door and Joan came into the room carrying tea things on a tray.

'Thank you, Joan,' said Hester and then turned to Silver. 'I usually have tea in here, but would you like some as well? There's more than one cup on the tray. You're a mind-reader, Joan.'

'Always do put two on, Hester,' Joan said, setting the tray down on a low coffee table. 'Saves going to get another and, in my experience, folk come out of the woodwork when there's tea on the go.'

She left the room and Hester said, 'I'm a great admirer of your work as well, you know. I missed *Swan Lake* but I did read the reviews. And I saw you in that interesting modern piece, what was it called? *Shades of Scarlet*, that's it. The Carradine Company is lucky to have you for *Sarabande*. Is it going well? Are you enjoying it?'

'I think it's okay. It's always hard to tell at this stage. So far we've mainly done our individual bits. Hugo works us very hard. Actually . . . ' she paused. 'He added a fiendish routine to my first solo today. I'm going to have my work cut out. Don't tell him I said so, of course.'

'No, of course not. Only I know from what Hugo tells me that he's only interested in the final result. He wants *Sarabande* to be wonderful, and I know he thinks you can be.'

'Yes, after he's bullied me unmercifully for hours at a time! No one else has ever treated me like that. Sometimes I feel as though I'm a schoolgirl or something, being ticked off . . . oh, I'm sorry, I shouldn't be doing this. Please ignore me. I'm just tired that's all. I'd much rather talk about you. I've loved your dancing since I was about six. My mum bought me a video for my birthday. It was you and Kaspar Beilin doing *Don Quixote* and I watched it so much that it just fell apart in the end. I had to buy another copy.'

'Thank you. It's always lovely to hear things like that,' Hester said. 'And don't worry about Hugo. It's not personal you know. Piers Cranley, who was the person who gave me my first chance, became a positive monster sometimes when things weren't up to standard. I'm sure Hugo's very friendly when you're not in the rehearsal room, isn't he?'

'I'm usually too annoyed by then to have much to say to him,' Silver said, and laughed. 'But it'll be okay, I think. I love the music.'

'That's by a friend of mine, you know. The original music, not the jazz variations that Hugo's using. Edmund Norland. I've known him for years and years and he's delighted that the piece is being revived. He'll be here in a couple of days, and I know he can't wait to see what's been done with his piece.'

'Yes, I knew you were friends. I read about it in an article in the

Sunday Times. It was all about how you had to stop dancing after an accident. That must have been ghastly, a real tragedy.'

'Not grand enough to be a tragedy. Just unlucky. It was one of those things that could have been trivial; could have healed very easily and allowed me to dance for a little while longer at least but no, it was a complex fracture and that was that.'

'I don't know what to say,' Silver said. 'How absolutely ghastly for you! I'd have been in complete despair.'

Hester sighed and then smiled to lighten the mood. 'I was. It was one of those times in my life when I lay in bed facing the wall for what seemed like weeks and weeks and didn't feel like talking to anyone or going out or doing anything really. If it hadn't been for Edmund, I might have just closed my eyes and decided not to open them again. Edmund and my old ballet teacher, Madame Olga. They pulled me round in the end, and made me see that there were other things I could do. Other ways of living. But it was hard, I won't deny it. I don't often speak about it, you know, but you're a very sympathetic listener. I hope you don't mind.'

'Oh, no,' Silver said, jumping up and crouching down next to Hester's armchair. She took hold of Hester's hands and squeezed them. 'I don't mind at all. I'm honoured that you told me about it. My retrospective sympathy won't help much, but I *do* feel for you, truly. And I think you're very, very brave. I'm so glad I took the part in *Sarabande*. I hesitated at first, but I did want to meet you and see Wychwood and I feel I made a fortunate choice.'

She leaned forward and kissed Hester on the cheek and then stood up. 'I'm not going to complain about Hugo again either. I shall try my very hardest. Really. I'm so happy to have talked to you.' She was gone before Hester had time to say anything.

The fragrance she wore, like vanilla and something else – sandalwood? – lingered in the drawing room. Hester couldn't deny that there was some satisfaction in meeting someone face to face who was a true fan; it was so good to be admired. It was probably vain of her to enjoy Silver's adulation, but she couldn't help it. It was true that she was very conscious of her reputation and her looks and if that was vanity, she was guilty of it. I don't think though, she reflected, that I've ever deluded myself. I don't think I've given myself airs, or I hope I haven't. I wasn't like Claudia. She was forever looking over her shoulder to see the effect she was having on people and I never did that. Silver seems confident yet somehow not in the least full of herself. She's a surprise, Hester thought. She looks so cool, and yet she's a kind young woman. It had been some time since anyone had kissed her as affectionately and impulsively as Silver had done and she felt as though she'd been given a gift.

'Are you going back to the house?' Nick was leaning against the wall of the rehearsal room, and Claudia could feel his eyes on her back as she bent forward to zip up her boots. He was undoubtedly staring at her thighs in black Lycra and the thought of what he might be thinking made her smile. I wish he'd touch me, she thought. He could. He's easily close enough, but perhaps he feels embarrassed with some of the others about. She straightened up. 'Yes, I am. But I thought I'd go along the outside path. I need a bit of air. And a cigarette, to be quite frank. Hester doesn't like us smoking in the house, so I'm going to have to brave the weather.' She smiled at him. 'It'd be much more fun if you were to come with me. If you can bear the cold, that is.'

'I don't notice things like that. Not when I'm with a beautiful woman.'

'How gallant!'

They made their way out of the Arcadia Theatre, laughing.

'I can't tell you,' Claudia said, pausing outside the doors of the foyer to light her cigarette 'how refreshing it is to laugh a bit. Hugo is such a worry guts. Takes everything hugely seriously. You know what I mean, don't you? He just never seems to relax these days.'

'He's mad,' Nick said. 'If I had you to *relax* with, I'd do nothing else.'

Oh, God, Claudia thought, staring into his eyes. Why does he have to be so gorgeous? The temptation to put out a hand and brush his hair off his forehead was almost overwhelming, but Claudia was a great believer in playing hard to get, at least for the first few skirmishes in the sex war. In the end, she realised with a thrill that originated in her womb and spread through her whole body, she would succumb. She always did. Nick kissing her . . . imagining that made her feel a little dizzy and she took a drag from the cigarette and blew smoke into the cold air. Then she set off along the path and Nick walked beside her. She said, 'That's not what I heard.'

'What's not what you heard?'

'That you'd like to *relax* with me. Or any woman, come to that.'

'Oh, I get it!' Nick laughed. 'It's the gay stories, isn't it? You've been listening to gossip, Claudia. You shouldn't. People are so *inaccurate* sometimes. You ought to know that.'

'Are you saying you don't . . . you've never?'

'No, I'm not. I have been known . . . well, let's say men haven't always been entirely out of the question. Especially when I was much younger. But these days, a person has to be extra careful, don't they? The whole AIDS thing terrifies me. Do you understand?'

'Yes, of course,' said Claudia. 'I understand perfectly.' And as far as AIDS was concerned, she did. She, too, along with everyone else, had been shocked into serious consideration of this ghastly new illness. But Nick was obviously one of those people (and there were plenty of them, she knew that) who would sleep with men or women, as long as they were attractive, and *that* she found harder to understand. How *could* they find both men and women attractive, she wondered. She hadn't a clue, but if Nick said he fancied her, then who was she to contradict him? A tiny voice in the deepest part of her head was saying *wait till he's been with you. He'll never want to look at another man again. Or woman if it comes to that.* Claudia tried as hard as she could not to listen. She was being plain conceited, she knew, but still. It was a tempting thought to have the kind of sex with Nick which would make him renounce everyone else for a while.

As they walked, they chatted and gossiped about *Sarabande*, the others in the company and Hester Fielding. The house was coming closer. They'd be there soon, and no longer alone together and she wouldn't have another chance to get near him till God knew when. Nothing venture, nothing gain. 'I'm off to have a bath. I wish you could come with me and scrub my back,' she said.

He stood quite still for a moment and looked at her. Then he put out a hand and lifted the hair that was hanging down over her shoulder. He stroked it gently and she felt as though the blood in her veins was fizzing. He put his hand on her arm and leaned towards her.

'I wish I could, too,' he whispered, speaking right into her ear, even though there was no one looking at them except a bunch of silly sheep. 'But I wouldn't stop at scrubbing your back, Claudia. You're killing me. Dancing with you is killing me. We're going to do something about it, right?'

Claudia nodded, struck dumb for once. How, she wanted to ask? How, with Hugo sharing a room with me, and my daughter never very far away?

'Trust me,' Nick said, and strode away from her and towards the front door. She followed, hoping that no one had been looking down at the drive from one of the windows. She had to get herself into a normal condition before Hugo came back from rehearsal. She smiled as she remembered Nick's words. *We're going to do something about it, right?* Oh, yes, Nick, she thought. Very very right indeed.

'Claudia's going to be okay,' Hugo said. Hester nodded and said nothing, so he went on. 'I was worried that she couldn't manage the part. She's lost a lot of her power as a dancer over the last couple of years, but just lately she's done quite well. Put a lot more energy into her work. It might be Nick, of course. Having a much younger partner does sometimes have that effect.'

'Yes, it does. Look at me and Kaspar Beilin. And Fonteyn and Nureyev. It's often just what a ballerina needs to galvanise her. I'm sure she'll be splendid.'

'And I think Silver will be all right too, if I'm lucky. I showed her the new sequence you suggested and she seemed to be happy to try it.' He sat back in his chair and took a sip from the wine that Hester had poured him. This, he thought, is the best part of every day, just sitting and talking things over with Hester. He said: 'I'm so glad I can chat to you about everything that's on my mind, you know. I look forward to our sessions. During rehearsals, I think of things I want to consult you about, or ask you. I'm grateful to you for letting me see you like this.'

Hester laughed. 'I look forward to it as well, you know, Hugo.

I've got nothing but time, really, once the visiting company is here, and talking to the choreographer every day is my way of keeping an eye on things. But it does make me feel nostalgic. I go for weeks thinking I've got everything under control and that I'm quite used to being middle-aged and no longer able to do things with my body that I was able to do for years and then, quite suddenly, I'll think of something or hear a snatch of music or see someone – like Silver for instance – and then this feeling sweeps over me and I'm longing with all my heart to be able to do it just once more. Go to rehearsal. Tie the ribbons on my ballet shoes. Stand in the wings with the stage flooded with light like a kind of desert stretching out in front of me.' She paused, and smiled at Hugo. 'I'm so sorry. I got carried away. I don't often talk like this. I'm not sure what it is about you, but it makes a person want to confide in you.'

Hugo leaned forward and took Hester's hand. 'I'm honoured that you feel you can say such things to me. I won't let you down. I'll make sure *Sarabande* is the best it can possibly be. I promise.'

'I know you will. Have another glass of wine before you go.'

'I shouldn't, really. There's a lot I want to do before dinner. But thanks, maybe half a glass.'

As he watched Hester pour the drink, Hugo felt himself relaxing. Really, it was quite remarkable how safe she made him feel. That was the exact word for it, safe. He closed his eyes for a moment and listened to Siggy, who was snoring slightly as he slept, curled up on a rug in front of the fire.

31 December 1986

Silver stood behind Alison and frowned as she looked over her head into the mirror.

'Not bad,' she said. 'Okay, open your mouth just a little. That's right. This lipstick's called *Tulip Touch*, I love it. You have to be careful when you're a brunette, usually. Sometimes brunettes have an olivey skin which hates certain shades of pink, but you're lucky. You seem to have your mother's complexion, even though you're not a redhead. Nice and creamy.'

'Shame about the spots, though, right?' Alison said, her voice sounding funny because of how she was holding her lips while Silver worked away at making her up for the New Year's Eve dinner party.

'Spots are what concealer and foundation were invented for. Can you see any spots? Have a look.'

'I look – I look not like myself at all,' Alison said, and it was true. Silver, she thought, was some sort of magician. 'I'm so glad it was you who found me, and not anyone else.'

Silver had bumped into Alison in the corridor. She'd just come out of Claudia and Hugo's room and her eyes were red-rimmed with crying. Almost before Alison knew what was happening, she was being led into Silver's own bedroom.

'What's the matter? You've been crying.'

'And now I'll look worse than ever.'

'Tell me what's wrong. Have you been having a fight with your mum? I spent half my teenage years in floods after one kind of row or another. Have a drink, it'll calm you down. I've only got mineral water, but what the hell. Next time I come to the middle of nowhere, I'll be sure to pack a bottle of gin or something. What were you rowing about?'

'Oh, nothing, really,' Alison sighed. 'Nothing different. I just went to ask her, my mum, what I should wear for the dinner tonight and she said it wouldn't make any difference what I wore. So I burst into tears.'

'Did she *really* say that?'

'She actually said, it doesn't matter what you wear. But I knew what she meant. She meant that nothing I wore would make any difference to the way I look, i.e., fat and ugly.'

'Rubbish and total nonsense!' Silver said. Then she looked carefully at Alison. 'Have you got a pair of clean black trousers?'

'Yes.'

'What about a black top? T-shirt with long sleeves, or something. A thin jumper, at a pinch. But black.'

Alison nodded.

'Okay,' said Silver. 'Go and get those on and come back here in, well, give it half an hour to let your eyes recover.' She stood on tiptoe suddenly and waved her hand in a circle over Alison's head and smiled so that you could almost feel the warmth of it on your skin. 'You, too, shall go to the ball, Cinders,' she said, and burst out laughing. 'Wait till I've finished with you and then see if you're fat and ugly. It's simply not true!'

Now, Alison gazed into the mirror and rubbed her lips gently together. Her Tulip-touched lips. Her eyes looked amazing. Greeny-brown eyeshadow, highlighter, a bit of a line drawn along the lid which she could hardly see but which Silver swore made all the difference and tons and tons of mascara which made her eyelashes look dark and thick and glamorous.

'Very important to emphasise the eyes if you wear glasses,' Silver said, and then, looking with satisfaction at her own handiwork, she went on, 'D'you know, if I hadn't been a dancer, I'd have loved to do stuff like this. Make-up and hair. Or making people over from scratch. See how fantastic you look.'

Alison smiled. Silver had persuaded her to wear her hair loose. It hung down to her shoulders and luckily she'd washed it just this morning so that it shone. She could actually see it shining, just like hair in advertisements. Silver had made a sort of necklace out of a scarf of hers that was silvery and pink and looked gorgeous. Apart from the scarf, Alison was all in black and that made her look, if not exactly slim, at least not huge.

'Pity about the shoes,' said Silver. 'I wish I could lend you some of mine, but those boots look reasonable. Just remember for next time, go for a bit of a heel. Add height. Always a good idea.'

'You're really kind, Silver.' Alison turned round to face her directly.

'That's okay. I love doing it. Any time, honestly.'

Alison stood up to leave and Silver hugged her.

'Don't let them grind you down,' she said, and Alison left the room feeling as though she was a completely different person from the one who'd gone in – braver, prettier, more glamorous. She was longing for dinner.

New Year's Eve. It was her favourite time of the year. She had a mental image of all the months, looking like a kind of mountain, sloping from the top left to bottom right. December was in the bottom right hand corner and then, on the first of January, you started all over again at the top of the slope, sliding down towards winter. And somehow, everything was much more wintry here in the country.

Suddenly there seemed to be a lot to look forward to. Going into Leeds with Ruby was good fun, and tomorrow she'd be helping her with the costumes and props that needed repairing and making. Before that, though, there was the New Year's Eve dinner. She was longing for it. Perhaps she'd be able to sit next to Nick, or opposite him. Most of the time, her head was like a television screen running a whole series of little scenes involving the two of them: she and Nick clinking champagne glasses at midnight, laughing together, dancing, and holding one another very close. There was even one in which they were kissing, but Alison tried not to think about that too much. It depressed her when the dream ended and she had to admit that it was all mad. Cloud cuckoo land. None of it would ever happen, and she was a silly fool. Some people said that Nick was gay, but even if he wasn't he wouldn't look at her.

Now Alison went to the staircase and pretended that Nick was going to meet her at the bottom. He'd be staring up at her as she tripped elegantly down, almost floating, with the ends of the pink and silver scarf trailing down her back, and he'd say something like *I never realised you were so beautiful, Alison. You must sit next to me tonight. This year will be the beginning . . .*

'Well, Lawks-a-mercy, child,' said a voice, and Alison blinked and realised in a flush of embarrassment that it *was* Nick, the real Nick not the fantasy, speaking. She'd been so caught up in her daydream that she didn't even notice him standing at the foot of the stairs and looking up at her. How stupid was that! As her blush subsided, she managed to speak.

'Hello.' Okay, it wasn't exactly scintillating but it was a beginning.

'You look fabulous, my love,' said Nick. He shook his finger at her, and said, 'Someone's been having a go at you. Someone who knows what's what in the slap department.'

'Silver made me up.'

'She did a splendid job. Now come along to the dining room, honey. We're in top posh party mode tonight. No eating in the kitchen. We're living it up in style. Come with me, and we'll go in together.'

He tucked Alison's arm under his and patted her hand as it rested on his sleeve. This has to be, Alison thought, the best moment of my whole life. She could feel his muscles under her fingers through the fabric of his shirt. How strong he was! And he smelled gorgeous. They went into the dining room. The table was set down at the far end, and Alison caught sight of white linen and flowers and glasses by every place setting. Everyone had gathered near the door for drinks and turned as they came in.

'Nick, darling,' said Claudia, gliding to his side. 'We've all been wondering where you were.' She looked searchingly at Alison. 'Well now, don't you look good! Who's persuaded you out of your usual outfits? Not to mention the make-up. Amazing.'

'Silver made me up. She lent me the scarf too.'

'Lovely. How kind of her.' She turned to Nick. 'No one ever listens to their mother, do they? I've been trying to get her to smarten up for years and years and then along comes Silver and in one second, hey presto, the battle is won.'

She spoke lightly and Nick would never have guessed, but Alison knew how furious Claudia was. She was jealous of Silver anyway, because of her being younger and a better dancer and now she'd come along and acted as though she was related to Alison, or her best friend or something and Claudia didn't like that one little bit. She couldn't say a word, of course, because that would make her look mean and grudging. Tee-hee, thought Alison. Serve her right.

'Now, darling,' Claudia said to her daughter 'I think you've monopolised this divine young man long enough. He's done his duty and brought the princess to the ball, and now,' (she touched his hand and looked up at him from under a sweep of eyelashes that made Alison's look sparse) 'he's coming along with me to get a glass of wine.'

She gathered him up and he went off with her, glancing over his shoulder at Alison as they made their way over to the drinks table as if to say *it's not my fault. I can't help it. I'd much rather be staying and chatting to you.* Anyway, that was how she interpreted his raised eyebrows and the funny thing he did with his mouth when he smiled at her.

Alison didn't care. I know he likes me, she told herself. And he thinks I look great, so I must do. Claudia's outfit was a catsuit (tight all over but with wide, floppy legs below the calf) in brown velvet, printed with a sort of leafy pattern in green which made her look like a rather glamorous pixie. Ilene was in a peacock-blue silky dress, and Ruby was wearing a long tartan skirt with a black silk blouse. Hester's dress had a tight bodice and a full skirt and was made of some dark red, soft material woven with gold threads. They glittered when she moved and the fabric caught the light.

When Silver appeared, though, everyone else, even Hester, suddenly seemed drab. You could almost hear the intake of breath as she stood in the doorway for a few seconds before coming into the room. Her dress was black and as plain as could be, just a long straight shift of silky stuff that fell from her shoulders to the floor. Her arms were bare and from her ears silver and crystal earrings hung almost to her shoulders. The scarf she'd thrown around her neck was like a length cut from the sea: blue and green and purple and silver and all shimmering together so that you couldn't tell where one colour ended and another began. It flowed down over the darkness of her dress like a bright wave and almost touched the silver shoes she was wearing. Height, Alison thought. She's done what she told me to do. In dizzying heels, Silver towered over everyone else in the room, except for Hugo.

'Silver, how lovely you look!' he said, coming across the polished floor towards her. He kissed her first on one cheek and then on the other. Everyone could see it was just a friendly greeting, but Alison chanced to catch sight of her mother as it happened and she looked enraged and sulky. Ha! thought Alison. She thinks he fancies Silver. The moment this occurred to her, she wondered whether it was true and the more she thought about it, the more likely it seemed. What would happen if Hugo and her mother split up? I'm not going to worry about that now, she told herself. It's New Year's Eve. I'm going to have fun.

This has to be, thought Alison, the best meal I've ever had in my whole life. She looked along the table at everyone else and saw that they weren't even enjoying it properly. Typical! She took a sip of wine, which she'd accepted just to seem grown-up, and wrinkled her nose. I'll have orange juice when I've finished this glass, she told herself, and went back to her plate, which was laden with crispy roast potatoes, goose or duck or something, and vegetables which didn't taste like the ones she was used to from school, but more sophisticated somehow. She knew she was the only person at the table tucking in, apart from Siggy the cat. He was sitting under the table near her ankles enjoying the tiny pieces of meat she had contrived to drop on the floor from time to time. Everyone else was fiddling: pushing bits of this and that round their plates and talking a lot and drinking even more and, in the end, she could tell, there'd be as much left on their plates as there was to begin with. Ballet dancers! She sighed. It was because she'd had the misfortune to have a mother who was one of them that she was so unused to nice meals in restaurants. Claudia never went out to eat if she could help it, and Alison felt she'd missed out. Dad used to take me to the Chinese restaurant, she thought, and a sudden memory of red lanterns swinging from the ceiling came to her. She must have been very little because she could also remember being frightened of a huge red and gold dragon mask on the wall. She could see it now, exactly how it was, and wished she could go back now and eat there, in that very same place with her dad. She wouldn't be scared of it now. She'd love every minute.

Joan and Emmie took away all the plates and Siggy followed them to the kitchen. He'd be having left-overs for weeks, probably. Then the pudding was brought in, on three enormous plates, and Alison knew you weren't supposed to call it pudding when it was as grand as this. Each plate had on it a huge, white circle made entirely of meringue with raspberries and cream spread all over it and another layer of meringue on top.

'How very appropriate!' said Andy, smiling at Alison. 'Raspberry Pavlova. What else could a ballet company possibly have as a dessert?' He helped himself to quite a large portion and actually began to eat it. 'You don't see it very often these days. Most people I know gave up this sort of thing years ago. More fools them, eh?'

Alison nodded. She finished her pudding – dessert – and wondered how long they'd have to sit here and just chat. It wasn't that she was bored exactly, but she wanted to get a little nearer to Nick, and there was no chance of that when he was locked in his chair. She looked at her mother and frowned. What was she doing? She was leaning right over so that almost all of her was sort of curled round Nick and her arm was on the back of his chair. She was obviously drinking too much. It made her even sillier than she normally was.

The others didn't seem to be paying attention. They were busy with their own conversations. George and Ruby were talking to Ilene. Alison wondered again if it was true that Nick was . . . no, she thought. I refuse to even think about it. She'd never told anyone and didn't often admit it to herself, but the idea of almost anyone in bed with anybody else made her feel a bit queasy. She knew the facts of life, of course she did, but still, trying to visualise all that heaving and grunting when it was people you'd actually met was a bit off-putting and Alison tried to avoid bringing it to mind. When she thought of Nick *doing it* with anyone, she began to feel quite faint, but it was different in his case. She couldn't help imagining her and Nick together, and that made her feel, well, most peculiar, but it was quite a pleasant feeling and she found that she was going back to those thoughts more often, just in order to feel that tingle, located not exactly in her stomach but sort of *under* it.

So far, Claudia thought, so not bad at all. This evening's shindig was progressing much better than she'd expected, mainly thanks to the seating plan for dinner. A forest of flowers took up most of the centre of the table and she had been placed quite far away from Hugo, but right next to Nick. She'd spent much of the meal flirting with him. Hugo must have been able to see this, which added to the fun. There wasn't any harm in it, and anyone who knew her would realise that she was just, well, just playing really. The wine was delicious and by the time the roast goose had been cleared away, she was feeling both randy and reckless.

'I wish we could get away from all of them,' she whispered. 'Go somewhere on our own.'

'Everyone would notice. Hugo wouldn't think much of that, would he?'

'He's drinking rather more than he's used to, I can see. And he's busy with Hester. He's very close to her you know. Goes and chats to her all the time. Perhaps I should be jealous. She's very attractive.'

She ran a finger down his thigh. 'Are you quite as unattached as you pretend to be? No nice young ladies anywhere? Or nice young men, if it comes to that?'

'Nope.' He smiled at her in a way that Claudia thought looked distinctly promising. 'I'm as free as a bird.' Then he winked. Claudia took another sip of wine to steady herself. Maybe, maybe it would be possible for them to creep away without anyone noticing?

She sat back and looked at Alison, down the other end of the table, and caught her eye. The child looked as though someone had just stabbed her in the stomach. Oh, God, thought Claudia. Will she burst into tears and disgrace herself? She ought to be grateful to me for preventing her making a total fool of herself.

'Pour me another glass, sweetie,' she said to Nick.

Nick sighed theatrically. 'You're not going to be in a fit state to dance tomorrow.'

'Oh, yes, I will. I've got a very strong cons . . . constituency.

Constitution. You know.' She giggled and swallowed the wine. The faces of everyone sitting round the table were becoming a little blurred around the edges.

'Do you mind me saying all this?' Hugo leaned closer to Hester. 'You must stop me if I get boring, only I've had rather a lot to drink. It was a dinner to remember.'

Hester smiled at him. 'I don't mind you talking to me one bit. It *was* a good meal, but look at the table now.'

He followed her glance as it took in the ruins of the meal: plates bearing the remains of biscuits and cheese, napkins lying crumpled on the white tablecloth, wine glasses stained with a hint of scarlet, and many of the chairs pushed away from the table. The rest of the company had wandered off to have coffee in the drawing room, but Hugo and Hester were still at the table, alone in the huge dining room.

Hugo said, 'Shall we go and have coffee with the others? I'm sure you're longing to leave; I feel like the Ancient Mariner.'

'No,' Hester put her hand on his wrist and he looked down at it in amazement. 'You've clearly got things on your mind and I'm happy to listen. After all, we haven't had our get-together today, what with one thing and another.'

She moved her hand in the air. Hugo saw, in that small gesture, a shadow of the wonderful dancer she'd been. It was as though everything she'd learned over a whole lifetime of classes was in her now, and she couldn't even move her hands without instinctively falling into a perfect *port de bras . . . Port de mains*. God, I'm pissed, he thought. Maybe I ought to go to bed.

'Well, apart from the fact that our costumes and props are still being made and we've a *prima ballerina* I don't really have total confidence in, things couldn't be better. No, I'm being nasty. Forgive me. It's the wine talking. And I *do* have confidence in Claudia only . . .'

Hester wasn't saying anything. She was looking into his eyes in a way he found soothing and comforting. She wouldn't judge him. She wouldn't think he was a cad. She'd know exactly what he meant. He sighed and took another gulp from his glass and continued. 'But I think Silver's working hard at that extra sequence. Not quite hard enough yet, but—'

'I'm sure she will, in the end. I had a chat with her yesterday and I'm sure she's going to do her best. She's a very intelligent person. I think she'll do everything you expect of her.'

'And of course I don't want to let *you* down, Hester. After you've chosen me to do this.'

'Of course you won't. *Sarabande* will be wonderful. You have to have confidence in your own vision.'

'I have, only it's other people. They do get in the way of the vision, sometimes. Having to deal with your changing feelings for them.'

'Don't think about that now. Keep the discipline. Work on the ballet and focus on that. I know you do. I know that at this very moment *Sarabande* is the most important thing in your life. When it's over, that's when you can allow yourself to see . . . well, to see how things stand with you and Claudia. That's what you're referring to, isn't it?'

Hugo nodded 'I'm mad, aren't I? But she's so . . . Did you see her at dinner? Flirting with Nick? She's gets so stupid when she's had too much to drink. When I think about her, I'm quite glad to have normal things to worry about, like getting *Sarabande* right. Fixing up the costumes and props.'

'Don't worry about those for a second,' said Hester. 'Ruby will have the whole thing under control. And Alison's her apprentice. Ruby says she's very artistic.'

'She is,' Hugo said. 'That's another problem. Alison. I'd miss her, if I ever left Claudia. I come between them quite often. Take Alison's side in fights and so on. Poor thing. Claudia's forever getting at her.'

'There are times when it doesn't matter how hard you try to be good and do the right thing, you just can't help yourself. You can't help what you do. The feelings, well, they're too strong. You're powerless against them. That's what I think. Then you just have to do the best you can.'

Hugo laughed. 'I can't imagine you ever behaving badly. I bet you've never hurt anyone in your whole life.'

'Then you're more naïve than I took you for. There are lots of things in my life which I shouldn't have done. Or should have done differently.'

'Can you tell me about them? Do you want to?'

Hester shook her head. 'No, not tonight. Maybe another time. Now I really do think we ought to go and join the others.'

'Ought we? I suppose we should. But it *has* been lovely talking to you. You are . . . you're a queen. That's what you are, Hester. Really. A queen.'

'And you're drunk and getting silly, Hugo. You need a good strong cup of coffee. Come on.'

Claudia found herself looking out of the drawing-room window. Everyone else had disappeared. It must be very late, she thought. But how beautiful the snow looks. It had thawed a little yesterday but more had fallen during the meal and filled in the footsteps everyone else had made earlier. She'd arranged with Nick to go for a walk. Were they completely mad? She'd gone upstairs straight after dinner and changed into trousers and a sweater and a pair of woolly socks. Suddenly, instead of being a lunatic idea, there was nothing in the world she wanted to do more than walk in that snow, mark it with her feet. Her coat and boots were in the hall, where she'd left them earlier in the day. Nick was sure to be there by now, on the bench where they'd arranged to meet.

She let herself out of the front door. The snow was frozen hard now; it made a loud, crunching noise under her boots as she followed what she thought was the path, though it was hard to tell. Shrubs blanketed in white loomed up on either side of her like small hills, and purple shadows gathered around the trees. Her breath turned into ribbons of mist and hung in the air.

There he was, waiting for her on the bench outside the theatre. Why on earth was his head slumped forward like that? Perhaps he'd passed out from the booze. Maybe it wasn't such a great idea to meet outside on a night as cold as this.

'Nick? Nick, are you all right? It's Claudia.'

'Claudia!' He sat up straight at once and shook himself. 'God, it's cold. I was wondering what had happened to you. I'm fine, really. I've had too much to drink, I think. But maybe this outside idea isn't such a good one. Let's go in. Let's thaw one another out. If we stay here, we'll freeze into living snow people.'

'Yes, let's,' Claudia said, and took his gloved hand. He might be a little drunk still, but at least he'd had the presence of mind to put on a coat and wind a knitted scarf round his neck. They made for the walkway that led from the theatre to the house.

'My room,' Nick whispered as they walked towards the dim light that was still on in the front hall of the house. 'We'll go to my room.'

Nick stopped suddenly in the dark passageway and turned to Claudia.

'They're all asleep, aren't they? Isn't it quiet? It's as though we're . . .' He fell silent.

'As though we're what?'

'The only people in the world. I wish we were!'

Claudia felt a leaping sensation in her stomach. She didn't know what to answer so she didn't say a word. Then she felt his hands on her shoulders. They stood like that for a few moments, not speaking, not moving and there was a current of feeling rising between them that Claudia felt in her belly as a kind of magnetic force. He pulled her towards him and her face was almost on a level with his and she could smell him and his hands were around her waist and drawing her closer. My mouth, she thought. I want him to cover my mouth with his and before she finished the thought she felt his tongue between her lips. She heard his voice whispering as he tore himself away from the kiss and began to murmur into her hair. His words sounded as though they were being spoken somewhere deep in her own head: *Claudia, oh God Claudia, have you any idea how much I want you? Can't think of anything except fucking you . . . oh Claudia, kiss me again. Don't say anything, just come here.*

Claudia closed her eyes and allowed herself to be drawn into the kiss, which seemed to her to go on and on and she was being pushed against the wall of the passageway and Nick's hands were in the opening of her coat and on her breasts and then one hand was behind her and thrusting up under her sweater and she could feel his fingers stroking the skin of her back and he was groaning quietly or maybe that was her making those sounds and then, just as she was falling into an ocean of sensation, Nick suddenly pulled away from her and stood trembling against the other wall of the passageway, leaving Claudia breathless and panting and with a whole yard of carpet yawning between them.

'Claudia, let's go upstairs.'

She kissed him again, curving her body into his. His coat was open now and she pressed up against him and put her hands behind his head and drew him to her. Her mouth opened and she let herself be lost in the kiss until she was dizzy and gasping for breath. Then they were staggering, walking together along the passageway to the hall and up the stairs. The house was in total silence and there was no one to be seen.

'Ssh,' Nick murmured. 'We don't want anyone waking up.'

Claudia nodded. *What about Hugo*, the tiny part of her brain that was still rational and sensible asked her. No, that was all right. He was sure to be asleep. He'd disappeared from the drawing room hours ago. And he'd had a fair amount to drink. If he found out that she'd got to bed so much later than he had, she'd think of something. A story to tell would come to her. For now, there was Nick and nothing but him. The door of his room was there, in front of them and then it was open and they were inside, and before she could draw breath she found herself pushed back on the bed and he was kissing her again. I wish, she thought, I wish he'd never stop.

As Hester lay in bed, she remembered another New Year and shivered. It was so long ago, she thought, but still, thinking about that time is difficult. Then, Ruby used to be her companion on walks.

Adam was being buried tomorrow. She'd been avoiding thinking about it, but now she imagined Edmund, who'd be getting ready in just a few hours to pay his last respects to his greatest friend. It was hard not to go back to the bad times, the months she tried to put out of her mind. As she closed her eyes and willed herself to sleep, she imagined that memories of those days followed her into her dreams like black shadows.

1952

Hester woke up on the morning after her parting from Adam feeling as though she hadn't slept all night. Maybe she hadn't, although the dreams she thought she'd had meant that she must have drifted off at some point. She went through her morning routine – vomiting, having a biscuit and a cup of tea, and then getting ready for class. She couldn't speak to anyone in the theatre. They all seemed to be moving behind a glass wall, mouthing things at her to which she made some kind of answer, saying she had a bad headache. Her own voice sounded to her as though she were speaking underwater.

'Are you with us, Hester?' Piers asked, looking at her rather too sharply.

She nodded. 'I'm fine. Really. I'll be all right.'

It was an effort to go through the usual *pliés, arabesques, pirouettes, grand jetés* and the rest. She moved as though lead weights were attached to her feet. I can't bear this, she thought. I can't bear not being able to dance properly. Is it the baby stopping me? Filling me up and making me heavy? She imagined a tiny copy of Adam inside her, eating her up as it grew and grew, and she was suddenly filled with revulsion. I've still got it, she thought. The piece of paper. I can get rid of this. I don't have to have this baby. That doctor of Dinah's will scrape every bit of Adam out of me, and I'll never have to think of him again. A surge of energy filled her and she made up her mind to phone the number as soon as class was over. As she'd kept the piece of paper, it must mean that part of her had always intended to consult him. Didn't it? Maybe it did. Hester didn't know very much about the progress of a pregnancy, but she did know that the sooner you could have an abortion the easier and safer it was. And what they take out looks far less like a real person early on said a voice in her head, which she pushed away and decided to ignore.

May isn't supposed to be like this, Hester thought. She was walking down a long road full of boring, ordinary houses and the rain was pouring down. She had an umbrella but her feet were soaked through. A woman (the doctor's receptionist, probably) told her on the phone that it was only a few minutes from the tube station, but it seemed as though she'd been walking for hours.

She'd made the appointment after class yesterday and now here she was, somewhere at the end of the District Line, in a part of London she'd never been to before. The people she passed on the street were blank-faced and wrapped up against the weather, but Hester imagined that they were looking at her, pointing at her as she passed, saying *there's the young woman who's going to have an abortion. Shame on her.*

She'd been to the bank and taken out enough money. It cost a hundred pounds to get rid of a baby, apparently. Was that reasonable? Dinah had said it was. Luckily, Hester had saved enough over the past few years to be able to pay for the operation herself, but it left her rather short. *I'll help you financially and so forth.* She could still hear Adam's words and they made her furious all over again.

This was the house. It looked just like all the others. A bay window; a green-painted front door with a skylight at the top. Number 56. A neglected garden, a little overgrown, with roses which had never been pruned already putting out buds at the end of long, leggy stems full of far too many thorns. She knocked at the door.

'Miss Gordon?' A woman stood in the dark of the hall and for a moment Hester wondered who Miss Gordon was, before remembering that she'd given a false name. She nodded. The woman stared at her, then said, 'Come in. The doctor will see you in a moment.'

She looked, Hester thought, as though she ought to take up residence in a coffin: pale, dressed in black, with a damp smell about her. She led the way to the front room of the house. This was supposed to be a waiting room. There were ancient magazines on the table in front of Hester, but as she was clearly the only patient, she couldn't help wondering why she was being kept waiting. The room was chilly.

'The doctor will see you now,' said the woman in black, returning. 'Follow me.'

The surgery, or whatever it was called, was across the hall from the waiting room. The doctor was sitting behind a desk and smiled and got to his feet as he introduced himself. He was thin and small, and as pale as his assistant or nurse or whatever she was. She stood, waiting – to do what? Help him with the operation? Hold the patient down? Give an injection? Mop up the blood? Hester could scarcely answer the doctor's questions because of a creeping feeling of terror and nausea that threatened to overwhelm her.

The room was full of shadows, she noticed. The light shining on to the doctor's desk made them gather in the corners. She became aware of the woman who had shown her in standing quietly behind her chair, waiting and growing. That was what it felt like. Hester felt that she was becoming larger and larger and looming over her, close enough to smell. She glanced at the woman's hands, white against the fabric of her dress, and thought she saw claws at the end of each finger, animal's claws, and she imagined those hands reaching inside her as the monster doctor pulled her legs apart, pulled apart her flesh, and Hester could feel the agony of those claws on her body, and she saw, quite clearly, fountains of blood gushing from between her legs and washing over the floor of this terrible room and then there would be . . . what? Something. Someone. Taken from her, drowned in blood and taken by the woman with the claw hands to be thrown away into a place she couldn't bring herself to picture.

'Please take your clothes off and lie on the bed behind that screen,' said the doctor. Hester stood up.

'I'm sorry to have wasted your time,' she said, every word she uttered almost choking her. 'I've changed my mind. I'm going to have the baby. I have to go now.'

'You've changed your mind?' The doctor sighed. 'You young girls don't know what you want, do you? Can't keep away from the sex, of course, but don't want to deal with the consequences. I suppose the father is long gone? Well, you know your own business best, but I do wish sometimes—'

'I'm sorry to have taken up your time,' Hester said again, cutting him off, and hurried from the room. She was losing her mind. Just yesterday, the thought of her baby filled her with a sick horror and now, here she was, feeling an overwhelming love for this *thing*, this scrap of nothing in her womb. Her baby. Not anyone else's. Hers. Her child. I'm mad, she thought. How could I let this person with his white cold fingers prod at me and prick me with needles and take away my baby. Kill it. Murder it. Wipe its blood, my blood, off his horrible plastic bed?

Hester ran down the ugly street in the rain, letting it fall on her head, soaking her. I can't, she thought, I can't do it. She sat on the tube to Lancaster Gate, looking at the ghost-image of herself on the window of the carriage, and felt as though she herself had escaped death. She was sick and cold and wet and there was nothing in her head but Madame Olga. She'll know what to do. She'll help me. I must go to her.

Hester was a little comforted by this thought and yet she knew that Madame Olga would be furious. I'll never be forgiven for throwing away my career, she thought, and started to cry. How would she reach Wychwood House without telling Piers the whole story? She couldn't imagine doing that. She said to herself, I could run away now, this minute, without even going back to Moscow Road. I've got a hundred pounds in my handbag. It's only four o'clock. I can be with Madame Olga tonight. Then she can explain to Piers. He'll send my things up to Yorkshire.

In a trance, she got off at the next stop and began to make her way to King's Cross. I want to go home, she thought, but where is that? She wanted *Grand-mère*, but she was dead and couldn't help her. She wanted not to be pregnant, but she couldn't murder her baby. She wanted to dance. How would she ever dance again? Her legs felt as though they could scarcely carry her on to the right platform. She was aware of other people on the edges of her vision, peering at her to see if she was all right. I must be crying, she thought. I must look like a mad person. I don't care. No one dared to approach her. Hester thought she might have been making strange sounds as she walked. The glittery, hard floors of the tunnels she was passing through rang with the sound of her footsteps and every advertisement was blurry and swam before her eyes and somewhere, somewhere inside her, her heart was breaking. Someone had taken hold of it and twisted it about, this way and that, until it broke at last. That was how it felt; exactly like that.

'*Moia golubchka!*' Madame Olga stood by the door and peered through a grey mist at Hester. 'My poor darling child.'

She was too exhausted to speak. The journey had taken longer than she thought, and every part of it was difficult. The train was crowded and she sat looking out of the window and seeing nothing, all the way to Leeds. She fell into a taxi and told him where she was going. She'd noticed the driver staring at her and knew that she looked distraught, but couldn't summon up the energy to smile and reassure him that he wasn't letting a madwoman into his cab. Rain began to fall as the car drove into the village and she roused herself a little to watch out for the gates of Wychwood House.

'This is it,' she told the driver. 'I'll get out here.'

'I'm happy to take you up to the house,' the man said. 'It's no trouble really.'

'No, I'd rather walk, thank you,' Hester said, congratulating herself on sounding almost normal. How could that be, when she felt as though there was nothing in her head but black space?

'Right, then,' said the driver, and took his money. Hester sat in the back seat, trying to work out which handle to press, how to get out of the taxi, and then saw that the driver had opened the door for her.

When the taxi had gone, she looked up at Wychwood House and down the road to the village. Beyond the shop and the church was the house where the Wellicks used to live. They'd moved south long ago, but just being here, in this place where she'd spent so many unhappy nights when she was a little girl, made Hester shiver. She turned her back on the village and opened the black gates that would lead her to Madame Olga.

It was raining again as Hester walked up the drive. At least I've got my umbrella, she thought. What will Madame Olga say? Will she send me away? Where to? Will she be angry with me? She'll ask me why I haven't got any luggage. I'll have to write to Nell and ask her to send it on. She won't mind. She always helps me. I wish I'd thought of phoning her from King's Cross. By the time Hester rang the bell and leaned, exhausted, against the inner wall of the porch, all she wanted was to be inside, out of the rain.

'Come in, come in, *moia bedniazhka*,' Madame Olga said. She had her arm around Hester's shoulders and led her to the kitchen. 'Sit, sit and I make tea for us, like we used to do. Remember? In the glasses. I have no chocolate, but I have biscuits. Where are the biscuits?'

Hester sat at the kitchen table and watched Madame Olga as she went from the sink to the kettle and then to the cupboard, getting everything ready. She kept up a constant stream of talk, as though she knew that when she stopped, there would be nothing to hear but bad news. It wasn't till Hester had drunk a few sips of the hot, sweet tea that she dared to speak.

'I'm going to have a baby, Madame,' she said, and waited for the whole house to fall down on her head. Madame Olga put a hand up in front of her mouth and made a small, whimpering noise. This was the only sound of weakness and distress Hester had ever heard her utter. She'd barely registered the cry when Madame Olga sat up straighter, took the hand away from her face and smiled bravely. She took Hester's right hand between both of hers and squeezed it tightly.

'Do not worry any more, my child. I will arrange everything. It will come out well in the end, you will see.'

'I've been to a doctor, Madame. I can't do that. I'm not having an abortion.' This made Madame Olga frown. 'You are sure? It is nothing in the early days, I promise you. You will recover quickly.'

Hester shook her head. 'I want this baby. I thought I didn't at first, and I went looking for a way to get rid of it, but now . . .' She blinked at Madame Olga through tears that threatened to brim over. 'I . . . will love the child. The baby will love me. Don't you think I'd make a good mother?'

Madame Olga snorted. 'To be a good mother is easy. To be a good ballerina is very difficult. How can you continue with the dancing if you become a mother? Tell me that. And where is the father?'

'I don't want to talk about him. He's married. He can't . . . he won't . . . I wouldn't consult with him about anything. This is *my* baby.' She put her hand on her stomach where, hard as it was to picture, there was someone, a real person, growing. It made her feel dizzy to think about it.

'You must decide nothing now. Stay here and I will speak to Piers and he will make up a story to tell everyone. You have been doing too much work, too much dancing and you must rest; something like that. I will look after you and we will have a class every day until you cannot dance any more. It will be good for you, the countryside, the fresh air, away from London. Then, when your stomach is very big, I will send you far away so that no one will know.'

'I don't care if everyone knows. How will you keep such a secret when the baby's born? She – he – will live with me, and I'll be looking after him – her – so what's the point of hiding away now?'

'Journalists, the public, the ones who pay to watch you, they must know nothing. Not now, and if it is possible, not for a long time. This is what I think. I will discuss with Piers what we have to do. Till then, you must say nothing. But please do not worry. Please. It is bad for you. You let me worry for all of us. Now you should sleep. I will run a bath and prepare a room for you. You understand, I did not expect you, but is good that you came to me. Yes. I will take good care of you.'

The days and weeks that followed ran into one another with nothing much to disturb them, each one tracing a similar pattern: class (more and more gentle as time went on; stopping in the end when she was too clumsy to move freely), a light lunch with Madame Olga, a walk on the moors beyond Wychwood House, early bedtimes. During those months her love for Adam was like a wound. She thought sometimes that it was healing over and forming a scab, and then something would happen, a tune on the radio, or a remark of Madame Olga's, that would tear the wound open again.

A letter came from Dinah:

Where are you? What have they done with you? I've come to the conclusion that you must be at Wychwood, but I've been told in no uncertain terms by Piers (yes, I telephoned him as soon as I heard) that I'm not to come looking for you. You were very ill. A nervous breakdown, he said. When I asked why, he said that people didn't generally need a reason to have one. Too much work and what he called 'personal difficulties'. I can read between the lines with the best of them, Hester and I'm sure I know what's going on. I've thought ever since you came to see me in Cardiff that you might be pregnant. Call me melodramatic if you like but it looks to me as though they're hiding you away because they don't want the press to find out. The last time I enquired I was told you had gone to Paris. Can this be true? Have you been in touch with Edmund? Or A?

Anyway, it's pointless me wanting to come and see you. I can't. I have to work or I'd starve and what's worse, lose my position in this company, where I'm doing quite well. But if you wanted me to, I'd come and see you wherever you were. On a Sunday, I suppose, but still – I do miss you, Hester. You know I'd do anything for you whenever you asked me to. Please write.

That was the first of many letters from her dear friend. Hester answered them and tried to explain to Dinah how sad and sorry for herself she was feeling:

I've become another person, Dinah. You wouldn't recognise me. I cry at the least little thing. It's probably hormones, but I'm frightened too, about what's going to happen, and I'm sure hormones aren't meant to make you feel fear. I'm not even sure what I'm scared of. What's it going to be like after the baby's born? Will I be able to look after it and carry on dancing?

Adam, she knew, would hear of the birth somehow, through Edmund perhaps, and then he'd try and send money or (worse or better? Hester couldn't decide) not send money. At the very heart of her fear lay the thought *I'll never be able to dance again once I've given birth. No one will want me as a principal any longer. The magic will vanish as though it had never existed and then what will become of me?* Hester understood that Madame Olga was probably right in everything she said, but she couldn't think of her baby being given away without wanting to die. She didn't allow it to enter her mind. Adoption would happen over her dead body. The only thing that gave her the strength to get up each morning during those months was the dream she had of her child.

Hester spent a long time trying names out in her head. She wrote them down in the blank pages of a notebook. Helen after her mother,

Celeste after her grandmother, or Elizabeth, Suzanna, Maria, Marguerite. Names for boys were harder. Matthew, Jonathan, Christopher, Michael. Two names she rejected at once were Adam and Henry. She wanted no memories of fathers – not hers and not her baby's. Edmund would be the godfather. Dinah would be better than a fairy godmother. Everything would be all right. There were days when Hester almost persuaded herself that she truly believed that she might resume her career and take care of her child in a perfectly normal way.

A letter came from Edmund, and Hester smiled to read it. She could hear his voice clearly in every word:

Darling Hester, I am going plumb loco worrying about you. I do wish you'd drop a single line just to reassure me you are really where Piers says you are, in a clinic far away recuperating after some sort of illness. He was amazingly and dazzlingly unspecific, and assumed, I think, that I had the usual male embarrassment about Women's Things. Ha! I pressed him and he confessed after a bit that a nervous breakdown was what you were suffering from and that the doctors had advised peace and quiet and absolutely no visitors. A bigger load of spherical objects I never heard in my life! The thing for depression is friends. Everyone knows that. I would come and cheer you up at the smallest sign from you. I must stop now. I am busy, busy, thank Heavens. If it weren't for constant work (a production of Red Riding Hood in Amsterdam next) I would seriously not be my usual cheery self. Write to me, Hester, if you can. I think of you constantly. Yours, Edmund.

P.S. I have ideas of my own about what's wrong with you. The passage of time will tell me if I'm right and if I am, then you have my word that I will look after you. Does that give you the courage to write to me? I hope so.

Hester smiled to think of Piers protecting her reputation and keeping her secret. She wrote to Edmund at once and told him everything. As soon as he heard from her, he began sending her postcards from Amsterdam to cheer her up. She wrote back, but knew that she could never match Edmund's sparkle and energy. She sometimes felt that every word she put down was as heavy and miserable as she was, but Edmund always ended his messages by begging her to write again, so she did.

When she was feeling particularly low, Hester would tell herself that maybe Adam *had* written and Madame Olga had intercepted the correspondence. Perhaps he was bombarding her with letters, begging her to come to him; telling her that yes, he was divorcing Virginia and that they would now be able to live together for ever and that these things never reached her because Madame Olga had looked out for them and torn them up from the very beginning. At moments when she felt particularly desperate, Hester imagined that he might decide to get her himself. Take her away with him to live happy ever after.

While they were still at Wychwood, she used to stand at the window for hours, peering down the drive, willing the postman to appear. When she saw him, she'd run down and see if she could get to the letters before Madame Olga and sometimes she did, but there was never anything from Adam. Not once, while Hester was on the lookout.

There were nights when she couldn't sleep and then she saw her, Virginia, lying next to Adam in bed. Hester imagined him wanting *her* as he made love to his wife. She went over everything that they'd ever said or done again and again till she was nearly demented. As the summer moved into autumn, she found it harder and harder to lie comfortably in bed and began to fear the birth. The pain. Madame Olga made a point of *not* dwelling on the agonies of childbirth, but her very silence terrified Hester. Madame had had no personal experience of it, but still, there were all the stories that circulate among women. She must, Hester felt sure, have a whole fund of those. She was saying nothing, Hester thought, because she knew the pain would be so bad that she daren't tell her the truth, and this made her more scared than ever. Piers arrived for what he called 'a conference'. The next morning, as soon as he'd left for London, Madame Olga told her what they had decided.

'It is all arranged. Ruby is going to leave Piers' house and come and look after you.'

'But I don't need looking after,' Hester frowned. 'Do I? I've got you after all.'

'Of course, of course. I do not speak of now. I speak of nearer the time of your confinement. I think you should go away from here, because I have a special doctor who is the one who should look after you. He is in Scotland. A place called Gullane.'

'Scotland? Why? Why on earth do I have to go all the way there? Surely there are doctors who can deliver a baby here in Yorkshire. I don't want to leave Wychwood.'

'It will be good for you. Sea air. You can relax. Raymond, Dr Crawford, has assured me he will look after you as though you were his own daughter.'

'Who is he? Where did you meet him?'

'That is not important. He looked after me when I was sick in Paris once. He was a junior doctor then but now he is a respected obstetrician. Very well respected. In those days, I think he was in love with me a little, but of course I did not encourage him. Still, he is very kind to me always and it is good to have someone to look after you who is a personal friend.'

'I don't see that it's necessary. None of it. I know why you're doing this, Madame. You want me out of the way. You've already told me that you don't want anyone to know that I'm pregnant.'

'What do you expect us to do? Piers says the papers have phoned to see what has happened to one of the Charleroi's principal dancers. This will get worse. The stories will grow and spread. The gossip will stop now because he has told them you are exhausted. You are resting, he says.'

'And they'll soon forget all about me if I'm somewhere out of the way.' Hester shrugged her shoulders. 'I suppose I have to do what you say. I can't manage on my own. At least Ruby will be with me in this Scottish wilderness.'

'This Scottish wilderness is a lovely place. Ruby tells me she used to go there for family holidays when she was a girl. Piers said it was a good omen, this coincidence. You and Ruby will go in October and I will come to join you nearer the birth. All will be well. You will like Raymond Crawford, I am quite sure of this.'

When Hester's father died at the end of June, that was, according to Madame Olga, a stroke of good fortune for them, though she didn't express it like that when she spoke to Hester. They could tell anyone who enquired that she was in Paris and give no more details. After a while, all but her closest friends stopped enquiring about where she was.

No one asked Hester whether she wanted to go to her father's funeral. Never mind that she hadn't been in touch with him; never mind that she'd left his house fifteen years ago. If anyone had consulted her, she would have said yes, but her desire to go to Paris was not so much to pay her respects to someone she regarded as a stranger but a longing to see again the place where she'd spent her first years; to move through the rooms that she remembered from childhood. Perhaps, too, she could visit *Grand-mère*'s grave, and mourn her properly, as she never had at the time of her death.

Madame Olga prepared for their visit to France as though they were going on holiday. She spent many hours deciding what to wear: what jewels, what hats, and what shawls. She tossed items from the cupboard to the bed and then picked up one thing after another for careful scrutiny.

'You will wear black, Hester? Or dark purple is good. Luckily you do not show yet. And a hat? Or a Spanish mantilla? Look, I have a piece of lace here which I have not worn for years, but it will be just right for you. And with it you can wear my pearls. I can take them out of the bank.'

'No, just this.' She fingered the gold of her grandmother's necklace.

Madame Olga sighed theatrically. 'This necklace of yours, it is mad. You can never wear anything else round your neck because of this necklace. I have in this house amber and jade and every kind of jewel and I am keeping it all just for you. Why do you not wear those instead?'

'I do, sometimes,' Hester answered. 'I hide this one under high-necked things. But I never take it off except on stage. Never.'

The Channel crossing was smooth and easy. The sun shone and the sea was like a sheet of pale grey satin. Hester stood on deck watching

England growing smaller and smaller and trying hard to feel something other than completely numb. I should be sadder, she thought. I should be crying for my father, who died before I could see him again. What would I have said to him? Hester found it hard to imagine that conversation. All her feelings had gathered in the very centre of her being, concentrated on nothing other than her baby, her growing baby.

Hester's thoughts, which should have been focused on the funeral, on wondering what she would say to her father's second wife, Yvonne, whom she'd never met, refused to fasten on to anything. She imagined them flitting round the inside of her head like moths trapped in the glass globe of a lamp, aimless and blundering.

'Oh, ma petite, je suis tellement . . . Mais entrez, entrez, et bienvenues à toutes les deux!'

Yvonne was a small woman with a thin mouth and eyes like currants. She wore her grey hair in a bun and was dressed from head to foot in black. Hester couldn't decide if this was her habitual dress or whether she was wearing it because her husband had just died. What, she couldn't help wondering, had made her father fall in love with such a woman, especially after being married to Hester's mother? Yvonne said, 'I will show you where you will sleep,' and led them up the stairs.

'This was my grandmother's room,' Hester said, running her hands over the counterpane. 'The wallpaper's been changed. This counterpane too. Grand-mère had yellow walls and a satin cover on the bed. Everything's different.'

'You,' said Madame Olga. 'It is you who are different. Not the house. Places stay the same and we change. It is always so.'

The house was smaller than Hester remembered, and everything was shabbier. The kitchen, which she'd held in her memory for years, had a new modern sink and cooker. The apricot-coloured curtains had been replaced with a pair made of some synthetic material printed with jolly-faced kettles and saucepans. The wooden table had gone and the room was dominated by something hideous and blueish in metal and Formica.

'Your father has arranged for money for you,' said Yvonne, when they were sitting in the drawing room having tea.

The teacups were her mother's. Hester recognised them and felt sorrow and regret wash over her as she drank. Madame Olga did the talking for both of them. She was the one who asked about the arrangements for the funeral tomorrow; who found out that Yvonne was the main beneficiary of Henri Prévert's will.

'I don't care about the money. I don't care about any of that,' Hester said next morning as she and Madame Olga were dressing for the ceremony. 'I just wanted to come back and see the house again. That's all. But *Grand-mère* – she's gone long ago. This isn't her house. Not really. The shape is the same but the colours are different, and the smells.'

'Smells?' Madame Olga paused in the middle of pulling on a black cloche hat with a jet brooch pinned to the front. 'What are these smells?'

Hester shook her head. It was too complicated to explain that when her grandmother was alive, the fragrance of cinnamon, or lemon, or rosemary or garlic haunted the air. *Grand-mère*'s violet perfume had lingered in the soft furnishings and the curtains, and had filled every corner of her bedroom. When Hester was a child, there were parquet floors in every room which smelled of the lavender and beeswax polish used to clean them.

She looked out of the window and saw the top of the black car that was to take them to the funeral. For a moment, she was dizzy. There was another car, wasn't there? Another time. Snow on the ground and her mother about to be taken out of the house in a long, wooden box and Hester not allowed to go because she was too small. Too young. She could feel herself trembling and sat down on the bed, her vision suddenly blurred with tears.

'You cry at last for your papa,' said Madame Olga. 'That is good. You have not felt it till now. It is the shock.' She misses nothing, Hester reflected. Whatever else is going on, she notices everything about me.

'I'm not really crying for Papa. My mother. I can remember . . . never mind. Let's go down now. They're waiting for us.'

As she stood beside her father's grave, it occurred to Hester that the cemetery was a miniature town, where the headstones were like the façades of houses. Gravel paths resembled small roads, winding between them, and summer trees and shrubs stood guard around these miniature houses of the dead. The weather was warm and she felt herself perspiring in her thin, wool coat. Madame Olga had prevailed on her to wear the black mantilla. It wasn't worth fighting over, though she was conscious of looking out of place, like someone from a production of *Don Quixote*.

Out of the corner of her eye, Hester could see that Yvonne was crying, dabbing at her eyes with a handkerchief edged in lace. Madame Olga stood very straight and still. Her own gaze was fixed on *Grand-mère*'s tombstone, which was near the hole in the earth into which they would soon be lowering her father. He's dead, Hester thought, and I should mourn him, but I can't because I never really knew him. Everyone thinks these tears are for him and they're not. She wanted to shout out, I'm not crying for *him*! Why should I? He sent me away when I was little more than a baby. He never loved me, not properly. I'm crying for my grandmother who died before I could say goodbye. She bit her lip and closed her eyes and prayed for the burial to be over.

While the others made their way down the neat grey paths to the gate, Hester stood by her grandmother's grave and fought an impulse to lie down on the tomb and fling her arms around the headstone. Suddenly, she saw herself as Giselle. At the end of the ballet she'd done exactly that – draped herself over a tomb made of some kind of cardboard and pretended to weep. I know all the positions for grief by heart, she reflected, and turned to walk away. The thought of her grandmother down there under the earth tormented her. She tried to comfort herself by thinking, it's not really her. It's nothing more than a skeleton. Not *Grand-mère*, who is alive in my mind. A real person.

Once they returned to Wychwood the days passed quietly, but for a few weeks bad dreams woke Hester almost every night. She'd lie there gasping, almost able to taste the earth on her tongue, as it was shovelled into a grave into which she'd been lowered and which was already half-full of petals from thousands of cream roses. When this nightmare came, she sat up in bed and turned on the bedside lamp and sometimes went down to the kitchen for a cup of tea, because she knew that sleep was out of the question.

One day towards the beginning of October, Hester and Madame Olga were walking in the garden. The trees were particularly beautiful, leaves covered the ground in a patchwork of gold and scarlet, and the sky was a clear, pale grey. Hester could still walk almost exactly as she used to, with her head high and her hands covering the rather small bump of her stomach. Madame Olga's chin was buried in the enormous Persian lamb collar of her coat.

'Now,' she said, 'the time has come that we must make plans for the future. Dr Crawford has introduced me to good adoption agency up there in Scotland, for afterwards.'

'*Adoption agency?*' Hester turned round, not quite believing what she was hearing. 'What are you saying? I told you! We discussed it right from the start. I'd never, never give up this baby for adoption. What makes you think I would? Did you think I'd changed my mind?' Hester knew that she was scarlet in the face.

Madame Olga shrugged. 'It's what's necessary. When you first came here, you were very sad. I said whatever you wanted to hear. What could I do?'

'I won't do it. I can look after him. Or her. I can keep him and be his mother.'

'Impossible! It would be cruel to leave him from the start when you go back to class. All his life, if he stays with you, he will be second-best. You are a dancer. You cannot also be mother. This I know. This I have seen, many times. You cannot be everything. And think of this: many women, millions of women can be good mothers. No one but you can be Hester Fielding, *prima ballerina*. I am right, am I not?'

Hester was so angry that she began shouting. 'No, you're *not* right. You're wrong. I'm a mother. That's what I want. I told you from the very first day I came to you. I want to be a mother to this baby. I know what it's like not to have a mother and my baby will have me. Every day. Every night. I'm not going to go back to dancing unless I can keep my baby. Why can't I have a nurse to help me, while I'm in class, or dancing? Someone to take care of the baby when I'm working?'

'This is stupid. If you have a nurse to do these things, how are you the mother? Will your baby not miss you when you are not with him? He is better with a mother who is there all the time. The adoption agency will put him, or her, of course, with the very best family, I can promise you that.'

'I'm not doing it!' She was shrieking now. 'I won't. I'm keeping my baby. I don't care what you and Piers have arranged. You can't make me. And I'm going to be a dancer as well. Why can't I? Why can't I do both?'

'You are a silly girl and you do not understand the feelings of the public! They will not love you if they see you are an unmarried mother. It is a disgrace. They like their ballerinas to be pure and good. They want to admire them. To be in awe of them. If you had a baby, it would show them that you are—'

'What? A slut? A slag? What?'

'Not any of those. Do not say those words to me. You know I do not think that. No, they will see you are human. Like them, not better than they are. Not different. They will ask themselves who the father might be, and there will be gossip and the years will go by and you will not be young any longer and the child will grow up without knowing who his father is. That is cruel to your child, not kind.'

'You can't say that! It's not true. I'll love him so much. Quite enough for two parents. He'll never, never be without love. I'll surround him with it. Or her. My baby might be a girl. She might become a dancer too. Have you thought of that? How can you make me give my child away? It's monstrous.'

'I think of you. Only of you. *Your* career. *Your* life. I think of *your* future. Who will marry you when you have a baby by another man?'

'I don't care if no one does. And I'm going to keep my baby. I won't let you bully me.'

'I do not bully!' Madame Olga was shouting now. 'I am doing what is right for you, *glupysh!* You will regret it, you see, if you keep it.'

'Then *let* me regret it. It's none of your business. You're not my mother. Or my grandmother. Go away and leave me alone.'

Madame Olga turned white. She stood up and Hester saw that her hands were trembling.

'I didn't . . . I *really* didn't mean that, Madame Olga,' she sobbed. The tears had come suddenly, and she wiped them away with her sleeve. 'You know I didn't. I love you. I can't bear to fight with you.' Hester sat down on the top step of the porch and put her head in her hands. Sounds came from her mouth that she couldn't seem to prevent – howls and moans, animal noises.

Madame Olga crouched down beside her and stroked her hair, gently, as though she were a wild creature that might turn on her and bite. Gradually, Hester's sobbing died down and there was nothing but the sound of the wind that had sprung up suddenly to shake the leaves from the trees.

'We will go inside now. And I will do what you want, of course. But you must think, yes? About what is best. You are only nineteen years old, do not forget. To me you are still a child. But I will not force you. We will do what we have to do, after the birth, but you must have the baby in Scotland. Piers has already paid the rent for a cottage. Near the sea. Very healthy for you. It will be like a holiday. That is how we must think of it, yes? Everything will be good. We will not tell the world yet. You agree? It is a good place. Peace and quiet.'

'It's not exactly a metropolis here, is it?' Hester said, sniffing and using the hankie Madame Olga had handed her. 'I hear nothing but silence and no one ever comes to visit. Except Piers.'

'Never mind. You will see, everything will be fine.'

At the beginning of November, Hester and Ruby moved to a cottage beside the sea in Gullane. This was a small house, with two bedrooms upstairs and a sitting room-cum-kitchen on the ground floor. It was a little way out of the town, set apart from other houses, and they had no immediate neighbours. Even here, Hester thought, where I know nobody, they're making sure that no one comes near me. I don't care. Soon, my baby will be here.

A bed had been booked in the hospital at Haddington and Dr Crawford ('Such a gentleman! You will love him, I am quite sure,' said Madame Olga) came to visit Hester a few days after her arrival. She hadn't summoned him, but when he appeared at their door, she realised that Madame Olga must have told him that she and Ruby were in residence.

Hester was reassured when she met him. While he took her blood pressure, she tried to imagine what he must have been like as a young man. He was short and square and tweedy, with a rather mournful face and thick iron-grey hair. His white hands felt cool on her skin. He smiled kindly at her and she found herself relaxing.

'You must rest, my dear,' he said. 'Your blood pressure tends towards the high, so we must keep an eye on that.'

'Is anything wrong? Will the baby be all right?'

'Nothing to concern yourself about at the moment, but don't excite yourself unduly and take regular gentle exercise. I'll come and visit you again in a few days.'

'Will you take a cup of tea, Doctor?' Ruby asked him, as he folded away his stethoscope.

'No, thank you, Ruby,' he said, going to the door. 'It's time I was off to see my other patients. Good day to you both.'

When he'd gone, Hester said, 'He's very nice but I can't imagine him ever being in love with Madame Olga, can you?'

'I'm not sure,' said Ruby. 'I think he might have been quite handsome as a young man. He's a comforting sort of person.'

'Anyway, I'm glad he's going to take such good care of me. I'll try to do what he says and avoid thinking of anything depressing. I'm going to rest and go for long walks and eat lovely food. And so are you, because you're here to keep me company.'

Ruby made sure that Hester kept to her resolution. Every day, they wrapped up in warm clothes and went for walks among the sand dunes and Hester tried not to worry. They talked as they went, about everything, and Ruby was always comforting and calm. Whenever Hester gave way to despair, or anxiety, Ruby was there with a sensible word and a distraction of some kind. She seemed to know that Hester was avoiding thinking about what lay ahead for both her and her baby. Ruby was in charge until Madame Olga arrived. She was due in Gullane in good time for the birth, towards the middle of December.

For the first seven months of her pregnancy, Hester had hardly noticed that her body was changing. She was fit and young, and went on feeling almost exactly as she always had. It was possible sometimes for her to forget that Adam's child was there, in the dark, growing and growing. Grief was the emotion she felt for the most part. She was grieving for her love and she gave little thought to what would become of her once the baby was born. She knew it would be hard to get back to dancing, but this was mostly because Madame Olga kept telling her so.

Then, towards the middle of October, Hester began to be aware of the changes. Suddenly, she was heavy and slow, and because of her distended stomach she was finding it difficult to walk or sit or even lie in bed normally. He (she always imagined her baby as a boy) was moving almost all the time, and Hester felt him turning and pushing and kicking in the silent dark, waving his tiny hands like fronds of seaweed in a kind of underwater dance. She dreamed of her baby at night. She saw his body enclosed in her body whenever she shut her eyes, and during the day she went slowly from place to place, feeling huge and swollen and totally unlike herself but like some strange, un-human creature.

In their little house, the days passed slowly. Late in the year, the nights seemed to come down almost after lunch, and they were very long. Hester didn't mind that. She'd found a new talent for sleeping. Ruby was in charge of the cooking, but she always found something soothing for Hester to do such as scraping carrots, or laying the table, or chopping what seemed to Hester like a thousand vegetables for the nourishing soups that were Ruby's speciality.

'You always say you're going to make shortbread, Ruby, but what we get is healthy soup! This is about the only time in my whole life when I could eat as much shortbread as I liked. No one cares if I'm fat at the moment.'

'I'll make some tomorrow. I'll use my mother's special recipe. It's not difficult, Hester. You'll learn how to make it yourself.'

'I'll need to, won't I? I'd like to be the kind of mother who makes shortbread.'

'When you come back from rehearsal, d'you mean? You'll put away your *pointe* shoes and get out your pinny . . .'

'Or maybe I could make shortbread *en pointe?* In a tutu?'

The two women burst out laughing and Ruby said, 'You're trying to avoid dealing with those turnips. This soup will never be ready at the rate we're going.'

Hester sat down obediently and smiled. How lucky she was to have Ruby as a companion!

During the day, when they walked on the dunes, she wore a thick overcoat and a hat that Ruby had knitted for her. Her hands were hidden in a fur muff that Madame Olga had found, left over from the Russian winters of her youth.

On these excursions, she watched the clouds streak across the colourless sky, and followed the line between the sea and the sky, and trudged through the sand with the wind blowing in her face. Hester was grateful for the fact that Ruby came with her, even though sometimes, Hester knew, she would have preferred to stay by the fireside doing her tapestry. There were days when she persuaded Ruby she was happy to go out on her own, and it was true. Sometimes, she wanted to be absolutely alone with her baby and the sky and the iron-grey sea.

Hester couldn't pretend that her sadness over Adam hadn't lifted since the night they parted, but every movement of his baby reminded her that he was out there, in the world that existed beyond the dunes, and the small town with its neat houses and quiet streets that Madame Olga had chosen to be the birthplace for his child. There was also, somewhere, another universe: of footlights and greasepaint and ballet shoes, and flowers tossed on to the stage, and this seemed so distant that sometimes Hester had trouble believing in it. Here: this was where the truth was, in her sore ankles and huge stomach and the bone-wrenching tiredness that took hold of her whenever she sat down.

After supper, she and Ruby talked. Hester watched Ruby work on her tapestry and enjoyed seeing it grow and spread over the canvas. This had no picture printed on it, and Ruby chose her colours according to some private scheme that she couldn't articulate when Hester asked her about it. Or perhaps (this sometimes occurred to Hester) she didn't want to describe her thought process. Maybe she was superstitious about it. Hester knew that sometimes when you tried to explain how you did something, it vanished or evaporated, or a part of the magic that accompanied the creation seemed to disappear.

Ruby told Hester a little about childbirth. She was trying to be encouraging, doing her best to make Hester brave about the ordeal to come, but the mere fact that she clearly *did* think of it as an ordeal was the opposite of heartening.

'The first baby's always the hardest,' she said one night. 'That's what my mam said, and of course I was the first. She was three days in labour with me. It's a wonder, really, that she dared go on to have my brothers and sisters.'

'I'm not going to have any more children, Ruby,' Hester said. 'You know I'm not.'

'Well, I'm quite sure not everyone has a three-day labour. And in any case, this was thirty years ago, don't forget. Things have moved on. I was born at home, in my parents' bed. It's all much more . . . more scientific now. Doctor Crawford is very clever and I'm sure you're in excellent hands. Don't forget that your body is much more flexible than my mother's ever was.'

'Tell me about the pains, Ruby. How bad are they?'

'I can't tell you properly, because I've never had them. But they can be bad, that's true.'

'Bad? How bad?'

'My mam used to say, like the whole of your insides being cramped up by burning tongs.'

'My God! And women go through this?'

'Everyone does. It soon passes, and then you've a pretty bairn in your arms and you forget about the pain entirely.'

Hester doubted that she would, but said nothing. Ruby went on stitching, picking one colour after another from the basket of wool at her feet. Hester fell silent, trying to imagine what it would be like, this pain, this agony that was coming towards her as surely as the mist rolled over the sand dunes, blown inland by the sea wind.

Madame Olga arrived to be with them in mid-December. She

installed herself in her modest hotel room with as much ceremony as though she were moving into the Ritz in Paris.

'You really didn't have to come here for the birth,' Hester told her, after she had been in Scotland for some days. She could see that Madame Olga was out of her element, uncomfortable. She visited them in the cottage every day, and returned to her hotel only to sleep. She didn't like the dark afternoons, the weather had turned cold, and something between a fog and a shower of rain seemed always to be sweeping across the windows.

'I will be here with you,' Madame Olga said. 'It is my duty and my pleasure. This child, she will be like my granddaughter.' She refused to consider the possibility of a male child. She took a sip from her teacup and put it down on the table. Ruby was sitting in an armchair beside the fire, working on her tapestry and Madame Olga and Hester were facing one another at the table. Hester's body was so awkward now that she found a straight-backed wooden chair the most comfortable place to sit. Madame Olga went on, 'We will not talk about babies now. I will give you the gossip from the Charleroi. I was with Piers in London before I came here. He is making a ballet from *The Snow Queen* of Hans Andersen for this Christmas. Most beautiful. It is Emily Harkness who will dance Gerda, the main role. Do you remember her?'

Hester nodded. Emily came into the company three years after she did. She was a fair-haired, rather austere girl when Hester knew her, silent and withdrawn, but undoubtedly talented. She listened to Madame Olga talking about her; about the others in the company; about the music and the kind of choreography that Piers was experimenting with and the words came to her as though from very far away. They meant nothing. Ballet. Hester felt as though it was a country from which she'd been exiled for so long that she'd completely forgotten what language they spoke there; what they did there; how they felt about everything. She had left that strange and beautiful place and because she couldn't imagine how she'd ever get back to it, hearing Madame Olga speaking about it filled her with such sorrow that she couldn't help crying. Madame Olga saw her wiping tears away with the back of her hand and rose to her feet at once.

'Please, please, do not cry, my darling,' she said, crouching down beside Hester and putting an arm around her. 'Please stop crying now, please. I am stupid, stupid. I am making you sad with talk of the dance when I came just to make you happy. I will not speak about it any more.'

'No, I *do* want to know. I want to hear all the news. I know it's my fault mostly, but I feel so cut off from everything. From my life, from my friends, from you. I'm tired. Tired of being fat and ugly and not being able to move and I'm scared. I'm scared of the pain and I don't know what's going to happen to me and how I'll ever get back to being *me*. Hester Fielding. I feel . . . I feel lost.'

Her quiet tears then turned into a storm of weeping. She couldn't stop herself. Ruby stood up and went to make tea. Madame Olga took Hester upstairs. She led her gently by the hand, and washed her face before helping her to undress, folding every garment carefully on to the chair before tucking her into bed as though she was a child.

'You sleep now,' she said. 'The taxi will come soon and I will go to my room in the hotel. In the morning, I will come again. It is nearly Christmas. Such a happy time to be born! Same birthday as the baby Jesus, maybe, if you are lucky. We must find a good tree and dress it with beautiful things. I will buy everything. We will light candles and sing the songs of Christmas and Ruby will cook us such food – food like you have never eaten before. There will be gifts and the angels will come down to visit us, you see. Dream of good things.'

Hester closed her eyes and shivered. This was the longest night of the year and also the coldest. The small electric fire in the bedroom, with its two horizontal scarlet bars gave out more light than heat but, in any case, it was always off at night, because Ruby said it was dangerous to have it on while you were asleep. The sheets on her bed felt like slicks of ice against her skin. She lay there in the dark after Madame Olga had gone downstairs to wait for her taxi, and listened to her own teeth chattering. The narrow cupboard against the opposite wall was painted white and Hester knew that inside it, her suitcase was ready. Ruby had packed it the week before, putting in a nightdress and a sponge bag and a bed jacket she'd knitted herself.

She could hear Madame Olga's taxi driving away and Ruby moving about, putting the kettle on to boil for the last cup of tea of the day. A comforting sound, Hester thought, and then she fell asleep.

She woke up suddenly with no idea of how long she had slept. She got out of bed to go to the lavatory and was suddenly seized with a pain in her head that was so dreadful that for a moment or two she thought she was going blind. She stumbled to the bathroom and turned on the light, but it was too bright, much too bright, and as well as the terrible agony splitting her head, flashes of brilliance exploded in front of her eyes and she closed them to keep out the glare, but that didn't seem to work. Here she was, ready to put up with the agonies of childbirth, and some malign fate had decided that this night, of all the nights of her life, was the time to show her what headaches really were. She started to cry, sitting on the edge of the bath.

Then she caught sight of her feet and didn't recognise them. Her ankles were thick and swollen and all she could think was, how will I dance? How will these monstrous feet fit into my ballet slippers? She was crying so much that she could hardly breathe.

'Ruby!' she shouted.

Ruby came at once and put her arms around her. 'There now, Hester,' she said, calmly. 'What's the matter? Tell me what the matter is.'

'I can't see, Ruby. My head is bursting with pain and look at my legs, look how swollen my ankles are. And I keep seeing these bright lights in front of my eyes. Oh Ruby, I'm so frightened.'

'I'll speak to Dr Crawford immediately. You stay here for a moment. I'll just get your dressing-gown. It's freezing. I'll be back at once.'

While she was gone, Hester stared down at her hands. She couldn't move because every movement felt as though a knife was being driven into the space between her eyes. Her hands were disgusting. Every finger was like a sausage, thick and red and hideous. She extended her arm a little, trying to perform even a poor imitation of a movement she might have made onstage. She looked ridiculous. Someone's hands, someone's fat, old and ungraceful hands had been grafted on to Hester's arms. Where was *she* in all of this? She felt as though someone had stolen her away and left a snivelling, swollen wreck in her place; a wreck whose head felt as though it was about to burst open like a ripe pumpkin.

Ruby came hurrying back into the bathroom and draped a dressing-gown around Hester's shoulders. 'We have to be quick, Hester. The ambulance'll be here soon. I'll get your case. And you'd best put on this coat, it's so cold. Dr Crawford says we have to get you into hospital at once.'

'Why?' A chill that had nothing to do with the weather had taken hold of her.

'It sounded to him, he said, like possible eclampsia.'

'Did you ask him what that was?'

Ruby shook her head. 'No, there's no time to lose. I didn't want to waste whole minutes talking. You need to be in hospital. He said he'd ring Madame Olga's hotel and arrange for her to meet us there. Are you nearly ready?'

The drive to the hospital was nothing but darkness and a kind of howling. Hester thought it was the wind but then wondered whether it could have been a siren. Or maybe even herself, making those ghastly sounds. Fuzzily, she thought, surely there's no need for a siren on quiet country roads in the early hours of the morning, long before sunrise? She was almost fainting with pain and then there was Dr Crawford's face, like a mask above her somewhere in a corridor.

She heard words . . . emergency . . . Caesarean . . . hurry . . . hurry. Was she lying down? On some kind of trolley? She didn't know. What she knew was that the pain went on and on and the lights kept flashing until suddenly there was nothing but darkness like a black cloth coming down over her eyes and after that, nothing. No pain, no feelings, no memories, no shame, no worries, no real world, only a deep well of unconsciousness into which she fell and in which she lay for hours.

Hester thought it was hours, but later she learned it was the best part of three days. Certain things came back to her in the way fragments of a bad dream return to your mind. You catch sight of them just as they slip away and vanish. If she thought hard, if she concentrated, she could remember seeing faces masked in white.

There were a lot of green tiles, and then a baby's face. She thought she could see her child's tiny face, with the eyes closed but then wondered whether maybe she'd imagined it.

Hester lost that time. She lost the days that were the whole life of her child. She missed his entire existence. By the time she woke up, slowly, uncomfortably, like a creature coming up from the black mud of a swamp, Madame Olga was there beside her bed.

'My darling girl,' she said. 'Such a terrible thing. Your poor little baby . . . he didn't live. He was not strong. He has gone to God.'

Hester wanted to scream. Where is he? What happened? How long did he live? Where have they taken him? What do they do with such tiny corpses? I can't do anything. Where are my tears?

She had no strength left. She felt the words without being able to say them. She was dimly aware of Madame Olga holding her hand, and Ruby standing at the end of the bed. Hester couldn't even see as far as the walls of the room. It was as though she was in a glass box of misery, all by herself.

The explanations came later, from Dr Crawford. Madame Olga and Ruby were there when he came to see Hester, but he sent them away. She could see that Madame Olga wasn't very happy about this, but even she obeyed the doctor.

'My poor dear girl,' he said once she'd gone. He seemed genuinely distressed as he tried to make her understand what had happened.

'There's little we can do in eclampsia cases like yours, dear Hester. When you came in four days ago, you had a seizure. A fit, you might call it. We had to consider your baby as well as you, of course, but the best way to deal with the raised blood pressure is to remove its cause. Which is the baby itself, of course. So we rushed you in for an emergency Caesarean, and I'm afraid . . . well, the baby doesn't always survive the operation. My dear, I can't tell you how sorry I am.'

'Why,' she whispered because it was hard for her to speak 'couldn't I see my baby? Why couldn't I hold him? Even dead, I would have wanted . . .'

'I know, I know. But the best treatment for the mother is sedation. For rather a long time, until the blood pressure is normal again. I couldn't risk losing you, too.'

I wish you had, Hester thought. I wish I'd died with my baby. Why did you let me live? To Dr Crawford she said, 'Thank you. Thank you for explaining to me.'

'There's something else,' he said. He took Hester's hand, which was lying outside the blankets. 'I'm so sorry, Hester. I'm very much afraid that you won't be able to have more children. The operation . . .' His voice tailed off. Hester managed to make a noise that sounded a little like a laugh. All she said was, 'I don't want any more children.'

This child. I wanted this child, she told herself, not any other.

Dr Crawford left Hester's bedside in the end, and she began to grieve. She developed a high fever, which made her delirious. She saw visions of monsters and dancers and hideous landscapes. She saw her grandmother wrapped in a shroud. She thought she was speaking, but Ruby told her later that she didn't say a word for more than a week. When she came to herself, she was no longer in the hospital but in a nursing home called The Laurels, run by Mrs McGreevey. She had her own room, and there was nothing wrong with it, but she was desperate to leave Scotland and go home to Wychwood.

The Laurels was a pleasant building of ivy-covered red-brick. Her window looked down on an uninteresting garden dotted with shrubs and she found herself longing for the moors in Yorkshire. Beyond the garden was a street, where the other houses resembled the Laurels in almost every particular. The corridors inside smelled of furniture polish and Mrs McGreevey's shoes made a squeaky sound on the greenish linoleum. There was a lounge for those patients who were well enough to get up from their beds, but Hester wasn't one of them. She had caught a brief glimpse of it from the corridor and that was enough. The walls were hung with paper chains, and there were sprigs of holly stuck to the frames of every picture. Christmas. Hester had forgotten about it, and thinking of the merriment and warmth and good cheer associated with the season roused such an ache of sorrow in her that she vowed she would never, ever keep the festival again.

She couldn't move. She was weak and sick and still feverish. Her breasts were like two open wounds somewhere near where her heart was supposed to be, and they burned and throbbed and sent waves of pain shooting through her body every time she moved. And her baby. Her baby was dead. Ruby sat beside her for hours, stitching and stitching and answering Hester's questions as best she could.

'Tell me. I can't remember anything. Tell me about the last few days. When did I come here? Why did they bring me here? Couldn't I go home? To Wychwood? Or at least to our cottage?'

'You've been very ill, Hester. You need time to recover. We'll go back presently. For the last few days, you've just lain here tossing and turning. We've had a nurse day and night, to sponge your forehead and try and keep the fever down. You didn't eat. Dr Crawford has been to see you every day. You were fed through a tube and Madame Olga and I took turns to be with you. We spoke to you, but you didn't hear us.'

'I think I did hear you. But I couldn't answer. I was down, down at the bottom of something. A pit, a deep pit. Perhaps I was at the bottom of his grave. My son's grave.'

Then the tears came. More than a week after the birth, she started to cry and couldn't stop. Then Ruby told her that Madame Olga had decided that the funeral would take place next day.

'But she doesn't think you should go,' she added. 'She thinks you're not well enough.'

'No! How can I? Stay away from my own baby's funeral? I must see him buried,' Hester cried. 'How can they put his body in the ground if I'm not there? And the necklace. What about that? I want the necklace to be buried with him. My grandmother's necklace. The other part of this.' She pulled the gold chain out of the neckline of her nightdress to show Ruby. 'It's important. I promised her that my child would have it. Please say it will be buried with him. Promise me. Both of you must promise me.' Hester was weeping so much that every word was nearly drowned by sobs and tears.

Just then, Madame Olga came into the room.

'My darling, why are you distressing yourself?' she asked.

'I want to come to the funeral,' Hester sobbed. 'Please say I can come. Please. I can walk a little, just to the car. I'll go straight back to bed afterwards. I promise.'

'We will see tomorrow. I will ask Raymond. Maybe it will be possible.'

For a moment, Hester couldn't think who 'Raymond' was and then remembered that it was Dr Crawford.

'Oh, thank you, thank you,' Hester said, and leaned back against the pillow. 'Then I can make sure the necklace is buried with him.'

'Where is it?' Madame Olga said. 'If you tell me, I will arrange this. I promise you, on my honour.'

'I know where it is,' Ruby said, and Hester closed her eyes, exhausted. It was enough. Maybe if I rest now, she thought, I really will be strong enough tomorrow. My son. He didn't have so much as a name. Adam's son. Hester couldn't find a word anywhere in her head to call him. Ruby had told her that they put him into her arms for a few seconds just before she was sedated, but Hester had no memory of that. She had no memory whatsoever of her son's face. She didn't know who her baby was. Her baby. She imagined him as beautiful even though she had no idea what he looked like. That was the very worst thing; the unbearable thing. He didn't exist for Hester except as an absence.

Next morning, Madame Olga helped her to dress. Hester was being allowed to say goodbye to her baby after all. She was silent as Madame Olga pulled the black dress over her head, and while she buttoned her coat. She was so weak she could hardly stand. How, she wondered, was she going to stay on her feet at the grave? Her head swam with blackness when she thought of it. Hester knew where the cemetery was. She and Ruby had often walked past it, and though Hester had scarcely moved her head to look at it as they went by, there's always something about a cemetery that makes you notice it. You can't pass one and not think about death, even if those thoughts just trail through your mind and are gone. Hester had a sudden longing for her baby's tiny grave to be next to *Grand-mère*'s and near her father's, far away in Paris, in the graveyard that resembled a small town of streets and houses inhabited by the dead. That was impossible, she knew. He'd be forever in the ground here, in this windswept place where you could stand on the dunes and watch the sun rising over the grey sea to the east.

'You are strong enough, darling?' Madame Olga said, frowning as she adjusted the black hat on Hester's head. 'You are sure?'

Hester nodded because she still didn't trust herself to speak. She stood up, shaking a little. Her legs! Her ballerina's legs, as strong, she'd always thought, as steel rods, were about to let her down. She stumbled against the chair and Madame Olga caught her and steadied her.

'You must drink. Take this. It will give you energy. Strength.' She put a glass into Hester's hand, and gave her a pill to take.

She took a couple of steps into the corridor. She was wearing black gloves. When had she put those on? She couldn't bring it to mind. She began to walk downstairs to the front hall of The Laurels. There was a grandfather clock on the landing, and the hands stood at ten to eleven. Rain was falling. She could hear it beating against the windows, which were tall and set with panes of stained glass high up. She blinked. And then she was in her bed again, waking as though from a deep sleep.

'Why?' she croaked. Her voice sounded rusty, unused. 'What am I doing here? There's the funeral. My baby . . .' she couldn't go on. Where was Madame Olga? Ruby? What was Mrs McCreevey doing leaning over her? She managed to say, 'Where is Madame Olga? And where's Ruby?'

'Don't worry yourself about them, dear,' said Mrs McCreevey. 'They're taking care of everything. They told me to tell you they'll be back as soon as . . .' Her voice failed her, and Hester could see tears in her eyes. Mrs McCreevey collected herself and went on, '. . . as soon as the wee bairn's buried. They told me to tell you they wouldn't be long.'

Hester turned her head to the wall and closed her eyes. The funeral was taking place without her. She'd failed her son. He's in his coffin, she thought. They're covering his coffin with black earth. The necklace . . .

'Mrs McCreevey, could you see if there's a box, there, in the left-hand drawer of the chest of drawers? A small, tortoiseshell box. Thank you.'

The woman looked relieved to have something to do. She opened the drawer and began looking through Hester's possessions.

'No, there's no box here, I'm afraid. Are you quite sure you put it in this drawer?'

'Yes, that's fine,' Hester answered. 'They must have taken it. Thank you. Madame Olga and Ruby. They've taken it to the funeral.'

She closed her eyes. She waited till she heard Mrs McCreevey tiptoe from the room and then she sat up. Her head felt as though someone had taken an axe and buried it in her skull. There was a mist in front of her eyes and anything she looked at seemed to have soft, wavering outlines. She lay down again and turned over so that her face was hidden in the pillows. At least her baby would have the necklace with him, something from his mother to comfort him down there in the earth. As the minutes passed, Hester's shame at lying there, not attending her own child's funeral, changed into another feeling altogether – one that she didn't want to acknowledge because she was so ashamed of it, but which felt to her like relief. She realised that she was being spared. If she never saw where her baby was buried, she could pretend that he wasn't there, turning into something that was no longer a person. That's what it came down to: his small bones, his soft skin, his new eyes and tiny fingers were rotting away under the earth and she didn't want to have to see the place where he lay hidden. I won't ask to visit the cemetery, she thought. I don't care how heartless Madame Olga and Ruby think I am. If I never see his grave, I don't have to admit that he's dead.

Hester and Ruby returned to the cottage on New Year's Eve. Everyone else in Scotland, Hester knew, was celebrating Hogmanay, but not them. Not this year, and maybe never again. Madame Olga came with them, and they were there to pack everything away, ready to travel back to Wychwood. The air in each room seemed stale to Hester, as though nobody had lived there for some time, and of course they hadn't. Ruby had spent every day at the nursing home with Hester, only returning to sleep in the cottage at night.

The suitcases were nearly packed when Hester saw it – a Christmas stocking made of felt, lying on top of the chest of drawers in her bedroom. 'What's this, Madame?' she asked.

'Oh, my God! I forgot to take it away. It is a Christmas stocking.' Madame Olga's lips trembled and she wrung her hands. 'It was for the baby.'

Hester threw herself on to the bed and burst into a paroxysm of grief, weeping, and beating her fists on the pillow. Dimly, she was aware of Madame Olga hurrying down the stairs and saying something to Ruby. How was she going to face the everyday things of the world when every single thing reminded her of her loss? How was her life to be borne? Hester wished she believed in life after death, but she didn't. She never had, but maybe she could start believing now, this minute. Maybe her baby really *was* with the angels now, and smiling down at her. She was not consoled, however. There was no life after death, she was convinced of it and she would be forever in mourning for her son. Hers and Adam's.

1 January 1987

Hester woke up on New Year's Day and got out of bed with some reluctance. Perhaps it hadn't been such a good idea to drink so much wine last night, but the New Year's Eve dinner was one of the highlights of the rehearsal period and she'd joined in the partying and enjoyed herself more than she'd expected to.

She washed and changed into her leotard. Then she went into the dressing room and took her place at the *barre*. A small tape recorder stood on a table just inside the door and sometimes she turned on the music to accompany her morning routine, but today she felt the need for silence. The sequence wouldn't suffer. She had the order and the rhythm of the steps she went through each day so deeply in her mind that she didn't need to think consciously about them. Her body obeyed instructions it had received years ago and although she knew she was older now, that didn't prevent her from stretching and bending and doing all the things she'd been doing every day for almost half a century.

She smiled. Who am I kidding, she thought. It might feel as if I'm doing the same things, but the elasticity isn't there in the same way and I used to be able to raise my leg so high and straight that I could touch my ear, which I certainly can't do now.

Never mind, she told herself, as she pulled a sweater and boots and a hat on over her exercise clothes. I'll go for a walk and that will blow away the last trace of hangover. Hester tiptoed downstairs and made her way quietly out of the house and down the drive. The snow had fallen for a while again last night, but a thaw must have set in early in the morning. Here and there on the lawn, large patches of white showed up in the pearly morning light. The clouds massing over the furthest moors but it was too warm for any more snow to fall, at least for the moment.

It wasn't as cold as she expected. The wind that had blown a little during the night had dropped and the only sound in the whole landscape was the crunching of her feet on the gravel of the drive.

Alison watched Ruby pulling down the ladder that led up to the attic. It took her a little while because the catch was stiff but soon the silver steps were there, ready to take them up. Ruby went first, because she knew where the light switch was. Alison wasn't quite sure what to expect. In her experience, which was entirely from books, attics were almost magical places, filled with things that couldn't be found anywhere else – secret documents or old photographs, or else something terrifying that someone had wanted to hide away. The room she saw as she climbed in after Ruby was full of shadows, but it was much neater than she expected it to be and someone had obviously been keeping it very clean and tidy. Four skips were lined up under the overhang of the roof, one beside the other, and each had a luggage label tied to it. *Costumes. Props and headdresses. Programmes and cuttings. Miscellaneous.*

'Right,' Ruby said. 'There's a lot here that's going to come in handy, shawls, and jewels and headdresses that we can put together with the things we got in Leeds. We'll do the props this morning and then the costumes. We haven't much time before the technical dress rehearsal. I'm going to start you off on crêpe-paper roses. We're going to need rather a lot of those.'

Alison leaned into the skip Ruby had just opened and pulled out a bunch of red flowers, slightly squashed by years of lying under other things.

'Like these?'

Ruby smiled. 'Yes, just like those. They're from *Sleeping Beauty*. Do you know the Rose Adagio from that ballet?'

Alison nodded. She'd seen Claudia as Aurora, and now that she thought about it, there were an awful lot of roses about in that scene. She remembered her mother objecting to the colour of most of them and the set designer almost walking out of the production. Claudia had gone on and on about it: *I'm the one that's got to be up there dancing the bloody thing. The least the designer can do is see to it that the flowers don't actually clash with my hair.*

'Then I'll just take some of these bits from down here' (she scooped up an armful of assorted garments and pushed them into a pillow case she'd brought with her), 'and we can go over to Wardrobe and get started.'

As they climbed down the ladder again, Alison found herself wondering about the contents of all the other skips. I wouldn't have minded getting a look inside them, she thought, and wondered if she'd get to go up to the attic again while she was here. Probably not. There wouldn't be any need for it.

'We're always at sixes and sevens after New Year's Eve dinner,' said Ruby. She and Alison were sitting on either side of the table in Wardrobe at one o'clock, which was after lunch for them, but after breakfast for the rest of the company. Everyone else had slept late and eaten at about half past eleven, and rehearsals weren't due to start till two. Siggy had followed them to the Arcadia and was now sitting on top of a small skip.

'He looks as though he's making sure we're getting on with our work and not slacking,' said Ruby.

Alison smiled. Siggy reminded her of another of her dad's verses, the one about the kitten, in the lullaby book:

> Here is a kitten
> with four white paws
> who dreams of creeping
> through the grass.
> She thinks of butterflies she has seen
> who tickle her white nose
> as they pass.

The postman wasn't going to come today. Maybe tomorrow there'd be a letter from him. It was getting harder and harder to believe that Dad would write to her while she was here, but she'd been very careful to put the Wychwood Hall address on the back of the envelope she'd sent her card in. She concentrated on twisting the strip of scarlet crêpe-paper she was holding into something she hoped resembled the perfect rose lying in front of her. Ruby had shown her how to make these flowers and they needed loads of them for the show, so she was going to be safe here for a bit, away from her mother and Nick and the rest of the company. Sometimes she wished she could just live on an island all by herself, like Robinson Crusoe. It would be restful, she thought, to have to worry about practical things like where your next meal was coming from, and not have the inside of your head taken up with sorting out what you felt about everything.

Ruby was busy embroidering brightly coloured, rather large flowers and leaves on a plain blue skirt with what was obviously tapestry wool. She didn't speak much and when she did, it was about practical things. She glanced up and explained what she was doing.

'If I used silks to do this work, it would take a very long time and be much too dainty. The wool is thick and so you can see the effect much better when it's on stage. It's louder and more obvious, and the work goes very quickly. Look at the size of my needle! It's the one I use for darning.'

Alison couldn't think of an answer. This morning, because she was so tired of waiting for some kind of communication from her father, she didn't really care too much what anything looked like, which she supposed was disloyal of her. *Sarabande* meant so much to her mother and Hugo, and he was really upset about what had happened to the costumes. But after what had gone on last night she was too pissed off with both of them to see things from their point of view.

'Are you all right?' Ruby asked, holding her needle still for a moment and looking searchingly at Alison. 'You must be tired. We all went to bed so late.'

'I didn't sleep very well, even when I did get to bed.' Alison summoned up what she hoped was a cheery smile. All she needed was Ruby interrogating her about what she'd seen. She turned to the crêpe-paper, cut off a length of green, and twisted it round a bit of wire to make a stem for her rose.

'You're getting good at those,' Ruby said encouragingly.

'I like making them,' Alison answered. 'I'm going to do some pink ones in a second.'

Ruby nodded and went back to her embroidery. Alison went on trying to puzzle out what she'd seen and not seen last night. Her mother had drunk too much wine. She was flirting with Nick and though Alison hoped and hoped that he wouldn't respond, he seemed to be enjoying it. Leaning towards her and looking down the front of her top. Alison had gone to bed straight after all the midnight kisses, which weren't really kisses, but just people making their mouths into kissing shapes and going about trying to catch everyone. She'd never in her life had so many people wish her Happy New Year. What she'd felt like doing was running away and being alone.

She'd fallen asleep almost at once. Then, just as suddenly, she was awake. She could hear voices. She lay in bed, wondering who it was and then thought she recognised her mother's laugh. Could it be? She debated getting up and looking out of her door to see if it was indeed Claudia, and then she heard whispering and giggling. She sat up in bed and listened. Was that Nick? Again, she heard her mother's laughter. What was Claudia doing, up so late? Was she with Nick? Alison jumped out of her bed and opened the door. She was just in time to see Nick's bedroom door closing. He'd gone to bed. Where was Claudia? Were they together? She couldn't really be sure and yet she'd certainly heard her mother's laugh. Alison went back to bed and lay staring up at the ceiling for ages.

As she thought about the events of last night, Alison gave the wire she was holding a vicious twist and put the finished rose in the basket with the others. Only about another twenty or so to go. She recalled her mother and Nick flirting at the table. It was completely revolting. She decided that she'd never been so miserable in her whole life, and wondered what her father was doing this New Year's Day. Not thinking of me, that's for sure, she told herself.

The number of roses in the basket was growing. It was such soothing work that a couple of times, her eyes had closed briefly. Once, Ruby looked up and saw her.

'Would you like a bit of a rest?'

'No, I'm fine, thanks.' Alison turned back to the flowers. She changed the subject deliberately. 'I wanted to ask you about Hester. You used to be her dresser when she was a dancer, didn't you?'

'Yes, indeed. I've known her since she was about your age. She started dancing very young, you know.'

'My mother told me about her before we came. It must have been awful for her to have to stop when she was so famous. I know about the accident. Didn't she fall over a cliff? In Cornwall?'

'It wasn't even as dramatic as that but it put an end to her career anyway.' Ruby sighed. 'Such a shame. That was in 1966. She was thirty-three and still had a few good years left, I think. She was walking along the cliff path with a friend, well, with Edmund Norland who wrote the music for *Sarabande*, as a matter of fact, and she just lost her footing. She broke her ankle, very badly and that's the kind of injury it's hard to come back from at that age for a dancer.'

'How awful!' Alison imagined Hester lying with her foot in plaster in a hospital bed, and understood how ghastly that would be for her. 'That's so sad.'

'She had . . . never mind.'

'Please tell me,' Alison begged. 'I won't say a word, really.'

'I shouldn't have . . . well, I don't imagine it matters after all this time. I was going to say she had something like a breakdown just after that. It hurt her dreadfully to have to give up the ballet. It was – it had been – her life for such a long time.' Ruby smiled suddenly. 'We should talk about something more cheerful. On the first day of the year, don't you think?'

Alison nodded.

'Hugo will be thrilled with those roses,' Ruby continued. 'And when we've finished those, we can go on to covering garden baskets and things with gold foil. I've always got some of that in the props cupboard. There's another thing I'd like you to help me with, if you don't mind.'

'No, I don't mind at all. What is it?'

'On the first night we always have a party and of course we don't want to do anything too elaborate, but I always try to decorate the place a little. To make up for not having Christmas decorations.'

'I'd love to help,' said Alison. 'What sort of thing will we do?'

'Well, I've got a lot of rather good branches put aside and I'm just thinking of what we could do with them.'

'I know!' Alison put down the rose she was making and almost jumped out of her chair. 'I've got an ace idea. Can I do it myself? I'm sure you'll be ever so busy. You won't want to be bothered with decorating and things, will you?'

'I'll have to see,' Ruby said. 'It depends on what your idea is!'

'I want it to be a surprise so if I tell you, do you promise to say nothing to anyone else?'

Ruby laughed. 'All right, then.'

'Thanks,' said Alison. She made sure to close the door of Wardrobe before she went round to Ruby's side of the table to tell her. You had to be careful with brilliant ideas. Anyone might be listening.

'Ah, Claudia.' Hugo was smiling, but she knew him well enough to realise that if they'd been on their own he'd have been snarling at her.

'Don't say it, darling. I know I'm *ghastly* late and I'm so sorry. Everyone, I truly am *so* sorry, but it was such a night last night. I haven't really recovered yet.'

She made for one of the chairs pushed against the wall of the rehearsal room and flung her big bag down beside it and sat down as quietly and unobtrusively as she could. She opened the bag and took out her ballet shoes.

'Get your breath back, Claudia,' said Hugo. 'We're all rather behind today and I've still got a bit to do with Andy and Ilene.'

Claudia nodded and sat down. Oh, GodGodGodGodGod, she thought. I am definitely getting too old for this. She'd stood in the shower for about half an hour with the hottest water she could stand pricking her all over before she felt sufficiently together to venture downstairs. Her head was throbbing. That was the booze. I ought to stop drinking, she said to herself. I wish I hadn't drunk so much. No power on earth could have kept her out of Nick's bed last night. She didn't regret it, but there had come a certain point during the New Year's Eve dinner (and it made her stomach shrink and shrivel into queasiness just to think about *that*, the goose fat, ugh!) when she'd stopped knowing exactly what was going on.

What she remembered was Nick leading her upstairs to his room, which was down the far end of the corridor. They seemed to be upright one moment and lying down on the bed the next and after that, her mind really did refuse to function. She'd opened her eyes hours later, and stumbled into the en suite bathroom with a raging thirst. Why had she been so surprised to see Nick, still asleep in the bed she'd just left? She shook him awake.

Claudia was finding it difficult to think. The music that accompanied Andy's appearances in *Sarabande* was plinking and plonking rather too merrily for her liking and her concentration was shot to hell, but she blushed as she recalled what Nick had said to her when they first kissed – how much he wanted her. Nothing had changed, he told her when she was on her way back to her room.

'Why are you going? Come back to bed.'

'You're joking! All we need is for Hugo to find out. You must promise not to say a single word to anyone. Promise?'

'Keep your hair on,' Nick said. 'I won't utter a squeak. And if you're really not coming back, then I'm going to sleep. We've got dancing to do tomorrow.'

Now, here they were, and in a moment, she'd have to do some dancing herself and it was the very last thing in the world she felt like doing. She looked at Hugo, taking Ilene through her paces. He'd been so fast asleep when she slipped into bed beside him that she got away with her lie very easily this morning, the one about coming to bed just after he had. 'You were dead to the world, darling,' she'd told him. 'It would have been cruel to wake you up. Even to wish you Happy New Year.'

'One and two and then turn,' Hugo was saying now. 'And up to Andy and down to the front of the stage again and turn and back. That's right. Claudia, are you ready to join in yet?'

'Sure.' She went to sit on the pile of cushions that was representing the Princess's bed. Soon she would have to move, to dance. Was she going to be able to do that? She lay back against the pillows. How typical of my luck, she thought. I spend a night with a beautiful young man and I can't tell anyone about it. And I feel sick. Damn and blast the booze. I am *definitely* going to stop drinking. Please let me get to the end of the rehearsal without throwing up.

Alison looked at the tarpaulin thrown over a pile of branches in the space at the back of the garage. Ruby was so reliable. Why couldn't everyone be like that? Why couldn't Claudia? She'd told Alison where to find everything, and there it was, in the exact spot that she said it would be, and all neat and carefully covered-up too. She could make a start now, because everyone in the company was busy having class and Ruby herself was up in Wardrobe. Alison had put everything that she thought she needed into a huge carrier bag. She had permission to leave it here in the garage when she'd finished for the day, and to come in and work on her idea whenever she got a chance.

She put the big scissors down on the floor. This was probably going to take longer than she thought at first, but it didn't matter. It was restful, this cutting and more cutting, and then deciding where everything was going to go. While she was busy transforming the branches, her mind wandered very pleasantly, and a thought that started on, say, Nick, could easily float off and settle on Silver or Siggy or what they were going to have for lunch. She thought of the tree her dad had drawn in the lullaby book and the verse that was written underneath drifted into her head:

> *This is the wish*
> *of every tree:*
> *for birds to settle*
> *among its leaves*
> *and flutter and cry*
> *and coo and call . . .*

It was one of her favourite pictures. The tree took up almost the whole page and there were birds perched on every single branch, hundreds of them. Her dad would love what she was doing to these branches. Maybe someone from the company could take a photo of the decorations. Then she could send it to America. I'll ask Hugo about it, Alison thought. He's got a camera.

Hester felt restless. She sat in Wardrobe, watching Ruby putting everything back in its proper place before going on to the next task. How typical of her that was! She was looking particularly striking today, Hester thought and nearly said so aloud but stopped herself at the last moment, knowing how Ruby hated compliments and how bad she was at acknowledging them. She's ten years older than me, Hester thought, and even though you couldn't call her pretty or even handsome, there was something regal about her. She was imposing – tall and strong-featured and wore her glasses, in their pale tortoiseshell frames, almost all the time these days. Ruby's clothes were always of the very best quality even though there was nothing showy about them. She still made them herself. Her skirts never bagged and were always perfectly lined. There was almost a Ruby uniform: skirts in heathery-coloured tweeds worn with cotton blouses, and cardigans she'd knitted herself. Her shoes were sensibly low-heeled and plain, but highly polished. Hester had never seen her with bare legs. Ruby wore stockings even in the hottest weather.

She wanted to talk about what was troubling her but didn't know how to broach it. Instead, she asked, 'How are the costumes coming on? Will it be all right? I told Hugo it would.'

Ruby looked up and smiled. 'Yes, everything's under control, but you didn't come all the way over here to talk about costumes. Is something worrying you?'

'Dear Ruby, you know me too well.' Hester stood up. She went to the window and looked out. She said, 'I suppose I'm a little nervous about what Edmund's going to say . . .'

'About the funeral, you mean?'

Hester nodded. 'I'll have to ask about it and part of me wants to know everything, every detail, but most of me can't bear to think about it.'

'Do you still . . .' Ruby didn't finish the thought and Hester knew why. She'd never, not in all the years Hester had known her, asked about her feelings for Adam. Hester suspected that there was a part of Ruby that disapproved of her affair with a married man, but she had never spoken about it. Hester said, 'Do I still love Adam? Is that what you were going to ask? The answer is no, not really. Love? No, I stopped feeling that a long time ago, but . . .' She hesitated. 'I suppose I had to convince myself that he was the love of my life to justify everything I went through. It's as though, until now, I haven't been able to breathe properly. To feel properly or think of anyone else in a way that's unclouded by my love for Adam. It's hard to explain.'

'I suspect it's much easier than you think.' Ruby was concentrating on stitching a frill to the sleeve of the Jester's shirt, but she looked up and stopped sewing for a moment. 'I think you don't have to consider what you feel about him. He's not a part of your life any longer. I think Adam's death has made you free. For the first time in years.'

'Yes, perhaps you're right. I *am* free and I feel it, but that's what they say about people who spend too long in prison, don't they? That the real world seems a scary place. That prison has become safe in a strange way and the freedom frightens them. I think I'm like that. I feel I can move on, but what lies ahead makes me a little nervous.

'I know it's not my business, Hester, but I'll say it all the same. I think it would be a sad thing for you to end your life all on your own.'

'I'm not on my own! I've got you. And George. And Edmund. And such a busy life with the master classes. And the festival – all those dancers every year.'

Ruby didn't answer. Hester said, 'You think I'll grow old all by myself, don't you, rather like Madame Olga.'

'I hope not. That's all I'm saying.'

Madame Olga had always been an awkward subject between them; a subject to be avoided. Hester knew that Ruby didn't like her, but had never been able to discover why this was. Ruby was now bent over the Jester's shirt again and her face had taken on that closed look it often wore when the past came up in conversation. Hester knew there was nothing to be done about it.

'I'll be off now, leave you in peace. See you later, Ruby.'

1953

Everywhere she looked, Hester could see nothing but grey. The grey Promenade or Front or whatever they called it, followed by the grey sea, and then more grey in the sky. The wind seemed to be taking lumps of water and flinging them against the panes of the Sunporch, and Hester drew her cardigan more closely round her shoulders. I should be out there, she thought. She imagined the storm blowing in her face, imagined the spray stinging her cheeks, and longed to run out from behind the glass and straight into the freezing gale. I could cry and no one would even notice. The Front was deserted. No one with any sense came down to Brighton in February. If I ran out there, Madame Olga would stop me, she told herself, and besides, I have to appear normal. I have to seem as though I'm recovering. I've been brought here to recover. I am supposed to be *getting over it*.

Madame Olga had offered her the South of France, Spain, somewhere hot.

'You need to recuperate, my darling,' she told Hester. 'You need sunshine. To lie in the sun and get the heat in your bones.'

'No, no sun,' Hester said. She wanted the cold. She wanted to step into a block of ice and stay there forever. 'But please as far away from Gullane as possible.'

Brighton was as distant from Scotland as you could get before falling into the sea, and she and Madame Olga were now residents of the White Cliffs Hotel, which was hardly the Royal Albion or the Grand, but which was quiet and pleasant enough. They had taken two adjoining rooms with full board for a whole month, and even after a week Hester wondered how she was going to survive the days.

Madame Olga loved the Sunporch, a kind of enclosed balcony furnished with overstuffed armchairs and small tables, and they spent a great deal of time there, with Hester staring at the vast swathe of steel-grey water stretching out before her and wishing that she could walk into it and never come back to the shore. The Sunporch was the pride and joy of Mrs Norrington, the manageress, and she regarded those few old people who sometimes sat there with maternal benevolence. For Hester, she had nothing but awed admiration. Madame Olga had exaggerated Hester's fame as a ballerina and the 'ill-health' that she was presently suffering and, as a consequence, they were being very well looked after.

Today, for example, Edmund was coming to tea. That meal was usually taken in the Residents' Lounge, but Mrs Norrington had said, 'For you, Madame Rakovska, I'm happy to serve it on the Sunporch. I'll keep an eye on comings and goings and as soon as your guest arrives, I'll bring everything in.'

'She is expecting maybe someone famous,' Madame Olga said, peering through the rain-streaked windows, on the lookout. 'And I did not tell her it was only Edmund, of course. Let her have some pleasant anticipations, yes?'

Hester nodded. Did she want to see Edmund? He had written to her often, begging her to let him come and talk to her; asking to see her over and over again until she had no strength left to say no. Now that she'd agreed, however, she no longer knew whether she was capable of sitting in a room and behaving normally. Part of her wanted to see him. She longed for someone who wasn't bound up in her agony to tell her about the rest of the world, about everything that was happening that wasn't about her, how *she* felt, how much *she* was hurting. But I don't know if I'm ready, she thought. A kind of panic was making it very hard for her to breathe. What will I say? How will I greet him? She blinked very hard to stop the already gathering tears from falling. Then she sat up a little straighter.

Don't be a fool. It's Edmund, she told herself. There's nothing to be afraid of. It will be wonderful to see him. I want to be comforted.

'I think,' Madame Olga was standing with her face almost pressed up against the glass, 'I think it is, yes, it is, Edmund, and . . .'

There were two men coming through the revolving doors. One of them was Edmund, hatless even in this weather and behind him . . . it was only two steps from the entrance to the Sunporch and there he was, behind Emund and striding towards her.

Hester closed her eyes. If I don't open them for a very long time, she thought, it won't be true. If I stop breathing now, this instant, then I'll never have to open my eyes and look at him. If it is him. It is. It's Adam. Edmund has brought Adam here. Brought him to see me without telling me. Without asking my permission.

The fury, the rage. It was as though someone had set a match to everything that she was, everything she felt, and had burned her heart to ashes.

'Hester, Hester darling,' Edmund said and hugged her, pressing her against his coat. Hester stood there, stiff and angry, unable to speak. 'I've brought Adam, Hester. He . . . I thought it best if we could, well, you know. Meet. And speak. Have tea or something.'

He laughed, but without mirth, and still Hester said nothing. She sat down on her chair and didn't lift her eyes from the carpet. One huge red flower merged into another and Hester concentrated on those. Don't look up, she told herself. Don't meet his eyes. But here he was, sitting down in the chair next to her. How did he dare? How could he? How could Edmund do such a thing? Of course he hadn't consulted her. He knew very well what her response would have been.

I can't stay here, she thought. I can't have tea with Edmund and Adam. I am *not* going to talk about what happened. I refuse. Mrs Norrington was in the Sunporch now, and two young women were following her, carrying cake stands and tea trays. Hester looked at her own hands in horror.

'Darling Hester,' said Madame Olga, 'we will drink some tea and then we will talk. Yes, I will go and let you speak with your friends alone. This is what you wish, isn't it?'

'No,' Hester said. She was aware, as she was often aware when she was on stage, of being somehow outside her own body. Here is a young woman and she is about to make a scene. She is going to make a spectacle of herself. She can't help it. If she doesn't say what she thinks, her heart will explode. She is not going to behave well. She turned to Edmund.

'Edmund, I thought I could trust you and I see I can't. I don't want to have tea with you. How *could* you? How could you have thought . . . You knew, you *knew* I wouldn't want to see him.'

Until that moment, she'd kept her eyes turned away from Adam.

In that first glimpse of him in the doorway, she'd absorbed everything about him, the hollow cheeks, the dark circles under his eyes. Good, she thought. He looks as though he hasn't slept for weeks and I hope that's true. But now I must say something to him. She took a deep breath and moved till she was standing in front of him.

'Adam,' she said, and as she spoke she surprised herself by how calm she sounded. 'I didn't want to see you ever again, but Edmund has done this and it can't be undone. I still don't want to see you. We had a son, and he died. That's all I have to say to you. Goodbye.'

'Hester, please,' Adam spoke and his voice made her shiver. 'Please speak to me. Please sit down.'

The calmness left her. She could feel every word tearing at her throat. 'Don't you dare to tell me when I should sit and when I should speak. I don't want to speak to you. There's nothing to say. Go away and don't come near me ever, ever again.'

She turned to Edmund and went on screaming. 'And I don't want to see you either, Edmund. You're always so sure you know what to do and what's best and this isn't. Do you hear me? This is *not* best. You've hurt me and I don't know how I'm going to be able to—'

She couldn't continue. She ran out of the Sunporch and through the revolving doors and out on to the Front before anyone could stop her. Good, good, she thought. Let it blow. Let it blow me away. She ran towards the sea and the wind pulled at her clothes and twisted her hair and tossed salt spray into her face where it mixed with the tears that were pouring down her cheeks. Oh, Edmund, Edmund, she thought. What have you done? Why did you bring him? How will I ever be able to speak to you again, when all I feel is fury and betrayal?

'Hester?' There he was, bloody Edmund, always trying to help. 'Hester, you can't do this. You'll catch pneumonia. Come back inside. He's gone. Adam's gone. He won't come back. I'm sorry.'

She let herself be led inside after a while. I've become, she thought, like one of those shells down on the seashore, thin and white and hollowed-out. *Sorry*, Edmund kept saying, *sorry*, as though that were any help at all. Hester wondered whether a time would ever come when she'd be able to forgive him.

2 January 1987

Hester stood at the window of the Office just after breakfast and thought, if you were to design the perfect winter day it would look exactly like what she could see at this moment. The sky was cloudless, and so pale a blue that it was nearer to white or silver. The temperature had fallen overnight, and on every blade of grass, every branch and leaf, the frost glittered and shone in the misty sunshine. The highest parts of the moors in the distance were covered with snow. There was even a bird – a robin? It was hard to see from where she was – perched Christmas-card style on the gate. She was happy that Edmund would see Wychwood looking its absolute winter best.

She could sense her heart beating rather more quickly than usual. Edmund . . . This is ridiculous, she thought, I've known him for over thirty years. We've been through so many things together. I'm not going to sit here waiting. I'll go for a walk, just up to the end of the village and back.

She put on her boots and coat and left the house, walking quickly and breathing in the clear air to calm herself. She recalled the bleak months that followed the only time in her life when she and Edmund had quarrelled. Those days were so lonely, she thought. For both of us. Poor Edmund not only had me refusing to see him but also quarrelled with Adam. When she and Edmund had at last put what happened in Brighton behind them, he confessed to her that Adam had also felt betrayed. *He said he thought you'd agreed*, said Edmund. *He said I told him you had, which I didn't. I would never have done that.*

It might be ages before he gets here, she thought. The last postcard she'd had from him wasn't very specific. The message on the back read, *Will be with you as soon as I can on Jan. 2nd. Can't wait to see you. All my love. Really. Edmund.*

She noticed that the gates were standing open as she walked back to Wychwood. Did that mean he was here already? Hester started to walk up the drive, and then she saw him. He was standing next to his car, holding his arms out. She flung herself at him and felt herself folded into his embrace. Then she burst into tears, unable to hold down what she was feeling for a moment longer.

'Oh, God, Edmund, I'm sorry, I can't help it. I'm so . . . oh, I must stop. I'm so happy to see you. That's it. I'm so relieved you're here.'

'Hester, darling! How lovely to see *you*. It's all right. I'm here now!'

Hester couldn't speak. She allowed herself to relax in Edmund's embrace for a moment and then stepped back. She smiled weakly. 'Crying into your coat again! How many garments of yours have I ruined over the years?' She smiled. 'Let's go inside. I've missed you. And it's freezing.'

Silver was making an effort to put everything but the music out of her head. She and Hugo were alone in the rehearsal room, and she was going through the fiendish sequence of steps that he'd devised for the Angel's solo, which just happened to come immediately before her *pas de deux* with Nick. There were the *jetés en tournant*, a whole run of *entrechats* and, in addition, there was the vibration that Hugo wanted for her arms. She'd pointed out to him that it was going to be a bit of a problem having wings, which would certainly interfere with her sightlines when she was trying to fix on a point during the turns. That was a challenge even without this new vibration idea he'd come up with. She'd tried to explain how hard it was going to be, all that turning; was there any other reason for having so much except to show off the wonderful wings she was going to be wearing? She'd asked Hugo and he'd explained.

'I want you to be airborne. The vibrations are to show the movement of air in your wings. I want your dancing to be almost like flight.'

'If you wanted flight, you should have hired a bird,' she muttered under her breath the last time they'd been through the routine.

'I heard that, Silver,' said Hugo. He was smiling. She didn't know any longer what she thought of him, which didn't make life easier. It would have been much simpler if she could hate him. Then she'd have been much ruder. I'm not afraid of being sharp with people, she thought, but it's very hard not to like Hugo.

She bent and swayed and fixed her eyes on a black mark on the far wall of the rehearsal room and went into the whirling storm of turns, all done *en pointe* and at top speed. She knew not many other dancers would have been capable of what she was trying to do. Hugo thought she was capable of it because she'd done so well with the famous thirty-two *fouettés* in Swan Lake. Okay, here goes, she thought. The arms. Trembling in the arms and don't lose your footing. Keep it steady. Listen to the rhythm. Round and round and listen to the beat and fly and fly and round and round and more and more and shiver the arms and lift them and float and leap and again and again. Silver had disappeared and there was nothing but a body moving through space; nothing but the body and the music and a burning sensation in every part of her lungs.

'You've done it!' He was hugging her in his delight and Silver felt her heart thumping in her chest. She was covered in sweat. Her face was running with it. She leaned against Hugo's chest and stayed there for a moment. He was still speaking. 'I knew you could! I knew you were better than you thought you were, better than everyone told you you were, and I've proved it.'

He stepped back a little and took hold of her hands. 'Have I been a most frightful bully, Silver?'

'No, not a bully. But demanding. You've been bloody demanding. And bossy. You always think you know best, like most choreographers.'

'Well, I do!' Hugo laughed. 'I *do* know best. About *Sarabande*, anyway. And about you.'

He was looking at her in a way that made her feel most peculiar. She suddenly had the impression that it was getting increasingly difficult to breathe. She and Hugo were standing very close to one another and she could feel the warmth of his body. Was she imagining it? Where was the cheeky remark that she should have made almost at once? Silver found that she had no words ready to say. Nothing in her head except a sudden, silly desire to be held by him.

Stop it, she told herself. Grow up and behave. He's practically married to Claudia. He's never shown the slightest interest in you except professionally. Don't let yourself be carried away simply because you're feeling good about having achieved something well-nigh impossible. She looked at him. 'I hope I can do it again, Hugo. What if I can't? What if that's it?'

'You'll do it again. You'll do it better. I have the utmost faith in you, Silver.'

He put out a hand and touched her hair, just at the nape of her neck, stroking it a little.

'I'll see you at lunch, Silver. Ilene and Andy'll be here in a minute. Thank you.'

'Yes, see you later.'

Hester got up to draw the curtains against the gathering dusk and the lamp on her desk cast a golden light into the room, dispersing some of the shadows. Edmund had joined the company for lunch and everyone had been thrilled to bits to have the composer of their ballet sitting with them.

'It's such terrific music to dance to,' Andy told him and Nick and Ilene nodded in agreement. Hester heard Claudia saying, 'You obviously understand women *so* well,' and she was practically purring. It wasn't surprising. Edmund was still handsome. He'd put on a little weight but Hester thought that it suited him. He looked solid and healthy. His eyes were just as blue as they ever were and the fair hair that used to fall over his brow was grey now and cut shorter.

Now everyone was in rehearsal and the house was quiet.

'Tell me about the funeral, Edmund,' she said.

'It was a very moving ceremony. Very cold at the actual burial, but a great many people were there. I didn't realise they had so many friends in America.'

Hester listened to him speaking and when he'd finished she said, 'Thank you so much for telling me, Edmund. I'm not good at funerals. Do you mind if we talk about something else now?'

'There's just one thing though.' Edmund hesitated. 'I'm sorry, Hester. This might be painful. I've got a letter for you. I suppose I could have left it until after the first night, but I want you to read it now. I think it's important that you . . .' He hesitated again before taking a deep breath and going on. 'I think I've been wanting to say something like this to you for years, Hester, and never could till now. Adam's dead and you have to face that fact.'

'I *have* faced it, Edmund. What do you mean? I haven't been . . . I haven't thought about him for years.'

'That might be how it's appeared to you, but for me, well, let's just say I always knew that Adam was still very much alive in your thoughts.'

'How could you have known? I said nothing. Nothing at all.' And, she thought to herself, *you were otherwise occupied with one or another of your women, anyway.*

'I watch you, Hester. I've been watching you since you were a young girl. I see things you think you're hiding. I want you to read this letter, whatever it says. I think you'll feel better after you've faced whatever's in it.'

'Have you read it?'

'No, of course not. The envelope was addressed to me, but what I found when I opened it was another sealed envelope and that's got your name on it, as you can see. Virginia gave it to me after the funeral. She found it among Adam's things and it wouldn't have occurred to her that it might be for you. Or if it did, she hid it very well.' Edmund took an envelope from the breast pocket of his jacket and handed it to her. 'Shall I go? D'you want to be by yourself?'

'No, please stay. I'm fine.' Hester took the folded page of thick, cream paper out of the envelope. The sight of Adam's handwriting made her throat close up. She shut her eyes for a second and took a deep breath.

Dearest Hester

I've wanted to write to you many times in the years since we last spoke to one another. I have left Edmund, in my will, a yearly allowance which is to be paid to you until your death and after you die, to your heirs whoever they may be. I hope that you won't feel you can't take this gift from me. I am doing it through Edmund because he's my oldest friend and because I don't want Virginia to discover after my death that I have thought of you every single day. With almost every breath, I've agonised over what happened between us and mourned the death of the only child I'll ever have. Edmund has told me about you over the years, and I've followed the public story of your career and felt a mixture of pride in your achievements and despair at my own behaviour. There have been so many times when I've nearly done it. Left Virginia and come to find you, Hester, but in the end, as in the beginning, I couldn't, could *not*, do that to a woman whom I saw as much weaker than you were; much more dependent on me for her survival. There's nothing else I can say now, Hester, except that if you're reading these words then I am dead and I have loved you all my life and will go on loving you from beyond the grave, if there is a beyond. Believe me, my darling. Adam.

Hester folded the letter and put it back in its envelope. She looked down at her lap. Her hands were shaking. A mass of sorrow had gathered in her throat and she felt that if she tried to speak, no sound would come out of her mouth. Her eyes blurred with tears and she was trembling. She made an effort to breathe and put her hands over her face and covered her eyes. I'm in shock, she thought. This is shock. I haven't seen Adam's handwriting for thirty years, and now, there it is, right in front of me. It's like seeing a ghost. I must make myself calm. She forced herself to breathe in and out and gradually began to feel more normal. She thought of Adam's words: *I have loved you all my life and will go on loving you from beyond the grave, if there is a beyond*. She tried to hear his voice saying them, but couldn't. It was as though the whole of him, his voice, face, everything, was fading and disappearing, like a stain dissolving in water.

'Hester?' Edmund's voice brought her back from her reverie. He'd come over and was crouched down beside her. He took her hand. 'Are you all right?'

She still couldn't trust herself to speak. She looked at him and nodded.

Claudia took a spoonful of the orange-coloured soup in front of her at dinner and wondered why even her normal small appetite had disappeared. She was aware that all around her at the table, the rest of the company seemed to be having a good time. Nick, in particular, was right up the other end (how did that happen when she tried her hardest to sit next to him or opposite him at every meal?) and giggling with Ilene and Andy like a young kid from the *corps de ballet*. She stared at him, hoping to make him aware of her presence, but it wasn't working. Instead, she had Ruby on one side of her and Hugo on the other and both of them were as far from pleasant dinner companions as it was possible to be. Ruby was talking to Alison on her other side and Hugo seemed fascinated by George's stories of the good old days, when he was a young feller-me-lad, out every night on the town, betting on the horses and not being too careful about the amount he drank. She could hear most of the anecdotes from where she was sitting.

Claudia sighed and looked at Alison, who seemed to be enjoying herself and who had, indeed, just laughed out loud. That was a good thing, wasn't it? Before coming to Wychwood, Claudia thought that having her daughter with her would be a pain, but it hadn't worked out like that. So why was it that instead of rejoicing she was faintly peeved? She wasn't in the habit of analysing her own feelings too closely, but the annoyance she felt towards Ruby, for no good reason in the world, must have been partly because Alison was so keen on her. I'm jealous, she thought. Jealous that Alison finds it so easy to chat with Ruby and so difficult to say a civil word to me. How ridiculous is that! She took another mouthful of soup and then put her spoon down. I will throw up, she thought, if so much as another drop crosses my lips. She noticed that Alison was tucking in as usual and had helped herself to a second roll with her soup, but she said nothing. They all, she reflected, looked at me as though I was beating her with sticks the last time I tried to stop her stuffing herself. I'm not saying a single word now.

She looked up and caught Silver, on the other side of the table, staring at Hugo. Her gaze was intense. Why? Why was she gawping at him like a love-struck youngster? Surely they couldn't . . . ? No, of course not. She would have spotted it. Hugo was still absorbed in conversation with George, but he, too, must have felt the force of

Silver's eyes on him. He glanced up and saw her. What was he doing? Claudia could hardly believe it. He had raised his glass to her as though it were full of champagne and he was smiling. Only his profile was visible to Claudia but she would have given anything to be able to see the expression in his eyes. Silver raised her own glass in response and smiled. What did that smile mean? Probably nothing. It was pointless to wonder about it. Claudia went back to looking at Nick and imagining what would happen the next time they were alone together. She closed her eyes briefly and shivered with pleasure. Fantasies like this could banish almost anything from her mind. They weren't as good as the real thing, but they came pretty close.

George, Hugo thought, was a good sort, but you had to watch it, or he could become boring. He was the kind of man who was always called a charmer. His hair was grey but still wavy, and his blue eyes did a great deal of twinkling. He was full of stories, which took the place of real conversation. Sometimes they were amusing and sometimes they weren't and, at the moment, Hugo was so taken up with thoughts of *Sarabande* that he was finding it hard to take in what the older man was saying.

George was momentarily distracted by his food and for a few seconds didn't say a word. What bliss the silence was, Hugo thought. Then he became aware of someone staring at him from the other side of the table. He looked up, thinking that perhaps Nick and Ilene and Andy were talking about him, and found himself gazing into Silver's eyes. He smiled at her and raised a glass, as though making a toast. He'd always known how beautiful she was. It was one of the reasons he'd chosen her for the part of the Angel, but this morning at their rehearsal he'd felt something else, an attraction so powerful that it made him feel a little breathless. He put his glass down quickly and blinked. Silver. He would have to think about what he was beginning to feel for her. They'd been a little at odds until today. She often told him how bossy and dictatorial he was, even though, admittedly, she was smiling while she said it. She'd been quite brilliant today, and perhaps part of the emotion had to do with the dancing and not him. There had been, till today, no sign from Silver that she was interested in him, but now here she was, looking at him intently, and he wanted to reach out and touch her hand. She was smiling at him as though she had a secret that she was longing to share. Was he imagining a blush? Yes, he probably was. Wishful thinking, he told himself. Get yourself under control. There's Claudia sitting right next to you and looking like a thundercloud. You do not need complications. But as he helped himself to biscuits and cheese, he couldn't help wishing for the time to go more quickly. He found that he was looking forward to the next rehearsal with Silver on her own. Looking forward? No, Hugo wasn't in the habit of deluding himself. He was longing for it.

The dinner had been fantastic and now there was an apple pie on the table which no one seemed to be eating. Alison, hoping she was safe from Claudia's attention on the other side of Ruby, helped herself to a big slice and added some cream from the jug in front of her. Her mother seemed out of sorts. Alison knew that this mood usually came over Claudia when she was being thwarted in some way. Not getting what she wanted. What could she possibly want that wasn't coming her way? Was it to do with Nick? It seemed to her that if anyone had a right to feel pissed off, it was her and not her mother. I'm the one whose dad doesn't answer letters. I'm the one who wishes Nick would think of me as something other than a nice kid. And I'm the one who has to go back to school and leave Wychwood. She realised, as she ate her apple pie, how much she would miss the place. She would also miss Hester and Siggy and Ruby, who was the only person she'd ever met who treated her as though she were just another person. Not a difficult teenager. Not a fatty who needed her food monitored. Just another pair of hands, getting everything ready. And Ruby was going to let her decorate the dining room. That showed she trusted her. Alison was feeling better than she'd felt for ages. The apple pie helped.

She looked at Claudia and saw that she was staring at Hugo and that Hugo was staring at Silver. Silver looked gorgeous. That wasn't surprising really. She always did. Today, she was wearing a grey cardigan that crossed over at the front and her skin looked pearly. Most people would have thought she had no make-up on, but Alison knew better. Silver said she always wore make-up and when Alison remarked that it didn't look as though she did, the answer came at once. *That's the whole point of the exercise. You want them to think it's your natural face.*

Alison considered taking another bit of apple pie because it was obvious to her that no one else was going to, but then she decided she wouldn't after all.

3 January 1987

The house lights were off. Alison was sitting in the stalls, two rows behind Andy and Nick, who wasn't aware she was there. She could stare at the back of Nick's head to her heart's content. The whole company was in the theatre for the technical dress rehearsal and to admire the set, which had just been put up. A large van had arrived early this morning and since then, George and the three young men from the village who usually did the gardening had assembled it.

Now George was in the lighting box and Hugo was on stage signalling him and speaking to him through a kind of walkie-talkie. Ilene and Claudia were also sitting in the stalls and Silver was in the front row, ready to go up on stage and walk through her moves. In a minute, the other dancers would follow her, taking turns to see if the cues were right. Lights kept going on and off. Blue, then orange, then pink. Hugo walked about a bit, and then made a thumbs-up or a thumbs-down sign and then everything changed again. Ruby was getting the props ready on the table in the wings, and soon, Alison would have to go and help her give the basket of fruit to Ilene, the ribbons and dolls to Andy and the flowers to Silver.

The set was brilliant. Later on, maybe tomorrow morning, she would go and examine all the detail, but it looked fantastic. There was a folding screen upstage right and another downstage left and these could be moved about between scenes very easily. The colours were so vibrant that they seemed to shimmer: purple and gold, moss-green and coral, chocolate brown and ocean blue and turquoise, bronze and black and scarlet. You couldn't follow one colour without it merging and blending into the next. Every part of the pattern seemed to curve and stream and flow into the next. Was the pattern nothing more than a pattern? Were there faces in the design? Trees? Landscapes? It was hard to tell, but you couldn't stop trying to find them. There were no hard lines anywhere. As George went through his cues, everything on the screen seemed to change, and there were times when they were in shadow and all you could see was the gold and bronze bits catching what light there was.

Andy was whispering, but some of what he was saying reached Alison and when she heard her mother's name, she paid more attention. She wondered whether she could creep a little closer and decided that was too risky, so she tried to block out the sounds that were coming from the stage and leaned forward to hear more.

She wondered whether Claudia was really keen on Nick or whether she flirted with him all the time in order to annoy Hugo. She'd overheard the two of them yesterday on the way back from rehearsal, and her mother was saying something about Hugo being obsessed with Silver. Hugo had just laughed and said *I'm trying to make her into a ballet dancer, darling*, but Alison wondered whether her mother might really have some reason to be jealous. Hugo did seem to be spending a lot of time instructing Silver. Her mother quite often behaved badly. She didn't seem to be able to stop herself.

Alison looked at the back of Nick's head again. I'm not stupid, she told herself. I know that he'd never be interested in me in that way. She felt like crying, but at the same time she knew that the adoration she felt for Nick had just grown a tiny bit weaker. He was like everyone else after all – Claudia had only to bat her eyelashes and he went with her wherever she wanted to take him. She'd seen her mother in action many times before and could recognise the signs. Hugo might be on his way out, she thought. I wonder if he knows? I wonder if I should tell him?

Claudia slipped into the seat beside her.

'I wish you wouldn't sneak up like that, Mum. You made me jump.'

'Hmmh. Fine welcome for your mother, I must say. God, I'm so late. Hugo'll kill me. Give us a kiss, darling. I never seem to see you these days, to talk to. Are you having fun?'

Not as much fun as you are, was what Alison nearly said, but controlled herself. 'Yeah, not bad. I like Ruby. It's okay here.'

'Grudging, but I think that's a thumbs-up, right darling? Coming from you.' Alison didn't bother to answer. 'You'll be pleased about this, though. I've got a letter for you from your dad.'

'Really? Where is it? Give it to me.'

'It's here somewhere.' Claudia plunged her hand into the depths of her handbag and rummaged round like someone at a bran tub. 'Is this it?' She pulled out a crumpled sheet of paper. 'No. Hang on . . .'

Alison wanted to hit her, but didn't because that would hold things up even more.

'Did it come today? I've been waiting for a letter for ages.'

'Can't honestly remember when it came. A few days ago. I know I picked it up and put it in here and then forgot completely about it.'

'You *what?*'

'Don't make that face at me, young lady. It's not as though there's anything important or urgent about it. It's a bloody Christmas card or something, for God's sake! What difference does it make when you get it? I forgot, that's all. I have a lot of things on my mind. Anyway, here's your precious letter. Take it and welcome.'

At that moment, Hugo called out into the stalls. 'Claudia? Can you come up here a moment, please?'

'Got to go, darling. Sorry about your letter, really. Forgive me?'

No, Alison said to herself. I don't forgive you. 'You'd better go. Hugo's waiting.'

Claudia hurried on to the stage and Alison opened the envelope. There was a card in it, but also a sheet of folded paper.

Hello, darling. Thanks so much for your letter. I'm sure that by the time you get this, you'll have settled in to the routine at Wychwood. Hope so anyway. I'm going to try and phone you when I get back from staying with Jeannette's parents at Christmas. Looking forward to speaking to you. I hate writing as you know. Lots of love as always, Dad.

Under his signature, he'd drawn a little snowman in ballet shoes, with his arms in the air, and scribbled a verse:

> Here is a snowman
> Wearing a hat
> And dancing a ballet
> On feet that are flat.
> Arabesques, pirouettes

Whirling and twirling
Too busy to chat.

Alison smiled. He did love her. He hadn't forgotten the book he'd made for her. This proved it. And he was going to phone her. She wished he'd been a bit more specific about when exactly. What would happen if the phone rang when she was in Wardrobe with Ruby? Would whoever took the call come and get her? She decided not to worry about this for the moment, but just thinking about her mother walking around with this lovely letter in her grotty handbag for days made her want to spit with rage.

'Alison?' Ruby was peering down at the auditorium now. 'Are you there?'

'Yes, Ruby. Coming.'

She ran up on to the stage, still carrying the letter. 'I've got a letter from my dad. Can I just run back to my bedroom and put it away? I don't want to lose it.'

'How lovely. Of course you can,' said Ruby. 'But be quick.'

'I'll be back in five minutes, I promise.'

When she returned after putting her father's letter away in the atlas, next to the lullaby book, she went to find Ruby in the wings.

'Hello again. You *were* quick. I'll be calling on you in a moment to go through the props with me, but could you go and put these on the table on the other side of the stage? Thank you.'

Alison picked up two baskets full of the roses she had helped to make and crossed the stage. The wings were nearly in darkness at the moment. George in the lighting box was obviously having a break. Hugo was on stage, ready to see the next pair of dancers through their routine. She'd almost reached the props table when she saw them. Nick and her mother, standing very close to one another, almost hidden behind a fold of the curtain.

Alison put the baskets down on the props table and out of the corner of her eye, she felt more than saw a slight movement. She turned her head. Nick had his left hand around Claudia's waist and she was leaning slightly sideways, away from him. It looked as though she was practising a step from one of the dances. Then her right hand came up and stroked the side of Nick's face from his hair down to his chin and she was bending the other way now, coming closer and closer to him until their bodies were so close you couldn't tell where one ended and the other began. He's kissing her, Alison thought, he must be. They've managed to slip even further behind the curtain. Just then, George must have flicked a switch and the whole stage area was suddenly bright with pinkish light.

'Right,' said Hugo, looking into the stalls. 'Let's get on, shall we? Ilene, Andy, can you get up here, please? Claudia and Nick? Ah, here you are.'

Nobody, she thought, seems to notice how flushed Nick and Claudia are. What would happen if she told Hugo what she'd seen? Would they have a row? Would he send her mother packing? No, that would put an end to *Sarabande*. She couldn't say a word. Not until after the first night anyway. The one thing she didn't want to do, both for Hester's sake and Ruby's, and also for her own, was to spoil the ballet in any way. It was silly, really, but she'd worked on the props and the costumes and that made her feel as though *Sarabande* was hers in a funny way.

Later, Alison watched her mother taking off her costume in the dressing room. Silver and Ilene had both been much quicker, but then they didn't seem to have to go through all the rituals that Claudia always insisted on: cream, then toner, then the application of a quite different foundation and blusher and eyeliner, which seemed stupid to Alison. If you were going to put on a whole lot of different make-up, why bother taking off what you had on in the first place? She knew the answer, which was that the stage make-up was much stronger, much more obvious, but what Claudia had on now looked much the same to her.

'I need something,' said Claudia, peering into the mirror and putting her hand into the V made by the lapels of the silk dressing-gown she always wore backstage. 'Just to lift the costume a bit. To catch the light onstage. Some kind of necklace or something. I don't feel like a princess without jewellery. But not beads. That would be too much, don't you think?'

Alison knew her mother was only consulting her about such things because there was no one else in the dressing room she could talk to.

'There's that chain Hugo sometimes wears. Ask him if you can borrow that,' she suggested.

'Not a bad idea, darling. How clever you are sometimes! I will, only I don't know if he's brought it with him. It's probably in a drawer at his flat. Just my luck. Come in!'

Claudia was answering a knock on the door.

'I heard that. What's just your luck?' said Hugo, coming in and sitting down on the only armchair, looking, Alison thought, completely exhausted.

'I was wondering if I could borrow your chain. To lift the costume a bit and make me look a little more like a princess. Did you bring it? It'd be perfect.'

'Yes, it's upstairs. Good idea. It'll go very well with your costume.' He sighed. 'I was so relieved to see that the others looked more or less okay that I didn't really pay proper attention to you, Claudia. I'm sorry, but you're always so good with your costumes. I know I can leave it to you.'

'Hmm,' said Claudia, unsure, Alison could see, whether to be pleased about being thought clever enough to deal with her own outfit or insulted that Hugo hadn't been looking at her properly. On balance, the annoyance she felt about that would probably win.

Hugo had just finished talking to Hester about the technical dress rehearsal, or tech, as it was generally called. She was looking at him, he thought, rather more carefully and sharply than usual.

'I'm pleased it went well, Hugo. And I knew that Silver would do it in the end. She's very gifted and also very determined.'

Silver was the last thing he wanted to talk about. He'd tried to put her out of his mind, at least during the run-up to the first night, but it was hard to ignore what he was feeling. He couldn't stop thinking about her. Last night he'd dreamed about her and shadows of the dream had been replaying themselves in his head all day, along with his other worry – what, if anything, to say to Claudia. More and more, he was sensing a kind of apartness in their relationship, as though they were yoked into it without necessarily wanting to be together. Was it just her silly flirting with Nick that had made him think that? Or the fact that his interest in Claudia, his desire to be in her company, was shrinking with every passing hour? Should he confess his doubts to Hester? Probably wiser at this point to say nothing to Claudia. He noticed that Hester seemed more relaxed than at any time since he'd been at Wychwood. He said, 'You're looking well, Hester.' He wanted to say she was looking happy, but that seemed too familiar.

'I feel as though one part of my life is over and something new is starting. Do you know what I mean?'

'I know exactly what you mean. I'm so pleased for you. I might be about to start a new phase in my life myself, but I can't say anything about it. Not yet.'

'No need to say a word, Hugo. I'm just delighted that the ballet is going to be what you want it to be.'

'So far, so good. But fingers are permanently crossed, it goes without saying.'

It was coming together, Hester knew. This was the stage, just before the dress rehearsal, when it became possible to see what the production would be like. Everyone had grown into their parts. They knew the other dancers well, but hadn't been together long enough to become cross and irritated with one another. She went to the window and looked out at the garden. The curtains should have been drawn ages ago, and she hurried to do it before Edmund arrived. He'd be here soon, for a cup of coffee with her, and how good it felt to know that!

She sat down at her desk because Siggy had taken up most of the *chaise-longue* and he looked so peaceful that she was reluctant to disturb him. On the walls, the photographs of herself and others in costume looked like the portraits of so many ghosts. She closed her eyes. That's what I miss, she thought. I'll always miss it. The way you feel just before a ballet opens. The thrill that's like nothing else in the world. Hester knew that, however successful she'd been in many ways since she stopped dancing, that was what had gone – the magic. She had lost that forever.

1966

They'd be here soon. The press, coming to interview her about the forthcoming American tour. Piers was going to talk to them about the company's visit to New York, Chicago and San Francisco. The ballet was a new production of *Les Sylphides*. Hester, as the *prima ballerina assoluta* of the Charleroi Company, was going to be there at his side to answer any questions the reporters cared to ask and, more importantly, to pose for the photographers. Kaspar Beilin, her blond dancing partner, had flown out early to visit his mother in Canada before the tour began.

'No one is interested in a fat old man,' said Piers. 'They want beauty, so I'm afraid you'll have to help me.'

His smile as he said this made Hester smile in return.

'I'm very flattered. But you're not an old man. I'll never think of you as that.'

'Fat then,' said Piers. 'All by itself. Though I'm no spring chicken as you know. Don't think I care for fat on its own. Not a bit.'

When Hester had come to London as a young girl, Piers had promised to look after her, and he'd been as good as his word. He'd been like a father to her. He'd made sure, along with Madame Olga, that as soon as she had recovered from the birth of her child, she began to train again. It was Piers who started to drop hints of her return, and who headed off any awkward questions anyone in the company might have had. Hester had been ill; that was the only thing anyone needed to know. His brisk manner silenced most people but Hester knew how they'd have been gossiping while she was away. Never mind, she'd told herself. They'll stop when I'm back. They'll stop when they see that I'm the dancer I always was. Maybe even better.

Madame Olga undertook to return her in a matter of weeks to the standard she'd reached when she stopped dancing. They worked every day in the studio at Wychwood. For hour after hour, Madame took her old pupil through everything that Hester thought she'd forgotten. As soon as she came out of the fever that followed the birth of her child, as soon as they left Scotland and were back in Yorkshire again, Hester vowed that nothing would stop her. She would dance again, and as soon as she possibly could.

Every day, she did little but practise. When she was moving her body, when she was bending and twisting and spinning, she felt nothing – thought of nothing – but the steps. She could feel the pain in her muscles, in her sinews, and that dulled the agony in her heart. With every day that passed, it was as though she were putting a wall up, brick by brick. She thought that if she built it strongly enough, made it high enough, then she would be protected forever. Safe. The sorrowful weeping Hester would be on one side of the wall and on the other would be the dancer, bathed in the light of stage lamps, receiving the adoration of the audience, a magical being, light as air, weightless, scarcely human at all.

Dancing was, for Hester, a way of stilling thought. It had been so from the day when Madame Olga showed her how to put her feet into the first position. From the very first time she started to go to class, she used the movement to keep the real world at a distance. Now, she understood that it was the discipline of the dance that had stopped her from yearning too much for her lost childhood. What else was there that could have blotted out the longing to go home, to see her grandmother before she died? What else could have anaesthetised her – yes, that was the exact word – against pain of every sort? In those days, when she danced Hester was unaware of the barrier she was building between herself and all kinds of events, but it was there. It had been there throughout her life, a kind of moat around her emotions, but now she was aware of it, and used the knowledge to help her return to the dance.

'All the newshounds are sitting in the stalls like good children at a matinée. Are you ready for them, Hester?' Piers had come into the dressing room, breaking into Hester's reverie. She shook her head. Those days were gone. It was now thirteen years since she had returned to the company, in the summer of 1953. She remembered what it had felt like to be that young dancer coming back. How she'd fought to recover not only her dancing, but her mental balance, and how she had taken on each role that Piers gave her as though it were a lifeline.

'Ready for anything.'

As Piers led her on to the stage of the recently refurbished Royalty theatre, Hester believed her own words. America! It was almost her favourite audience in the world, and she knew that her fans would be longing for the tour to begin. Tonight, after this press conference was over, she would be getting on a train and going down to Edmund's cottage in Cornwall for the weekend. When she'd announced her intention to Piers, he'd frowned and said, 'Goodness me, Hester, that's a very long way to go just for a rest. You do deserve a short break after your hard work on *Sylphides* but I was thinking more in terms of a walk in Hyde Park. Cornwall does seem so distant, somehow.'

'Not much further than Wychwood, really. And I do want to see Edmund before we go on tour.'

The questions from the press were what Hester expected. She could have written down a list of them beforehand. She smiled, and talked through what was different about this production, where they would be going, what she thought of the design, what she felt about the mini-skirt, and did she consider the Beatles to be the new Schubert? Then, after some remarks from Piers, and as Hester was preparing to leave the stage, a young woman spoke up from the darkness of the auditorium.

'Miss Fielding, may I ask you, is there any truth about the rumour that you and Hans Werner have split up?'

'You should know me better by now,' said Hester, standing up and coming to the front of the stage. She knew, even as she was speaking, that it would have been more diplomatic to smile and say nothing, but she was sick, sick, sick of prying reporters. 'I never, ever talk about my private life. Now if you'll forgive me, I've a train to catch.'

She swept offstage without a backward glance. When Piers came to the dressing room, Hester smiled ruefully and said, 'I've done it again, haven't I? Chewed out a poor reporter who meant no harm.

But honestly, Piers, I'm not prepared for my life to be picked over. I'm sorry if I didn't give the right impression.'

Piers chuckled. 'On the contrary, I think you've given exactly the right impression. The public adore it when their idols behave temperamentally. They almost expect it. You wouldn't have half the following you've got if you were a milk and water sort of person. Still, you can't stop them speculating. The mere fact that you don't discuss it makes them think that there's something thrilling going on. They'd love an affair between you and Kaspar. But a bit of fire never comes amiss, though I have to confess I don't enjoy it when you turn prima ballerina-ish on me.'

Hester stood up and kissed Piers on the forehead. 'That's because you're the only one allowed to be temperamental in this company.'

'Quite right. Well, I shall wish you *bon voyage*. See you again on Monday.'

Sitting on the train heading west, Hester looked out of the window at the sun, which was just beginning to spread gold and red into the sky as the afternoon turned into evening. Edmund always said he lived so far west that the sun practically bumped into the roof of his cottage as it set. Hester smiled. I'm going to forget about the press conference, she thought, but she wondered what the answer was to the young reporter's question about Hans. Had she split up with him? On the whole she thought she had. She sighed. She'd long ago come to the conclusion that she wasn't very good at love. She'd lost the gift for it when she left Adam.

In the last few years, there had been no shortage of men doing everything that men in love traditionally did. They sent her presents and came to see her dance and wrote her letters and took her out to dinners where they stared into her eyes and declared her the most beautiful, the most wonderful, the one they couldn't live without, and sometimes Hester felt a spark of something – desire, affection, friendship. When she did, she began a relationship which seemed to follow an increasingly predictable pattern.

For a few months, she could become quite caught up. Sometimes, especially if she was attracted to the man, she became half of a couple. They would be photographed smiling at one another at parties and spend nights together that almost convinced Hester that this was it, this was a man with whom she might find happiness. But then, boredom always crept in. She caught herself wanting to relate conversations to Edmund to see whether he found them as ridiculous as she did. When this happened, Hester always told her lover at once that this was the end of the affair. I don't let them go on hoping, she thought. Surely no man would choose to go on living with a woman who wasn't a hundred percent committed to him?

Was it just the memory of Adam and what she still felt for him that stopped her falling properly in love with anyone else? Edmund always avoided talking about Adam, but Hester knew that the two of them were in touch. Adam and Virginia lived part-time in America now. That was one piece of information Edmund had let slip. Hester routinely avoided bookshops for fear of seeing Adam's photograph on a dustjacket, but sometimes she'd come across a review in a newspaper and when that happened she had to throw the newspaper out at once. If she'd left it lying about, she'd have been tempted to go back and read the words that someone else had written about Adam.

Did that mean she was still in love with him? The dreams she had from time to time, the pain that prolonged thinking about him made her feel, the fact that she and Edmund never talked about him: all those things led Hester to admit that, yes, a part of her still yearned for Adam. It was only a tiny part, and she tried not to bring him to mind. She had determined to concentrate on other things, and she was good at that. She could, however, do nothing whatsoever about the core of sadness that refused to be moved from the very heart of her.

Edmund made her feel happy. Or as happy as she was ever going to be. He was very, very dear to her. He was so affectionate and cheerful that it was impossible to be gloomy in his presence. He loved her. There had been more than enough proof of that, but Hester was sure that it was the friendship kind of love. He looked after her. He shared his secrets with her. He wrote to her all the time, funny postcards and letters from wherever he was. He sought out her company. But he had never shown the least interest in her as a woman, and when he kissed her, it was in a brotherly kind of way. He's not interested in me as a lover and that's all there is to it. He's always got some woman in tow, though. He's never shown the least sign of pining over anyone. A woman would appear at his side and then, after a few months, she was replaced and Edmund sailed through from one to the other with a smile. Even more surprisingly, everyone he split up from seemed delighted to go on being friendly with him.

'Hester! How lovely!' Edmund was bounding down the platform towards her, his voice raised so that everyone around turned to look at him. In her last letter, Dinah had called him 'puppyish' and even though he was now practically middle-aged, it was true. His face and bearing made him look much younger than his years.

'Edmund, super to see you too,' Hester said, submitting to a hug that nearly squeezed the breath out of her. He was so tall that her face was squashed into the fabric of his jacket. She stepped back. Edmund was talking and talking.

'You don't know Marisa, do you?' he said. 'There she is, by the barrier. She's such a sweetie, really. I'm sure you'll get on.'

Hester felt a plummeting sensation in her chest. She hated to be caught unawares and Edmund knew that.

'I wish you'd told me,' she said, as they walked towards the waiting Marisa. 'I'd have come another time.'

'That's why I didn't,' Edmund grinned at her. 'I wanted you to come now. You're off to the States for months and months and I won't see you for such ages. I couldn't bear that, you know.'

'Don't talk nonsense, Edmund.' Hester wasn't mollified, but knew that she had to make the best of this situation. They were standing in front of Marisa and the introductions had begun.

'Marisa is an oboe player, Hester. Very talented.' Edmund presented her to Hester for approval. Marisa was tall and brown: tanned face, long brown hair, and long brown legs under a very short skirt indeed. She couldn't be more than twenty-five, Hester judged. I'll have to have a word with Edmund about cradle-snatching. She shook Marisa's hand and smiled. It's not this poor woman's fault that Edmund has no tact, she thought. And then something occurred to her. What did Marisa think of having an old friend of Edmund's turning up in the middle of their romantic Cornish idyll? She must have been more than a little put out. She decided to forgive Edmund, and got into the passenger seat of the car next to him almost before Marisa herself suggested it.

Hester lay in bed, looked up at the sloping ceiling of Edmund's spare room and listened to the sound of the sea. Fortunately, Edmund and Marisa's room was on the other side of the cottage, through the sitting room and up a short flight of steps. At least she wouldn't be disturbed by the noise of their lovemaking.

The sea. Hester loved it and was frightened by it. The sight of it from the window earlier in the day, twinkling and sparkling in the spring sunshine, was the kind of image you'd expect to find on the front of a tourist brochure. But she'd seen it when the wind was blowing. When gales lifted the waves and whipped them towards the coast, it wasn't hard to see in your mind's eye ships broken on black rocks and drowned men; what you heard was a wailing and shrieking in the air quite different from the gentle murmuring swish she was listening to now. Tomorrow, they'd be off along the cliff path. Maybe she'd make some excuse. Let the lovebirds go off into the distance together without her. Well, perhaps she'd go with them. She fell asleep before she'd made up her mind.

She did go with them. Edmund parked the car at the beginning of the cliff path and they set off on a slow walk towards the pub about two miles further up the coast. She had made an attempt, out of tact, to stay behind at the cottage but Edmund was having none of it.

'Nonsense, Hester. We won't hear of it. It's a lovely day and I know you're a great walker. And look at the sea. How can you resist? Turquoise stripes all the way to the horizon.'

She was following Edmund and Marisa now. The path was too narrow for three of them to walk abreast, but it was good to be alone with her thoughts for a short while. The sea was just as beautiful as Edmund had promised and she made up her mind to try and buy a postcard to send to Dinah that would show her what she was missing by living so far away from England.

Every so often, Edmund looked over his shoulder at her and called out, 'Hester? You okay?' and she would nod and wave at him and

Marisa to show that yes, she was fine, and they mustn't wait for her. She kicked some pebbles along the path with the toe of her walking shoe and thought how different they were from her ballet shoes. She'd be back in those soon enough.

Edmund and Marisa were ahead of her now and waiting for her to catch up with them. The wind was blowing a little more strongly, whipping Marisa's long hair over her face. Hester began to walk a little faster to catch up with them.

Her eyes were on the horizon and not on the ground ahead of her. She didn't see it. A rabbit hole on the edge of the path, hidden by a clump of grass. A rabbit hole just at the top of a small slope. Her left foot caught in the hole and she twisted herself to free it and fell a little way – only a very short distance – but she fell on the same foot and her twisting and falling ended in an explosion of agony. She had no breath in her body left to scream with, but she could hear a shrieking in her head. Her last thought was: *Sylphides*. How will I dance *Sylphides?*

'Oh, you're such a lucky lady,' the nurse squeaked. She couldn't have been more than twenty. 'Look at all these flowers. I don't think I've ever looked after anyone who's had so many flowers. Well, it stands to reason, doesn't it? You being famous and everything. My mum couldn't believe it. When I told her, she said now be sure and get her autograph, Noreen, because she's famous. A ballet dancer! Fancy!'

Was she going to stop now? No, Hester thought. Not yet. The words kept on coming.

'You can't imagine the fuss there's been. Press and photographers in the car park there were, till they were sent packing. Well, it's such a story, isn't it? How that nice Mr Norland carried you in his arms all the way to his car and then drove you to hospital and came with you when you were brought here. Ambulance brought you all the way from Cornwall; I didn't know they did long distances. *And* you were on the news. They said you were – I can't remember, but something very good, anyway. Oh yes, a legend in her own lifetime, that was it.

'I've kept all the papers for you. They're in a pile over there. Every single one had you on the front page, you know.'

Hester looked at her. She was carrying a vase of flowers. More flowers. The whole of the little room was full of them, like some funeral parlour.

'Are you feeling all right?' The nurse was still holding the vase in one hand. She put it down on Hester's bedside table. How can I possibly feel all right, Hester thought. That has to be one of the stupidest questions I've ever been asked. I'm a dancer and I've been told I'll never dance again. I want to kill myself. I want to take every single bloody flower that I'm so lucky to have and burn it in a huge fire. I don't want to read about myself in the bloody papers. They can go on the fire as well.

Hester reached out and swept her arm over the surface of the bedside table in a wide arc and knocked the vase to the floor. Water spread over the linoleum. Flowers scattered under the bed. She burst into tears. The nurse stood in the middle of the whirlwind blinking, not knowing what to do.

'Hester?' Edmund had pushed open the door and was looking in at her. 'What on earth's been going on? Oh, Hester, darling . . . poor darling!'

Hester couldn't speak. There were sounds in her head, a kind of keening. Were those noises coming from her? Edmund came and sat on the bed and put his arms around her.

'I'll look after you, Hester. You know I will. And Piers and Madame Olga. We all will. You must get better. You have to.'

'Why do I have to?' Hester's voice, muffled against Edmund's shoulder, broke through her sobs. 'What for? What use am I to anyone if I can't dance? That's all I'm good for. Don't tell me it could have been worse. I don't want to have platitudes pushed at me. I won't. I . . . oh, Edmund, I don't want to go on living like this! Save me, Edmund. You always save me. Get me some pills. Lots and lots of pills so that I can take them and sleep and never have to wake up ever again.'

Hester waited for Edmund to object. She waited for him to cajole her, to comfort her, to say something, anything, that he thought might make her feel better, but he didn't. He just sat on the bed and held her, in silence, for a long time. He stroked her hair and rocked her backwards and forwards, as if she were a small child. The tears kept falling and falling. There was no end to them. Hester felt, madly, that she was nothing but a vase herself, a thin, fragile vessel of glass filled with tears.

She calmed down in the end. It had been clear from the beginning that the compound fractures of both tibia and fibula in her lower leg meant she would never dance on stage as a professional ballerina again. Having the protection of the ballet suddenly removed was too much for her to bear. She became like a sea creature suddenly pulled wriggling out of her shell and left open to everything. She felt vulnerable and raw, as though her skin had been stripped away. Her career was over. What was to become of her? There was, she could feel it, a crust of ice around her heart. She couldn't bear talking to anyone except Madame Olga and Edmund. She would have spoken to Piers too, but he'd taken the company to America. Because the show must go on, mustn't it? Thinking of them dancing without her; thinking of her understudy, Patricia Blake, being partnered by Kaspar, taking her part, wearing her shoes, and the costume that had been designed for her, was a form of torture.

Hester stayed in hospital for two weeks, and then returned to Wychwood to recuperate. For a long time there was nothing anyone could say to her or do for her that made things better. The weather didn't help. It was supposed to be spring, but there was rain always slanting across every window and the moors were grey and cold. The trees were late with their leaves that year and what she saw through them was a grid fashioned out of black branches. The chilliness of everything froze her up and she longed for the sun. Then, one morning, Madame Olga came to tell her that she was expecting a visitor.

'Look,' said Madame Olga, plumping the cushions behind her back 'here is sun. Today will be a good day.'

Hester looked out of the window and saw that the weather was making an effort. It wasn't sunshine, exactly, that was pouring into her room, but a kind of diluted glow. The next best thing to real warmth.

'What visitor?'

'You'll see. I will help you to dress. Take the crutches and come here. We will make you very pretty today.'

This was a ritual they went through every day. Hester saw that Madame Olga had laid out the blue dress. She'd worn it last just before the accident, on the afternoon of the press conference announcing the American tour. They're in San Francisco now, Hester thought. The whole company but not me. Never me again. Thinking about this made the tears rise to her eyes. She blinked them away and put the dress on as quickly as she could. Madame Olga handed her a powder puff, a lipstick and a hairbrush and she went through the motions.

Someone who wasn't really her was staring out of the mirror. This was a person with dark shadows under her eyes. There was a greenish pallor to her skin. I'm like something that's lived under a stone for a very long time, she thought. Which is just about right. Something – a tiny impulse of determination or anger or disgust rising within her – was perhaps the first sign of recovery. I can't be like this, Hester thought. I must become myself again.

She had no idea how she would make that happen, but felt, for the first time in weeks and weeks that she wanted to change herself. Also, she noticed that she was curious. She wanted to know what the surprise was, and had started to experience something other than despair. It was the first time she'd cared about anything since before the accident. This, she felt, was a mark of progress. She finished brushing her hair with something like a lift in her heart.

Edmund was in the drawing room, waiting for her. She stood at the door on her crutches as he came towards her.

'Hester, Hester.' He held her upper arms. 'How lovely to see you looking so good. So, so much better. And you're on your feet. How long will you be on those things?'

She leaned against him. 'Just one more week. Oh, Edmund, it's so wonderful to see you.'

'And you.' The gaze he turned on her was full of tenderness. Had she ever seen that in his eyes before?

'I have to sit down, Edmund. And I'm glad to hear I *look* okay. It's nothing but a show, I'm afraid. You know how good I am at pretending. I feel . . . well, I feel empty inside. As though there's a long black road stretching out in front of me and I have no idea where it's leading or what's at the end of it. Oh, God, you don't want to hear this. It's boring. It's depressing. Cheer me up, Edmund. You're always so good at that. How I've missed talking to you!'

'Glad to hear it.' Edmund grinned. 'I'd have been here days ago. I've been begging poor Madame Olga to let me come, but no go. She judged that you were ready for a visit now, so here I am. I don't know if I can cheer you up, but I'll certainly try.'

'Do you honestly think there's a life for me outside ballet?'

'Of course there is! I've been thinking about that. You'll be a wonderful teacher. You could lecture all over the world. Earn a lot of money while you're at it. And there's another thing, Hester. You're thirty-three. You can't . . . you couldn't . . . have gone on dancing forever. It's a brutal thing to say I know, but your career as a *prima ballerina* wouldn't have lasted much longer anyway. That may sound cruel, but it's true.'

'But a few years. I could have managed a few more years. I wasn't completely decrepit, was I? I'd have known. Someone would have told me.'

'You might have known, but no one would have dared tell you. The great Hester Fielding? Your name alone means a full house. Not even Piers would have been in a hurry to stop you if you'd had a mind to continue.'

'What you're saying is, I've had a narrow escape. I should thank my lucky stars that I managed to break my leg so thoroughly otherwise I might have been tempted to go on until I was a real old crock. Do you think I'm an idiot, Edmund? I'd know. I'd have known the minute I couldn't do the work any longer.'

'You're angry, Hester.' Edmund took her hand. 'That's good. That shows that you're still in there somewhere, the old Hester, buried under all that silence and misery you've been in for the last few weeks. And yes, fair enough, of course you'd have known. What I'm saying is, you won't have to agonise over the decision now. It's been made for you, and you should come out. Join in the world again. I'll help you. Lots of people will help you. You have many friends, you know.'

Hester tried to smile at him. 'You're right. I will try. I'll try and get back to some sort of something. I'm not sure what. But I will make an effort, I promise you.'

'Let's change the subject then. I've brought you a present.'

'You didn't need to bring anything, but how lovely!.'

'No, but I have and it's fantastic, though I say so myself.' He went over to the piano and opened it. 'I've written something for you. Listen. All the sumptuous laziness of the East. It'll make you feel better just to hear it. No more Northern gloom for you from now on.'

Hester leaned against the cushions and closed her eyes. Edmund began to play and the melody poured into the room like liquid gold. She saw turquoise water and slender towers; cool shadows and fountains, and lemon trees heavy with fruit. She saw scarlet flowers and balconies and perfumed oils on newly-bathed skin; moonlight and the black silhouettes of small boats rocking on water; lovers lying on silk cushions, roses, fragrant cream roses. She opened her eyes in the end. The mind-pictures were becoming too strong, too vivid.

'It's quite beautiful, Edmund,' she said, when the piece was finished.

'It's called *Sarabande*. That's a stately Spanish dance in triple time, for your information. It's also a Persian rug with a pattern of leaves and pears. I don't think I've ever seen such a thing.'

'I'm honoured, Edmund. And it *has* cheered me up, I think. I'm going to make a new start tomorrow. I promise.'

He left his seat at the piano and came to sit beside her on the sofa.

'There! Lazy and pleasure-loving is how you're supposed to feel when you hear that.'

'I do,' said Hester. 'I feel as though I never want to do anything energetic ever again.'

'I'd do anything for you, Hester. I'll help however I can to get you back to something like normal. Just ask me, if there's anything you want.'

He smiled at her and she smiled back. Suddenly, he leaned forward and kissed her lightly on the mouth and she felt a small shiver of warmth running through her and then the kiss was over.

4 January 1987

'I love it out here,' Hester said. 'I try and walk for an hour every day before breakfast. It's good to have you with me.'

She and Edmund were walking through the village on their way to the moors behind the house. 'I almost never come past here, you know. That's the Wellick house. I've pointed it out to you before, haven't I?'

Edmund nodded. 'Yes, you have, and quite honestly, from what you've told me, I'm not a bit surprised that you avoid it. Such an ugly little house!'

'I think the poor old Wellicks did their best, you know. I can't have been the easiest person in the world to look after. But the place looks much better now. The present owners have put a sort of garden in at least. The Wellicks weren't interested in plants. They were too messy for Auntie Rhoda. It was nothing but a square of grass in front here, when I was a girl.'

She shivered, and saw that Edmund had noticed.

'Are you cold, Hester?'

'Not really. Just makes me feel funny sometimes, thinking about those days.'

They walked along in silence till the village was left behind and the moorland path rose up in front of them. Most of the snow had melted away, but a little still lay on the ground. The sky was like a stage backcloth of palest blue with streaks of white cloud painted on it. The wintry sun had just come up and every word they spoke turned into a plume of white.

'The snow may have melted, but it's still freezing,' Edmund said.

'I'm used to the weather up here. And I'm used to getting up early from years and years of going to class. And I feel . . . I feel as though something that's squeezed me and stifled me has been opened.'

'Like taking off a corset?'

'In a way, yes. I think this is the first day for years and years that I've woken up and thought of Adam as someone in the past. Before today . . .'

'I know. You don't have to tell me, Hester. You felt that he still had to be considered, you thought he was part of your life. Or could be one day?'

'No. No, I knew he'd never be that. But I *did* take him into account. I thought of him often, had nightmares about him, too, and I used to wonder whether I still loved him. Surely the fact that I did that means that I must have, in a way? That I couldn't let him go?'

'You never allowed yourself to love anyone else, did you?'

She laughed. 'It's not as though I've been besieged by a thousand suitors! I haven't been sweeping them away, you know.'

Hester was talking with such animation that she wasn't concentrating on where her feet were. Suddenly, she stumbled over a tussock of grass. She put out a hand to catch at Edmund's arm and he leaned forward quickly and took hold of her round the waist. For a moment, Hester was somewhere else, dragged back in memory to another fall on a sunny headland with Edmund and Marisa waiting for her on the cliff path. But this wasn't like that. Not in the least. She blinked to dispel the memory, straightened up, and made circles with her foot to make sure she'd done no real damage, trying to hide the shock she was feeling. Her heart was thumping and she could feel her legs trembling, not under her control.

'Hester?' Edmund put his hand gently on her chin and turned her face so that she was looking straight into his eyes. She was about to say something, about to reassure him that no, she hadn't hurt herself when she saw that his gaze was full of love. His eyes shone with it. Its warmth, its intensity fell on her like the beam of a spotlight. She was aware of the weight of his hand on her shoulder through the fabric of her coat. He said her name again and then closed his eyes and brought his mouth down to meet hers. In the cold air, his lips were burning. She let herself be drawn into his arms and opened her mouth in response, and had the sensation of falling. Of spinning down into a softness and sweetness that she'd forgotten could exist. Edmund. This was Edmund.

When the kiss ended, neither of them could think of a word to say. They sat down on a ledge of rock, out of the wind and then they both started to speak at the same time.

'I . . .'

'I . . .'

'You first,' Edmund said. 'You speak first.'

'I don't know what to say. I'm shaking.'

'Me too. Hester?'

'Yes?'

'I love you.'

Hester looked at him. She expected him to be smiling, but his expression was serious. She said nothing. Edmund went on, 'It's not a sudden thing, you know. I'm not being impulsive. I've loved you since the first day I met you.'

'But you never said. Why didn't you say?'

'I saw how you felt about Adam. From the beginning and even after everything that happened.'

'You should have tried, Edmund. You could have said something.'

'I thought about it many times, but in the end I was too frightened of what you might say. I wasn't going to risk our friendship.'

'Was it such a risk? I don't know. I don't know what I'd have said. I might have forgotten about Adam altogether if you'd only . . .'

Edmund shook his head. 'No, you were still in love with him. Part of you. And I had no idea whether or not you found me attractive.'

'I did,' Hester said. 'I do. But I thought . . .'

'What? What did you think?' He leaned his head into her shoulder and began to kiss her neck in the gap between her hat and her scarf. She shivered and turned her face to him and they were kissing again, and Hester felt a hunger for Edmund, for his mouth and his body, that she hadn't felt for anyone in years. She wanted to press every inch of her skin against his. She wanted to hold him close and enfold him in her body. She moved away from him a little because sitting so close to him made it impossible to concentrate.

At last she spoke. 'I thought I was like a kind of younger sister to you. You've always looked after me. And you *always* had a girlfriend. I didn't even know that you found me attractive.'

'Girlfriends. Yes, well, I wasn't going to pine away entirely. I could see how much in love you were with Adam. For years after you parted. Perhaps until his death.'

'I'm not in love with Adam any longer.' She stood up and put out her hand for Edmund. 'And we have to make up for lost time,' she said. 'I think we should go back to Wychwood now.'

'I love you, Hester. Did you hear me saying it before? I mean it.'

'And I love you, Edmund.'

'Not like a brother? Not like a friend?'

'No,' Hester said. 'Properly. Truly.'

They walked down to the village arm in arm. All the way back to Wychwood House, as they spoke of things they should have talked about long before, one thought filled Hester's mind to the exclusion of everything else: *He'll come to my room tonight. He'll be there when I wake up tomorrow. He loves me.*

'Excuse me,' said Alison, putting her head round the door of the Office, where Hester was sitting at her desk. Siggy had the *chaise-longue* all to himself.

'Come in, come in. I'm just writing to a dear friend of mine in New Zealand. I haven't seen you about lately.'

'Sorry to disturb you, but I wanted to ask you something, if that's okay.'

'Of course. You look worried, Alison. Is anything the matter?'

Alison sat down on the *chaise-longue* next to Siggy and began to stroke his back. He opened one eye to see who was caressing him, and then closed it again. 'He knows me, I think,' said Alison. 'He's so gorgeous. I'll miss him like anything when we go.'

'You should get a cat of your own.'

'My mum'd never let me. I'm at school during the term and she's out such a lot.'

'That's a shame. Tell me what's wrong, then. You look tired.'

'I didn't sleep very well.' She pushed her hair back from her forehead and went on. 'I'm worried about my dad. He said he was going to phone and we're in the Arcadia for so much of the day that I'm afraid I'll miss the call and then I'd . . . I don't really know what I'd do. He wrote to me, you see. Saying he'd phone.'

'Well, I'm here most of the time and I'd make sure to let you know if I took the call. And if I'm not here, there's the answering machine. I'm sure your father would leave a number where you could phone him, don't you think?'

'An answering machine! That's brilliant. Thanks so much. I'll stop worrying about it now.'

'Good. I'm glad we sorted it out. It's funny, isn't it, how things that worry us tremendously turn out not to be so dreadful after all?'

'I suppose so. Thanks very much, anyway. I've got to go and help Ruby now. She's ironing stuff for the dress rehearsal.'

'I can't wait. I've been busy sorting out the first of the master classes for February, but I'm longing to see what Hugo's done with Edmund's music.'

'I don't like ballets usually, but this is a bit different because I've helped with the props and costumes. And I like the music.'

As she left the Office and closed the door behind her, Alison almost bumped into Hugo, striding at high speed towards the corridor leading to the Arcadia. He stopped when he saw her.

'Hello, you!' he said in a very cheerful voice.

'Hello.' Alison fell into step beside him. 'Are you going to the theatre?'

'Yes,' said Hugo. 'I'm just checking up on things before the dress. You okay? You look a bit tired.'

'I didn't sleep very well. But I'm fine now.' A thought occurred to Alison. 'Did Claudia tell you there was a letter from my dad?'

Hugo shook his head. 'No, not a word. But then I'm a bit too busy to chat to Claudia as much as I'd like to. *Sarabande* takes up all my thoughts.'

'Is it going to be okay?'

'Yes, I think it is. I was a bit worried about some things earlier on, but I think it's going to be great. Silver's going to be amazing.'

Alison heard the warmth in his voice and wondered whether she was imagining it.

'You like her, don't you?' The words were out of her mouth before she could stop them. Hugo sighed.

'Is it obvious? I do like her, Alison. I hoped that I was keeping it hidden. For the moment at least. I don't want anything upsetting

Claudia now. The ballet, she must be able to concentrate on that. After it's over, well, then, we'll see. I'm not going to lie to you. I'm . . . I don't think your mum and I are going to be together for very much longer.'

'Don't you love her any more?'

Hugo shook his head. 'It's not as simple as that. It's just . . . well, it's complicated.'

Alison found herself, surprisingly, feeling sorry for Claudia. That was funny. Yesterday, she was ready to punish her for keeping Dad's letter but now, how would she react if Hugo left her? Alison said, before she'd had time to think about how it sounded, 'What about me?'

'I'd miss you, Alison. You know I would. You're a great kid. I've really got to like you so much. I'd try to keep in touch. You know that, I hope.'

'I suppose so,' Alison was almost whispering. 'I'll miss you as well.'

She hadn't realised it till just this moment, but it was true. If Hugo went off and left them, she might never see him again. People always said they'd keep in touch and then they didn't after all. How horrible life was! You could meet all kinds of nice people and get to like them and then what happened? They disappeared. She wouldn't see Nick again either, after she left for school on the seventh. Alison felt like weeping.

'I promise you that we'll still see one another. I'll write to you.'

'My dad's supposed to write to me, but he's useless,' Alison said.

'Ah, but I'm a super-duper letter-writer. Honestly, I will write to you. Promise. And not a word to Claudia, okay? All I need is for her to throw a wobbly before the first night.'

'Okay,' said Alison, and Hugo leaned forward and gave her a quick kiss on the top of her head.

'See you at the dress rehearsal, then.'

'Right,' said Alison and watched Hugo going into the Arcadia. He was moving as though he was in a great hurry.

Claudia sat in front of the mirror in the dressing room and considered her face in the unforgiving lights. She tried to work out what she was feeling and came to the conclusion that it was disappointment. Patrick once told her that she had about as much interior life as a prawn, and she'd thrown a ballet shoe at his head on that occasion because it simply wasn't true. Look at me now, she thought. I'm in turmoil. Inner turmoil. All my emotions are in a terrible state and my interior life is about the only kind of life I've got. The rest of my existence is just plain disappointing.

She wiped her face with a piece of cotton wool soaked in cleansing lotion and frowned. Her face usually cheered her up. She was beautiful, wasn't she? Everyone said so and she knew they were right, but what had happened over the last couple of days? She drew closer to the mirror. A network of fine lines was visible at the corners of her eyes and something about her expression – a sort of sulkiness – displeased her. She tried a smile and that was even worse. The lines were deeper and her face had taken on, in this ghastly bright light at least, the look of a mask. Horrible. She reached quickly for her make-up box.

Okay, she thought, and smoothed foundation over her skin. Immediately she felt better when she saw how it covered up the small imperfections that she didn't even like to think about for fear of becoming terminally depressed – those patches of skin that were slightly red, or blotchy, or uneven in texture. I'll look fine, she told herself, and then couldn't think why she was still feeling dissatisfied. Why was that? It must be Nick. Nick and Hugo. There was something seriously wrong with her relationship with Hugo, and what she and Nick had together could scarcely be called a relationship. Claudia was too old to kid herself. As soon as they got back to civilisation he'd drop her like a hot potato. I'm good enough as a bit of fun while he's here in the middle of nowhere, but once he's back with the girls and boys in the company in London, he'll drop me like a pair of laddered tights.

And Hugo didn't seem that keen any longer. Was that because of his preoccupation with *Sarabande?* Or something else? Was he going off her? We'll see, Claudia said to herself. The dress rehearsal is only an hour or so away and then the first night'll be here, and let's see if he changes back to how he used to be when that's all over. She wasn't altogether sure herself if she wanted to go back to the life, practically a married life, that they used to have.

She picked up a small pot of turquoise eyeshadow and began dabbing it on her left eyelid. Maybe he knows about Nick, she thought. I shouldn't have been so stupid as to go off with him like that on New Year's Eve, but Hugo was completely ignoring me and anyway I'd had a bit too much to drink. Can it be that I regret it? It certainly added something to each rehearsal. The occasional snatched kiss did make things a bit less boring – and what about another night together. Was that going to be possible? The dressing room arrangements in the Arcadia Theatre were not what was required for privacy, which was a real shame. She searched her conscience (Patrick said she was born without one) and decided that no, she didn't regret what had happened with Nick. She was being paranoid. No one knew about that night, she was sure, so no harm had been done. But perhaps I should tell Hugo, she thought. It might make him think about what he's been missing. Perhaps he'll be jealous and realise he has to pay me proper attention if he wants to keep me interested.

Alison. Claudia sighed as her daughter came into her mind. She's always had this effect on me, she told herself. She's a problem. Actually, she'd been less of a liability than usual at Wychwood, but ever since New Year's Eve there'd been nothing but glowering and frowning coming from her direction the whole time. She's got a crush on Nick and is jealous of me, that's the problem. She began to work on her other eye, reflecting that it was a bit silly of her to have forgotten that bloody letter from Patrick, but honestly, you'd think Alison had been stabbed in the gut or something, the way she'd reacted.

'Hello, Claudia.' Silver had come into the room without making a sound. Why couldn't the bloody woman walk like normal mortals instead of gliding silently everywhere?

'Oh, hello.' Claudia hoped she sounded more welcoming than she felt. There it was, right there, the main reason for the way she was feeling. Bloody Silver with her flawless complexion and her ridiculously perfect figure and her fucking niceness to everyone. How come a place as luxurious as the Arcadia couldn't run to a star dressing room? Why was she having to share at her age, like a kid from the *corps de ballet*, for Heaven's sake?

'It's getting colder,' Silver said. 'I think it might even snow again.'

'Mmm,' said Claudia, making a big thing of outlining her lips. Am I the star any longer, she wondered. Am I still the *prima ballerina* of this company? The misery she felt as she asked herself these questions brought tears to her eyes. She was quick to blink them away. Damned if I'm going to cry in front of sodding Silver, she thought, and gritted her teeth. She put the lipstick down on the dressing table and surveyed the results of her labours. Not bad. She'd still pass with a kick and a shove, but for how much longer? She opened the pretty little box that Hugo had given her, and tipped it up so that the filigree chain poured on to the dressing-table like a tiny stream of gold. It was old, that much was clear. The loud, rather vulgar shine that often marred gold jewellery had been worn into a glow like candlelight. Claudia held it up against her neck. Yes, she thought. That's going to make all the difference. And it picks out the gold in the fabric of my costume. I'm going to be wonderful in *Sarabande* if it kills me, she decided, even though she knew that moving in the ways she had to move was becoming increasingly difficult and she was growing more tired after each performance. What would become of her if she could no longer dance? She said, 'I think I'm going to put my coat on and have a smoke outside, Silver. I'll see you later.'

She left the room, wrapping her coat tightly round her, and didn't look back.

'Can I come in, Silver? Just for a moment.'

'Are you looking for Claudia? She's gone out to have a cigarette, but I'm sure she'll be back soon.'

'I'm not looking for Claudia. I thought I'd come and speak to you before the rehearsal. Are you nervous?'

Hugo sat down on the only armchair, which was pushed up against the wall next to the costume-rail. Silver could see him smiling at her reflection in the mirror. He was looking at her with great tenderness. She turned her attention to putting on the Angel's rather elaborate headdress, concentrating on that to distract herself from what she was feeling. She had done nothing but think about Hugo ever since she'd danced for him and he'd touched her hair. Was it only yesterday? Then he'd raised his glass to her at dinner. She'd taken ages to get to sleep, and when she had finally drifted off, Hugo's face was there in her dreams. She and Hugo were dancing together. He'd taken the place of Nick in the *pas de deux* and he was whispering to her, *more, you can do it better. Don't think I'm going to stop watching you.*

'You haven't answered. How do you feel about this afternoon?'

'You mean the dress rehearsal? I'm fine. I'm looking forward to it, really.' Could he honestly be intending to say nothing? Silver noticed that she was holding her breath.

'Silver?' (Yes, yes, she thought. He's getting up. He's coming over here. She could see him in the mirror, standing behind her now.)

She half-turned so that she was looking into the black expanse of his sweater. If she leaned against it, she knew how soft it would feel. She could smell him from this distance, some sort of wonderful aftershave or cologne or something, mixed with the fragrance of his skin, which made her want to hold him and breathe him in and fold him into her arms. She tried to say something but her voice wouldn't obey her.

'I've made you really, really work for the first time in your life, haven't I?'

'You have. I suppose I should be grateful and I am, even though you're a monster.'

'Silver . . .' Something in his voice made her get up from the dressing-table stool. She turned to face him. She closed her eyes and stepped — it was only a very tiny step — even closer to Hugo so that their bodies were nearly touching. It's up to him she thought. I can't do it by myself. He has to show me, prove to me, that I know what he's thinking. And then his hands were on her face and he was drawing her even closer so that their lips were almost, almost touching. She felt his breath on her skin and she opened her mouth as Hugo kissed her. Oh, please don't let him say anything. No words. I don't want any words. I want him to touch me. I want to touch him, drink in his scent. She stood on tiptoe and wound her arms round Hugo's neck and they clung together and the sound of their breathing was the only sound in the whole world and Silver's skin was on fire.

She lost track of everything – where she was, time passing, what they'd just been saying to one another. The whole universe had shrunk into this sensation, this emotion. She broke away after . . . how long?

'Someone might come in, Hugo,' she whispered.

'I don't care.' He drew her gently into another kiss. Her legs, legs that she must stretch and bend and dance on felt as though they were melting.

'Oh, Hugo, I've got to dance in a moment. I have to get hold of myself before I go on stage. I won't be able to concentrate. Please. I think you ought to go.'

'Okay. But later. I'll see you after the dress rehearsal.'

He kissed her once more, briefly, and left. Silver sat down again in front of the mirror. She was trembling all over. Her legs still felt weak. Pull yourself together, she said to her reflection, you're an angel. She smiled, and lifted her arms and imagined the wings she would soon be wearing. I'm going to do it, she thought. I'm going to fly.

Hester loved dress rehearsals. There was a particular moment, just before the curtain went up to reveal what the Wychwood Festival ballet was to be that year, which was almost pure happiness. All her attention was concentrated on the stage, dark for the moment but about to be illuminated by light that was like no other she could think of – warm with colour, and capable of transforming everything it fell on into something magical. The Mike Spreckley Trio, who were going to provide the live music, had already set up their instruments downstage left. Edmund had spent half an hour with them before the start of the rehearsal and they'd been overwhelmed to meet the composer of the original score.

She could remember, also, exactly what the dancers would be feeling as the time approached to come out on to the bright stage – a slightly sick feeling in the pit of the stomach, a sudden sweatiness of the hands, and, as you dipped your shoes into the rosin box in the wings, a blinkered vision that reduced everything to what you were about to do when you began to dance.

Edmund was sitting next to her. He was excited at the thought of seeing how his music had inspired Hugo, and his eyes shone. How young he looked! It was all Hester could do to stop herself touching him. Ever since they'd kissed earlier that morning, she'd wanted to kiss him again. Part of her wished that the rehearsal was already over. She longed to be alone with him, and he held her hand as though he didn't intend to let it go. He'd always been the perfect dress rehearsal companion, not too serious and ready with a light-hearted remark to cheer her up if he felt she needed it. He was also knowledgeable enough about ballet to discuss with her the finer points of anything they were watching.

'Don't look so anxious, Hester,' he whispered. 'It's going to be a great year, this year, I'm quite sure.'

'I hope you're right.'

'Oh, I am, I am. Look who's written the music. And those players are the best, you know. Great chaps. It'll be fantastic. Hugo's obviously very talented and so's his company, aren't they?'

'I think so. I hope so. I'm really longing to see them. Especially Silver. Hugo's been concerned about her.'

'Many people say she reminds them of you. I don't see it myself. She's very much taller. Probably more energetic and less lyrical.'

Hester smiled. 'You're so lovely to me, Edmund. It's wonderful to have someone around who remembers how I used to be.'

'I remember everything about you, Hester. I don't think there's been a single day since I met you that I haven't thought of you.'

'And I've thought of you, too. But now I'm thinking of you in an altogether different way.' She leaned over and whispered in his ear. 'You'll come to my room tonight, won't you?'

Edmund was silent for a moment and then he turned his face so that his mouth was very near Hester's. She could feel his answer whispered against her lips: *yes, my darling.*

The door which led from the stage to the auditorium opened and Hugo emerged, looking pale and rather worried. He saw Hester and Edmund sitting in the fourth row of the stalls and, waving, made his way towards them. They sat up straighter as he approached.

'May I sit with you? I need the company. I don't know why I'm so nervous,' he said, sitting down beside Hester.

'Of course, of course,' said Edmund, and Hester smiled at him.

'I'm sure you've no need to be nervous, Hugo,' she said. 'They're fine up there without you breathing down their necks. Everyone knows what they're doing.'

Edmund sat forward in his seat as the music started. 'They're great, aren't they? I never thought my stuff could become such wonderful jazz.'

Alison stood in the wings and looked at the list she'd taped to the props table. She went through everything again, just to make sure, even though she knew she'd put each prop where it was supposed to be. Cushions on the couch thingie her mother lay about on rather a lot; basket of roses downstage left, and Silver's wings hanging up and waiting for her to have them put on just before she went on stage. Ruby didn't want them mixed in with the rest of the costumes in the dressing room.

'You look efficient, dear.' Claudia came up behind her. 'Quite the little stage person, after all.'

'Break a leg, Mum,' Alison murmured, and thought again how beautiful her mother was. You had to admit it, even when you wanted to hit her. Alison had learned how to whisper backstage. You had to make almost no sound at all, and form the shapes of the words very clearly with your lips, so that the person you were speaking to was practically lipreading in the light that spread even into this darkest of corners. She looked at Silver coming down to get her wings put on, and thought she'd never seen anything quite so beautiful in her whole life. She really was exactly like an angel. Her white dress, more drifting and chiffony than the usual rather stiff ballet skirt, floated round her legs; her ballet shoes were white satin and her hair and skin and face glowed as though she were made of some pearly substance. Alison knew it was just glittery face powder because Silver had shown it to her, and even dusted a bit of it on her nose, but it made her look silly and she'd rubbed it off at once.

Silver smiled at Alison and went to stand in front of Ruby, who had the wings in her hands, ready to put on.

'How's it going so far?' she mouthed. Alison made a thumbs-up signal. Signals were used a lot in the wings as well. On stage, her mother was bending and swaying, Andy was prancing around downstage left, juggling three glittery balls, in an effort to amuse Claudia's Princess, who remained defiantly unimpressed by his efforts. The musicians sitting on stage made the music wash over everything, louder than it was in the rehearsal room and somehow sharper, and for the first time Alison understood what the fuss was about; why Hugo loved it so much. It was like a stream of sweetness poured out over the dancers, over everything, and it made you want to dance yourself.

Silver's arms were raised, so that Ruby could pass the bands (made of wide ribbon, sewn with feathers) round them, and then tie them up at the back, where they would be hidden by the wings. Alison was rather proud of these: her job had been to sew feathers and stick sequins on to the gauze.

'Turn round, please,' Ruby whispered. Now Silver was facing her, with her arms down. Alison waited for someone to say something – that the wings looked great; that they were very comfortable; even a mere 'thank you' would have been okay, but Ruby looked as though she'd been punched in the stomach. She was staring past Silver and seemed to be completely absorbed in Claudia and the dance she was in the middle of performing. Her hands gripped Silver's shoulders and she had stiffened all over. 'Is anything the matter, Ruby?' Silver asked her.

No answer. Ruby was stumbling backwards, with one hand over her mouth because there were funny sounds coming from it, stifled cries and a cross between gasping and sobbing. Her eyes behind the lenses of her spectacles were panic-stricken. She had her other hand stretched out, pointing, as though she'd seen a ghost, somewhere behind Silver's shoulder, pointing at Claudia on stage.

'Hester,' she whispered. 'Fetch Hester.'

'But it's the dress rehearsal . . .' Alison ventured, but then Ruby made a choking sound and slid to the ground in a faint. Silver bent to catch her and break her fall. She sounded fearful. 'She's fainted, Alison. Quick! Call Hester and Hugo. Go out on stage and tell them.'

'On stage?'

'Yes, at once. *Go on*. This is an emergency.'

Alison ran out on to the stage and was nearly blinded by the light. She put her hand up in front of her eyes. She could hear her mother exclaiming angrily somewhere behind her, 'What's the bloody child think she's up to . . .' and noises of seats springing back as everyone in the stalls stood up to see what was going on.

'It's Ruby,' Alison said anxiously into the blaze. 'She's ill. She's fainted in the wings.'

The stage lights went off at once and the house lights came on. George would be down immediately, Alison realised. Hugo had vaulted on to the stage, and Hester was at the door that led from the auditorium.

'Okay, everyone, take a few minutes,' said Hugo. 'We can resume when we see what's going on.'

Alison went back into the wings. Hester was there now. She was kneeling next to Ruby who had revived a little and was sitting up. Silver stood over them.

'Hester, she'd just finished fixing my wings and suddenly she looked at Claudia, who was just here, near this side of the stage, as though she'd seen a ghost, and then she fainted. I don't know what could possibly be the matter.'

Hester helped Ruby to her feet. 'Ruby, what's wrong? Are you in pain? Could someone please find a chair for her to sit on?'

Claudia had rushed in now, anxious not to miss anything, and was standing next to Alison.

Hester had her arm around Ruby when she suddenly stared fixedly at Claudia and seemed to freeze.

'Where,' she said quietly, 'did you get the necklace you're wearing?'

Alison thought her voice sounded funny. She'd turned pale and she looked terrified. She had started trembling too.

'Hugo gave it to me,' Claudia answered, fingering the necklace. 'I felt the costume needed something to cheer it up, if you know what I mean. Isn't it lovely? I'm so pleased you noticed . . .'

Hester looked utterly bewildered. She put a hand to her neck and shut her eyes. She was making an effort to breathe, you could see that. Andy had appeared next to Ruby with a chair.

'Here you go, Ruby. Sit down here,' he said. 'You'll be okay in a moment. The lights have all gone out on stage, so your George'll be here in a mo, I'm sure.'

As he spoke, George came through the door from the auditorium. 'Ruby? Ruby, darling, what's wrong? Tell me.'

He knelt beside his wife, and Alison saw, from the way he held her to him, from the way he touched her hair, stroking it over and over as though he were soothing an animal in distress, how much he loved her. For one moment Alison thought everything was going to be okay again. Ruby would say *It's all right, I've just been having a funny turn* and the rehearsal would start up once more.

But Ruby didn't do that. She turned her face so that it was buried in George's sweater and began to howl. That was the only word Alison could think of to describe the storm of wailing and sobbing that seemed to go on and on, as though everything that used to be Ruby was dissolving. The strangest thing of all was that Hester seemed not to be hearing what was going on. As though she's forgotten Ruby's existence altogether, Alison thought. She was standing in front of Claudia, looking dazed and frighteningly pale. Then she walked out on the stage.

The others were sitting around, waiting to see what was going to happen. Nick and Ilene were perched on the edge of Claudia's stage bed and Hugo and Edmund were standing together, peering into the wings. Edmund quickly moved to stand beside her and put his hand on her arm. She stood quite still for a moment and then spoke. Her voice sounded stiff and as though every single word was hurting her throat as she spoke it.

'Hugo, I'm terribly sorry. Something has happened. I'm afraid you must cancel this rehearsal. Please would you come to the Office at once, Hugo. I'm sorry, everyone.'

She turned to Edmund, who put his arm around her and they left the stage together. Alison could hear what Edmund was saying. 'My darling? Hester, what is it? Tell me what's the matter.'

Hester didn't answer him. They made their way quickly back into the auditorium and out of the swing doors at the back the theatre. Alison watched them go. Hester's left her shawl down in the stalls, she thought. I'll take it back to the house. Everyone up on stage was buzzing and whispering. What on earth was going on?

Hester saw nothing. The sleet that had been falling earlier that morning had stopped now, but the wind was higher and blew her hair into her eyes. She wasn't aware of that, or of anything. She was walking so fast that she'd almost broken into a run and behind her somewhere she could hear a voice calling 'Hester! Hester wait!', and part of her knew it was Edmund, running after her, but he was far away and what he was saying was blown off into the grey air and she didn't hear him. Someone – was it her? – was sobbing. The sound of it filled her head and her eyes stung from the tears. There was nothing as definite as a thought in her mind, only a throbbing pain all over her.

What had she just seen? A gold necklace. There must be thousands – no, millions – of gold necklaces in the world, so maybe this one wasn't the one she thought it was? But it was, *it was*. Why, otherwise, would Ruby have fainted? I've seen it, she thought. It's the one. The one exactly like mine. Impossible for me to mistake it. It's *Grand-mère*'s chain that Madame Olga and Ruby buried in Gullane with my poor baby. Claudia said Hugo gave it to her, but how did he get it? How has it come to be around the neck of a ballet dancer on the stage at the Arcadia? Hester had no idea, but one thing came to her clearly through the unhappiness that had come down around her like a mist: if the necklace was here at Wychwood, then it wasn't there, in her baby's coffin. Rage rose in her. Someone had stolen it, that must be the answer. Hester stopped walking, horrified.

'Hester! Hester, don't . . . please. Come, let's go inside where it's warm. You'll feel better inside.'

There he was, Edmund, standing in the wind, with no coat against the cold and his hair blowing on to his forehead, making him look exactly how he used to look years ago.

'Edmund, darling Edmund, it's always you, isn't it? Coming to help me.'

'Come inside now. Tell me what's happened.'

'The necklace. It's hard to explain.'

'Try.'

'I'm not clear myself what happened, but Ruby saw a ghost of sorts. Me too. The necklace Claudia was wearing is just like this one.'

She put her hand into the neck of the thin jumper she was wearing and pulled out a chain. 'This chain was cut in two by my grandmother. The other half was buried in Scotland with my baby. At least, I thought it was.'

Edmund said nothing but put his arms around Hester and she breathed in the smell of his jacket and felt herself relax against him. 'Poor Hester. Poor darling.'

She stepped a little away from him and squared her shoulders. 'I'm so glad you're here. I'll be all right now. It was the shock. Let's go in. Let's face it, whatever it is we have to face.'

They went up the front steps of Wychwood House together and Hester felt the blood draining from her face. I won't. I won't faint, she told herself. Whatever happens, whatever I discover, I'll try and keep myself under control.

She pushed out of her mind the image that was always with her – her baby in his coffin, nothing now but a tiny skeleton with mountains of earth heaped on top of him. She had imagined the chain in some way lighting up the darkness of his grave and the thought that it hadn't, hadn't ever, couldn't ever have done was almost unbearable.

They were like a lot of kids, Claudia thought. Pleased at being let off school early. Everything had come to a complete standstill just because Ruby had fainted in the wings. Probably, Claudia thought, a lot of fuss about nothing, but Hugo had made it clear that there would be nothing else happening here in the theatre for today and they'd all trooped off together to watch TV. It would be fun, as Andy put it, to do stuff most people do every day, but which are special treats for us.

Alison had some sort of secret going with Ruby and had vanished altogether. Claudia couldn't be bothered to find out the details, even though she knew her daughter would let her in on it if she pushed it, but the fact was, she wasn't all that interested.

Someone was knocking at the door of the dressing room. Who the hell was this? Claudia called out, 'Come in.'

'It's me, Claudia,' said Nick. 'Are you decent?'

'Would you rather I was –' her mood suddenly improved measurably – 'or wasn't?'

Nick ignored the innuendo and went to sit down on the chair next to the costume-rail. He smiled at her and she felt herself going soft all over.

'I've been having ideas.'

'Really? Whatever sort of ideas?'

'Subversive and naughty ones. You could come and see my etchings. In my room.'

Claudia giggled. 'How frightfully original. But I don't think it would be wise, do you? Everyone else is in the house. Someone will notice that we're missing, won't they?'

'Not necessarily. They've just started watching a movie on TV. They'll be there for a bit.'

'A bit? Don't you want something more than "a bit?"' She went over to stand in front of Nick's chair.

'Beggars,' he pulled her down on to his lap, 'can't be choosers.' He began to nibble at her neck and ears. 'Or,' he murmured, 'there's no one in the theatre. The whole place is quite deserted. We could stay here.'

His hands seemed to be everywhere. Claudia closed her eyes.

'You are very bad for me,' she whispered. 'You are very bad altogether. I shouldn't be doing this.'

'Why not?' Nick's hands were now under her robe, one on her breast and the other sliding slowly up her thigh. Claudia let *Sarabande*, Alison, Hugo, Ruby, her worries about her dancing career – everything that had previously been taking up space in her head – slide out of it and allowed herself to dissolve into pleasure.

Sex with Nick was all very well, Claudia thought twenty minutes later, but when it was over the bloody man seemed quite ready to go and find some other amusement almost at once, instead of . . . instead of what? What did she want from him, really? Would she have liked Nick to fling himself at her feet and declare endless love? That wasn't going to happen. He'd never said a word to make her think so. All he was feeling, all *she* was feeling, if she was honest with herself, was strong desire added to a bit of boredom and distance from the normal world. Claudia had been telling herself this ever since New Year's Eve and it hadn't helped much. She wouldn't have wanted a permanent relationship but the fact that he was so clearly not interested in one either wasn't exactly flattering.

He was standing by the door now, on the point of going back to the house.

'I'll see you later, then,' he smiled. '*Ciao.*'

He was off and away with a wave of his hand. Blast and damn his casual attitude! She peered at herself in the mirror. Better pull myself together before Hugo sees me, she thought. I look as though I've been unravelled.

Hugo didn't know where to sit. If this had been a scene he was directing, he would probably have said that there was no logical reason for this man, himself, to be standing next to the door, leaning against the wall. Go and find a chair for God's sake, he'd have cried. Balance things up a bit. He glanced to his left and there was the famous portrait of Hester Fielding, the one known as *A Backward Glance*. This was the image people all over the world had of her, a beautiful, perfectly dressed, delicate and ethereal ballerina. If they could see her now, sitting very upright on the *chaise-longue*, they'd probably not recognise her. Edmund was standing behind her, with his hand very near her, ready, it seemed to Hugo, to comfort her.

For the first time since he came to Wychwood, Hugo saw things about Hester that he'd never noticed before: dark violet shadows under her eyes, threads of grey at her hairline, a tremor around her mouth and her graceful hands looking older than they should have done, with the beginnings of what Claudia called 'grave-spots' here and there. Poor Claudia! She was forever holding her arms out in front of her, flapping her wrists as she examined her skin, in dread of their sudden appearance. Hester's head was bent. She was waiting for Ruby to speak.

I have not the slightest notion of what's going on, Hugo thought, but it's serious. He looked at Ruby. She was even more changed than Hester. She sat on an upright chair on the other side of the small table by the *chaise-longue*. Her face looked as though it was melting. The tears she'd shed seemed to have eroded the flesh of her cheeks and dragged it out of shape. Her normally neat, rather schoolmarm-ish appearance had utterly disintegrated. While she was still in her faint Hester had opened the neck of her blouse, undoing the first few buttons and Ruby hadn't done them up again. Her hair was disordered, messy. She was like someone coming round after being drunk. George had come in with his wife and was uncharacteristically quiet. He was standing at the window, a little removed from everyone else, but his eyes remained fixed on Ruby.

Hester was the first to speak.

'Tell us everything. Take as long as you like. There's no hurry at all.'

Ruby wiped her nose with a handkerchief.

'I don't know how to say it, except to say it straight out, Hester. Your little baby, he never died. He was adopted. I didn't bury the necklace. As you saw. I gave it to the lady from the adoption agency.'

'My baby? What are you saying? My baby *lived?*' Hester was short of breath. She closed her eyes for a few seconds. Then she opened them and looked at Hugo. 'Does the chain belong to you, Hugo?'

He nodded. 'Yes.'

'And, I remember this now, almost the first time we met, you told me you were adopted.'

Hugo felt as though something had shifted in his brain. Had he understood correctly? What was Hester really saying. He couldn't take it in, not any of it. He concentrated only on answering what he'd been asked.

'My mother never hid it,' he said. 'She made much of it, actually. She used to say that they'd chosen me specially. That they hadn't been able to have their own children, but the moment they saw me, they knew I was theirs. I never felt as though I wasn't their child. When I was twenty-one, my mother gave me the tortoiseshell box and explained that, well, that it had belonged to my birth mother, who wanted me to keep it safe. And I have. I have kept it safe. Forgive me if I've got it wrong, but I think that maybe . . .'

'Look at my chain, Hugo. It's the other half of what was once a single chain. My grandmother had it cut in half. Your half. I thought I'd buried it with my dead son, but . . .' Her voice faltered. When she spoke again, Hugo had to strain to hear what she was saying. 'I think you're my son. I can't . . . haven't . . . I don't know the words to say what I'm feeling. All the different pieces of my life, everything's different now. I'm your mother, Hugo.'

Hugo felt a mixture of complete bewilderment and shock. He found that his heart was beating far too quickly and he knew that if he spoke his voice wouldn't be steady. He longed to do something, go to Hester, put his arms around her. Her voice – she hadn't sounded in the least like herself. He could hear that she was almost breathless with emotion. But the moment passed and she was talking to Ruby again, and sitting up straighter.

'There's so much I want to ask you, Ruby,' she said. 'And I've just remembered something Madame Olga said to me on her deathbed. She asked me to forgive her. I've never understood why till now. Oh, I can't . . . I don't know where to begin.'

Edmund put his hand on Hester's shoulder and spoke gently to Ruby. 'Why don't you tell us what happened? Tell us everything. Hugo needs to know about it as much as Hester does.'

'And please,' Hester added, 'don't leave anything out to spare our feelings. I want to know the truth; every detail.'

Ruby took the damp handkerchief she was holding and began to pick at the lace trimming.

'It was Madame Olga's idea. She was the one who thought of it, though Mr Cranley helped her. He helped her do everything. The money mostly came from her, but he told the stories that everyone believed, that you'd had some kind of nervous breakdown. They never wanted you to have a baby, Hester. Madame Olga said it would be the ruin of your career. Impossible to be a dancer *and* a mother was how she put it.'

Hugo noticed Hester shivering.

'No one wanted to hurt you, Hester. You must believe that. I didn't know you properly when I was hired to look after you, but Madame Olga and Mr Cranley were devoted to you. I know how that sounds. Ridiculous and downright wrong when I think about what we did to you, how we deceived you over years and years. But that's the thing, isn't it? You can't start a lie without carrying it through to the end. While Madame Olga was alive, she persuaded me every day that we'd done the right thing. How can this not be good, she'd say as the reviews came in for your performances. Don't forget that, Hester. The whole world has watched you dance and been made happier, made better, Madame Olga would say, because of your work. You've added something to their lives and it's not something insignificant or trivial. And you've created all this.' She waved a hand to take in the room and more than that, the whole of Wychwood and the Arcadia and the Festival. 'I'm crying again. I'm sorry . . . I'll stop . . .' She put her handkerchief to her eyes again.

Hugo spoke. 'I had no idea about any of this. I feel . . . I feel quite shaken. I wasn't even one of those adopted children who long to know who their birth parents are. I was happy in my family. I'm ashamed to say I scarcely gave my adoption any thought. But poor Hester.'

'Yes,' said Edmund gently. 'It's Hester who's spent more than thirty years mourning a dead baby. Unable even to let the world know that she'd *had* a baby, because that old Russian dragon decided it would be bad for her image. And we all fell in with her wishes. You can't believe it now, Hugo, but in those days, not so long ago, either, stars were supposed to be unblemished. Perfect and better than ordinary mortals. I knew about it, but no one else did as far as I know. Everyone was very discreet.'

Ruby wiped her eyes again. 'I'm sorry. I can't stop crying. I don't know what to say to any of you. I've done something so dreadful.'

Hugo saw that George was frowning. He wanted, you could see, to go to Ruby and take her in his arms, but was stopping himself. Ruby was still speaking.

'You've always known there was something, haven't you?' she said to Hester. 'I've seen you looking at me sometimes. Wondering what was wrong if I was unhappy. Poor George thought when he married me that I sometimes had bad moods. He got used to it, but it's been hard for us. George and me, we've been through everything together. If only you knew how often I nearly told you everything!'

'Why didn't you? *Why* couldn't you have told me when I stopped dancing? That was years and years ago. I needn't have—'

'I'd given my word, and they'd paid me good money to keep my silence. Money that made such a difference to my family. There are so many of us. My poor mother could never cope on her own and I saw the money as a chance for them to . . . well, never mind, I shouldn't have taken the job. That's what I say to myself, but then I think if it hadn't been me, it would have been someone else, and they wouldn't have looked after you properly. Not like me. I've . . .' Ruby looked up at Hester. 'I've loved you, Hester. It'll sound strange to you, I know, but everything I did was because I loved you.'

Hester began to cry. Edmund knelt beside her.

'Take this.' He handed her a white handkerchief.

'Thank you,' she said and wiped her eyes, then she turned to Ruby. 'How could you, Ruby? I don't understand how you could have deceived me, all these years. Surely you could have . . . But of course I know you love me, and you've helped me so much, for years and years. I can't take it in. I'd never have done anything, any of this, at Wychwood without you. I'm sorry. I can't help the tears.'

Hugo approached Hester's chair and put his hand on her shoulder. 'We'll wait till you're ready, Hester. It's all right.'

Ruby went on, 'I know I should never have given in to Madame Olga. She had these eyes, you see. They'd look right into you, as though she was hypnotising you, and they were a kind of browny-yellow and you couldn't argue with her. Hester has possibilities of greatness, that's what she said. Imagine if we were to deprive her of fame that will last for ever. Imagine how sad she will be if she does not dance. Think of what you are helping to create, Ruby. So I agreed. I said I'd look after you till the birth was over, but after that, well, I asked if I could stay. That's the truth. It wasn't Madame Olga's fault. She and Mr Cranley would have let me go, given me my money and sent me away, but I couldn't bear to leave you. You had no mother to look after you. I begged her to find me something I could do for you once you began to dance again. But what is there for you in a theatre, Madame Olga said. I told her about the sewing and Mr Cranley mentioned that I'd sometimes helped out in the wardrobe department at the Royalty and so—'

'My baby.' Hester interrupted her. 'Tell me about my baby.'

'They had it all planned. Dr Crawford, Mrs McGreevey, the adoption agency. Everything was arranged before we ever got to Gullane. They made sure that you were unconscious for some while after the birth, and then, well, you know what happened. They told you that your child died.'

Ruby covered her face, shaken by a new storm of tears.

'I need you to tell me, Ruby. I was unconscious because of the eclampsia. No one could have known I was going to get that. What would've happened if I'd had a normal delivery?'

'The eclampsia was a stroke of luck for them. Three days of sedation after your Caesarean was exactly what they needed. But there were other things they could have done. They had pills, and they wouldn't have hesitated. After all, Madame Olga made sure you didn't attend the funeral, didn't she? There was a pill she gave you, d'you remember?'

Hester put her hands over her face. 'I can't believe it! It's . . . it was so risky! What if I'd insisted on seeing where my child was buried? Madame Olga couldn't have known how cowardly I'd be, how I wouldn't ever want to face the pain of seeing my baby's grave. How I wanted to try and forget it, erase it from my mind. Oh, Ruby, if only you knew how many times I've nearly gone back there, to Gullane, to try and find it.'

'And you would've found it, too,' said Ruby. 'Dr Crawford took care of that, he and the funeral director between them. Just in case. It's not so difficult to persuade people to do things if you also convince them that they're acting for the good of someone. If you say, this woman will go mad and even kill herself if you don't act at once. Sitting here, it's easy to condemn everyone, but they all thought they were doing the best for you.'

Hester looked at Hugo. 'His father. Hugo's father. What about him? Did Madame Olga give him any thought?'

Ruby shook her head. 'She said, he cares nothing for my darling girl. He nearly destroyed her. Such a man does not deserve a child. Let him know his son is dead. As a punishment. She and Mr Cranley told Edmund the story of the child's death and knew that he would tell the father.'

Edmund spoke quietly. 'Yes, I told him, and it was one of the hardest things I've ever done. He didn't say much but he was deeply hurt. He changed from that day in very many ways. One of them was distancing himself from everything. Partly living in America. Seeing less of me because I reminded him of you, Hester.'

He took Hester's hand and she smiled at him. 'I was so grateful to you for doing that for me. I couldn't have written to him. I wasn't . . . I wasn't myself. People say "heartbroken" don't they, when they mean something quite different? But I was. Everything in me was broken.'

For a few moments, no one said anything and the only sound was a slight snoring from Siggy, who was fast asleep under the curtain near the radiator. Then Hugo said, almost whispering. 'Will you tell me about my father, Hester?'

She nodded. 'Yes, of course I will. But not now. Now I need time to think, and there's *Sarabande*. We mustn't forget that.' She smiled at him. 'Shall we talk tomorrow morning, Hugo, just after breakfast? You'll have time before class, I think?'

'Yes, I've already worked out a timetable. Class at eleven, early lunch and dress rehearsal at three.'

'Good. I want you to know the truth as soon as possible, Hugo. But no one else needs to know about this, I don't think. It's not their business and in any case, you want to keep the company focused on the ballet, don't you?'

Hugo nodded. 'What shall we tell them?'

'I'll do it,' Edmund said. 'I'll say Ruby was taken ill and needed time to recover. That's all. I'll say Hester was very distressed to see this because she's so used to Ruby being in the best of health. But I'll stress that everything will be back to normal tomorrow. Will you be able to face them then, Hester?'

'The show must go on,' she said, smiling a little. 'I've always believed that.'

Hugo looked down at the floor. He felt embarrassed. 'May I ask you one thing, though?'

'Anything.'

'Did you love him? My father?'

'Very much. Too much. I loved him more than I can tell you. And then I hated him, but that was part of the same thing. That's all over now. I've . . .' She looked at Edmund. 'I've let him go.'

'Thank you. I'll go and talk to the others.'

He went to the door and stood there for a moment, looking at the woman he would have to get used to thinking of as his mother. It was too much to take in. I'm Hester Fielding's son, he thought, and a pang of sorrow for the woman who had adopted him and cared for him all his life, the woman he'd loved since he was a baby, made him catch his breath. This new relationship would need to be worked on. He and Hester would have to grow used to one another.

'He's gone, Ruby,' said Hester. 'I can ask you something else now. I'm surprised it didn't occur to Hugo. Or perhaps it did and he was just being tactful in not mentioning it.'

She stood up and went to the window. Edmund and George had now sat down and were talking quietly. Dusk had fallen over the garden and Hester could see the moors, a black mass outlined against the sky. She knew that Ruby's eyes were on her back, and she deliberately didn't turn to face her as she spoke. Let her guess at my feelings, she told herself. Let her wonder whether there are tears in my eyes. 'There's one thing I don't understand. How could you not have told me the truth after Madame Olga died? What possible reason was there for hiding it from me then, when she couldn't hurt you or dismiss you? I'd have been spared years, whole years of anguish. Why didn't you speak, Ruby?'

'Because I was terrified, that's why. I asked myself over and over, what would you do if you knew? That question haunted me all the time, every day. George and I spoke about it again and again. Didn't we, George?'

George nodded and took his wife's hand. She went on, 'I couldn't believe you wouldn't hate me. Oh, I imagined the scene so many times and I knew, I thought I knew, exactly what you'd do. You'd throw me out, however long I'd been with you. And I wanted to go sometimes, too. No, that's not right. I didn't want to go, but just seeing you every day was like a torture, because I knew how much I'd hurt you. How much pain you were still feeling, in spite of the fame and the dancing and the money and the glitter of the rest of your life. I saw you at your lowest moments. I saw you when you were tired and injured and sick and depressed and I couldn't, I just couldn't, let you send me away. And I didn't know the answer to the question you were bound to have asked me.'

'What question?'

'Where he was. Who'd adopted him. I knew nothing about that. You'd have been tormented knowing your child was in the world and yet nowhere to be found.'

Hester turned from the window. 'You're right. That would have been the worst thing of all. And I probably would have sacked you just because I was so unhappy.'

Ruby got up from her chair. 'I always find it easier to keep quiet than to speak.' She came up to Hester and stood next to her with her head bowed. 'I was never told who'd adopted your baby. That used to keep me awake often. I used to worry about the poor wee boy.' She smiled. 'Now I feel as though I've found him too, you know.'

Hester gathered Ruby into her arms. 'Oh, Ruby, I know I'll forgive you completely, but I have to get used to everything that's happened. I just need a little time. You've been better than a sister to me. I realise that now. Why haven't I ever told you that? Why have we never spoken about the things we should have spoken about?'

'I don't know. Things have a way of continuing in the way you start them. That's all. It's easy to let the days pass. I've never hidden anything else from you. You do know that, don't you?'

'Of course.' For the first time since they'd come into the Office from the Arcadia, she reflected, Ruby sounded like herself, like the person Hester was used to – the safe, strong, efficient Ruby. She stepped out of Hester's embrace and did up the buttons on her blouse and smoothed down her hair.

'I've a great deal to see to, so I'll be going now. It's been . . .' She smiled. 'I don't know what it's been. Not like other days.'

'Not a bit like other days.'

'I'll come with you.' George put an arm around Ruby's shoulders. 'See to what I have to do in the lighting box before tomorrow.'

They left the room, and Hester sank into the armchair. 'Tell me again, Edmund,' she said. 'Tell me everything's going to be all right.'

'I'd never say that, my darling,' Edmund said, and the way he looked at her made Hester feel warm all over. 'Everything probably won't be all right, but whatever happens now, I'll be here. And you have a *son*, Hester.'

'I can't take it in, Edmund. It's too soon. Too much of a shock.'

'But how wonderful that you seem to get on so well. Imagine the odds against that!'

'It's true. I did feel a sort of connection with him from the moment we met. I'm going to my room for a moment. I am completely exhausted.'

'Of course, my darling. I'll go and potter about somewhere else for a while. I'll come up and see you later.'

Hugo didn't know where to go to think. He wanted to be alone and didn't feel like going for a walk in the miserable sleet that had started to fall. The theatre was out of the question. That'd be full of members of the company. He opened the door of the drawing room and was relieved to find no one there.

He went to sit on the window seat, looking out at the garden. He could see the gates standing open and thought, my whole life's turned upside down since I drove through them a few days ago. I'm not used to being in such confusion. Claudia called him a control freak and it was true, he *did* like things to be organised, laid out neatly. He liked imposing an order on things, and knowing what was what in every department of his life. At the moment he had no idea what was going on in any of them. The news Hester had just broken made his head spin. Every time he tried to consider it dispassionately, he became dizzy as one implication after another occurred to him. Hester was his mother. Did that mean that he was heir to Wychwood? It was much too early to mention it, but the thought had come into his mind and he didn't like himself for thinking it. Hester. He could allow himself to love her. *His mother*. However much he said the word, it didn't sound true. You couldn't wipe out thirty years of care and tenderness and he still felt like a son to Sheila Carradine. He couldn't help it. He'd always love her.

He got up and went to stand in front of the fire, staring into the flames. Silver. One of the reasons he couldn't think about Hester properly was because of Silver. *I'm falling in love with her.* Ever since their kiss, he'd felt as though she was imprinted on every part of him. He'd thought of nothing but her for hours. It was hard to concentrate on anything else. Even *Sarabande*, which had obsessed him for months, became less important in comparison. I feel like a teenager, he thought. I want her. And I must leave Claudia. He sighed. How could they go on sharing a room? Impossible. He'd have to speak to her. He couldn't put it off any longer. Maybe she was upstairs now. He went to find her. As he strode up the stairs two at a time, he thought, I'll ask Hester if I can move into another room, and then into his head came a vision of Silver, stretched out on the bed, naked, her skin glowing like a pearl, waiting for him. Oh, God, with everything else that was going on, how could he also be feeling such overwhelming desire?

Hugo was sitting on the end of the bed. Claudia had just come out of the shower. She had a towel wrapped round her head and was wearing her robe. She seemed to be in a good mood, too, which was a change from how she'd been with him recently. He decided to speak before his courage left him.

'Can we talk, Claudia?'

'Of course. How's Ruby? What's going on there?'

'Nothing going on . . . she fainted. Probably been working too hard. But she's okay now and we're going to have the dress tomorrow.'

'That's good. I'm pleased she's all right.' Claudia sat down in the armchair and started towelling her wet hair.

'Claudia? It's not easy, what I've got to say, but I think I have to say it now. I did think I'd wait till after we got back to London, but—'

'Say what?' The towel had fallen out of her hand 'It sounds a bit ominous.'

'I think our . . . our relationship isn't what it used to be. Have you felt that? Am I right?'

For once in her life, Claudia was reflecting. He could almost see the possible answers she might make tumbling through her head. She was wondering how to react. For a moment he thought that she was going to throw one of her perfume bottles at him and shout obscenities, but then he could see her thinking better of it.

'No, I don't suppose you're entirely wrong. But why now? Have you stopped loving me?' Tears stood in her eyes. What on earth could he say? Why did women always ask such impossible questions? Ones you couldn't answer honestly without being hurtful? He sighed and decided that this was the perfect time for a lie.

'Of course I love you. You can't live with a person for as long as we've lived together and just stop loving them. Do you love me?'

There. Attack is the best form of defence, someone or other said.

'Of course, Hugo!' she cried, with only the tiniest hint of lack of conviction in her voice. 'You know I do! But I agree, things haven't been that great. I thought you were preoccupied, but it seems you're fed up with me.' A sudden idea seemed to strike her. 'Is it Silver?'

'Silver?' How could she have guessed that, when he'd only just admitted it to himself? One thing was certain. He wasn't about to tell Claudia of his feelings before he'd spoken to Silver about them.

'No. Not at all. It's just that, well, I feel we've changed. Am I wrong?'

'No, Hugo, I don't suppose you are, but that doesn't stop me feeling – oh, so many different things. I feel wounded, Hugo. I feel *hurt*.'

Hugo didn't say what he thought, that Claudia's pride was injured and that *she* liked to be the person who ended any relationship she was in.

'I don't mean to hurt you, Claudia. You know that. But it's foolish continuing with something that's, well, that's not what it used to be.'

'It was wonderful, Hugo, wasn't it? Tell me it was wonderful.'

'Of course it was. You're an amazing woman, Claudia.'

'You're pretty amazing yourself. But I still, well, I don't know what to say. It's a lot to take in. I'll miss you.'

'But I hope you'll feel we can be friends, Claudia. Can't we? I don't want to stop seeing Alison, apart from anything else. And we'll still be working together, won't we?'

'I'm not sure about that. I think I might be getting a bit past it.'

Say it, he told himself. Quickly, before she realises that you're agreeing with her. He shook his head hurriedly. 'Not at all, Claudia. I've been most impressed with how you've done with the Princess.'

'Really? That's fantastic. So you think there'll be a place in the company for me?'

'Of course there will.'

She smiled a wintry smile at him. He thought, later. I'll deal with that later, when the first night is over. There's enough going on without having to think about Claudia's future. For the moment, he felt nothing but relief that the scene he was dreading hadn't materialised. Claudia must have been more fed up with him than she admitted.

5 January 1987

Silver helped herself to another cup of tea and looked around at everyone sitting at the kitchen table. They'd all made the effort, even Claudia, because Hugo had told them the previous evening that Hester was going to say a few words about what had happened at yesterday's dress rehearsal. There she was at the head of the long table and you had to take your hat off to her, you really did. Not a trace of yesterday's problem, whatever it had been, was visible on her face, and okay, Silver knew enough about make-up to realise that Hester had applied it very well, but still. She seemed very upbeat, and quite different from the grim-faced person they'd all seen rushing out of the Arcadia yesterday.

Alison was looking fed-up and Claudia was looking tired. This was far too early in the morning for her. Hugo was pale but seemed cheerful enough. Silver didn't dare meet his eyes. She'd hoped to have a word with him in private last night, after dinner, but he'd disappeared somewhere and she hadn't been able to find him.

Hester stood up. Silver looked at her and wondered what was different about her. Something was, and for a moment, Silver couldn't think what it could be and then she realised. Hester, who favoured polo necked jumpers or scarves tied around her neck was wearing a blouse with the top button undone, and she was wearing a chain that from here looked very like the one Claudia had worn yesterday. When Hester began to speak, Silver forgot all about the coincidence, and listened to what she was saying.

'Thanks so much for getting up at this very early hour, all of you,' Hester said, smiling at everyone. 'I do appreciate it. I know that what happened yesterday must be puzzling for you and I apologise for the disturbance. I know that you'd counted on today as a rest day, but I'm afraid that's impossible now. Hugo will tell you about the timing of the dress rehearsal and so forth, but I'd just like to explain. Ruby was taken ill, as some of you saw. She suffers, though she wouldn't like it generally talked about, from dreadful migraine headaches from time to time, and these appear without warning and often at times of stress. She had, well, I can only describe it as a seizure of some kind, but the doctor's been to see her and she's fine now and won't hear of anyone else taking over her duties backstage. That's typical of Ruby, but of course she had Alison to help her and between them they'll manage very well, I'm sure. There's the matter of the decoration of the dining room of course but . . . yes, Alison, what is it?'

Alison had her hand up. That's brave of her, Silver thought. I wouldn't dare interrupt Hester Fielding in the middle of a speech.

'I'm doing it. The dining room I mean. Ruby's agreed and I'm going to put it up straight after breakfast today. George said he'd help me.'

'Thanks so much, Alison. That's very kind of you. I'm sure it'll look wonderful.'

Alison was blushing with pleasure. 'I'll leave you now and let Hugo tell you about today's class and the rearranged schedule. Good luck for this afternoon. What I saw of *Sarabande* yesterday makes me long to see the rest.' She paused. 'Hugo, could you come to the Office when you're finished here? I'd like a quick word with you, if I may.'

'Of course. I'll be there in a minute.'

Hester left the room and everyone started talking at once. Silver went round to where Alison was sitting and slid into the chair next to her.

'What's wrong, Alison? You look really miserable.'

'I am. I'm pissed off. Mum hates me saying that but I don't care. I'd like to break something.'

'Have you had a fight with your mum?'

'No, I'm used to my mum. It's my dad I'm really cross with. He said in his letter he'd phone and he hasn't.'

'Maybe he will. If he didn't give you a particular day or time, then he can still do it, right?'

'I suppose so, but you'd think he'd know how much I wanted to hear from him, wouldn't you? After not talking to him for ages and ages. You'd think he'd be hurrying, rushing, to phone me. But he isn't. He's obviously got better things to think about and that pisses me off.'

'Alison!' Claudia's voice sliced through all the other conversations going on at the table. 'I heard that! Honestly, everyone will think you've been dragged up. Behave yourself, please.'

'Sorry.' Under her breath she muttered to Silver, 'I *have* been dragged up. She dragged me up, so she ought to know. I'm going. I'm going to see to those decorations.'

She got up and walked out of the kitchen. Hugo stood up. 'Right, everyone,' he said. 'This is the timetable for today . . .'

Silver took in what he was saying with part of her mind, but she was thinking *Hugo – How beautiful he is*. She became so absorbed in the shape of his mouth that she missed most of what he said and then all at once he was gone. What about Claudia? What was she going to do? Silver took another sip of tea to calm herself down. Her blood was racing through her body and she tried to concentrate on getting herself back to normal before class.

'Is that it?' Claudia was speaking to her daughter and watching her as she fixed a branch to the top of the mirror above the mantelpiece, and Alison made up her mind not to turn round. Quite apart from the fact that she was at the top of a stepladder, it was clear that Claudia didn't think much of her efforts and she wasn't going to give her the satisfaction of appearing to care. Claudia went on, 'It doesn't look very decorative to me.'

'Full of kind remarks as usual, Mother dear.'

'Oh, don't be so teenagery, for Heaven's sake. As if we haven't got enough on our plates. I only came to ask you not to forget about my costume. You do know it's got to be ironed before this afternoon, don't you? I told Ruby, only she's been in such a state that I thought I'd better ask you to check up on her.'

'Ruby's fine. She had a migraine, but she's better now.'

Alison was only half-listening to her mother. She wanted to finish this bit before it was time to go over to the theatre. Everything had to be ready today because they weren't going to be allowed in here tomorrow. The caterers would be doing their thing, George said.

'I'm not altogether sure about this look, you know,' Claudia said.
'What's the matter with it?'

'Well, it looks . . . it looks a bit strange, that's all. Perhaps there's time for someone to drive into Keighley and get some last-minute flowers or something. What do you think?'

Alison thought that if she'd been on ground level and had the scissors in her hands she would have stabbed her mother with them. She opened her mouth and closed it again. I'm not going to cry. I'm not going to give her the satisfaction. 'What you know about decorations,' she amazed herself by sounding almost normal, although she felt like that person in the fairytale who had toads and snakes coming out of her mouth, 'could be put in a walnut shell and there'd be room left over for the walnut. You're ignorant.'

'How dare you? How dare you call me ignorant? You're nothing but a terminally untalented brat.'

Alison wanted to say *and you're a has-been. Everyone knows that, even Hugo but they're too kind to tell you.* But she kept her mouth shut and went, on putting up the branches. Instead she said, 'Do you love him? Hugo?'

'Hugo? Well, I wasn't going to tell you but since you've brought it up. He's leaving me, Alison. He's had enough. Can't say I'm surprised, really and to tell you the truth, I think I'm ready to move on myself, but . . .'

Alison looked at her mother. 'Are you going to be okay for the dress rehearsal? You're not upset?'

'Oh, yes,' said Claudia, getting up. 'I'll be more than all right, believe me. I'm going to show the whole lot of them what I'm capable of. They think, Hugo thinks, I'm past my best and he's besotted with Silver with her legs and that technique, but I'll give him something to watch this afternoon. Something that'll make him think twice about me as a dancer, even if he's given up on me as a woman. Oh, God, I'm not going to cry, am I?'

'No, of course you're not,' said Alison. She was used to cheering Claudia up when she felt neglected or ill-used by the critics and now she went through the routine once again. 'You're still Claudia Drake. You're a huge star. Your face is in all the magazines. You're miles more famous than Silver. You know you are.'

'How long for, though? I'm well over thirty. I can't go on for ever. That's the trouble with ballet. What's to become of me when no one wants me as a dancer any longer?'

'I expect you could be a model or something, couldn't you?'

Claudia smiled. 'They like their models even younger than their dancers, but it's true that some photographers have been after me to do what they call "celebrity shoots". They've said I have the bones for it. It's certainly worth thinking about. Thank you, darling! You've made me feel a little better.'

She walked to the door and looked back at Alison, who had started to climb up the stepladder again.

'Maybe I was wrong about those,' she said casually. 'They are quite effective, actually. On second thoughts.'

When she'd gone, Alison went on working on the decorations. She'd be finished before lunch. Everyone was having sandwiches in the Arcadia bar to save time, and she didn't want to miss that. How typical of Mum to change her mind, she reflected. She can't even stick to an opinion for more than two seconds. But this room is going to look fantastic and it was all my idea. She continued to cut and tie, cut and tie, until the carrier bag she'd placed carefully on the mantelpiece was quite empty.

'I'm sure we'll get used to it.' Hester smiled at Hugo. 'We have so much in common, after all, don't we? I'm sure there are lots of mothers who find it difficult to talk to their children.'

'I've never found it hard to talk to you. Don't you remember? On New Year's Eve I have a memory of wanting to lay my head on your shoulder and tell you all my troubles.'

'Yes, I do remember. I was touched.' She was sitting behind her writing table in the Office and Hugo was on the *chaise-longue*, Siggy on his lap. 'Siggy seems to think you're a member of the family, so I suppose you must be. It'll be a while before I absorb it fully, but he's a very wise old cat.'

'I feel a bit like Cinderella just after the slipper's been put on her foot. After our talk this morning, I'm a bit less confused. Everything's fallen into place. This all . . .' he waved a hand to include Hester and the room and the house beyond the room, 'seems somehow right. I've always admired you from afar. I liked you from the very first time I met you and actually I've even thought that we were a little alike and then decided I was flattering myself.'

'Perhaps we are alike. Imagine if someone else had been given the commission this year. Imagine that.'

'I can't. I can't imagine it. What would have happened?'

'Nothing. Nothing dramatic. We'd each have gone on with our separate lives, that's all. I would have mourned my dead baby every day for the rest of my life.'

'And I'd never have known you were my mother. Which would have been sad, though nothing like as sad as your situation. I had a mother, after all, who loved me and brought me up and I loved her too.'

'I'm grateful to her. You can't begin to understand how grateful. She must have been a wonderful person too, because you're a credit to her.'

'And to you and my father . . .'

'Your father, yes.' Hester looked searchingly at Hugo. 'Are you prepared to do what I asked you when we discussed it earlier? Not to say a word about Adam? Not ever? You know my reasons. I can't do that to Adam's wife, suddenly appear in public with his son. It would hurt her so badly. I hope you agree that I'm right. I don't know about Claudia. Do you feel you have to tell her?'

Hugo shook his head. 'We're not going to be together very much longer.'

'Oh, I'm so sorry. Is it going to be hard for you? Or for her?'

'No, I think we agree that we're not – our relationship isn't what it was. I won't tell her.'

'But if you get married, of course your wife will need to know everything.'

'I'll tell you before I confide in anyone, I promise.' A thought occurred to him. 'This situation must be hard for you. I'm glad you felt that you could tell me about my father. Do I look like him?'

'You have his smile. He was tall, like you, but broader shouldered. Ever since I met you, you've reminded me of someone and now I see that it's actually two people. One of them is my father. He had your build, but when I was a child, he seemed to be so stiff. I used to think he looked like a scarecrow, but you don't. Not a bit.'

'I hope I don't. Who's the other person?'

'Me. I think you look like me. I've watched you in rehearsal and class and you move in just the same way. Your *port de bras* – everything.'

'D'you know something? I can't think of anyone I'd rather look like.'

He got to his feet gently and Siggy took his place on the *chaise-longue*, looking only slightly put out.

Hester was just about to set off down the covered corridor to the Arcadia for the dress rehearsal when she remembered that Alison must have finished decorating the dining room. Not much time, she thought, but I'll just go and see.

She opened the door and stood for a long moment on the threshold, taking it in. The room had never looked like this, not in all the years since the Festival was first launched. All around the dado-rails, piled on the mantelpiece and on the mirror above it, along the front of the raised platform at the end of the room were more branches than she'd ever seen in her life. Ruby and George must have been out in the countryside collecting them for weeks. They'd been sprayed with silver paint and all along each one, someone – Alison, she was sure – had tied elaborate bows of satin ribbon. Such colours! Red and black and pink; blue and violet and yellow; pale green and silver and gold. It took Hester a little while to understand what the ribbons were. She realised it when she noticed the ballet shoes, dotted here and there. The ribbons came from Ruby's box in Wardrobe which was always stocked with every possible colour visiting ballerinas might require. Alison had stuffed the toe of every shoe and balanced them all so that it seemed as though an invisible creature had left them there, poised and ready to move into a dance.

Beautiful. It was so beautiful that Hester found herself blinking away tears. I must thank her properly, she thought, for this magical idea. She hadn't thought the house was capable of such beauty when she'd first inherited it from Madame Olga.

1970

Six months after her accident, Hester took on the most demanding role of her career. After she'd made up her mind that she was no longer a dancer, she threw herself into teaching with an energy that surprised everyone, herself most of all. She found that there was an enormous satisfaction from creating a ballerina out of someone who up till then was only an awkward child. She acquired, very quickly, a reputation for strictness and not suffering fools gladly. Liking her own way, and seeing that she got it, which had brought her into conflict with more than one choreographer, was exactly the quality that seemed *de rigueur* if you were a teacher. Hester played up to the part, and even though she stopped short of copying Madame Olga's dress and manner, she adopted a uniform and a style of her own, dressing always in very well-cut black trousers and a variety of silk shirts in jewel colours. Her hair, which she'd worn long throughout her dancing career, had been cut into a chin-length bob.

Hester also began to travel all over the world, amazed that there were people from Australia to Moscow longing to hear about her career, to listen to her views on the latest developments in modern dance, and on a whole variety of subjects about which she was magically supposed to know everything simply by virtue of who she'd once been. The legendary Hester Fielding, that's what they called her now. Dinah, who had been living in New Zealand since her marriage ten years ago, was overjoyed that they could meet again. 'It means you can come and see me and we can talk properly for the first time in years,' she wrote. 'Letters are all very well, but I can't wait to see you.'

It was in the spring of 1970, while Hester was staying with Dinah in Christchurch, that a phone call came from Piers. The line was crackly and difficult and he sounded as though he were talking underwater, but Hester heard him. Madame Olga had suffered a stroke. Hester returned to England at once. While she was on her way home, Piers had arranged for Madame Olga to be moved from Wychwood House to St Thomas's Hospital in London so that they could visit her every day. They expected her to make a complete recovery and convalesce in the luxury of Piers' house. What illness would dare lay Madame Olga low?

'She'll tell those doctor chappies what's what,' Piers said, in the hearty voice and bluff manner he reserved for particularly sad occasions when he thought people needed cheering up. Hester believed him. It was impossible to think of Madame Olga, who was so self-possessed and elegant and in charge of everything, lying in bed like a sick person; like an old woman. She's only seventy-two, Hester told herself. That's not really old. She was strong, too. Hester had never known her to suffer from anything worse than a cold in all the years she'd known her. She would definitely be fine.

Then the second stroke came and Hester and Piers rushed through the streets of London in the dark to visit her. They took a taxi from the theatre after watching the first night of a production of *Swan Lake* in which one of Hester's own pupils was appearing. Piers was waiting at the stage door at the end of the performance, ready to take her to the hospital.

Something was different. Hester knew it at once. Madame Olga had been moved to a small side-room near the entrance to the ward. They only did that for patients who were very ill indeed. Hester began to sweat, in spite of feeling cold all over.

'Madame?' she whispered, going to sit on the chair drawn up beside the bed. 'Madame, it's me. Hester. Please open your eyes.'

She'd shrunk. She was a little old lady lying in a bed. Her thinning hair had been plaited by one of the nursing staff and she wore a white nightgown with lace at the neck. Her hands looked like pieces of bleached wood, gnarled and swollen at the joints, but still arranged in a graceful way on the blanket, as though she had decided on this particular position for them. Her eyes were closed and her skin, which had always been smooth and pale and unblemished was dark under her eyes and saggy and loose near her chin. She had lost something of herself, and Hester begun weeping because her Madame

Olga had gone and this poor, sick woman, this old and feeble person had replaced her.

Hester took her hand and held it. 'The ballet was good tonight. Dulcie's very promising, I think.'

'You are now like me,' Madame Olga spoke so quietly that Hester had to lean forward to catch her words. Every one of them was an effort. 'The dancers become the teachers, yes?'

Hester nodded and tried not to cry. 'It doesn't seem so long ago that you came down to the Royalty to see me in *Sleeping Beauty*, when I did the Bluebird. Do you remember?'

'Everything. I forget nothing. This is the curse of old age. All remains and you cannot clean your head. But listen to me, child.'

She seized Hester's wrist then and her hand was like a bird's claw. She tried to sit up a little but that was too much for her and she fell back against the pillows. Hester said, 'Don't distress yourself, Madame. I'm here. I can hear you. Speak to me.'

'I want to say something to you,' she whispered. 'I have wanted to say it for many years. This. All of it is yours. All my jewels. You remember them, I think. I have left them to you and also the house. What will you do with such a house? It is not my business. But Wychwood is yours.'

Hester couldn't move her hand from Madame Olga's grip, so the tears ran down her face unchecked and she barely noticed. She heard what the old lady was saying and part of her took it in. Madame Olga was leaving everything she owned to Hester, and at this very moment, she didn't care two figs for any of it. She couldn't bear the way Madame Olga's voice was leaving her. The power of her lungs, which was almost as great as the power of her will, had gone, and now only a thin, thin breath of air was left to carry what she still wanted to tell Hester.

Hester knelt down beside the bed and thanked her.

'I love you, Madame,' she whispered, her mouth close to Madame Olga's ear, but it was hard to see whether she was aware of the words. In the end, a nurse came to tell Hester it was time to leave. She said, 'Come again tomorrow, dear. Madame Rakovska needs her rest now.'

Hester was already by the door when she heard a sound, a hoarse cry that was a version of her name, 'Hester. Hester come to me.'

She went back to the bed. Madame Olga was struggling to sit up and Hester put an arm around her to help her. She could feel every bone in Madame's back through her nightdress, and thought that if she moved too quickly, the old woman might break into a million separate fragments. Madame was struggling to speak. 'You forgive me, yes? Say this. Say you forgive me. I beg of you. Please.'

'Forgive you? There's nothing to forgive, Madame. You've been like a mother to me. You've done everything for me. Please don't say such things.'

'Say it,' she insisted. 'Say you forgive me. I beg. Please, I am dying, darling child. Let me know this before I go. Please. Say it.'

Hester didn't know what she was talking about. 'I forgive you. Of course I do. But there's nothing to forgive.'

She closed her eyes and smiled as Hester laid her gently down again. She looked as though she was dreaming of good things. Madame Olga died that night and Hester never saw her again. From time to time, in the years following her death, Hester would wonder what she'd meant. Why was she asking for my forgiveness? What could she possibly think she'd done?

On the morning following her visit, Hester answered the telephone and a voice on the other end, a voice she didn't know, told her the bad news. She closed her eyes and breathed deeply. I will have to ring Piers at once, she thought. The funeral. We must arrange the funeral. Her hand was trembling uncontrollably as she dialled his number, but the tears remained unshed for many hours. It was only when she was quite alone, in her bed that night, that Hester allowed herself to weep. I will never, she thought, stop missing Madame Olga. Never.

Wychwood House was looking particularly grim and grey when Hester and Edmund went to look round it. They walked through the rooms, where dust sheets covered every piece of furniture. The carpets were threadbare, the curtains eaten by moths and heavy with the dirt of years. Madame Olga had brought very little with her to

London, so the cavernous wardrobes were full of her dresses and coats. The bright scarves and shawls she always wore were in two drawers of the chest in her bedroom, and in another were albums and boxes bursting with photographs of dancers and other vanished friends from the days when snapshots were small, black and white and indistinct.

'Look at all this stuff,' Hester told Edmund, faint with the thought that she'd have to clear it up; deal with everything.

'We'll cope with it,' said Edmund. 'I've already spoken to various chaps who're going to come and clear the house. Auctioneers in Keighley. You never know, some of the furniture might fetch a bob or two. Don't forget that this isn't what she's left you. Not really. Not these old clothes and things. You have to look at the house as full of possibilities. Potential, the estate agents would say.'

'But potential for what? It looks like the House of Usher to me. How can I possibly live in it?'

'Well, not in its present condition, of course you can't. But if it's done up. Decorated, and that wilderness outside cleared and made into a garden . . .'

They went for a walk that afternoon, over the moors. The sun had come out for what Edmund called 'a special guest appearance' before night fell. The sky was streaked with purple and rose pink and orange as it made its way down behind the slope of a hill to the west. They talked about Wychwood House.

'I'd like to do something spectacular,' Hester said. 'Something unexpected. I'd like Wychwood to be known for ballet in the way that Glyndebourne is known for opera. A festival. I wish I could do that, but you'd need a theatre, wouldn't you? And no one would dream of putting a theatre in the middle of nowhere.'

'I don't see why not. You could build it down there, in that dip behind the house. I can see it now. A small theatre, of course, about two hundred seats. But very beautiful. And we must call it something romantic. The Alhambra.'

'No, that sounds like a music hall. What about the Princess?'

'Princess? No, that's terrible. Why that?'

'After Princess Margaret, I thought. She loves the ballet. Perhaps she could be a patron of the festival?'

'Well, perhaps she could, but the name is still awful. I've got it!'

'Tell me,' said Hester. 'Though I reserve the right to hate it.'

Edmund stood quite still and announced the name in a ringing voice that seemed to fill the whole landscape on this still afternoon. 'The Arcadia Theatre.'

Hester said nothing for a moment, and he went on. 'The classical paradise. *Et in Arcadia ego* . . . I, too, have been in Paradise.'

'It's lovely, Edmund. How clever you are! Thank you. It couldn't possibly be anything else. But that means it's got to be traditional. Not modern. It has to fit in with the house and the surroundings. Are people really going to come all the way up here?'

'They will if the ballet's good enough. And it will be. With you in charge, of course it will. You could have a competition every year, choose your choreographer that way. Then let whoever it is choose what he wants to do. Or she wants to do, I suppose, though I don't think there are that many women choreographers.'

'Brilliant, Edmund!' said Hester and hugged him. 'But you'll have to help me.'

'Don't I always?' Edmund smiled at her.

'You do. Always.'

The Wychwood Festival was launched in 1976 and the first night of the ballet was the sixth of January. The invited audience of critics and ballet lovers from all over the country sat in the beautiful interior of the Arcadia Theatre and watched a production of *Rosemary for Remembrance*, a piece based on *Hamlet*, seen from Ophelia's point of view. The applause at the end of the evening went on for nearly ten minutes. Edmund timed it on his watch.

At the end of the party after the first night, Hester and Edmund went upstairs together.

'It's going to be the best ballet festival ever, Hester,' Edmund said, putting his arm around her waist. 'I'm so proud to be part of it, through you.'

They were standing at the top of the staircase and he pulled her to him.

'You smell so lovely,' he said and buried his face in Hester's hair. He stepped away and touched her cheek.

'Goodnight, darling girl.' He turned and walked quickly towards his room. She was left there, not knowing what to do. She went to her bedroom and sat at the dressing-table. The chain, the gold chain that she always wore, caught the light, and Hester examined the face that she saw reflected in the mirror. I'm not a girl any longer, she thought. I must stop myself from thinking about love and kisses like a green young thing. I'm a business woman now. A festival director. I'm going to be good at it, too. Tears came into Hester's eyes as she thought of how much Madame Olga would have enjoyed tonight. How happy she would have been in the foyer of the theatre, trailing one of her more magnificent scarves and with her hands weighed down by silver rings studded with pieces of amber the size of small onions. She would have been proud of me, Hester thought. The ballets will be wonderful and people will come and see them from all over the world. They'll come to the Arcadia Theatre. Hester Fielding's theatre. My theatre.

6 January 1987

Alison sat on one of the hard chairs in the dining room and watched George giving instructions to the catering staff, who'd arrived that morning. They'd come so early that breakfast wasn't even properly over, and now there was already a table set up all along one side of the room, with white tablecloths laid over it.

George was hurrying towards her. 'Hello Alison! You don't look very happy, I must say. Whatever's wrong?'

Alison tried to smile. She wasn't going to moan about her dad. He wasn't going to phone, and that was that and she ought to get over it. She should've been used to being let down by now.

'I'm okay. I'm just at a bit of a loose end. The decorations are up and Ruby doesn't need me till this afternoon and I'm not sure what to do. I might go for a walk. The sun looks quite warm from in here.'

'Don't you believe it. You'll need to wrap up if you don't want to freeze your proverbials off.' He looked around him and was about to go back to the caterers when he turned back to speak to Alison. 'I won't have time probably to say this later, but what you've done with these ribbons and shoes is inspired. In all my days with the Wychwood Festival, we've never had decorations like these. Never. You're obviously going to be an extraordinary set designer. Extraordinary.'

He went off before she had time to answer, which was probably a good thing, because she'd never have been able to tell him how thrilled she was at his words. Now she began to wonder how she was going to fill the afternoon.

'Alison?' Hester was standing in the doorway, and beckoning to her. Alison stood up at once. What on earth could she possibly want?

'There's someone on the telephone for you. Take it in the Office.'

Alison stared stupidly at Hester for a few seconds before coming to her senses. 'Is it my dad? Did he say?'

'Patrick Drake, yes. Go on, off you go. I'll follow you later. You'll want to speak to him on your own.'

'Thank you!' said Alison, and flew along the corridor and into the Office. The telephone handset was lying on the desk and she seized it as though it were about to disappear if she didn't hurry.

'Dad? It's me. Alison. Is that you?'

'Yes, my darling, how are you? Did you get my present? I sent it to your London address. Did it come in time for Christmas?'

'No, I thought you'd forgotten all about me.'

'As if I would! I phoned you on Christmas Eve, remember?'

'I know. It's okay.' She hadn't enjoyed *that* phone call one little bit. It was supposed to be to her, but most of the time, Dad and Claudia were moaning at one another down the line. She'd only had a few minutes right at the end of the conversation.

'I'd have phoned you there before now, too, only things have been frantic. No excuse, I know, but still. Did you get my letter? I sent that to Wychwood.'

'Yes. Yes I did. Thanks.' She didn't tell him about Claudia giving it to her so late.

She sank down on to the chair by the desk and started to talk. Hearing her dad's voice was amazing, wonderful, the best thing she could think of to happen.

'Are you here? In England? Am I going to see you?'

'I'm still in America. But you'd love it here, Alison. You have to come over. Can you do that? Can you come here for your next holiday? I didn't get it together before Christmas, but can we make a date for Easter?'

'Oh, yes!' Alison's head was filled with a vision of herself stepping off a plane in America. Her father hugging her. 'I'll ask Mum. I'm sure it'll be okay.' She wanted to ask all sorts of questions, the main one being, how long for? How long could she stay with him?

'A couple of weeks? Would Claudia object to losing you for so long? It's ages since we saw you. I miss you, my darling.'

'I miss you, too,' said Alison, and she didn't add that it would be easy to keep in touch, if he really wanted to. 'And I'm sure Claudia won't mind if I'm with you.'

She didn't say, *she'll be glad to see the back of me,* but she knew that

Claudia would be thrilled to bits. The irritation her mother always felt towards Patrick would be gone in a minute when she realised that he was going to take Alison off her hands for the whole, the entire Easter holidays. She settled down in Hester's chair and listened to her dad telling her what he'd been doing over Christmas, and apologising yet again for not having phoned before.

When she put the handset down, she felt a little sad. She couldn't help it. The phone call was over now, and there was nothing more to look forward to for the moment. Tears came to her eyes and she blinked them away. Easter. Think of that. He's going to send me a ticket for the Easter holiday. The time'll go quickly. It's not true that he doesn't love me. He does. He loves me a lot. It's not his fault he's not here.

Alison looked up as someone knocked at the door.

'Come in,' she called.

'It's me.' Hester was carrying a long cardboard box under one arm. 'Have you finished your phone call?'

'Yes, it was brilliant. Thanks so much for letting me use your phone.'

'You're more than welcome. And I'm glad you're still here. I saw the decorations yesterday and wanted to tell you then how thrilled I was, but I thought I'd wait till we had a chance to talk. I *love* what you've done, Alison. It's completely beautiful.'

'Thank you. I loved doing it. Really. I was dreading coming here, but it's been brilliant.' Alison smiled and looked at her feet. 'I'd better go now, I suppose.'

'I've brought you something, a thank you present.' She put the box she'd been carrying on the desk and opened the lid. 'I hope you don't think it's too babyish, but it's of great sentimental value to me. It's a doll. My doll, from when I was a little girl. Her name's Antoinette. She's rather old and tatty, but I did have her cleaned about five years ago, and she's lived in this box since then, so she ought to be quite presentable.'

'Oh!' Alison took the doll out of the tissue paper sheets in which she was wrapped. 'She is so beautiful! What a lovely lacy skirt. I don't know what to say. No one's ever given me anything like this before. I love her!'

'I thought you might. That's why I decided to give her to you. She's been lying in the dark for much too long. I took her with me everywhere for years and years. It'll make me happy to know that you're taking care of her.'

'I will. I'll look after her, I promise.'

'And there's something else I want to say to you, Alison. You're welcome at Wychwood whenever you like. I'm always here, and I'd be delighted to see you at any time. I'm sure Ruby would be too. I mean it.'

'Thanks so much! I'd love to come and visit you. May I write to you? Will you answer?'

'Of course. I'm a good letter-writer. It'll be good to hear your news. I must go and get ready for the first night. Are you looking forward to it?'

Alison nodded. 'I've never looked forward to a ballet before, but *Sarabande's* different. I'm one of the backstage staff.'

'An *important* member of the backstage staff. See you later then.'

'Yes. And thank you.' On an impulse, she put her arms around Hester and hugged her. 'Thank you for everything.'

'Are you going to be able to cope, Ruby?' Hester put down her teacup and looked across the kitchen table at Ruby. 'You're not too tired?'

'No, I shall manage very well. In fact, it's strange. I feel so much better about everything. You cannot imagine how badly I've felt all these years. I'm sure that's what gave me the headaches. Perhaps they'll ease off now. D'you think you can forgive me, Hester?'

'I'm sure I shall. I might have done the same thing, if I'd been in your shoes. And you've been such a good friend, and so loyal to me for so many years. That's what I'm trying to concentrate on. I'm going to focus on that and not on the mistakes. And if I could have chosen the sort of child I wanted, I don't think I'd have been able to come up with someone as, as wonderful as Hugo. It's not just me, is it, Ruby? He is a good person? And he's gifted.'

'His adoptive mother brought him up very well.'

'Better than I could have done, I daresay.' Hester was fiddling with the teaspoon, turning it over and over in her hand. 'I think Madame Olga might have been right, you know.'

'About what? She was wrong about quite a few things, but no one ever seemed willing to cross her, did they?'

'I don't know if I'd have been a good mother. I don't think I'd have had the patience to deal with baby things. I probably would have let nurses and nannies do all that. I'm also sure I'd never have given up dancing a single role for my baby. What sort of mother would that have made me?'

'People become the kind of mothers they are, that's all. You would have done the best you could, like everyone else.'

'But what I mean is, I think I'll be a good mother for a grown-up person. And Hugo and I got on long before we even knew . . .'

Ruby didn't respond and Hester wondered what she was thinking. I've known her all these years and yet I've never asked her.

'Ruby, do you mind if I ask you something? I never have before because I didn't want to pry, but I want to know. Why haven't you and George ever had any children?'

For a moment, Hester thought she might have made a mistake. She oughtn't to have asked after all. Ruby was offended. She was going to say something sharp and silence all questions for ever. She might even go into a sulk.

'We weren't able to. That's all.'

'Oh, Ruby, I'm sorry. Really sorry.'

'We haven't let it spoil our lives,' Ruby said calmly. 'We've been very happy, just the two of us.'

Hester nodded in agreement and wondered how truthful Ruby was being. I'll never know that, she reflected. I'm not going to ask any more questions.

'Silver?' Silver almost let go of the armful of clothes she was carrying and turned to see Hugo following her down the covered passage towards the Arcadia. 'Can I help you carry some of that? What is it, anyway?'

He'd caught up with her now and she handed over the plastic dry-cleaner's bag she'd been holding. She said, 'It's only my stuff for the party. My dress and shoes. I wanted to get changed into it straight after the performance.'

Hugo pushed against one of the foyer doors with his shoulder and held it open for Silver. 'Can you spare a moment? I'd like . . . that is, I want to say . . .'

'D'you want to come to the dressing room?'

'No, I want to go somewhere where we're not going to be interrupted. There are things . . . how about this?'

'This' was the props room. A table, which still held the covered-up model of the *Sarabande* set, stood in the middle of the floor. On shelves from floor to ceiling all sorts of things were lined up – goblets made of *papier-mâché*, swords, lamps, jewel-boxes studded with glass gems. Two chairs were drawn up to the table and with one hand Hugo pulled one out for Silver to sit on.

'Just a step removed from an interrogation room, isn't it?' he said. 'It's the lack of windows. Horrible. Still, no one will disturb us here. I have to say something to you, Silver.'

She couldn't speak. Her heart was beating so hard that she wondered for a moment whether Hugo could hear it too. He smiled at her.

'There's no need to look so worried. I just wanted to say this. I've spoken to Claudia and we've decided – well, I told her and she agreed – that we're no longer . . . that we've split up, I mean. That's all I wanted to say. Claudia and I have split up.'

Silver concentrated hard on not reacting. She felt like leaping out of the chair and shouting for joy, but she controlled herself. Maybe Hugo simply meant to keep her informed. Perhaps his breaking up with Claudia wouldn't affect them.

'I'm sorry. I don't know what you want me to say. Are you all right?'

Hugo reached out and stroked Silver's wrist with the tips of his fingers. 'I've never been more all right in my life. But what about you? Do you still think I'm a monster?'

'Yes, I think you're disgustingly bossy as a choreographer and completely dictatorial when it comes to your dancers.'

'Anything else apart from that?'

'I'd have thought it was perfectly obvious. I don't just kiss any old person who happens to come along, you know. What kind of a girl do you think I am?'

'A magical girl. A wonderful girl.' He stood up and reached out to pull her towards him. 'I wanted to make sure, that's all. That I wasn't imagining it. That what seemed to be happening between us wasn't part of some pre-ballet excitement, or something. I mean, we've hardly talked, only about *Sarabande*. There's a whole lot of stuff I'm uncertain about. I'm older than you. You scarcely know me, outside the rehearsal room.'

'I do know you,' she said. 'You talk a lot of nonsense. I know you care about *Sarabande* and so do I and I have to go and get ready for the first night. But I don't want you wondering about me. About how I feel, I mean.' She wrapped her arms around him. 'Kiss me,' she murmured. He bent down to obey her, his mouth open and his hands stroking her back, her neck, her hair.

'Silver . . .' he breathed when she moved away from him. 'Oh, my Silver girl . . .'

'I'd better go, Hugo. I'm dancing for you tonight. Just for you.'

She picked up her bag of clothes and stepped into the corridor, wondering how long Hugo was going to sit in the props room. She needed time alone to stop the trembling that had suddenly affected all her limbs. On the way to the auditorium, she glanced out of the window and saw a quarter moon rising over the moors, looking like a slice of lemon floating in the dark sky. Only five o'clock and it was nearly night time.

Bloody bloody Hugo, Claudia thought. She peered at the necklace that she'd had to substitute for the gold chain which he'd taken away from her. He didn't want her to wear it, he said, and that was that. No explanation forthcoming, or at least none until she'd insisted on a reason. It then turned out that George didn't like the way it caught the light. She sighed and considered the strand of jade pieces that she happened to have packed in her suitcase because the colour brought out the green of her eyes. It'll do, she told herself, but she couldn't help thinking that the removal of the gold chain was a kind of omen.

She felt uncharacteristically nervous and when Alison had come in to wish her luck, she'd been rather chilly to her. Never mind, she would make sure to be extra nice after the first night was over. She turned to look at Silver, who was applying her make-up and being very silent about it. She wondered whether Hugo had had a chance to tell Silver about breaking up with her. She wasn't going to mention it. Hugo denied it had anything to do with Silver, and Claudia didn't know whether to believe him or not. She said, 'Oh, well. Let's hope that all Hugo's work on your scene with Nick pays off. I hear you've managed to do what he wanted. He's so unreasonable sometimes.'

'I think I have. We'll have to see if I can do it again tonight.'

Silver was making a great thing about outlining her lips in such a way that talk was impossible. Oh sod it, thought Claudia. If you don't want to talk, I'm not going to put myself out. She turned to Ilene. 'Shall we go down and lie about on the set, Ilene? I need to think myself into Princess mode.'

'I'll be ready in a sec,' Ilene answered. Claudia stood up to wait for her, thinking that Princess mode was the furthest thing in the world from the way she was feeling at this very moment. Nick hadn't come to wish her luck. No future in that relationship, Claudia knew, and she was somewhat depressed by how little she seemed to be caring about it. Let him go back to his boys and girls and welcome. He'd do for the run here at Wychwood, but she wasn't going to waste time on him when they went back to London. Dump before you're dumped yourself. That had always been her rule in the past and she wished she'd had a chance to put it into use where Hugo was concerned.

'I can't believe it yet,' Hester said. She and Edmund were sitting in the Arcadia stalls. The house lights were still up, and around them, the audience was chatting and laughing in the slightly hushed voices of people who knew they would very soon be watching a ballet that no one had ever seen before. There was no doubt in Hester's mind that it was this desire to be first, to be there when something was born, that filled her theatre every year. The people who came to the Arcadia knew that excellence was guaranteed. She had a reputation as someone who wouldn't accept anything less than perfection.

'What can't you believe?' Edmund turned to face her.

'All this,' Hester indicated the theatre, 'going on as usual, the same as it does every year, and me, the way I feel, so very different. I'm . . .'

Edmund said nothing, but Hester could see he was waiting for her to gather her words into some kind of sense. That was going to be harder than he knew, because she couldn't have expressed everything that was going through her mind even if her life depended on it. There was Hugo, at the back of the theatre. He'd told her, days ago, that he could never sit down to watch the first night and Hester understood that. He'd be anxious about every single thing that could go wrong. He'd be worrying about all the tiny details that others couldn't even imagine. And on top of that, he'd had to contend with finding out that she was his mother. He seemed calm enough about it, but it was bound to have shaken him, as it had her. The fact, the mere fact of his life, was taking time to sink in.

As she thought this, Hester shivered. My child. He's my baby, and I can't believe it yet. How long will it be before I take him, take his life, for granted? What will happen now? We'll have to decide if anyone has to be told, and if so, what to tell them. We have to talk about the future. All of this, the theatre, the house, everything, will be his one day. Has he worked that out yet? And Edmund. There's Edmund to take into consideration too. She smiled. 'I was thinking that in spite of having so many friends and being part of something like the Festival, in the most important ways I've been alone and I'm not alone any longer. That's an amazing feeling'

Edmund took her hand and kissed it. She knew that if she tried to speak, the tears would come. As it was, they were threatening to fall and she took a deep breath. The house lights went down and she squeezed Edmund's hand. As the music poured out of the speakers and filled the auditorium, he leaned close to her and whispered, 'They're playing our tune!'

She'd always known that that was one of the best things about Edmund – he made her laugh. He made her laugh and he was the kindest man she'd ever known. But when he kissed her, she felt eighteen again. Images – bright, glowing pictures of their lovemaking – returned to her mind. He'd touched her and stroked her and spoken soft words to her and kissed every part of her till she was transported, swept away, and now she felt herself flooded with desire, all over again. It's me, she thought. I'm the one who's changed. Hester stole a glance at his profile and leaned over to kiss him in the half-light. 'My darling Edmund, do you know how much I love you?'

Ruby and Alison stood in the wings together, watching *Sarabande*. There was something different about a performance, Alison realised. It didn't matter how many rehearsals you'd seen, how many times you'd walked through the stalls and around the different parts of the theatre, it wasn't a bit like this. A special smell, a special kind of atmosphere, filled the whole building and Alison had noticed it the minute she came into the dressing room carrying the ironed costumes for her mother, Silver and Ilene.

All three of them had been sitting at the mirror, which had good luck cards stuck all over it. Flowers in vases were lined up on a table in the corner, out of the way of the make-up, which had taken over the whole surface of the dressing-table. Ilene was drawing black lines under her eyes; Silver was applying gold eyeshadow, and Claudia was making her mouth as red as she possibly could.

'Good luck,' Alison said, as she hung the costumes on a rail. 'I can't wait to see it.'

'I'd have thought you'd have had enough of it by now,' Silver said. 'You've watched us going through our paces every day, almost.'

'It's going to be different though, isn't it? It feels different.'

She went back to the side of the stage and took her place next to Ruby. The house lights were still up and she could see them: the audience. They were talking quietly but the noise they made sounded like a hum from where she was. All the ladies were dressed up. You could tell because their necklaces and earrings caught the light. There was Hester, in her usual place in the sixth row.

'Doesn't Hester look great?' she whispered to Ruby.

'She always does. And that moss-green velvet is one of my favourites. I made it for her.'

'Really? That's amazing.'

'Wait till you see the skirt. Yards and yards of fabric. She looks like a queen when she's wearing it.'

'Silver's dress is hanging up in the dressing room. I saw it. It's very dark red. She's said she'll make me up after the show for the party. That's really nice of her, don't you think? And she's going to lend me one of her scarves, like she did on New Year's Eve. I could kill my mother. She never said I should bring anything partyish. I haven't got anything anyway – at least, nothing I like.'

Alison stopped abruptly, aware that she was gabbling, talking for the sake of it, because suddenly there was a feeling in her stomach that was exactly like butterflies fluttering around. How funny! People were always saying they felt that, but she hadn't realised that it was true.

The musicians started to play and the house lights dimmed. George in his lighting box at the back of the auditorium turned one of his magic switches and the stage was bathed in pinkish-yellow light. There was the set, which was so beautiful that everyone started to clap before one single step had been danced. Claudia, lying among the cushions on her couch, looked like part of a painting and Alison found that she was holding her breath. Then Ilene came in, carrying a basket of fruit, and presented it to Claudia and the music swelled and grew and filled the whole auditorium with a melody so luscious that it reminded Alison of melted chocolate.

'We'd better go and do some work,' Ruby said. 'Andy'll be there looking for his stuff in a minute, and I must make sure that those wings are ready for Silver.'

They sat together on their chairs as the ballet progressed. There were quite long periods when they just watched what was happening on stage, but during one of Nick and Silver's *pas-de-deux*, Ruby touched Alison on the arm.

'I don't know if I'll get a chance to say this later, so I'll say it now. It's been so good to have you working on this.' She waved her hand towards the props table. 'You've been a great help to me, and it's been . . . it's been fun, too. I've enjoyed it. Thank you for everything, Alison.'

'That's okay,' Alison blushed with pleasure. 'I've had a good time.

It's made me, well, it's made me understand a bit what everyone gets so excited about. I've never really known before.'

'Are you a ballet fan now, then?'

'I don't know about that, but I like it better than I used to. It's okay. It'd be even better if they said the odd word every now and again.'

Ruby had to cover her mouth with her hand, to make sure that her laughter wasn't heard on stage, where Silver was looming over Claudia, hiding her face with the white wings they'd taken such ages to make.

Hugo always stood in the same place for every first night – at the back of the auditorium, – too nervous to sit in a seat, and yet wanting to see the ballet, the result of his work, unfolding on the stage. He was much more nervous tonight than usual, and not only because this ballet meant so much to him, but also because he was waiting to see Silver appear. And, he knew, also because of everything that had happened in the last couple of days. He'd been so preoccupied with *Sarabande* he'd not had the chance to take any of it in properly.

There they were, Hester and Edmund, sitting together in the sixth row of the stalls, right in the middle. Hester had her hair up in a kind of bun at the top of her head, which made her look younger than usual and more like a ballerina than ever. How could such a person be his mother? His *mother*.

Part of him still felt like Sheila Carradine's boy. She'd loved and cared for him for more than thirty years. How could he not love her? Love her memory and honour it? That was impossible. But Hester – he was flesh of her flesh, blood of her blood. It made him feel dizzy to think of such a thing. Later, he thought. I'll think about the implications later.

He blinked. Part of him was still the choreographer, the creator of everything that was appearing in front of this audience, but there was another part which wanted simply to watch Silver. He stood up straighter as she moved into the sequence he'd devised for her. She was so beautiful that Hugo found he was holding his breath for most of the time that she was dancing. How she moved! Here it comes, he thought. The music swelled and soared and she flew up and up into the air in a way that seemed to defy gravity and then down again as though she weighed less than nothing. She landed on the stage in total silence, not like a human being but like some ethereal creature. Like an angel. Her wings stretched out and glittered where the gold threads caught the light and, for a moment, Hugo's eyes were filled with tears at the perfection of it. Silver achieved what every dancer aspired to: she came as near to flying as humanly possible. He leaned against the back wall of the auditorium and thought of how it would feel to hold her again.

Nothing in the whole world was like this. The dancers at the edge of the stage, bowing and curtseying and looking up to the circle, and picking up the flowers that the Friends of the Wychwood Festival always threw on to the stage at the end of every performance – and the applause, like a kind of music, rising and falling. For a moment, Hester longed to be one of them, wished more than anything she could be there, there on the stage with the others, sweating and happy after having danced and danced. That's me, she thought. I'm not this middle-aged person, sitting in the front stalls looking at everything, wearing my best dress. I'm one of them. One of the dancers. That's what I want to be, what I've always wanted. Madness. She shook her head and immediately the madness left her. There was still the same trace of deep envy she always felt at the end of every performance, but looking at Edmund, sitting beside her and clapping and clapping and shouting out 'Bravo!' at the top of his voice, she returned to the real world, in which she was about to be happy. Hugo was up there now, embracing Silver, then Claudia, calling Ruby and Alison out of the wings to take a bow, and then beckoning to her.

'Ladies and gentlemen. Please welcome to the stage the real star of the Wychwood Festival, Hester Fielding.'

Hester would stand in the golden light again, and some of the flowers would be for her. She would pick them up and bury her face in their fragrance and remember to make the kind of deep *révérence* on which Madame Olga had always insisted. Edmund stood up and kissed her briefly, sweetly on the lips as she passed him and made her way to the small door that would lead her from the stalls and up on to the stage.